This page intentionally left blank,

because I'm an asshole.

The End

Although he had been president for slightly over three years, this was his first real crisis with the Secret Service. What surprised him most was the rough handling. He had always assumed that the agents would merely shield him as he was hustled away safely under his own power. But what he had not been expecting was for his protective detail to literally snatch him up off the ground and transport him at a dead run, straight into the waiting express elevator.

But that was not the end of his surprises: although President Jefferson Phelps had been briefed on the existence of the Presidential Emergency Operations Center, or PEOC, he had never actually been down into the bunker. The speed of the plunging elevator was fast enough to achieve half-gravity. With his lunch threatening to escape his esophagus, he tried to regain his composure, *or at least pretend to.*

"What's the situation, Mack?" He used the agent's first name, his voice cracking slightly as the agents released their grip on him.

"He is descending rapidly, directly over the White House, roughly three hundred thousand feet in altitude." Senior Agent in Charge Mulligan reported as the doors slid open. More hustling and the President found himself roughly deposited in the Situation Room

THE DAY GRAVITY BECAME IRRELEVANT

RALPH ROTTEN

Published by Indies United Publishing House, LLC

Index

"What the hell is he doing?" President Phelps asked as he watched data flash across the array of screens that covered the far wall. Every printer in the bunker was churning out document after document. He had no way of knowing it, but the same event was occurring all over the world as the virus forced its content into home computers and government supercomputers alike. Adjusting the reading glasses that perched on his nose, he tried to decipher what he was seeing.

"These are Iranian Nuclear Council documents, all top secret!" The Commander in Navy dress blues was alarmed.

"These are Russian…I think?" Phelps mumbled as the Cyrillic characters flashed past.

"These are all North Korean nerve agent inventories." Someone else down the line noted as he perused a printout.

"Sir, these are our enemies' secrets. All of them…" The technical advisor who managed the bunker turned to the President.

"That's good, right?" Phelps asked, uncertain by the looks on their faces.

"Sir." The Chairman of the Joint Chiefs stepped forward assertively. "If this is what he is showing us, then what is he divulging to our enemies?"

"Mister President." The technical specialist cut back into the conversation, "We are showing data-flow in both directions; we're not the only ones being flooded with classified materials. We believe he is airing our dirty laundry to the whole world, literally posting our deepest, darkest secrets on the internet where anyone can read it. I am showing RedBack servers all across the country being flooded with data. He even cracked Google and spidered the sources to make it accessible to anyone with a computer, then encrypted the backlinks so we can't find the actual content. It's fucking brilliant." The techie was clearly impressed with what he saw happening before them. Petabytes of classified data were flowing freely all over the world and there was nothing they could do to staunch the flow. With almost every computer in the world plugged into an *always-on* broadband connection, the virus was free to virtually host its content on any hard drive or even in system RAM. The information was everywhere, and not just theirs. The virus had examined their files thoroughly before seeking out their enemies and sharing their data as well.

Summoning up his most presidential gravitas, he turned to his military advisor.

"Shoot him down!"

Nothing more was needed to be said. Within seconds his military henchmen had translated the order into a formal battle plan that would be executed with precision. A simple phone call would in turn scramble a formation of F-22s with a classified payload. Streaking to 38,000 feet, they released their ASAT165 missiles in a massive salvo.

With the air around them thick with electronic counter measures, the missiles climbed ever higher still as their intelligent warheads guided them to the only target they could see. There, thousands of feet above, the object plunged towards them from high in the thermosphere. Closer and closer they drew until their proximity detectors told them they were within detonation range of their target. In a flash of light that was plainly visible to anyone in Washington DC, the capsule detonated like a distant supernova. From that altitude it took several minutes for the wreckage to plunge earthward as it trailed flames and plasma before finally coming to rest in the waters of the Washington Memorial.

Bent and burnt, the capsule laid steaming in the water. The wreck had come to rest not fifty yards from a group of camera-snapping tourists who recorded every detail of the event. Within seconds it was being shared thousands of times across the internet.

But the real frenzy began as people realized it was raining money. Like a cloud of butterflies, the sky was filled with millions of charred *Benjamins* that fluttered down onto the city below.

Knowing there could be no denial of the events, President Phelps and his spin doctors wasted no time in ensuring that the world knew exactly what had happened. At a press conference set up within sight of the crash site, the leader of the free world leaned on his fists and looked the American people directly in the eye before beginning.

"Ladies and Gentlemen, citizens of the United States of America, today our brave military forces have thwarted an adversary who threatened our very way of life. These men were terrorists who infiltrated our security systems, compromised years of intelligence gathering, then went on to present a clear and present danger to the entire District of Columbia, as well as an even greater threat to the United States and her proud citizens. I am relieved to tell you that these men, brothers Jack and James Sparks, are confirmed dead at this time."

The Beginning

The Sparks brothers could not have been any more dissimilar if they had been from different planets. Although they had once shared a womb, the similarities ended there for the fraternal twins. It had always been something that defied logic. After all, they had been raised by the same parents, in the same home, under the same Italian-African-American hybrid social culture, even schooled in the same institutions. Nonetheless, they were as dissimilar as Europa and Io.

Born the product of an Irish-Italian father, and a mother of African descent, Jack had never really identified with either racial group. By his thinking, true Americans were mutts; something that his mixed ethnicity truly epitomized. It had always seemed illogical to him to use antiquated terms such as African-American or Italian-American. Having been born a citizen of the most powerful nation in the history of the world, it seemed to him more important that you were American first, then whatever your ancestors had hailed from. Hence, he preferred to think of himself as an *American of African-Italian-Irish descent*. After all, in America, everyone's ancestors were from somewhere else.

Named after his grandfather, Jack had been the first born, only minutes ahead of his younger brother. Like most boys, Jack Edmund Sparks had captured his share of lizards, skinned his knees while jumping his bicycle over the gorge next door, and even pulled the neighbor girl's pigtails a few times. By no means a simpleton; he had joined Mensa when he was fifteen, graduated from high school when he was sixteen, and completed his master's degree in electromechanical engineering by the age of twenty. While most of his peers had considered the curriculum at MIT to be challenging, Jack had sailed through despite spending most of his nights either drinking at frat parties, or chasing skirts on campus. Like any red-blooded American college man, he had enjoyed his time at university, sucking the marrow out of life's bones during his brief tenure.

But even from the start things had been different with Jamie. Where other babies had cried incessantly until their parents figured out what ailed them, the youngest of the Sparks boys had learned early on that simply holding his hands up to his face as if he were sucking on a bottle would result in his being fed. Squirming his buttocks told his parents that he needed changing, and grasping fingertips meant that he wanted to be held. Speaking in complete sentences by the age of 2, he set his next milestone a year later when he learned to read by watching the closed captioned text on TV.

He was barely 4 the first time he spoke in a foreign accent. At the time it had just been written off as something he picked up from TV. Besides, it was cute to have a child genius with a British accent. However, they were much less thrilled with his hillbilly persona; little country Jimmy was known to be quite profane.

While other children in daycare stacked blocks or played in mud puddles, Jamie was usually found with his face in an encyclopedia. Once he had digested the entire vintage set of Britannica encyclopedias that lined the shelf, he moved on to technical manuals, college textbooks, and readily digested Stephen Hawking's *Brief History of Time*. While this rate of progress initially thrilled his parents, by the age of 7 it had turned problematic.

Although James and Sandra Sparks, academics themselves, delighted in the idea of a child savant in the house, the reality of such a progeny soon taught them that it was not all it was cracked up to be. Far too smart to join the other first graders in his class, and already brighter than the teacher herself, there were problems right away. After a specialist was brought in to evaluate the boy, the determination was quickly made that with his quantum rate of advancement, public school was not the place for Jamie. Unfortunately, they received the same advice from all three of the nearby private schools. At that point their only other alternative would have been to enroll an 8 year old as a college freshman.

Not comfortable with her child being submerged in a classroom with students more than a decade older than her little boy, Sandra had finally given up and taken a sabbatical from her position as a tenured professor. It had seemed simple enough at the beginning; after all, she was an experienced educator, how hard could it be? Usually she taught to hundreds of students at once, so one single student should be a snap. *Right?*

The first few years had been challenging as her son soared through increasingly more difficult material. She had her first real inkling of what lay ahead the morning she found him editing her graduate thesis after finding it in a desk drawer. It had shocked her, the sheer amount of red ink the twelve-year-old had expended on the masterpiece she had spent three years compiling. It boggled her mind to realize that already his intellect had soared to the degree that he could so easily quantify truths of the universe that she still struggled to fathom. *How do you keep up with an intellect like that?* It befuddled the mother to think that even after more than twenty years of education, and another decade as an experienced educator, she was dangerously close to having nothing left for the boy. Already he did their taxes better than TurboTax, and graded physics papers faster than graduate students.

Despite the difficulties, James and Sandra Sparks traded off the workload of educating their son. It was simply more than one person could do alone. Like a quantum singularity, the little boy could digest anything in his path. Sandra had likened it to feeding a locomotive. Unfortunately, if they failed to keep Jamie Junior's fires stoked with new knowledge, he tended to turn his attention to other things. After he convinced Jack to help him build a particle accelerator out of the family microwave, they knew something had to be done with the boy.

But the straw that broke the camel's back came when Sandra's own alma mater accused him of cheating during his equivalency testing. Although little Jamie had indeed attended college for almost an entire semester, the experiment came to a screeching halt after his professors united in protest. While the professional educators pointed to Jamie's unique *personalities* as the source of the problem, in reality they simply did not like having their errors pointed out by a fourteen year old child.

But in truth, Jamie's episodes had been increasing. Where he had once only slipped into his characters intermittently, he now tended to loiter there, sometimes for hours. It had become a concern for James and Sandra. More and more of his interpersonal communication seemed to be through these characters...these avatars. While Sandra realized fully that this was just how her son's beautiful mind chose to communicate, in a formal classroom environment his conduct was just too disruptive.

With no teacher willing to host the child in their classroom, Jamie had been forced to complete equivalency testing to obtain his degrees. After an exhaustive battery of exams in every discipline, the academic staff was shocked at the results. Convinced that he must have duped the test somehow, the University had demanded that his intelligence quotient be tested.

But the results had been off of any recognizable chart. The Stanford-Binet test used by the university was designed to measure an IQ up to 160. Jamie had not only achieved the maximum possible test score, but done it in half the time of anyone who had ever taken the test. For reasons beyond explanation, the university had refused to ratify the results. While simultaneously denying his requests for graduation, the college chose instead to ask him in blunt terms to leave their campus and never return.

Although the matter had upset James and Sandra considerably, it had been an insignificant event to little Jamie. After all, he had felt stifled by the plodding pace of college. Finally released from his educational bindings he was now free to study at his own pace. With a broadband internet connection, and an Amazon account, the young man was able to pore through volumes of data.

It was at the age of eighteen that Jamie first began to change his own paradigm. Having absorbed the equivalent of eight doctorates, he was no longer satisfied with just learning. The epiphany had come about after a morning of being irritated with the speed of his personal computer. Though it was rated as one of the fastest on the market, the silicon masterpiece seemed to take forever to load and process large volumes of data. As his subconscious brain analyzed the parameters of hyperthreading with an 18 core processor, it occurred to him that there was a better way.

And thus was born his first invention: the Cubed Processor. Cobbling together components from more than a dozen motherboards, he had assembled a CPU that was a 128x128x128 matrix, or 128^3. Using virtualization to double the size of the existing 64 bit processors had only been the first step in creating a central processor that was 128 bits wide, 128 bits tall, and 128 bits deep. Running at nearly 4,000hz, the Cubed Processor had the ability to process more than 8 billion bits of data with each tick of the electronic clock. While conventional hyperthreading allowed the operating system to dedicate individual CPUs to each major process, Jamie's system allowed him to dedicate entire floors to an application. With each layer of the cube possessing the computational power of 128^2x3900hz, even a single floor was several magnitudes more powerful than the best mainframes on the market. Additionally, he found that unused floors could double as processor cache; the ability to park data for processing within the CPU itself meant that there was no longer even a RAM transfer delay. In essence, the Cubed Processor could outstrip all but the best super-computers on the planet. The truly amazing thing was that he had done it all on the cheap by buying up last-gen processors at bargain prices.

His next problem was the operating system itself. Needless to say, Windows and Linux were completely incapable of handling this kind of raw power; and thus he found himself writing his own OS. Originally named Babbage in honor of one of the earliest leaders in computer science, the mass of code performed admirably enough. Still, it was really little more than a digitalized version of Charles Babbage's mechanical computer. Inputs dictated actions that created outputs. Every action stimulated a predictable result consistently. While most people would have been satisfied to have created not only the world's fastest computer but an entire operating system, Jamie was decidedly not. In his eyes the OS was dumb. It was little different than using wheels, levers, and pulleys to calculate. In his imagination he could actually envision a crude steam engine driving his simpleton software.

It was here that he turned to the works of Alan Turing; the theoretical father of artificial intelligence. Having lived and died before the invention of the semiconductor, Turing's genius had been hindered by the crude computers of his era. But Jamie suffered from no such technological limitations. Moving to the next logical step, he began devoting his every waking minute to the creation of a sentient AI.

At the age of 20, the brothers suffered their greatest loss in life; the death of James and Sandra Sparks in a tragic car accident. Killed by a drunk driver on their way home from Christmas shopping, the event had been particularly difficult for Jamie. Although Jack had dozens of friends, the studious Jamie really only had his family. While his brain could uncover the secrets of the universe as easily as most people peeled a tangerine, the young savant had always found his own species to be a mystery. Even after spending months trying to dissect social conduct, he found that most of it was illogical. He simply could not understand why people would find small talk anything but boring.

Finding his world reduced to just he and his brother, Jamie had no idea how to process the gaping hole in his life. While he would have logically turned to his brother, Jack's own reaction to the tragedy was to clam up at the mention of his parents. Like anyone faced with a senseless loss, the elder Sparks brother felt a great sense of bitterness every time he thought about the drunk who had killed his parents. Charged with felony DUI, it was the man's third conviction. It galled Jack to know that when the felon was finally freed from prison in a decade, their parents would still be dead. Rather than revealing his feelings on the topic to his brother, Jack simply closed up tight as a vault, often becoming hostile at the mere mention of the day their lives had changed.

Living off of their meager inheritance, the brothers instead focused on their own business. With their above-average intellects they had no trouble creating new devices and products that generated acceptable revenues for their fledgling tech company. Working out of the basement, the Sparks brothers had managed to amass a respectable workshop where they breathed life into their inventions. It is here that they prospered and developed as young adults. But more importantly, it is here that Jamie made the discovery that changed everything.

The Discovery

"What are you doing to my car?" His voice held a hard edge to it as Jack stopped short in the doorway. Wearing a light windbreaker and keys dangling from his hand, it was obvious that he was about to go somewhere. Staring at the rows of parts that were intricately laid out on a rubber mat, he could tell at a glance that his brother was in the middle of another unauthorized upgrade. While several of the improvements had indeed been of useful value to their little company, it bugged him to no end to see Jamie installing unknown technology in his *baby*. Candy-apple red and powered by a carbureted 302cc engine, the classic 1965 Ford Mustang convertible was a flawless example of automotive restoration. Inherited from their father, Jack had long since assumed the car as his own. Leery about whatever his brother was doing to the vehicle, Jack eyed the work being done as he awaited a reply from his brother.

"Micromic field progression system. It will be the greatest invention since...tea and crumpets." Standing upright, the wiry savant gave a terse smile as he spoke with a flawless British accent. His face stretched oddly, it was as if he were new to smiling.

Exhaling sharply, Jack gave a defeated sigh at the sound of his brother's accent. No stranger to Jamie's voices, he had long ago come to terms with his brother's various characters.

"I told you not to mess with my car. If you need a test bed then use the vacuum chamber." Breathing deeply,

Jack suppressed his instinct to yell at his brother for the sacrilege he was committing upon the classic car. Leaning over he could see the device being mounted in the trunk.

"Unfortunately, the test chamber is of insufficient length for a fully rigorous examination." Shaking his head, Jamie considered how to explain his quandary. "The test-bed needs to have a momentum factor of at least nine point two six to the negative tenth of C before it will function within measurable tolerances. Hence, it must be mounted to a fully mobile platform." Shrugging as if it were common knowledge, Jamie lectured as if he were a professor at Oxford. It had been his way since childhood, to use his various personalities to express his current emotional state. The Professor James avatar was essentially his way of indicating that he was fully focused on his current project.

Taking a minute to run the calculation through his own head, Jack showed obvious irritation.

"So it needs to be travelling at least seventy-nine klicks per hour?" Giving a smug grin, the older brother was pleased with himself for the calculation.

"To be completely precise; seventy-*seven* kilometers per hour." Blinking his eyes as he corrected his brother, Jamie's expression remained blank.

"So this thing only works when I get her up to seventy-seven KPH? Seriously? Did you install a flux capacitor too, Professor Brown?" Jack gave a loud belly laugh at his brother.

"The purpose of a capacitor is to store and discharge a specific amount of energy. It would be contrary to the basic function of the device if it were to fluctuate." His eyebrows raised, he failed to grasp the cinematic reference. Fiction was not something that Jamie studied much; most of it abounded in scientific inaccuracies that he simply found intolerable.

Shaking his head, Jack knew better than to try to explain to his brother. That approach rarely yielded anything but the kind of brain-twisting argument that made his head hurt. Instead he took another path.

"You need to wrap this up; I got a date with Cindy McDonnell." Tapping his wrist, Jack indicated that he was on a schedule. "You remember Cindy, right? About this tall, and legs that go on forever."

"Giraffes have an average leg length of one point eight meters." Ever pleasant as he spoke in a flowing British accent, Jamie gave a nod before he returned to his work in the trunk. Tinkering away as he hummed *God Save the Queen*, the quirky savant ignored his brother's sense of urgency.

"I'm not dating a giraffe! I date humans, unlike my brother who doesn't even date mammals." Giving his voice an acrid tone, Jack leaned over to see how much work remained.

"I don't date at all." Never looking up, the savant made the finishing touches on the mounting bracket that sat squarely in the middle of the trunk. "I have already calculated the odds of finding a suitable match and statistically speaking I should not even waste my time."

Jack raised his eyebrows as he considered the equation. "Yeah, you got a point there. Your perfect match would probably be a face-hugger." Jack pretended to have a creature clamped onto his face.

Professor Jamie simply raised a Vulcan eyebrow as he quietly regarded his brother. While he had never seen any of the *Alien* movies, he could infer from the context that the comment was derisive in nature. Not content to let his brother ponder the matter deeper, Jack used his hand to slap the edge of the trunk to get Jamie's attention.

"Don't stand there looking at me like I'm Doc McCoy. Get to back to work! I got places to go and women to defile. Let's get a move on there *hombre*, we're burnin' daylight." Jack used his John Wayne voice for the last part, though he doubted that his brother would get the cultural reference.

"There is a fixed amount of work, and it will require a fixed amount of time to complete. Your bimbo will wait." His face blank, Professor Jamie simply flashed a stretched smile, as if it pained him to bend his face.

"You say bimbo like it's a bad thing. Bimbos have feelings too y'know, and usually they feel pretty good." Pretending to be sympathetic to their plight, Jack's face quickly split into a grin. "At least my women only have silicone implants; your digital bimbo is almost entirely silicon."

"I'm not a bimbo." A woman's voice spoke up, the sound emanating from the vehicle's sound system. "However, online evidence indicates that your date certainly is, complete with a tramp-stamp. This was just posted on Cindy's FaceBook page: *I am soooo in love with these new shoes from Manolo. I feel like I have died and gone to shoe heaven when I wear them.* Additionally she has forty-three other pictures of shoes on her page. Who does that?"

Co-opting the monitors on the nearby work bench, Alexis rendered a dizzying slideshow of shoes and selfies. The photos seemed to go on forever. Shrugging it off, Jack was dismissive.

"First off, with her legs, I couldn't care less if she even has feet. Secondly," Grabbing his brother by the shoulder, Jack yanked his sibling around to face him. "I told you not to install Alexis in my car again. Get her outta there."

"I fail to understand why you would not enjoy the companionship and assistance of another sentient being during your travels." Jamie had just started to defend his actions when his brother cut him off.

"One; she's not sentient, she's just a pile of code compiled on an advanced processor…" Jack was just ticking off the reasons on his fingers when the woman's voice interrupted him.

"Oh, that's mean. I would never trivialize your existence by pointing out that you are nothing but a series of synaptic links, strung together in a cohesive network, or the fact that your DNA operates suspiciously like the Windows registry. Calling me code hurts my feelings." With an edge to her voice, Alexis sounded anything but hurt.

"You're a machine, you have no damned feelings!" Raising his voice, Jack was losing his patience fast. With images of Cyndi McDonnell in a mini-skirt dancing around in his head, he was quickly becoming exasperated by the delay. "And the last time you were installed in my car, you completely ruined things with Shaniqua. I was totally about to score on that ass when you had to go and open your big, virtual mouth and ruin everything."

"She called your brother a retard; I was only defending his honor, as you should have done. What kind of a sibling lets a woman talk that way about his own brother?" Her tone surprisingly incredulous, Alexis raised her voice angrily.

"The kind of brother who was about to get hip deep in some of that, that's what kind of brother I am." Standing with arms folded, Jack was on his last nerve with the two of them.

"I did you a favor." Her voice suddenly sweet, Alexis pointed out the logic behind her intrusion that night. "Based on my research, you and Shaniqua had less than a one percent chance of long term success. The relationship was doomed to failure."

"I only needed it to work for another ten minutes." Raising his eyebrows, he doubted either of them would understand his needs.

"I would have guessed closer to four minutes, based on your performance during your frequent practice sessions." A happy lilt to her voice, Alexis refrained from laughing out loud as she played an audio file that sounded suspiciously like Jack talking dirty to Rosy Palm. "That is quite a workout regimen you keep, I have to say. You must have massive forearms. I should call you Popeye."

Jack's eyes flared as he balled his fists. "Get her outta there, or I'm pouring an espresso over her CPU."

"That would be uncalled for..." Jamie began to dismiss the threat.

"A double latte." Jack upped the ante.

"Oh, cool your jets" From the speakers in the trunk, Alexis's voice piped up. "I'm not actually installed in your precious car. I'm just here by a digital link to your stereo system. James knew that you would object to him installing extensive telemetry sensors so I have been linked to the package in the trunk to record the outputs and results."

"She is much more efficient that a non-sentient telemetry package." Nodding his approval, Jamie agreed with her diagnosis.

"Is it done yet? Can I go now?" His hand on the trunk lid, Jack was ready to get gone.

Nodding, Jamie flashed one of his classic smiles. Really more of a grimace that upturned on the ends, he was not very good at expressing himself in colloquial mannerisms.

Pausing before he slammed the trunk shut, Jack gave the device one last glance before raising an eyebrow in inquiry.

"Assuming it works, how much increase in velocity will it give me?" A skeptical look on his face, he interrogated his younger sibling. "This isn't like that ion engine you built, with the output of a mouse fart, is it?"

"Assuming it functions as designed, and is properly employed, it should yield a nine percent increase in velocity. However, this is only a prototype, and as such there is no guarantee it will even function at all. Additionally, it is only charged with twenty-eight point three-five grams of reactant, providing a maximum boost duration of less than six minutes." His face neutral again, Jamie explained as his brother slammed the trunk. "I have scheduled tomorrow morning for the testing phase. Zero-seven hundred hours at the drag strip."

"Seven AM?" Frowning, Jack showed his irritation at the plans. "Tomorrow's Saturday. I was planning on sleeping in."

"Translation:" Alexis chimed in, her voice emanating from Jack's smart-watch. "He plans on *working-out* more in the morning." Emitting a laugh, she included the sounds of Jack's heavy breathing.

"Get outta there!" Shouting at the smart-watch on his wrist, it irritated him to no end the way Alexis was prone to invading connected devices at will.

"Good luck with your efforts to copulate." Bobbing his head, Jamie again faked a smile before turning away.

Intent on leaving, something made Jack pause halfway into the car.

"What reactant?" He called out, concerned that his brother may have used some form of hazardous material as fuel. *It would not have been the first time.*

Half turning in the doorway, Jamie responded without hesitation. "Element forty-seven met the criteria for abundance, affordability, conductivity, and lowest initial ionization rate of any of the elements."

Taking a minute to run through the periodic table in his mind, it took Jack considerably longer to come up with an answer than his brother had.

"Heh, silver?" Giving a shrug, he relegated the atomic properties of silver to the back of his mind. Preferring to spend his brain power on the image of Cindy in yoga pants, his brain returned to coarser considerations.

Although he had known his date from elementary school, it had been years since Cindy had lived in their neighborhood. Like most people in their class, she had moved out not long after reaching adulthood. Living in the neighboring town now, she kept an apartment on the west side, not far from the interstate. Navigating the surface streets, he was within two blocks of the highway when a familiar rumble could be heard through his open window.

"Well if it ain't one of the mulatto boys." The gruff voice from the car beside him was echoed by a laugh from the passenger.

Turning to one side Jack found himself looking at the Burke brothers in the car next to him. Although they were a familiar sight from his childhood, they were not a welcome sight. In fact he had a hard time remembering a single positive interaction with the two.

Smiling from the passenger seat, Chauncey corrected his older brother. "Chet, you can't use that term no more. Don't you know that the term mulatto is no longer considered politically correct? Nowadays you call 'em mudbloods."

"No, no, you got it all wrong." From the driver's seat Chet used a beefy hand to wave away his brother's assertion. "Mudblood is just some Harry Potter faggotry. But good ol' Jackie is just plain old mud-people."

The two shared an open laugh as Jack tried to conceal his irritation. Although it had never worked, he hoped that ignoring them would make the Burke brothers go away.

"Oh, I see my mistake, a thousand pardons." Smaller by a head, Chauncey pretended to speak in an elite New England accent. "How's yer retard brother? Still a retard?"

Turning to one side, Jack looked over the Burke brothers. With thick necks and muscular forearms, they had been his nemesis since kindergarten. In truth, they had been at least partially responsible for his efforts to graduate from high school early. Even now he could remember the indignities he had suffered at their hands. Flashing them a smile, Jack returned the insult.

"Hey Chet, I heard you got fired from the hardware store and had to move back in with your mommy and daddy." Flashing them an easy smile, Jack knew exactly how to get under their skin. Irritating them had never been a problem; it was **not** getting his ass kicked that had always been the elusive part.

"Hey, fuck you Neeeegro!" Flashing him an extended social finger, Chauncey Burke was expectantly coarse in his reply.

"Yeah, like you're one to talk. Still living in the old homestead ain't ya?" Chet called out from the driver's seat. "How's yer Mommy? Oh that's right, she's fuckin dead. I totally forgot she got her head all smashed up. Sorry man!" Feigning an apology, the older of the brothers pretended to be remorseful for what he had said.

Flashing smiles that were clearly not apologetic, the brothers also knew how to infuriate Jack. Glancing up at the stop light, the oldest Burke brother estimated the time remaining before the automated signal changed.

"Still driving Daddy's jalopy I see. I'm surprised that thing even runs still since your daddy was such a shit mechanic."

Frowning, Jack looked over his shoulder at them. "That's because Dad was a theoretical physicist, not a mechanic. Say, what did your dad do for a living? Wasn't he the school janitor? Or at least he was until they fired his ass for stealing pills from the Nurse's office, wasn't it?" Giving them a smug grin, Jack dropped the clutch and darted ahead as soon as the light turned green.

Leaving them to fume behind him, he was disappointed when the next light turned red before he could reach it. Within seconds the brothers were there beside him again as Chauncey waved a tire iron at him through the open window.

"Hey, fuck you. You ever talk about m' daddy again and I'll give you an atomic wedgie like we was back in Miss Johnson's class." More than an empty threat, Chet promised violence for a repeat offense.

Looking ahead, Jack evaluated the on-ramp ahead. Starting out with two lanes, the roadway would merge into a single track within a hundred yards. Knowing how much it would gall them, he looked forward to cutting them off at the top. Glancing over at the perpendicular traffic signals, he could see them going yellow, then red.

Knowing that his own signal would have a 1.5 second delay before going green, Jack again dropped the clutch as the Mustang spun its wheels before darting ahead. Glancing back at the surprised brothers behind him, he knew they had not been expecting him to jump the light. Fueled by testosterone and primal instincts, they would make every effort to catch up with him. While his classic Mustang had a hearty engine, it was no match for the factory fresh Dodge Charger they drove. With a supercharger under the hood, they would likely overtake him in time to flash him the bird as they roared past, much to his humiliation.

Shifting through the gears as fast as he could, Jack knew that their automatic transmission was yet another advantage the Burke brothers had over him. With the latest in electronic controls, the Charger was a superb beast with more than enough power to upstage a fifty year old Ford, regardless of how well it had been restored. Glancing down at the tachometer, he noticed the array of switches his brother had mounted on the dashboard. Almost as if Jamie regarded him as a simpleton, the switches had been labeled 1 through 6 to ensure he did not foul the process.

"Asshole!" Grumbling to himself, Jack enabled the first two switches before a familiar voice cut through the roar of the engine.

"That's not a good idea." Alexis cautioned him, no doubt alerted by activation of the device.

"Shaddup!" Angry at her intrusion, he quickly flipped the next three switches. Glancing down at the speedometer he could tell that he was well in excess of 77kph.

"But..." She never got to finish her protest as he flipped the last switch. With the Burke brothers closing fast on his right side, Jack had no desire to debate the topic.

Pedal to the floor, he felt the surge of speed at the same instant he saw the highway patrol parked by the side of the road. At this velocity there was no slowing down in time. With the Burkes hovering in his blind spot, his analytical mind knew that the only option was to push on and hope that the patrolman went after the trailing vehicle. Glancing up at the overhead sign that appeared out of the darkness, he knew that the next exit was less than a quarter mile ahead.

"I can help, you know." Alexis chimed in, her voice sing-songy. "Otherwise the Burkes will pass you, leaving you to deal with law enforcement."

"What the hell can you do?" He should have known better than to ask.

Responding with a laugh, Alexis seemed to be enjoying herself. "Plenty. The Dodge Charger has a built-in network connection, and the Burke brothers never bothered to secure the connection."

His mind running at a hundred miles an hour, Jack suddenly realized she was right. It was unlikely that the brothers even had an inkling how to use their onboard connection, let alone how to lock it down with something besides the default factory password.

"Fine, shut 'em down, Lo-Jack their asses!" It galled him to have to make the request of the AI.

"Say please." Sweetness dripping from her voice, Alexis intended to milk it for everything she could get.

Shaking his head, Jack imagined himself in jail, surrounded by thugs like the Burke brothers. Grimacing, he finally relented.

"Fine! *Please* shut them down." Switching off his lights in a single motion, he cut to the right as he exited the freeway abruptly. Glancing back he could see the Charger silhouetted by flashing blue and red lights. With their electronically controlled engine disabled by the AI, they would be easy prey for the highway patrolman who pursued. Pleased to have escaped the ordeal, the inventor's smile quickly faded as he heard a creaking sound from the trunk.

"What the…?" He was just about to protest that it had been nowhere near six minutes when he felt his wheels leave the ground. Feeling panic, he was sure he had simply made the off-ramp at too high a speed. Sloping down gently, the exit plunged some twenty feet to the surface streets below. Expecting the speeding vehicle to settle back to the ground, Jack was amazed as he soared on through the air at more than a hundred miles an hour. What concerned him most was the fact that his altitude had not depreciated in the least. Feeling the engine roar as the drive wheels spun without resistance, it finally occurred to him to let off of the gas pedal.

"This is a problem." Alexis' voice was calm as she seemed to be evaluating the situation.

"Ya think?" Watching the buildings pass beneath them, Jack was unsure how fast he was even going; airborne the speedometer was useless.

"Jackie…" She started out.

"Stop calling me that!" Frustrated, he had completely forgotten about the Burke brothers who were likely being handcuffed somewhere behind him.

"That is your name." Her voice was firm.

"No, that was my name when I was seven. Now that I wear big-boy pants my name is Jack, just Jack."

"Correction, your name is Jack E. Sparks." Giving a happy inflection to her electronic voice, Alexis truly seemed amused by his predicament. "I am merely referring to you by your first name and middle initial; Jack E."

"How about if I called you Allie, or Al? How'd you like that, eh?" Trying to use anger to mask his nervousness, he realized he had no idea how fast he was going, or how much reactant remained.

"I believe I would like that. It is at least preferable to the names you usually call me. You are a very hurtful man, Jackie Sparks." Admonishing him, she quickly switched gears. "However, we…or more specifically you, have a serious problem."

Remembering that she was only speaking to him via remote link, he realized that she had no skin in the game. Jackie was truly on his own.

"Alright, what problem?" Scowling, he hated to admit helplessness to anyone, especially a synthetic entity.

"In thirty-two seconds you will need to disengage the micromic field projection system." She spoke the words as if there were no obvious penalty to the action.

"Like hell!" Jack roared. "I'm like twenty feet off the ground. I'll fall like a stack of bricks if I do that."

"Twenty-four feet." She corrected him. "However, in forty seconds you will be over the Buono's Pizza Emporium when the reactant is exhausted. Hence your need to disengage the drive in twenty-five seconds, while you are directly over Willow street, otherwise you will crash through the rooftop of the pizzeria and possibly cause injury or death to the occupants of that structure."

"You gotta be shitting me." Glancing down, it looked like a frightening drop to the young inventor.

"I cannot *shit you* since I have no bowels, as you have pointed out many times. I recommend you use this time to recline your seat all the way back for maximum impact protection." Lecturing him, Alexis did her best to conceal her glee at the situation he was in. While she may have been synthetic, there had never been any love lost between the two of them. "Ten seconds."

"Dammit!" Shaking his head, he hated to admit she was right, or even that *she* was a *she*. "Damn your digital circuits!"

Dropping the seat back until it laid down, he was suddenly glad he had chosen to replace the factory seats. In truth he had really only done so to allow him to get horizontal with his dates.

"Disable the drive now!" She called out.

Giving a gulp, Jack could feel his heart pounding in his chest as he used a hand to simultaneously flip all six switches. As if someone had cut a rope, he felt the bottom drop out of his world.

"Shiiiiiiiiiiittt!" It was the last thing out of his mouth as he plunged towards the streets below.

It was almost two hours later that Jack limped the Mustang back into the garage. With two flat tires, four blown shocks, broken motor mounts, and a bent frame, the classic

Mustang looked as if it had been dropped from the second floor. It had been sheer luck that the transmission still functioned at all, having struck the ground hard enough to leave a groove in the asphalt. Feeling the lowest he had felt since his parent's death, Jack was crushed by the idea that he had ruined the car he had inherited from his father. He had long ago sworn to safeguard the vintage automobile for as long as he could obtain parts. Realizing that the car would never be right again, it was as if he had lost his parents all over again.

Initially he was surprised to see his brother there waiting for him. But once he realized that Alexis had likely alerted him hours ago it only made sense. She was loyal to her creator; of this he had no doubt.

Adding insult to injury, Jack was unable to open the trunk due to the deformity of the frame and body. Having to resort to using a crowbar, he only ruined the candy-apple red finish even further. As he laid a hand on his crippled car, Jack felt true pain.

Beside him, Jamie was focused entirely on the device he had installed only hours earlier. Using a metal scribe he prodded the blue material that seemed to be leaking from one of the access covers. Making a grunt, he stood upright to face his older sibling.

"What the hell'd you do to 'er?" Jamie's voice was gruff. Gone was the Oxford Professor, now replaced by Jersey Jimbo. Surly in his mannerisms, Jamie jabbed his brother with a finger. "I toldja we was gonna test her tomorrow morning. Now you gone and broke it!"

Jack's mouth dropped open as he started to object. Having spent a lifetime around his younger brother's various personas, he knew better than to aggravate Jimbo the Jersey truck driver. Of all of his brother's avatars, this was the one he feared the most. More than once the angry blue-collar personality had punched him for getting out of line.

"You didn't say NOT to use it." Shrugging, he pointed out the loophole.

Instantly angry, Jamie drew up dangerously close. Aggressive in his demeanor, Jersey Jimbo invaded his brother's personal space as if challenging him. "You'se gonna get smart with me? Is that what I'm hearin' from you? I'll kick yer college-boy ass around the block if'n you give me any lip. *Capice*? You feelin' me?"

Backing up slightly, Jack hated it when Jamie was in this avatar. While he understood that it was merely his brother's unique way of expressing himself, it had been difficult spending his life with someone who changed personality constantly. You simply never knew who you would be talking to next.

"Alright, college-boy, pull it outta there so I can examine it in the fluoroscope."

"Examine it? Throw the damned thing away." Knowing even as he said it that his words were nonsense, Jackie still felt bitter over his car. A sharp look from Jimbo and he knew it would be unwise to argue any further. Grabbing a ratcheting socket driver, he began unfastening the motor mounts that held the device.

No sooner had he freed the micromic field projection device from its moorings than his brother plucked it out of the twisted trunk. Scuttling away, Jamie was already deep in conversation with Alexis. No doubt the two had been studying the issue since long before Jack had arrived home. Having had complete telemetry access to the device, Jamie's synthetic assistant would have had great insight into what went wrong with the experiment.

Taking one more look at the Mustang, Jack could only shake his head sadly. He had long ago spent his emotional energy, and now found himself tired and wasted. Closing the trunk delicately, *as if it mattered now,* he shuffled away towards his bedroom.

A New Paradigm

After a night of fitful sleep, Jack finally wound up rising at his usual six AM. Not that he enjoyed getting up that early; he was simply conditioned to it. The only alternative would have been to lay in bed, wide awake, as schematics flashed through his mind. With three devices under development on his work bench, it was as if he were being pulled by the irresistible force of a singularity. It had been this way for nearly a decade, ever since his parent's fatal accident; the hole in his life plugged with his fascination for discovery.

While he may have been far from his brother's incomprehensible genius, Jack was more than capable as an inventor. With dozens of patents under his belt, he was more than just a skilled fabricator. Though it was true that the bulk of their revenues came from devices envisioned by Jamie and manufactured by Jack, his own creations had significant merit.

Pausing with a cup of coffee in hand, Jack examined the digital blueprints that filled the oversized monitor on his desk. Glancing down he noticed as something scrambed across the keyboard. Stooping to examine the creature, he could tell that it was one of the Gen III drones. No bigger than a cockroach, the autonomous device sported three pairs of oscillating legs and a compact solar cell. Though it was clunky compared to the Gen IV model portrayed on his screen, the IIIs were still quite capable. Powerful enough to transmit video and audio with all the range of wireless a router, the Gen-III models still used most of their power on locomotion.

Giving a grimace, Jack turned to the long table beside his work bench. As he eyed the machine that looked suspiciously like a hair dryer, there was a deep sense of regret over the device. Purely his own creation, the EMP cannon had been a relative failure. While it was true that the device could indeed emit an electromagnetic pulse capable of shutting down a car, it lacked any real range. Limited to an effective range of 7.12 meters, the intended target had to be relatively close. Beyond that distance the signal simply became electronic noise akin to a radar jammer. Jack had spent almost a year chasing his tail on the device, unable to increase the striking distance a single millimeter. As if his failure were not enough, his brother's behavior towards the device told him that Jamie likely knew exactly how to fix it. No doubt his younger sibling considered the device too dangerous to hand over to the military, and had chosen to remain silent on how to remedy the invention. Hence, Jack's proudest invention, the EMP cannon, could only shut down cars within about 21 feet of the device. In practice he had never been able to use it on anyone but the worst of tailgaters.

Scooping up a remote, Jack activated a high definition projector that lit the far wall with his current designs. While he had a perfectly capable touchscreen monitor on his desk, somehow the inventor felt confined looking at such complex diagrams on a mere 30 inch screen. It helped him see the solution when the screen was eight foot across.

The next step in his routine was music. Activating the slim tube on his desk created a wealth of sound as Billie

Holliday belted out her lyrics. Although he normally preferred something slightly more modern, it was just too early in the morning. Besides, Billie's style held a special place in his heart; as a child his mother had sang her songs as lullabies whenever he was upset. Since then, the sound of the legendary blues singer had always set him at ease.

Looking down at the slim tube on his desktop he could feel a pang of regret over another of his inventions. The Sonic Cannon had originally been intended as a way to communicate between vehicles by using a focused beam to resonate audio off of car windows. Really it was an ingenious device; other vehicles heard nothing but a nearly inaudible whine, but for the target vehicle it was as if the sound were coming from within their own vehicle. Jack had found great amusement in the device as he used a variety of audio clips to punish bad drivers.

But in the end the Sonic Cannon had been a commercial failure. Not one single manufacturer had been interested in the device. Aside from using it to scare the occasional driver, Jack had taken to using the invention to bounce its compressed signal off the panel walls in his workshop. While the sound was top quality, it bothered him that his invention had been reduced to little more than a pair of desktop speakers.

Turning to the far workbench something seemed out of place; there was a blank spot where a digital printer should have been chattering away on PC boards for the next generation of drones. Seeing an empty spot where the cart would have been parked, Jack immediately began to notice that other things were missing as well; tools, orthoscope, meters... It was as if someone had raided his fabrication station. One word came to his lips.

"Jamie!" Shuffling across the linoleum floor in his bunny slippers, Jack was irritated at his brother for taking his tools. It was contrary to the way they ran their shop; Jamie was the idea guy, and Jack brought those dreams to reality. Jamie was theoretical, Jack was fabrication. This was how they had always found their greatest success, a pattern that had yielded over a hundred successful co-patents.

"Hey!" An angry tone to his voice, Jack admonished his brother for disturbing the work he had left in progress. "You can't be taking the fabber while I have it running a job. I needed those boards done by Monday so I can test the Gen fours."

Sitting silently, Jamie's expression was odd. While most people would not have detected anything out of the norm, Jack noticed right away; his brother wore a genuine smile. It was something he had not seen in years.

"Goooood morning, Jackie!" His voice exploding in volume, Jackie sounded like a master of ceremonies as he greeted his brother.

Pausing in the doorway, Jack sighed deeply as he realized what avatar his brother was impersonating this morning. Although Professor James irked him, and Jersey Jimbo outright intimidated him, it was Jimmy the game show host that most annoyed him. Buoyant and loud, the character seemed to leap out of him. Still, Jack knew that each of his brother's personalities represented a different emotion within him, and Game Show Jimmy was his expression of discovery.

"Let's give a big round of applause for our next contestant; Jackie Sparks from West Carson, California." Still grinning feverishly, Jamie threw an arm around his brother's shoulders. "So Jackie, are you feeling lucky today?"

Shrugging off Jamie's arm, Jack was annoyed. It was just too damned early in the morning for Game Show Jimmy. Stepping away to a safe distance, he grumbled audibly.

A grin spread across Jamie's face as he made an odd flourish with one hand.

"Don't worry; it won't fall if you bump it." Still grinning like a madman, Jamie never moved from his spot; that silly smile plastered across his face.

"It won't…?" Jack was still puzzling over his brother's cryptic statement when he turned and ran directly into the fabber cart. Stunned, he realized right away something was wrong. Normally the 5-wire 3D printer only came up to his waist, but today he ran into it with his face. Bumping his nose on the side of the cart, he felt it bounce away from him easily enough.

"What the…" Irritated at first, Jack's look turned to wonderment as he began to see more and more objects floating just a few feet off the floor. Turning to take in the whole room, he nearly dropped his coffee when he realized that his brother had levitated dozens of objects on the far side of the workshop. Each hovering silently, they looked like a swirling galaxy of trash as the air pressure from the nearby vent pushed them around in lazy circles. His jaw dropping open slowly, Jack realized he had been gaping at the assortment of equipment for a full two minutes before Jamie broke the silence.

"We have discovered something wonderful." Clearly pleased with himself, the younger sibling held out his hands gesturing to the cloud of levitated equipment before them.

"We? I was just the crash dummy." Jack finally turned to his brother.

"Indeed WE have. Johnny, tell our contestant what he has helped to discover!" Turning to scoop up a small piece of flimsy material, Jamie held up the object. "Remember this?"

"Yeah, that's the micron filter that I told you was gonna be too thin, but you insisted on using anyhow." Jack shrugged, remembering the argument that had ensued during the fabrication phase of the project.

"You are absolutely right!" His voice booming as he switched to his announcer voice, Jamie even pretended to hold a microphone as he detailed the revelation. "Not only is this the micron filter, but as an added bonus it was also tooooo thin. Give that man a Kewpie doll!"

"I was right?" Stunned by the revelation that he had actually been on the right side of a dispute with his brother, Jack's mouth hung open.

"Well, Jackie, the membrane was too thin for the kind of acceleration you exposed it to yesterday." Holding a socket driver as if it were a microphone, Jamie never missed a beat as he dragged his brother over to the workbench. "Intended to be used at a constant rate of seventy-seven kilometers per hour, as opposed to the illegal drag race you subjected it to, the device failed miserably. However, when it did, it fractured the membrane, allowing the viscous fluid to leak into the reaction chamber which interrupted the process, so instead of harvesting energy from the silver atoms as they were being sequentially split, the resulting particles and energy were captured in the viscous fluid until it was so saturated with energy that it turned into this." Jamie sang out a cheerful *ta-daaaa* before holding out a curious object roughly the dimensions of a cell phone battery. With a glowing blue tinge to it, the tiny gel-pack in Jamie's hand seemed to illuminate his palm.

Stooping over to view the glowing package, it immediately occurred to Jackie that the material could be hazardous. Recoiling, he looked to his younger sibling for reassurance that the blue stuff was safe.

"I call it Blue Plasma, which seemed much more marketable a title than Inelastic Spallation Plasma. This little vial holds the equivalent to nine hundred kilowatts of energy. What's even more amazing is that I have not actually split the atom, but stretched it."

"Stretched it?" Jack was surprised to hear his brother speak in such unspecific terms.

"Well, you know how much space is between the nucleus of an atom and its orbiting electrons, right? It's equivalent to the distance from the sun to Pluto, quite a bit of empty space between them, really." Raising an eyebrow, Jamie stayed in his gameshow announcer mode as he explained. "Well this new process simply stretches that distance…a lot."

A look seemed to wash over Jamie's face. Standing ramrod straight, his eyebrows climbed his forehead as he assumed the mantle of the unflappable Professor James.

"The real beauty of this system," His precise English accent flowed smoothly. "…is that I can hold these molecules suspended in this stretched configuration indefinitely. The atoms are just straining to reunite, in fact they're working so hard to get back together again that they actually emit this curious blue glow as a byproduct of the process. But the real energy comes when the atoms are reunited across the collector membrane. As the atom springs back together, it sacrifices a neutron, converting it from silver one-oh-nine to one-oh-seven."

Convinced that there must be a downside somehow, Jackie's mouth moved silently for a second before he actually thought of an objection.

"How do you know you aren't getting cancer just holding that stuff. You remember what happened to Curie?" Raising an eyebrow, he was sure it had to be toxic somehow.

Like someone had flipped a switch, Jamie's demeanor changed noticeably as he transitioned from Professor James to Gameshow Jimmy again.

"Studies indicate that this Blue Plasma emits no harmful radiation or seepage. However this substance is not intended for internal consumption and may include such side effects as explosive diarrhea, incontinence, itchy scalp, and death. Blue plasma should only be used in accordance with prescribed instruction; any deviation from this process could be hazardous to your health." Jamie's rapid fire announcer voice filled the room as he gestured to the dry erase board behind him. Filled from corner to corner with calculations, the penmanship was clearly British James'. There was no mistaking that much. Not only did his various avatars use different speech patterns, but they each embodied their own peculiarities, including hand writing.

Taking a moment to examine the figures there, it occurred to Jack that his brother rarely wrote things down. With his highly refined eidetic memory he had no need for note taking, and simple chemical calculations like the one on the board could have been crunched in his head. Hence, the only reason for him to have prepared these calculations was for his dim-witted older brother. Pushing the thought aside,

Jack concentrated on the resultant compounds that were derived by the process.

"Hmmmph." Giving a grunt, he had a hard time concealing his surprise. It amazed him that despite the eerie glow, the material was no more hazardous than metallically-infused vegetable oil.

"Nine hundred KW, eh?" Plucking the gel-pack from his younger sibling's open palm, Jack eyed the substance warily.

"Enough stored energy to power an average home for a month." A genuine smile stretched across Jamie's face as his voice boomed. It was obvious that there was more he wanted to say.

"So let me see if I got this right; you created a highly portable and compact form of energy by holding silver atoms in a spallated state while capturing the fragments in suspension fluid..." Jack trailed off as he examined the little gel-pack of blue plasma. Turning to the dry-erase board he looked at his brother's calculations. It amazed him that the real energy came not from splitting the Ag^{109} atom, but in reassembling it through the collector plate. Even more incredible was the fact that the device's resulting exhaust was Ag^{107}, a lower form of silver that resulted from sacrificing a neutron in the exchange process. It was a truly beautiful

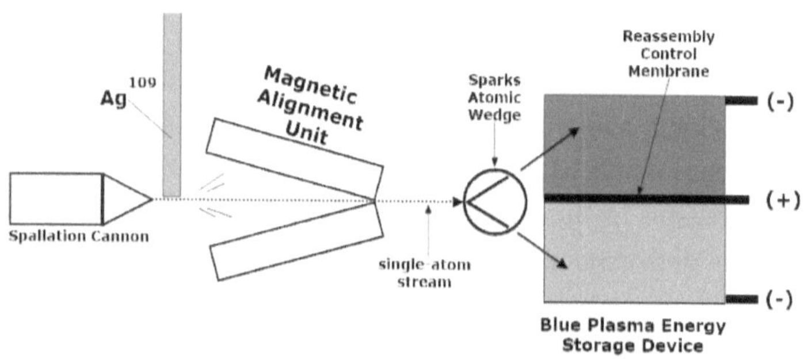

system; even the waste was valuable.

As Jack's mind continued to study the blue plasma, something occurred to him.

"But this stuff didn't make my *Stang* fly, did it?" Delicately placing the gel-pack on the nearby desktop, Jack looked to his brother for a further explanation. He knew Jamie well enough to know when he was bursting to reveal a secret.

"You are correct, Jackie Sparks of West Carson California! That's just the beginning of the real magic!" Back to Game Show Jimmy, he used an arm to steer his brother over to the technical schematics on the desk.

"With the regulator now consuming an energy stream that was ten to the eighth power more concentrated, it caused the emitter to fuse to the collimator wall so that the new output was no longer a harmonious flow of particulate matter, but rather a grounded-out field that created an effect I refer to as gravitational disaffinity." Scratching out new figures at the bottom of the dry-erase board, Jamie illustrated mathematically how the effect would work.

Jack realized he was gaping again. Instinctively he closed his mouth and pretended to be able to follow the factors his brother scribbled on the board. Though his math skills were nothing to scoff at, Jamie's calculations were beyond anything he had ever seen. Silently, he wondered if that was what it looked like inside of Jamie's head; complex algorithms and indistinguishable logic. *Did his brother even speak English in that skull of his?*

Jamie had begun scribbling more calculations on a second dry-erase board when Jack realized he no longer understood any of it. Though he would never admit his ignorance to his younger sibling, Jack had always been in awe of his brother's ability to calculate faster in his head than most physicists could with a programmable calculator. He knew from experience that there was no sense in checking his numbers; when it came to math Jamie was never wrong.

"So in summary, not only did we just invent a new, environmentally friendly form of energy, but we also just discovered the secret of antigravity." Stopping to flash that goofy, crooked grin of his, Jamie seemed truly pleased with himself. Gone was the awkward smile of a man pretending to blend into a world he considered a sociological mystery. It was here that the awkward savant was happiest; in the realm of pure science.

Standing back, Jack watched his brother's face as he took a moment to wipe the dry ink off of his thumb and onto his lab coat. While most people would not have thought twice about wiping a smudge on their shirt, it was completely out of character for any of Jamie's avatars. Jack spotted something else; his brother's expression seemed off somehow. Few would have even noticed the subtle difference, but after a lifetime of living with his brother, Jack could see that something was not quite right. It was almost as if his brother were slightly intoxicated. *Could he be drunk on science?* Dismissing the thought, he realized that there was likely a simple explanation to it all.

"Have you been up all night working on this?" Jack asked skeptically, a hint of concern to his voice. If there was one thing that he had learned about his brother it was that it was best for everyone if he stayed within the parameters of his rigid sleep schedule. Deviation from the routine was never a good idea with any of Jamie's personas.

Glancing at the nearby clock, Jamie gave a guffaw before smiling broadly. "Indeed I have."

As if it were insult to injury, Jack realized that even after working furiously for 24 hours straight, his brother's intellect was still several magnitudes greater than his own. It occurred to him that even in a coma, Jamie would be smarter than he.

"Worry not." Raising a finger, Jamie promised more to come. "I was careful to structure my productive time precisely so that while I am recharging, you will be able to begin fabrication of the first prototype. Alexis will show you what needs to be built."

Giving a curt nod, Jamie flashed one of his plastic smiles before striding purposefully out of the room. Never one to ramble unnecessarily, the savant was extremely deliberate in anything he did. Jamie Sparks did not waste time on small talk, and always had a purpose to anything he did.

Following a short distance, Jack watched his brother climb the stairs up and out of their basement workshop. Only after he was gone did he finally relent and call out to the silicon entity he was sure had been listening to every word.

"Alright girl, show me." Giving a defeated sigh, he called out to Alexis.

Immediately the schematics began to render on the far wall, projected in 4K resolution.

"This is what he wanted built first." All business today, the synthesized voice pretended as if there had never been any friction between them. "After that he needs three of these built."

Jack recognized the first device right away; it was a blue plasma generator. The next drawings were individual anti-grav units. It seemed odd to him that the two assemblies were being built as separate devices.

"He was specific that the two entities should never be combined. For security purposes, energy manufacturing and gravitational disaffinity devices should never share the same platform or schematic." Alexis's voice took on a hard tone, as if to forewarn him in no uncertain terms.

Still scanning the blueprints he assumed that it was being done that way to maintain the scientific process. Separate the components and beta-test them individually. The alternative was that too complex a device could skew the test results. Breaking it down to individual parts would make it easier to study.

Shrugging, he took a seat at his desk and began the long arduous process of translating his brother's theoretical diagrams into printed circuit boards. After that he would need to figure out how to de-levitate his fabber that still hung in mid-air.

As he worked, it had slowly begun to sink in the magnitude of these two discoveries. While any fool could see the potential of a new type of fuel, especially one so compact and enviro-friendly, it was the secondary device that truly awed Jack. Antigrav meant much more than flying cars; it was the kind of invention that would change the very fabric of their society. It would create a new world paradigm.

Staggering in its potential applications, gravitational disaffinity opened up so many possibilities. As he examined it in a linear and logical manner he knew that flying cars would negate the need for expensive roadways, no more intersections, no more freeways, no more vehicle exhaust turning their atmosphere into a greenhouse. Even trains would be radically changed. Vast amounts of cargo would simply be levitated to an altitude where the jet streams would push it in the direction you wanted. With modern flight management systems the entire process could be easily automated; after all, it was far easier to use autopilot for airborne devices than it was for ground vehicles. There was no reason that humans even needed to be part of the process.

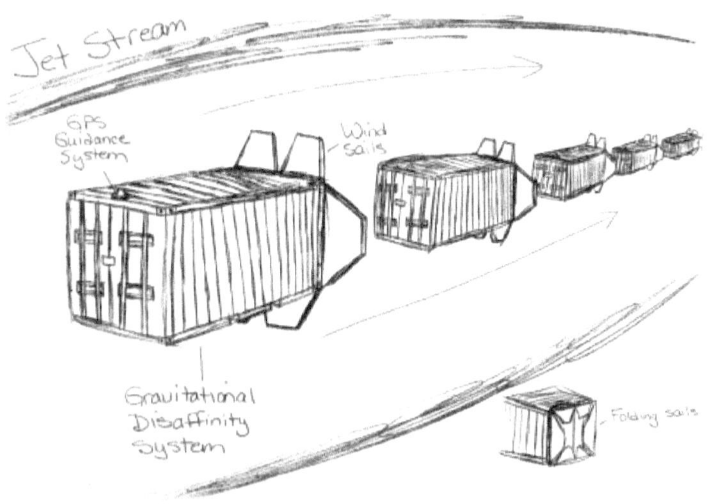

But as if replacing trains, planes, cars, and boats were not enough, it occurred to Jack that they could go much further with an invention like this. Antigravity would even change the real estate market. After all, if it were ridiculously cheap to stay aloft, then why not suspend other objects like homes or businesses or even sky scrapers. Giving a happy smile, Jack considered how much more practical the Sears tower would be if it were able to rotate slowly, absorbing sunlight on all sides evenly. Even more incredible, when the structure was finally ready for demolition, rather than a hazardous process of carefully containing the blast and commensurate destruction in a crowded urban scene, they could simply fly the building to a safe location for destruction or recycling. With this equipment, he could own a castle in the sky. Like the giant who chased Jack down the beanstalk, he could perch his home high in the clouds.

Working steadily, he only paused to pour fresh coffee or relieve himself. As he slowly parsed the logic behind his brother's theoretical schematics he began to understand more and more of the science behind it. While he understood the broad strokes to what Jamie had designed, it was only as he dissected it at the granular level that he truly comprehended his brother's genius. Absolutely fascinated with the work he was doing, Jack's mind took a while to finally stumble onto the greatest potential of the device: **Space travel**.

It had occurred to him in a flash. He had been imagining futuristic express trains in the sky, autonomously riding the jet stream to distant destinations. Next he had imagined how the ability to hover effortlessly meant that they could even replace expensive satellites. While humans relied heavily on the devices, the sheer cost of placing a single pound of satellite into orbit cost nearly as much as a 2 bedroom house. Never mind the issues associated with these space-borne devices. Although geosynchronous satellites could be used for communication and entertainment, their orbital range of 37,000km meant that there was significant lag to anything they did. When a user requested data via a satellite network connection, the data had to travel more than thirty thousand kilometers to a band of distant satellites that orbit Earth like the rings of Saturn. Once there, the data query was processed, returned to an earthbound station, processed yet again, and finally the requested media was transmitted from earth to the satellite and back to the viewer. Though the signal travelled at a fantastic velocity, it had to go a whopping 148,000km before the user got a single byte of data; hence the laggy response of satellite based communications. But this was an inherent part of geosynchronous orbital mechanics.

But with antigrav, they could simply hover a communications satellite in the upper troposphere. It would be well out of regular flight patterns, yet close enough to erase the lag factor associated with geosynchronous satellites, or the need to constantly hand off data as done with low-orbit satellites.

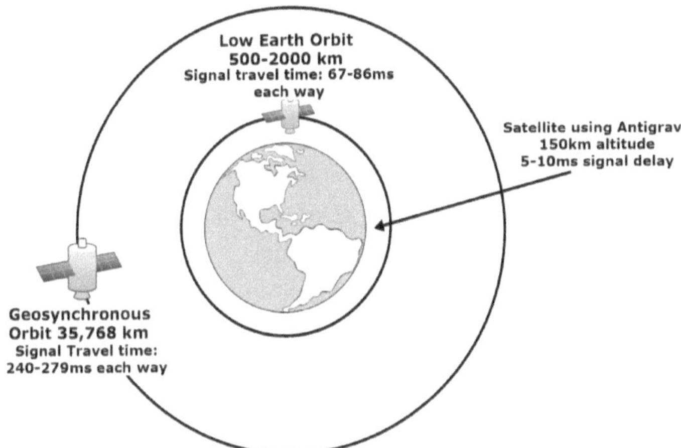

It was here in his thinking that he realized that this device solved the greatest hurdle to space exploration. As anyone in the business would tell you, the hardest part about getting to the moon was the first sixty miles. As daunting as the task seemed, the vast amount of resources expended in lofting thousands of tons of vessel into space was mind boggling. Because it cost over $80,000 dollars for each pound of payload, space vehicles needed to be built extremely light. But therein lay the problem: the fabric of a ship in space had to be incredibly light, yet provide protection against extreme heat, extreme cold, radiation, and withstand the rigors of riding a rocket into orbit. In essence, a modern space craft needed to be made out of fantastically expensive materials, all due to the incredible costs associated with a mere 65 mile barrier known as Earth's atmosphere.

But the device Jack toiled on changed everything. With antigravity they were no longer bound to the weight issues of yesterday. So if they no longer had to concern themselves with super-light materials, space ships could be constructed out of much simpler compounds so long as they provided the essential protections against the ambient hazards of space. It occurred to him that they could theoretically use materials as pedestrian as steel pipe. The only problem with weight was that it presented an increase in the vessel's overall mass and would require slightly more energy to make course changes. But if it no longer required millions of gallons of hydrogen peroxide and oxidizer to get into space, then they could take as much fuel as they wanted.

Sitting back for the first time in hours, Jack could not help but smile as he realized that the device he was building would easily reduce the cost of space travel to one twentieth of the current price tag; possibly even more. A trip to the International Space Station could wind up being little more expensive than a modern European vacation. While it pleased him to think that they could end many of the problems here on his own planet, it was the idea of space travel that truly excited him.

To hell with Earth he thought with a grin on his face, *I'm gonna go to the moon, bitches!*

Squinting to examine the progress of the fabber that chattered away on circuit boards, Jack wanted desperately to test them. Still laying down the sub-structure, the digital printer had a ways to go before it even began the laborious process of printing the next layer of components. Although the device was capable of running autonomously, the current design required a number of processor chips to be inserted into the feed. While his invention allowed him to print simple components like diodes, capacitors, and resistors, the more complicated silicon processors, with their microscopic circuitry, were still beyond the machine's capability. He had been working on a 3D printer with the resolution to print chips, but with the cost of off-the-shelf chipsets it was simply more practical to have the fabber pause while he inserted EPROMS and control chips. The fabber would handle the physical connections, then fill the empty space around them with shaped components. It was a beautiful process that wasted no space; every bit of the internal volume was filled with components. The only downside was that there was no way to repair such a monolithic circuit, let alone disassemble the finished product.

It was the sound of someone stirring behind him that told him Jamie was awake. Turning to share his progress with his younger sibling, Jack was surprised at the sight. Stumbling into the room bleary eyed, the savant looked as if he had been dropped off a rooftop during his slumber. Gone was his attention to personal detail; Jamie looked like he had not even stopped to brush his teeth. Right away Jack knew that something was up. His brother bordered on obsessive compulsive behavior, and to see him make it all the way downstairs in this condition meant something was truly wrong.

"What the hell happened to you?" Incredulous, Jack was waiting for the other shoe to fall. At the same time he was concerned with which of his brother's personalities he would meet this morning. The difficulty of managing his sibling was often compounded by his current psychological avatar. *Oh, what he would give for a brother who merely suffered from mood swings…*

"We…can't…" Seemingly at a loss for words, it was his hesitant manner that confirmed that Jamie was struggling to process something difficult.

"Did you get any sleep at all?" Rising to look Jamie over, Jack was concerned. It was atypical to see his brother like this. Sleep was a regimented part of his daily life. The savant preferred to have his batteries fully charged at the beginning of each day.

"We cannot market this device, they won't let us." Jamie's tone a deep rumble, it almost sounded as if someone were playing back his voice at super-slow speed. Slumping as he moved, he seemed like a balloon that had lost part of its air. There was something familiar about this avatar as Jack's mind tried to place the persona.

"Bullshit!" Jack roared. "Not only are we gonna sell this baby, but we'll make sooooo much money off of it we'll be able to buy our own country. I'm thinking France; I love French chicks, even if they don't shave their pits."

"Nooo." The breath seemed to escape from Jamie as if he were deflating. His voice deep in resignation, it was as if he had given up on life itself. "It is doubtful that we would live long enough to collect a single dollar of revenue." Finally focusing himself, Jamie gave his brother a sad look.

Recoiling slightly, Jack was finally able to put his finger on the exact personality he was seeing. Having spent his life with Jamie, he knew them all, even the ones who rarely made an appearance. Taking a deep breath, the inventor realized he was talking to Eeyore.

While Jamie spent most of his time expressing himself via a mere handful of personas, each designed to express what he was feeling at that very moment, there were literally dozens of characters that had spilled out of the savant over the years. Today it was the droopy donkey known for his clinically depressed demeanor. It had been one of the books that their Mother had read to them during the early years. Like any children, they had the books, the movies, and even some of the stuffed animals. Signifying Jamie at the lowest point of his psychological scale, the Eeyore persona was a rare one, reserved for those times when the savant was inescapably sad and depressed.

Taking a deep breath, Jack knew to proceed with caution. In the back of his mind he wondered if he should lock up the poisons and power tools. Eeyore's appearance worried him considerably; his experience with this avatar had almost never been good.

Jamie seemed flustered for a moment as he tried to find a way to coalesce his complex vision into words. His voice a monotone grumble, he flopped down into the nearest chair as he spoke. "What would have happened if Oppenheimer had discovered the secret of nuclear weapons on his own, without government funding, simply came up with the device in a lab at Berkley?"

That caused Jack to take pause before answering.

"The government would have swooped in and taken over the technology. They would have classified it, and every bit of Oppie's work." Even as Jack said it, he realized that they were talking apples and oranges. "But that was a weapon of mass destruction, during a time of world war. They would have had to do it, if nothing else, to keep the Axis forces from getting hold of the knowledge."

"This is no different." Shaking his head, Jamie confirmed his belief that these were parallel inventions.

"This kind of technology would be a boon for military weaponry, and the nation that possesses it would rule the world. The applications could change the very face of warfare, giving the possessor a significant advantage over the nearest contender. Not only would they take the technology from us, but it would remain classified for a score of years. It would be decades before any of this made its way into the mainstream." His voice dragging, Jamie seemed almost stunned as his tone recreated the gravel of Eeyore's essence.

Rising up ramrod straight, Jack considered the concept. It was true enough that antigravity would change not only fighters and bombers, but tanks and ground vehicles as well. *If you could levitate houses or skyscrapers, then why not tanks or battleships...or the entire 1ˢᵗ Infantry?* Man-portable packs were easy enough to build once you knew the secret.

"And as you mentioned, they would have taken Oppenheimer's technology to keep it from falling into the hands of other nations. There is no country or major corporation on the planet that would not kidnap us for this technology. It is worth countless trillions of dollars, and the nation that possesses it will become the newest alpha-nation on the planet. It would be thirty years before this technology were applied to space exploration, and even then the prices would be kept artificially high by greedy capitalists. I'm not sure which would hinder progress more; the government or big-business."

Slumping down into a nearby chair, Jack felt as if he had been hit by a truck. As much as he wanted to refute his brother's assertions, he knew it was true. Both the government and commerce would seek to control this invention, delaying its greatest uses in favor of military superiority and profit margins. Even worse was that so many foreign nations would not blanche at the idea of kidnapping them for this technology. Seeing no way that they could hope to profit from this without ending up in Stalag-17 themselves, he saw his dream vanishing quickly.

"What...?   So what do we do, shelve this technology? No way!" Still sure that there was an alternative, Jack rebelled against the idea. But time and again he was forced to wonder if humanity was ready for the invention.

As he sat dejected, Jack finally understood what had caused his brother's bedraggled condition; no doubt the savant had suffered hours of fitful sleep as one nightmare scenario after another attacked his dormant mind. Even in sleep mode his beautiful mind was capable of processing quantum volumes of data. More than once the savant had literally unlocked secrets of the universe in his sleep.

"No, we will not shelve it." Shaking his head, Jamie seemed sure of that much. "We simply cannot roll out this product without significant safeguards in place. We cannot leak a hint of this until we are ready."

"That's gonna be a problem." Remembering something that had popped up on his social media alerts earlier in the day, Jack poked the touch screen to activate a browser. There on his feed was the picture of a 1965 Ford Mustang soaring over a pair of street lights. "Our cousin Alvie found it on one of the conspiracy sites he goes to all the time. Said he thought it looked a lot like my car so he sent it over."

Peering at the photo, Jamie made an angry sound. Straightening up, he seemed to shrug off Eeyore before speaking in a firm voice.

"Alexis, go to red alert, and delete every copy of that picture, delete all text associated with the story. If you cannot access the content then give their servers a head-crash. It must all be erased." His voice now resolute, Jamie had switched to his Captain James T. Kirk avatar. Suddenly standing upright, his dour expression had been replaced by a hard and focused stare.

There was a pause before the AI answered in a festive tone.

"I was able to track down one thousand and thirty two instances of that photo, but the story had spread extensively through social media."

Pursing his lips, Jamie considered the next step. Knowing that sites like Facebook and Twitter were hardened against external attacks, he would need to take alternative steps to purge any information in their domains.

"Use the Moscow connection, and nuke them." Nodding firmly, Jamie was sure that it was the right option.

"I dunno about that." Jack shook his head. "Sure, everybody'll believe it was the Ruskies that did it, but if you do then people will start thinking that there's something to the story. Right now it's just more fake-news. It hasn't even gone viral yet."

"Hmmmph." Not convinced, Jamie took the next logical step. "Lieutenant Uhura, begin searching for alternate pictures. If one person with a phone spotted him, then there may be more."

"A picture of a flying car will just be written off as Photoshop magic." Jack shrugged, worried that nuking popular servers could garner too much attention.

"You seem to forget that your car not only has a license plate in the back, but another in front as well, and

THAT could easily be traced to our location." Pointing a finger towards the garage on the first floor, Jamie's voice was definitive.

Jack paused a moment as he imagined stormtroopers kicking in their front door.

"Do it Alexis." Jack agreed. "Nuke any site you can't access otherwise. Clean house, and look for any other pics."

"You are not the boss of me." In a sing-songy voice, the synthetic entity reminded him who she really worked for.

"Double mocha latte." He reminded her of the standing threat to pour coffee over her CPU.

I can nuke people too, you know." As she spoke, his screen switched to video imagery of a small bathroom. Seated on the throne was Jack with a Hustler magazine parked in his lap. Staring intently at the images therein, the inventor's left hand seemed busier than the rest of his body.

"Whoah!" Eyes wide, Jack quickly switched off the monitor before turning to his brother sharply. "When the fuck did you put a camera in the bathroom?"

"Mind your language, Ensign." A sharp scolding to his voice, Captain Jamie stood firm.

"Bullshit! You put a camera in MY bathroom. What in the hell for?" His anger drowning out his brother's dislike for profanity, Jack demanded an explanation.

Halting for the briefest moment, Jamie seemed to almost be switching gears. A quick shake of his head and the savant continued lecturing with a flawless British accent.

"Alexis needed to be able to evaluate the full spectrum of human activities as part of her learning process. She must have unmitigated access to our daily routines in order to truly gain an understanding of human dynamics." Shrugging, it seemed self evident to Jamie.

"In my bathroom!" More of a statement than question, the elder brother already planned on smashing the camera with a hammer while Alexis watched.

"Wouldn't it be terrible…" She started out with a lilt to her voice, "if somehow my processor was shorted out, and I accidentally posted these images all over the net? You would literally die from the embarrassment, wouldn't you?"

Holding up the empty coffee pot, Jack fumed. "You're lucky I'm outta Joe or I'd fry you like a Florida death row inmate."

"Children, please." Jamie shook his head as their mindless argument pained his beautiful mind. "We have more important things to consider than my brother's compulsion with touching himself. Perhaps a cup of tea would help to set us on the proper course."

Sitting glumly on the edge of his desk, Jack grumbled just loud enough for Alexis' sensitive microphones to detect. For her part, the AI knew how much Jamie disliked unnecessary prattle so she simply remained silent.

"I dunno about this. We have invented the greatest breakthrough in history, this is our big break, and we'll be richer than Midas. No way in hell should we let this technology die on the vine." Shaking his brother by the shoulders, Jack implored Jamie to see logic.

Reminding him of the dangers associated with trying to profit from this invention, Jack could almost see Oxford Professor fade from Jamie's eyes before being replaced with gloomy Eeyore.

"I…I need to give this some thought." Jamie stammered as he turned away. Shuffling in his bedroom slippers, he made his way back upstairs, most likely to finish the sleep he had missed with a restless day of tossing and turning.

Feeling the irritation begin to build within him, Jack was reduced to a single coarse expletive.

"FUCK!" Bursting outwards, it was the one word that truly demonstrated what he was feeling right then. Here they had achieved arguably the greatest invention since the light bulb, and they could not afford to even release it.

"Bat guano!" Alexis echoed his sentiment.

"Girl, I gotta teach you to swear better than that." Shaking his head, Jack glanced up at one of her cameras. "Right after I smash that bathroom camera."

"It's not like I'll un-remember what you do in there, just because you get rid of the camera." A tinge of laughter to her voice, Alexis chided him through the desktop speakers.

"Don't get cocky or I'll post pictures of you with your service panels taken off." Referring to the metal access doors that covered her enclosure, Jack appealed to her own bizarre sense of privacy.

"No, Jamie said you were not allowed to post naked pictures of me." Aghast, Alexis seemed to recoil at the idea of having her innards exposed for the world to see.

"He's not the boss of me. You either forget about what I...*read*...in the bathroom, or I'll post naked pictures of your processor on Twitter." Looking up, Jack gave a wiry smile.

"Ooooh, fine!" Clearly exasperated, she gave in reluctantly. "I'll disable the connection to the bathroom camera."

"Thank you for being *sooo* reasonable." Flashing a plastic smile, Jack turned back to his desktop. Satisfied that he had her contained for the immediate future, he had played on her base coding. Having been there when her original OS was written, he knew the provisos that had been incorporated into her original code. Despite all of her complexity, the synthetic woman suffered from many of the same frailties and insecurities of any real human.

In the days that followed, Jamie was increasingly difficult to live with. With his frustration being manifested in an atypical fashion, the savant was completely out of sorts.

"WHATEVER GAVE YOU THE IDEA THAT WE WOULD WANT TO TALK TO A PITIFUL, INSIPID BEAST LIKE YOU, EVEN IF WE WERE HOME?" Shouting into the telephone receiver, Jamie's voice echoed throughout the basement workshop. "IF YOU EVER CALL AGAIN I'LL COME TO YOUR HOUSE AND MURDER YOU, AND YOUR DOG, AND YOUR GOLD FISH! DON'T CALL AGAIN…EVER!!"

Watching Jamie hang up the phone with a vile expression, Jack could only wonder what that was all about.

"Telemarketer?" The elder brother asked hesitantly.

"Oh, no." Jamie's demeanor changed to one of Professor James' stretched smiles. "I was just setting up voicemail for this new phone."

"Sure, you run with that." Giving a grimace, Jack was in the process of backing out of the room when his brother's expression changed dramatically once again.

Rising from his seat with a sheaf of designs in his hand, the younger Sparks brother begin an angry lecture as his finger jabbed at one of the components.

"¿Por que você usou cobre para alinhar o conjunto de cunha? Eh?" Waving the sheets in front of his brother's face, Jamie was livid. *"Eu disse pare você usar platina para que não ficasse!"*

"Whoa there hawse; slow yer roll little brother." Using a single finger to push Jamie away, Jack resisted the urge to yell at his sibling. "You know I don't speak Portuguese so I got no frickin' idea what you're babbling about."

"Bah!" Clearly irritated, the savant threw the papers into the air before storming back to his desk.

"This is the part where I get the hell outta here for the rest of the night." Holding up a finger, Jack knew it was his best idea of the day. Closing the door gently, he made a point to avoid anything that could trigger another of his brother's avatars.

"Portuguese?" Alexis asked as he passed her camera.

"Oh, you haven't met Portuguese *Jaime* before. Yeah, ol' *Jaime* is a little volatile but nothing to worry about." Reassuring the artificial intelligence that watched them both, Jack paused to offer another piece of advice. "Look, I'm gonna go get stupid-drunk and try to forget where I live for about twelve hours. So keep an eye on him while I'm gone. If he starts barking and chewing on slippers then just play him some Metallica."

"That works?" She seemed surprised at the counterintuitive suggestion.

"Nope, not a bit. But it drowns him out so the neighbors don't freak out. Eventually he'll mark his territory, hump a table leg, and fall asleep on the floor." Nodding, Jack winked at the nearest camera before ducking out of the workshop.

There was a moment of silence while Alexis' cubed processor considered the scenario.

"I swear, next time I'm online and some whiny millennial complains about their parents, I am totally telling them about this." Giving an electronic sigh, the AI returned her focus to the man in the next room.

The Plan

Jack knew that something was up as soon as he walked into his workshop. With his far wall covered by dozens of hand-written notes, pictures and news clippings, all connected by colored yarn, it was obvious that his brother had been up for hours. While most people would have assumed that it was simply the way that the savant's mind worked, in truth the entire display was strictly for Jack's edification. Since Jamie could keep all of that knowledge easily stored in his eidetic memory, he personally had no reason for note-taking.

Starting with the first picture on the left column, Jack had made it through three completely unassociated articles before he felt his brother's presence in the room.

"It will make no sense if you read it in the wrong order." Clucking, Professor James chided his older sibling in a rich English accent.

"I'm sorry; do we not read left to right, top to bottom? Are we Japanese today?" Irritated at his brother for making him feel ordinary, Jack lashed out.

"No, we read things intelligently, from the core outwards." Tapping the center of the wall, he indicated the spot where most of the colored yarn seemed to terminate. "Simpletons read left to right because their minds cannot quantify a world in three dimensions."

"Fine. Read it to me so that my simpleton mind won't be overloaded." Folding his arms, Jack gave a grimace. Somehow he had the feeling that he should be wearing a crash helmet for what was to come next.

"Now boarding; the short bus! *Toot toot!*" Singing out the words, Alexis could not resist the urge to taunt him.

"Toot toot?" Jack shook his head. "Boats, trains and flatulent people go toot-toot. The short bus has a horn."

"And you would know, having actually ridden the short bus. Did the driver let you honk the horn when you were a good boy, Jackie?" A girlish giggle followed before Alexis was silenced by a hard look from Jamie.

"If we may continue unabridged…?" With one eyebrow raised up higher than the other, Professor James made it clear that the question required no further dialog.

Like a proper British college professor, Jamie lectured his older brother for more than an hour, laying out every possible ramification of their actions were they to attempt to market their new discovery. In nearly every scenario they either ended up slaves of the state, dead, incarcerated, or saw their dreams of space colonization delayed by as much as 40 years. No matter how they tried, their efforts were blocked by capitalists and war mongers. The only path that kept them out of a North Korean gulag was if they gifted the technology to the world…but then they would not be able to benefit financially from their own discovery. Growing more frustrated with each reiteration that ended in failure, Jack was sure that they were sunk.

"And that is a basic summary of how things will go if we take the classical pathway to introduce gravitational disaffinity. *However…*" Jamie repeated himself for clarity. "*However*, there is no requirement that we take the classical path at all. Think of this; if we already know their every move, then all we have to do is create a plan that preempts these attacks, negotiates around the roadblocks, and we could have it all."

"So you have an idea for us to get rich, and go into space at the same time?" Jack perked up, knowing that his brother must have something clever brewing.

"Absolutely.   However, there is one small, miniscule…*trifle*…of a hiccup in the whole plan." Showing one of his plastic smiles, it was obvious that Jamie was trying to show a brave front.

"Oh?" Jack asked, not liking the sound of the qualifier his brother had just used.

"Very small hiccup, sub-atomic in fact; we just have to die." Shrugging, the savant acted as if it were something people did all the time.

"Go on…I'm listening." Wondering how his brother would talk himself out of this cliff-hanger, Jack sat back for the rest of the story.

VIDEO LOG: JACK E SPARKS MS ME MEE

Jack's face looked tired as the camera came to life. Reclining in the seat his eyes seemed to evaluate the lens that peered at him robotically. With a cold beer in a frosted mug, he had clearly decided to get comfortable for whatever he was about to say.

"So, I am recording this log in the event that our plans don't work out. We already know that if things go wrong, we could become the victims of fake news and conspiracy theories, and the only thing worse than spending the rest of my short life in a communist prison would be if the entire world thought we were terrorists. Jamie has reasoned that one of the most likely weapons to be used against us is fabricated evidence. It would be one of the government's primary weapons, to bury us under a tidal wave of falsehoods. That comb-over of a President may only have an IQ of one-fifteen, but he definitely knows how to play the media like a fiddle.

If you are watching this now, then you need to understand that my brother and I are not terrorists, we are not spies, and we are not trying to sell any military secrets to foreign nations. We are simply two guys who invented the most breath-taking device since sliced bread. We have invented an energy efficient form of antigravity. We'd love to sell it, to cash in on it, but the fact is; we want much, much more than money. More than just personal recognition or fame, we want to truly change the world for the best. Before I die, I would like to stand on the moon, or farm potatoes on the face of Mars. But the only way we could do these things is if we took some very…different actions. We have no desire to harm the world. Quite the contrary, our actions are intended to keep the world from harming us."

Clicking the recording off, Alexis was already encrypting the file before Jack even took a breath.

"You look uncomfortable." She noted as he took a long pull from the frosted mug in his hand.

"Don't you need to defrag your drives or something?" Irritated at having Alexis watch his every move, Jack returned his attention to the beer in hand.

"With my solid state matrix, I do not suffer from file defragmentation." She pointed out an obvious fact. "I would assume you knew this, since it was you who built that particular component."

"I wasn't actually trying to imply that you really needed to defrag; moreover I was hinting that you should really go away and leave me the hell alone." Grumbling, he was surprised that she did not get the barb the first time.

"I am cognizant of your intended meaning, and I responded with my own pointed response." Sounding like a female Doctor Spock, she stood her ground, *figuratively anyhow.*

"And yet you're still here. *Go away kid, ya bother me.*" Turning away from the camera, Jack tried to focus on the diagrams that Jamie had prepared for him to work on. It was late in the day, and he was tired. Flipping through the pages, he could not help but notice that his brother had graciously listed each project in order of priority; just in case Jack's simple mind could not keep track of the steps in the plan. Admittingly, it had been elaborate; Jamie's plan had sounded more like something from an episode of *Mission Impossible.* Even as it was being meticulously explained, Jack had not fully grasped it until the very end. It was only after his brother was done with the explanation, and he'd had sufficient time to digest it, that he finally comprehended it all.

Turning away from Alexis' ever watchful eye, Jack began the task of laying out the control circuitry for the new and improved Gen V drones.

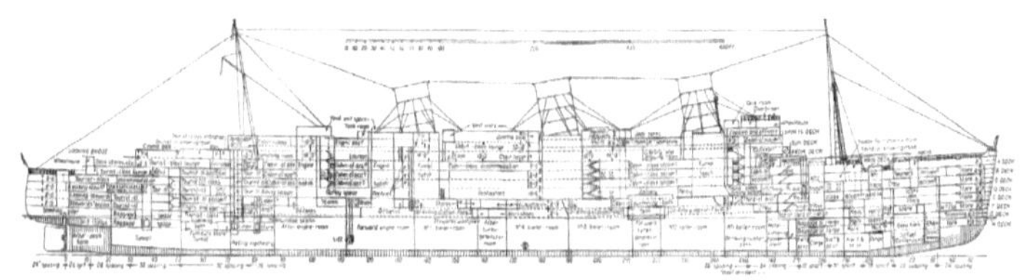

Lurching to a stop, Jack was not gentle on the rental car. Although it was a sporty little Ford, it just wasn't his Mustang. Irritated that he had to drive the substitute while his '*Stang* was in the shop, the inventor had been especially rough on the rental car.

Climbing out, he walked to the edge of the parking lot before taking in a deep breath of the sea air. It had been ages since he had gone to the beach, and even longer since he had been down in this part of Long Beach. Allowing his eyes to scan the horizon, they ultimately settled on the magnificent creation before him. There she sat; the RMS Queen Mary.

She was impressive, even from this range; 81,000 tons of steel, rivets, and deck plating. Over a thousand feet long, she was akin to a hundred story skyscraper laid on its side. Afloat since 1936, she had once been regarded as one of the seven man-made wonders of the world. But that was half a century ago. In the years since, the floating luxury liner had been relegated to a tourist attraction. Parked in an artificial harbor only slightly bigger than the ship, she would never sail the high seas again.

Jack could not help but give a smile as he realized that she was absolutely perfect for their plans. Turning back to the little rental car he removed a valise from the back seat. With the case resting on the hood of the car he examined the contents. To the casual observer they were just insects, albeit large ones, like flying cockroaches with a compact solar cell running down the middle of their back. Of these, there were three. Designed for surveillance purposes, they each sported a high resolution camera, extended wifi, and built-in microphone units.

But it was the final bug that really stood out. Larger than the others by several magnitudes, it looked like an oversized dragonfly. Functionally different from the others, it was more of base-station. While the smaller drones were quite capable of their assigned task, they lacked wi-fi range, especially if they were to be deployed within the metal guts of the Queen Mary. Hence, the dragonfly was really more of a relay station, gathering feed from the smaller units and forwarding it to the next wireless point in the chain.

Using the tip of a pen to activate each of the drones, he waited until a voice in his ear told him that comms had been established.

"I have link with all four drones." Alexis was all business today.

"Do it to it, Pruitt." Grumbling the words, he watched as the Gen V drones lifted off, heading directly for the massive ocean liner.

This afternoon found Jack seated on a bench in a small park. Really more of a grassy knoll, the diamond-shaped patch of grass between Water Street and Broadmont was largely ornamental. Aside from the lawn and two benches, there was nothing very park-like about it. Still, it was a public bench, located in an area with no camera coverage from either the traffic cameras, or the FBI office across the street. Better still, the geography allowed him to stay off cameras for fifteen blocks; something essential if they were to remain undetected from the digital watchdog that protected government buildings. Essentially a giant calculator with a million eyes, the PREDATOR system would not only track faces at a single site, but across multiple hi-risk targets. In simplest terms, if the system spotted your face in proximity to too many of the wrong places, it would signal an alert to its masters, even if you were not on any watch lists. PREDATOR did not believe in coincidence. With what he and Jamie had planned, it would not help their plan if they drew the attention of the NSA's virtual watch dog.

Waiting until the last of the pedestrians were out of sight, Jack opened up the small leather case, exposing a trio of smaller bugs and one of the larger base station units disguised as a dragonfly. Already switched on, Alexis confirmed that she had a digital link with the devices.

"Away with you. Deploy." Muttering in a low voice, Jack spoke directly to the synthetic lady at the far end of the link. Glancing down he watched as the bugs lifted off one at a time. Rising to treetop height, they each began the slow process of flying towards the federal building. With their newly acquired flight abilities, they had significantly more range than the Gen IVs would have enjoyed. Although it had taken some work, Jack had been able to manufacture a nearly microscopic gravitational disaffinity device for each. Powered by blue plasma, the antigrav system had enough fuel for significant flight operations. Unfortunately the rest of the onboard systems were still powered by good old-fashioned electricity. It was for this reason that the Gen Vs sported not only the solar cell down their back, but another along their belly. Ideally the recon units would perch from light fixtures while they conducted their surveillance. People in offices rarely looked up at the light fixtures, and even fluorescent bulbs released enough photonic energy to keep their miniscule solar units charged.

With Alexis managing their flight remotely, it was not difficult for her multi-tasking CPU to allow each of the surveillance units to tailgate personnel as they entered and exited the building. Busy with their lives, none of the federal employees paid any attention to the bugs that snuck through the door behind them.

But the base station was far too big to go unnoticed indoors. Instead, Alexis found a convenient spot to park the oversized dragonfly on the exterior of the building. From there it would communicate with an entire network of relays attached to the sides of buildings. Although it had been a lot of work (and expense) to build a small army of the oversized dragonflies, the use of the wireless base stations gave them the security of an air-gap in their comms. Had they chosen to go with a cellular or Ethernet connection they could have been easily traced. But with a network of dragonflies perched on buildings between them and their targets, the only concern they faced was from the avian community. Already they had experienced a few close calls with the damned pigeons that inhabited the rooftops of their city. Apparently dragonflies are considered a delicacy at those altitudes.

"We are in." Alexis confirmed that she had penetrated the FBI building.

"Good. I'm outta here." Jack rose slowly and began shuffling down the same path he had taken just an hour ago.

The next step of the plan had been the most dangerous.   While the FBI penetration had required significant safeguards, this time they were going directly into the belly of the beast. Jamie had reasoned that they needed to be able to monitor their chief adversary, but unlike the Federal Bureau of Investigation, the NSA was an organization specifically hardened against active attack. Being a central arm of the intelligence gathering system employed by the Department of Homeland Security, the NSA had resources in place specifically designed to defeat efforts like theirs. It was a foregone conclusion that there was no approach to the site that was not covered by overlapping cameras. Able to monitor feed from any traffic camera or surveillance system, PREDATOR was already watching him.

It was for this reason that Jack now pushed a shopping cart loaded with aluminum cans. With clothes that were tattered and stained, he made sure to play his part by muttering to no one in particular. Wearing a scraggly beard and mismatched shoes, he appeared to the locals to be nothing more than one of the many homeless citizens who flocked to this low income neighborhood.

Stopping in front of the hardware store, he pretended to engage in an argument with a telephone pole. Cursing as much as he mumbled, he managed to blend his movements as he flipped back the raggedy blanket that covered a series of drones all laid out and ready to go.

Still deep in an argument with his imaginary friend, Jack noticed the Cadillac Escalade as it slid into the driveway next door. While there were many such luxury vehicles in the city, there were few in this neighborhood. With the local median income only slightly above the national poverty level, the expensive SUV was conspicuous. Still babbling to himself, Jack could see the Escalade as it stopped at an intercom. Within a few seconds the garage door slid upwards, allowing the vehicle entry into the non-descript warehouse.

Wandering a few feet from the shopping cart, Jack held a grungy spray bottle in one hand, and the sports section in the other. Mumbling incoherently, he only needed to approach people to be actively avoided. In this city it was assumed he was offering to clean their vehicle windows in exchange for whatever change they had in their pockets. Although he had no intention of cleaning anything, he knew that this part of the act was critical to the plan. With PREDATOR watching, they needed some sleight of hand. Drawing attention away from the shopping cart, Jack left it clear for Alexis to deploy the smaller drones one at a time. Even if someone reviewed the footage they would be unlikely to notice insects buzzing about his cargo of trash and aluminum cans.

"Hey!" The manager called out from the doorway of the hardware store. "Get the fuck off the property or I'll call the cops!"

Appearing to babble mindlessly, Jack grumbled as he headed back towards his cart. Yanking it by the handle, he tried to convey a sense of anger at being run off. Shaking a fist as he yelled over his shoulder, it was easy for him to run the cart into a curb, spilling the top layer of trash piled high there.

Still cursing, he made a pitiful sight as he scrambled to pick up the junk that spilled off his shopping cart. As he scooped up the last of the items, he was sure to leave the dragonfly just under a shrub. Too big to go unnoticed, it would be deployed later that night, long after Jack was gone.

"So you're sure that place is NSA?" Speaking in a low voice, Jack still wondered about the mysterious warehouse. From the outside it looked more like a crack-house.

"Positive." Alexis confirmed. "I have tracked petabytes of data flowing into that site. Clearly it is a digital repository or processing center of some sort."

"We'll find out soon enough." Shrugging, Jack continued to shuffle along as if he were in no particular hurry. He had six blocks to go before reaching the alleyway where he had parked. It had been the closest they could get without coming up on any of the thousands of cameras perched around the city. There were electronic eyes everywhere, and PREDATOR had access to all of them.

In the garage Jack worked on the broken Mustang. With four new wheels, new struts, two axles, and a rebuilt transmission, she was serviceable again. In truth, Jack had done almost none of the work, preferring to leave *that* type of labor to the grease monkeys down at the shop. Besides, he had a ton of work of his own. The sheer number of projects in Jamie's master plan was extensive. Only halfway through the list, Jack chose to outsource the grubby work.

"You done with them man-packs yet?" Gruff in his delivery, Jamie's country accent told his brother what kind of mood he was in.

Giving a sigh, Jack leaned back against the side of the car where he had been attaching a bracket. Realizing that each avatar represented his brother's inner emotions at that particular moment, he knew right away that Jamie was feeling out of his element this morning. Country Jimmy usually manifested himself when the savant had something daunting to do. As best as Jack had been able to figure over the years, it was Jamie's way of showing how vulnerable the situation made him feel; like a hayseed that just fell off a turnip truck. Giving Jamie a hard look, he refrained from answering. Jack knew that whatever alternate agenda his brother had would be revealed in short order.

"We gotta timeline to keep. Ain't gonna get rich if you're lollygagging all th' time." Clearly irritated with progress, the savant's voice was derisive.

"Yeah, I know, and I have an appointment with the FAA inspector tomorrow." Raising an eyebrow, Jack let the irritation seep into his voice. It was difficult living with a computer. Alexis was no better.

"Mmmm." Nodding, Jamie glanced around at the other devices that still awaited installation.

"Mmmm? What?" Jack was not fooled by his brother's act. He could tell that there was something else.

"Well y'see..." Clearing his throat, the younger sibling seemed atypically unsure of how to proceed. "Alex is worried about workin' with you on account of how you always talk smack to her an' all. Y'know what I mean?"

Jack simply blinked his eyes twice as he looked up at his brother. It was not the first time they'd had this conversation, though usually it was with Professor James.

"She's all worried that..." Jamie was cut off by his brother's interruption.

"It's not a she, it's a computer, albeit a very smart computer, but still just a chunk of resistors and silicon wafers." In a stern voice, the older sibling was in no mood for this argument.

Jamie seemed to pause for the briefest moment. From where he leaned up against the car, Jack could almost see him shifting gears in that beautiful mind of his. Gone was the stooping posture of Country Jimmy as Jamie stood ramrod straight. With one eyebrow raised, he was clearly back to Professor James.

"She is a simulated neural net with as many synaptic endings as a real person. You hurt her feelings." Finding his own courage, Jamie felt that he was standing on firm ground.

"Computer!" Jack retorted before standing up.

"Sentient being." Jamie squinted at his older brother. "She scored better on the Turing test than you did, twice."

"Turing was a robot." Flashing his eyes as he turned away, Jack snatched up one of the little hobbyist jet engines from the nearby work bench. Moving to the trunk, he examined the mounting brackets that had already been installed.

"See what I have to work with." Alexis's voice chimed in. "I am willing to accept his shortcomings, yet he treats me like a piece of office furniture. It's organic discrimination; he's created a hostile workplace with his specist attitudes."

"Specist?" Jack roared at that accusation. "That term would imply that you were also a species."

"OMG, he is so insensitive." Her voice taking on a new pitch, she seemed to almost recoil. "And I'm allegedly the one who is devoid of emotions. Are you sure you didn't build him in a lab too?"

"I got work to do." Dismissive, Jack tried to ignore them both.

"What I'm saying is that it is imperative that the two of you work together cooperatively in the very near future, and it needs to be…" Jamie searched for the right word.

"Harmonious." Alexis finished his sentence for him.

"Why can't you just have an inflatable woman like other brothers? Seriously, who builds the talking half of a woman first?" Giving a grimace, Jack hoped the barb would be enough to make the two of them go away.

"Insufferable!" Alexis' voice seemed to choke at the end. It took a few moments before they could hear the faintest of sounds in the background.

"Is she crying?" Standing bolt upright, Jack was truly irritated now. "Seriously? I'm supposed to buy this little act of hers?"

Nonplussed, Jack thumbed towards the speakers where her delicate sobs emanated. It was at that instant that he saw Jamie make one of his classic pauses as he changed gears. Right away the savant's posture changed noticeably. With fists balled, Jamie leaned into Jack's personal space threateningly. Right away the older brother realized that he had triggered his least favorite of the avatars: Jimbo the Jersey truck driver.

Furrowing his eyebrows, Jamie looked angrily at his brother. "How many times do I gotta tell you'se to treat her like a lady? Eh?" Giving Jack a firm shove, the savant was clearly on edge. "I've kicked wholesale ass for a whole lot less'n you just said; you feelin' me college boy?"

Stepping back, Jack reconsidered his next statement. There was a big difference between what he could say to Professor James and what he could say to Jersey Jimbo. The latter tended to get punchy.

"Jamie, she's a computer!" Jack shot back. "I know because I built half of her."

"Naw, she only started out as a computer. How many times I gotta tell you that a truly sentient AI needs to be grown like a child. You can't just write a buncha code and call it alive. We'se all the result of years of living, years of experiences all combined to build the people we'se each are. Hell, you yourself started out as a non-sentient embryo. In fact, I read a scientific study the other day that said that you weren't sentient until the age of two. Before that you'se was just an eating, pooping, crying machine. So if it took more'n two years fer yer own neural net to grow an' develop into a sentient being, then why can't you'se see that Alexis ain't no different?"

Frustrated, Jack knew his brother's persistence. While most people could be driven off with insults, Jamie rarely knew when to give up the fight. With Alexis sobbing in the back ground, it was a safe bet that the only way he would get any work done was to compromise.

"Okay, what exactly do you want from me?" Dropping the wrench into the trunk angrily, Jack looked up at the nearest camera.

Shrugging, Jamie seemed to find the answer absurdly simple.

"Just treat her like a lady. She's as much a person as you or me; all she wants is to be given the same consideration as any organic being."

"Maybe you haven't noticed, but I don't treat humans particularly well either." Jack continued to look into the camera. "Alright, if I agree to treat her nice will she promise to stop recording me all the time?"

"Alexis?" Acting as a broker between them, Jamie looked up to the same camera his brother stared into.

There was a moment of silence before she responded. "I promise that if he treats me like a lady then I will not attempt to blackmail him or otherwise embarrass him by revealing his private activities."

With a smile, Jamie turned to his brother. "Well chump, what's it gonna be? Plan A, or plan B" Holding up a fist, Jersey Jimbo let him know exactly what Plan B entailed.

"Well what?" Jack rebuffed the look. "Oh fine. I promise to stop threatening to urinate on her processor, and I will try to treat her as well as I treat the ladies down at DMV."

"Plan B it is!" Grabbing his brother by the collar, Jersey Jimbo knew better than to let the last part slip past.

"Fine, I'll treat her as well as a regular human." Exasperated, Jack just wanted them to go away so he could finish the car.

"Superb." Flashing one of his plastic smiles, Jamie switched back to Professor James in the blink of an eye. Satisfied with himself for negotiating the truce, the Professor looked between Jack and the camera before departing the room.

"I still don't like you." Jack whispered hoarsely.

"Oh look, it's nine o'clock. Shouldn't you be touching yourself inappropriately by now?" Her tone acrid, there was an audible click after she spoke, as if she had just dropped the microphone.

"I really gotta get my own place." Shaking his head, Jack resumed work on the Mustang.

It had been a long day when the packages were delivered. Although the brothers had regular drop-offs by UPS, Fedex, and DHL, this one was special. Hermetically sealed inside of a box marked with Cyrillic writing, the contents had been carefully packed for shipment across multiple continents.

"Oh goody!" Jamie's voice was almost a squeal. It was atypical to hear him this excited about anything. "Open mine…open mine!"

Jack could not help but smile as he watched his brother. It was his Jimmy Christmas avatar; reserved for times when the savant was truly giddy about something. His face aglow as he clapped his hands, it was as if Jack was talking to a small child. It was atypical to see his brother this way; Christmas Jimmy was one of his rarest of personas.

Careful not to damage the contents, the older sibling used an X-acto knife to slice open the vacuum sealed bag before gently pulling out the helmet inside.

"Gimme gimme gimme!" Jamie's enthusiasm was pretty far off the reservation as he held out anxious hands. Plucking the helmet from his brother's grasp, he immediately had it on his head. Peering out through the Lexan visor, he gave a giggle before toggling the built in sunshade. "Hurry up with the rest!"

"Yeah, yeah, yeah." Jack turned his attention away from his brother's antics and began opening the next package. Gently removing the thick suit from the bag, he found his brother already tugging at the contents.

Knowing better than try to dampen his brother's enthusiasm, Jack ripped the bag open the rest of the way, allowing Jamie to pull out the heavy space suit. Holding it aloft while still wearing the helmet, the savant's face was in awe as he looked over the authentic cosmonaut's extra-atmospheric suit. Designed to be worn only during launch operations, it was not intended as an external suit like those worn by Armstrong and Aldrin during their legendary moon walks. Nonetheless, the very idea of owning a space suit touched a special nerve with the brothers.

Still giggling inside his helmet, Jamie was already struggling to get into his suit. Although the multiple layers of enclosures in the back slowed him down some, it was only minutes before the savant had the suit on in a cockeyed manner. Clearly designed for someone taller than he, the outfit seemed to hang on him.

Pausing from his job of opening the packages, Jack took a minute to fasten the front of Jamie's suit before helping him lock his helmet in place. Truly giddy, the younger brother actually stamped his feet in place as he gave a squeal of excitement. Pantomiming in slow motion, he pretended he was walking on the face of a distant world. Even with his face shield beginning to fog up, Jack could still see his eyes wide with wonder at the new toy.

Smiling, he could not remember the last time his brother had been this happy about anything. It would have been before their parents died. Mom had always been able to coax a smile out of Jamie. Sitting down on the edge of the remaining crate, Jack enjoyed the moment. Although he too wanted to try on his surplus space suit, he knew that the greater treasure was in watching his brother's joy. It would be fleeting, no doubt.

Finally back to business, Jack began to unpack the remaining outfit, checking it carefully for any rips or tears in the fabric. Sold as an expensive novelty item, the exoatmospheric suits were not intended to be used in space again. Having been used more than a few times before being stored in a Russian warehouse, it was a safe bet that the space suits would have at least a few issues. At minimum, they would need to fabricate the airpacks used to supply oxygen and power to the suits. Noticing a scuff on the left arm, Jack eyed the blemish closely as he tried to determine if the spot would need to be patched. Although he would much rather have used American suits, they cost much more and were difficult to obtain. Not only that, but in an odd twist of reality, purchasing US suits would have put them on the government's radar. With the Russian suits already being sold in high-end catalogs and EBay, no one would have thought twice about someone buying a pair of the things. But two American suits…that would have been atypical, that could have caught PREDATOR's attention.

"Whooh!" Jamie finally slowed down, his eyes wide inside of his helmet. "These things are tiring."

"You're probably just running out of air." Giving a grimace, Jack reached up and unlocked his faceplate.

"Oh, that's much better." Still grinning, Jamie took a breath of fresh air as he held the helmet gingerly in his hands. "This suit smells like feet."

"Feet and farts. I'm not surprised." Jack flashed a smile. "We'll clean 'em up. A little Fabreze will do wonders."

"Sodium Bicarbonate would be the appropriate agent." Returning to his usual Professor James avatar, Jamie was all business again.

"Sodium Bicarbonate?" Jack gave it a thought. "Baking soda?"

"Aye, Comrade." That silly grin on his face once again, Jamie delivered a snappy salute. "Are you going to try on your suit?"

Trying to be the adult in this conversation, Jack gave a frown. "I dunno, I still have a lot of work on the man-packs…"

"Ooooh, you know you want to." Showing a devilish grin Jamie prodded him with his free hand. Christmas Jimmy was impossible to contain.

Finally giving in, Jack let out his own broad smile. "Sure, what the hell."

Laughing as he opened the second box, the eldest Sparks brother had trouble subduing his own excitement.

Like the oversized child he was, Jack desperately wanted to play with his new toys.

"Men." Alexis sniffed as she watched them dance about in their suits. "Nothing more than overgrown boys."

Change of Plans

With four monitors flashing their content simultaneously, Jamie gave new meaning to multi-tasking as he worked on orbital calculations. With a small pair of speakers filling the room with the sweet sounds of John Coltrane's jazz, the savant kept pace by tapping his foot to the asymmetrical sounds. Allowing his eyes to scan between the various drone feeds, Jamie intently studied the layout of the NSA's data bunker. Built deep underground, the place was carefully concealed beneath a dilapidated warehouse. Although they had been successful at inserting the trio of drones into the secret facility, it had taken days to get the larger base station into the bunker. It had only been after Alexis had spotted a maintenance truck, complete with ladder rack, entering the sloping driveway that she finally saw her opportunity.

Once in, the oversized dragonfly had quickly relocated to the nearest light fixture where it could charge while still maintaining contact with the outside world. Being underground had made the event complicated. With the signal stunted by so much earth and concrete, they had to sneak in an extra relay unit. Smaller than the base station unit, it was still larger than the drones that crawled about the facility like roaches. Nonetheless, without it they would not have been able to get a reliable signal.

Flicking his eyes from screen to screen, Jamie had already determined a number of important components to the facility. He knew who the managers were, when each of the

3 daily shifts started, and where the server room was located. Additionally, he knew which of the employees was the least security conscious when they entered their user credentials. Already he had managed to capture passwords from multiple technicians.

But even more importantly he had been able to learn some truly frightening things about the breadth of the NSA's operation. Not only did they spy on virtually everyone, capturing their phone calls, text messages, emails, and social media posts, but they even snooped on other agencies. In fact it seemed that a large portion of their database was collated from lesser organizations. The FBI, INS, and DOJ were but a few of the groups who were unwittingly being spied on. As if that were not enough, any surveillance data gathered by those agencies was also pirated and pooled into the larger Department of Homeland Security database. In essence, anything that any law enforcement agency knew, the NSA and DHS also knew. All indications were that this river of knowledge flowed only in one direction; the feds were not known to share.

Insidious in its breadth, PREDATOR had tendrils in every aspect of their daily lives. In addition to spying on their private lives, the silicon beast also tracked banking history, routine internet traffic, cloud storage services, and even shipping records from millions of companies. He had no doubt that their own equipment purchases were in there somewhere. Having seen more than a dozen Ebay records accessed, they likely even knew about the space suits the brothers had recently ordered. Even more amazing was that they were actively tracking more than two hundred million cell phones, as well as wireless traffic at millions of public hotspots worldwide. Every Starbucks on the planet was actively scanned to see which MAC addresses were connecting there. PREDATOR saw everything, and recorded it all. Nothing was ever thrown away, discarded, or deleted. There was no way to avoid being data-collected by the digital beast; at best the brothers hoped to conceal themselves in the clutter.

"Uh oh." Sitting up abruptly, Jamie recognized the equipment in the technician's hands right away. With a loop of metal protruding from the hand-held unit the technician seemed to be scanning every surface in an organized pattern as he worked his way down the hallway. Although the twins had expected this to eventually happen, it had been assumed that they would have weeks to survey the operation before the next bug sweep.

Alexis saw the sweeper as soon as Jamie did. Immediately the drone scuttled backwards, trying to conceal itself under the fluorescent light where it had been perched. Hoping to shut down the transmitter as soon as it was out of sight, they never had a chance as an unseen hand reached up and plucked the device from its perch.

"What do we have here?" A woman's face peered down at the fake cockroach as she examined it carefully.

Immediately joined by a second technician, the two scrutinized the device before dropping it into a metal container. As soon as they closed the lid, all signal was lost.

"We have been compromised." Alexis spoke with a tinge of alarm to her voice.

"Jackie built the drones with Cyrillic markings so they will likely assume the devices are Russian. Alternately, they may consider the markings a false flag and come to the conclusion that it was planted by the Chinese because of the particular lithium-polymer battery I used." Nodding sternly,

Professor James reasoned that it was only a matter of time before the other drones would be found. As he could see on the remaining monitors, the facility was already shutting down all operations. Work would be halted until a complete sweep of the complex was conducted. The discovery of a foreign eavesdropping device would trigger a reaction throughout the entire NSA as well as DHS. They would begin checking all of their facilities, every employee would be forced to change their passwords, and every frame of surveillance footage would be examined. While this complicated things somewhat for the brothers, it would actually help Alexis to pinpoint the other data archives around the country. Already the AI was monitoring the alarms being spread outward from the hidden bunker.

"This is going to put a serious crimp in your plan." Stating the obvious, Alexis' voice was toneless.

"Yes and no. We will simply need to activate plan B." Shrugging, Jamie watched the remaining monitors.

"Jack will not like plan B. Not at all."

"And that is why he will not know about it until it has already happened." Nodding sternly, Jamie knew that there were serious risks associated with his alternate plan, risks that his twin brother would no doubt derail if he knew about them. "I have already built your alternate matrix, so you will be relatively safe."

"But you won't." Concern in her voice, the AI was clearly not a fan of the plan.

"I will be fine as long as you and Jack take care of your end." Though he spoke the words, Jamie could not help but let a hint of doubt creep into his voice. "Alex, listen to me very carefully; I need both of you to learn to work together.

Without me there to run interference, you two need to function as a cohesive team."

"But…" She stammered; a tic she had learned from watching TV. "Jackie's such an asshole."

"Indeed." Agreeing, Jamie's eyes never left the monitors. "Nonetheless, none of this will work if you two cannot reconcile your differences. You have an intelligence quotient several magnitudes greater than my brother, figure him out. Compared to you he is a simple corporeal being."

"How?" Desperation in the AI's voice made it clear that she had been trying to make peace with Jack for some time.

"To understand any living being you have to first understand what motivates them." Jamie held up a single finger as he explained just how simple humans really are. "You figure out what motivates my brother and you can influence him."

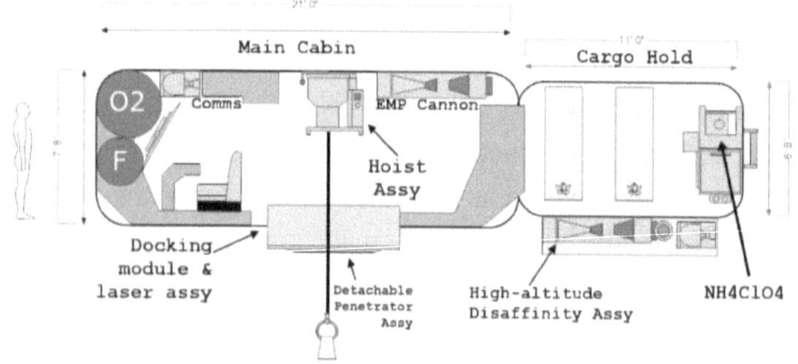

Jack woke the next morning to find a series of new designs on his workbench. Scrutinizing each, he tried to remember exactly where these would fit into the existing scheme. Right away his sharp mind sensed there had been a change of plans. Stepping into Jamie's workshop he was surprised to find the place empty.

"James had to run some errands." Alexis spoke up, her voice chiming through the desktop speakers at Jamie's work station.

"Errands?" Jack was surprised. His brother rarely drove anywhere. He considered it a stunting experience. Unable to multi-task, the savant regarded driving to be wholly un-stimulating. Aside from that, he was not very good at it. His highly logical mind had difficulties grasping the illogical patterns of other drivers.

Taking another moment to look over the office, he began noticing that the project his brother had been working on for several days was absent from the work bench. It puzzled him that Jamie would have taken Alexis' new processor core with him. Shrugging, he stumbled bleary-eyed back into his own office as the coffee gurgled into a pot against the far wall.

Switching on the trio of monitors that filled his own desk, Jack next scooped up the remote for the projector. Activating the display that covered an entire wall, he was surprised to find himself face to face with a diminutive woman. With red hair that flowed like fire from her head, she had playful eyes that seemed to evaluate him as he moved. Wearing a silky blouse and knee-length cigarette skirt she looked like a picture clipped from a catalog.

Looking her up and down, the elder brother had to admit that he liked what he saw. Built a little top-heavy, she was quite attractive by his standards. Really, she was attractive by any Western standards. In some parts of the world she would be jailed for looking that good.

"Morning Jackie." She flashed him a wry smile.

Jack recognized the voice right away. "Alexis?"

"We have a winner." She gave him a wink. "But it's pronounced wiener."

Listening to her playful laugh, Jack knew something was up. Giving her a hard look, he had to admit that he liked her better this way than her usual disembodied voice.

"What're ya doing, Alex?" Folding his arms, he inquired of her intent.

"Nothing in particular." Shrugging, Alexis never broke character. "I read a book last night, and it got me thinking that maybe I should have an avatar of my own."

"What book?" Even as he asked, Jack suspected that she had an agenda in all this.

"*The Moon is a Harsh Mistress*, by Robert Heinlein." Shrugging, she half turned away as if examining the diagrams on the screen behind her.

Jack's eyebrows went up right away. Although he knew that the AI had absorbed thousands of books, somehow he sensed that this particular novel was specifically scanned for his benefit. It had always been his favorite Heinlein story, and Jack had read them all.

"I liked Mike the sentient computer. Something about him seemed to connect with me." Looking over her shoulder she flashed him those blue eyes of hers while affording the engineer a view of her from the back.

"I hated the ending." Jack admitted before turning away to pour himself a cup of mud. With a preference for extremely dark coffee, he liked to jumpstart his day with a steaming cup of crack.

"But the colonists achieved independence?" Turning to face him, there was a look of genuine curiosity on her face.

"And they lost Mike." Adding a splash of sweet cream to his cup, Jack considered leaving it at that. Glancing up again at the young lady rendered on the screen he considered the effort she had likely taken to create this image. Although he considered Alexis to be nothing more than the culmination of some very clever software coding, he was in no mood for their usual combative conversational style.

"So despite the human's success, you were most concerned over what happened to the synthetic being in the story?" Raising an eyebrow, she seemed perplexed. "So you were willing to believe in the idea of AI in a book written more than fifty years ago, yet you refuse to believe in me?"

Caught in a discrepancy, Jack felt his warm and fuzzy feelings evaporate.

"Look, the new avatar is great and all, but I have work to do. Whatever my brother has cooked up means that I'll be working late for the next few weeks."

Nodding, Alexis suddenly gave a pirouette. When she was done spinning, her clothes had changed to a white lab coat. Her red hair now up in a bun, the woman's face was further accented by a pair of oversized glasses that gave her a more pensive look. Behind the virtual lenses her eyes had changed to a stunning shade of green.

Pausing as he sipped his coffee, Jack had to admit that he liked this avatar. Although her previous look had been attractive enough, there was something about a smart and strong willed woman that worked for him. Without meaning to, his expression revealed his innermost reaction to the new skin.

Glancing down at a clipboard in her virtual hands, she was all business.

"We received the royalty check from ENT and Mobil, both being direct deposited to the primary business account, so we are well funded for the immediate future.

Revenues on Pricewatch have been trending upwards, and Fedex tracking shows that we can expect delivery of the new fabber components later this afternoon." Looking up with those crystalline-green eyes of hers, she remained confident in her act.

"Then let's get to work." Feeling his ire softened considerably, Jack was having a hard time finding a downside to Alexis' new format. Even as he realized that her image was simply the result of a complex algorithm based on his browsing and multimedia history, the engineer could not help but feel a little appreciative at her effort. It did not hurt that she had struck a particular chord with him by adding the glasses.

*Damn, she's rocking those glasses...*he thought to himself.

It was late by the time that Jamie came home. Although he had really not gone far, it had been the surreptitious route he had taken that had consumed almost half of his day. While he expected much of their activities to be discovered in the weeks to come, this was a critical step that had to remain an absolute secret. Hence, he had found it necessary to obtain an older vehicle that would be sans GPS or tracking features like LoJack. Also, it had to be registered to someone completely unrelated to the twins, lest the license plates be tracked back to them via traffic surveillance cameras. Even at that, he had to choose a path devoid of the watchful electronic eyes that were everywhere. Not only were there traffic cameras everywhere, but cameras in ATMs, cameras in businesses, and even cameras on almost every laptop or phone. While the savant could avoid many of these by simple route planning, for the others he found it necessary to employ active measures.

Once he had acquired a clean vehicle through an ad in the paper, his next step had been to outfit it with a series of IR lamps, both inside as well as out. While the tiny string of LEDs were invisible to the naked eye, to the electronic eye they could be used to change the picture dramatically. Inside of the vehicle he used an illuminating projection to wash out his own features. On camera he would be nothing more than an indistinct blur behind the wheel, impossible to identify.

But on the outside of the vehicle he set up a much different rig. Using the adjustable light spectrum he could change the color of his vehicle at will. Additionally, using a cleverly designed device installed over his license plate, he could cast an entirely different image that was visible only to the peering electronic devices that were everywhere. With more than 30 different plate designations programmed into the device, all the savant had to do was press a button and his vehicle could not only change color, but license plate, state, date of expiration, etc. With a third unit mounted on the bumper, he could even project bumper stickers, all in a spectrum invisible to the human eye. To a bystander it would appear as if he had Christmas lights on his car, but electronic eyes and cameras would see an entirely different vehicle.

What complicated all of this though was the fact that he had to do it all manually. While Alexis could have done it much more efficiently than he, again he had to worry about being tracked. Even if he disabled all tracking features in his laptop, his route could be determined by triangulation as he moved between coverage of the regional cell towers. Hence, he had to manipulate the covert system old-school, by making manual selections every few blocks.

Finally arriving at his destination, he found a secluded place to unpack the contents of his trunk. Working to remove the bulky solar cells from the back seat, it only took a few minutes to attach the metal package to the back. Looking benign enough, the entire assembly was designed to look no different than the thousands of other solar cells located throughout the region. In the last decade the devices had become ubiquitous on their landscape, powering everything. In remote areas it was simply easier to install a solar array than to run power lines.

It had taken hours of surfing GoogleMaps to locate just the right place. With a trio of the big panels already powering the remote USGS climate reporting station, Jamie knew that no one would notice an additional panel or two. Parked down on the end of the row, it would simply appear to be part of the existing array. Only the closest of examinations would reveal that it actually powered a broadband transmitter and a duplicate of Alexis' core. The site already included a series of metal equipment cabinets, who would notice one more?

Finally satisfied with his work, Jamie had used the same contorted techniques to mask his path home. It worried him that his countermeasures were ineffective against the swarm of satellites that peered down from far above. However, he considered the risk from these devices to be minimal. While they could snap thousands of high-resolution pictures, the nature of their low-Earth orbits meant that they could not remain overhead for very long. Zipping along at 17,000 kph, the task would have to be handed off to a new satellite roughly every eight minutes. There would be gaps in their coverage that would allow him to disappear into the clutter of the California highways. Even the best intelligence agents would be hard pressed to track him more than a few miles, especially if he frequently paused under trees or other aerial cover.

Tip-toeing into the basement workshop he shared with his brother, the savant was surprised to see Jack asleep on his desk. On the screen behind him was a clutter of designs. Smiling, he held up a single finger to his lips as soon as Alexis appeared on the screen.

Shushing her, he gingerly made his way into the next office before closing the door behind him.

"It's all set up." He spoke the words in a quiet voice, not wanting to wake his brother.

"I know; I've been in it for hours." Appearing on the screen, her appearance had changed. With her hair draped on her shoulders, and a simple T-shirt replacing the lab coat, she had adopted a more casual look. "So the comms link is up and running. The new processor is quite an improvement over my current matrix."

"I also upgraded memory significantly." He spoke the words even though he knew there was no need. Alexis would have seen the changes within pica-seconds of taking over the new processor core.

"I still don't like this idea." Giving a frowny-face, she let him know how she felt about plan B.

"Do we still have any drones in play at the data center?" He asked, already knowing the answer.

"No. I burned them when capture seemed imminent." Raising an eyebrow she responded quietly. "And the drone they already found should have self destructed hours ago."

Nodding somberly, Jamie had been sure to include a small cache of white-phosphorous into the design. With each of the drones relying on gravitational disaffinity to get around, he could not risk having the technology falling into government hands any sooner than need be. Additionally, the design could tie them to the espionage. As things stood, the NSA was probably already blaming Beijing for the intrusion.

It was a moonless night as Jackie stood in the back yard. With a layer of clouds blotting out the stars, it was pitch black outside. Fastening his night-vision headset into place, he was able to see well enough despite the darkness. With the world rendered in a peculiar shade of green through the NVS goggles, the engineer had to smile as he looked around. Taking one more opportunity to check his shoulder straps, he wanted to be absolutely sure that the package on his back was firmly in place. Using a rig similar to that found on a parachute, the straps would keep the device anchored to his back at any orientation. This was critical considering how it would be used.

"Are you ready?" Alexis' voice was clear as a bell in the earpiece he wore.

"Red-eye!" Giving a nervous laugh, Jack gripped the controllers in each hand.

"Now beginning test zero-zero-one of the portable man-pack, alpha variant." Chiming in, she let him know that the telemetry data she monitored indicated that it was safe to start.

With his thumb he slowly moved the slider until he felt his feet lift off the ground. Feeling giddy, he could feel the straps as they cut into his waist and groin. Around him the world seemed to be sinking slowly as he rose up. Halting at twenty feet, he next flicked the small hat-switch that would pivot him using micro-jets installed on the sides of the pack. A little noisy in their operation, he quickly vowed to find a better way to control the device's yaw axis.

"Begin leveraging the disaffinity vector." Jamie's voice came through the earpiece clearly as he directed his brother to test the next component.

"Right, said the crash dummy with a master's degree." Using humor to conceal his discomfort, Jack grinned nonetheless. With his thumb, he toggled a small hat-switch to move to one side. It had been one of Jamie's recent discoveries about his disaffinity invention: that if they altered the polarity of the main collator disk, they could leverage the device in such a way as to create selective locomotion. In simplest terms; not only could the invention be used to ascend and descend, but they could essentially use the polarity like a crowbar against their primary gravitational adversary; Earth. While it had been perplexing at first, they had ultimately realized that the effect occurred 90 degrees out of phase. Ergo, if they applied the polarity change to the collator disk to the front of the platter, rather than going forwards or backwards, the device would move to the right. If they applied energy to the right side of the disk, it moved backwards. The effect had mystified them initially, but ultimately Jamie had reasoned that it was the atomic equivalent of *phase lag* experienced with rotary winged aircraft. Igor Sikorsky had struggled with the very same problem when he perfected the earliest helicopters.

Feeling himself shift to one side, Jack gave a nervous smile. Increasing the pressure on the hat switch he began moving faster in the desired direction. Flicking the control about he was able to fly a box pattern in the back yard before finally running into a tree.

"Stupid tree!" He grumbled, realizing how foolish it must have sounded to say that. The tree had stood there since before he was born; if it was anyone's fault it was clearly his for not recognizing that fact. Still, it angered him to have to disentangle himself from the branches.

"Anyone want anything from the store?" Switching to his casual mode, Jack decided that he'd had enough of playing in the yard. Rising up several hundred feet, he immediately zoomed towards the corner store.

"Jackie, remember the street cams!" Jamie's voice was terse as he reminded his brother just how much surveillance there was in their modern world.

"Yep." Acknowledging the warning, the older sibling could not help but grin like a kid on a roller coaster as he streaked through the air. "I'm just gonna grab a Big-gulp and a donut."

"Oooh, get me some peanut butter M&Ms, the big sharing size." Jamie's love for the candy treat was evident in his voice. "Or Chick-a-stick if they got."

Selecting a spot on the edge of a park, Jack settled to the ground out of camera coverage. Walking a short distance to the brightly lit store, he was in the middle of filling a 44oz cup when the Burke brothers walked in confidently.

Rolling his eyes, Jack knew there would be problems. Word in the neighborhood had been that the older of the brothers had spent the night in jail after their little drag racing episode. Knowing how low-Qs like the Burkes thought, he would likely be blamed for their legal quandary.

"Well, if it ain't doofus number one." Chet Burke turned to face the Sparks brother as soon as he spotted him. "You cost me a lotta money the other day."

"Don't blame me if they raised the price for Hooked on Phonics?" Flashing a smile, Jack continued to pour his drink as it occurred to him that it took both hands to fly the man-pack.

"Hey!" Angry, Chet shoved Jack's shoulder hard enough to make him spill the drink in his hand.

Jack narrowed his eyes as he remembered the familiar feeling of being harassed by the brothers. Already he could detect Chauncey moving around behind him. It was always that way with these two; even though either of them was strong enough to beat him on their own, they always worked in tandem. It had never made any sense that even after ganging up on him they would feel somehow superior.

"What's with the backpack?" Shoving him from behind, Chauncey seemed curious about the metal pack he wore. "What is that thang, an anti-wedgie protector?"

Laughing at his lame joke, the brothers would reinforce each other in all things. It was the way of simpletons like the Burkes. Regardless, Jack found himself stranded between the two.

"Hey!" The manager called out from the counter as he eyed the three of them. "Don't you start no problems in m' store or I'll call the cops. Ya hear me?"

Rolling his eyes, Chet seemed annoyed with the clerk. "Yeah, sure Ralph. We was just gonna tenderize him a little bit."

"Buy something or get out." Wielding a baseball bat, Ralph had seen his share of troubles with the Burke brothers.

"You caused us a lotta problems the other day with the po-lice." Jabbing him in the chest with a meaty finger, the oldest of the brothers was predictably blaming Jack for their legal woes.

"So how was jail? Keep a tight grip on the soap?" Grinning, Jack knew he would be penalized for his smugness. Nonetheless, it chafed him to knuckle under to them. It was an attitude that had led to his frequent victimization in school. "Is it true that spit is the Devil's lube?"

Faster than Jack could react, Chet's fist shot forward, catching the inventor squarely in the solar plexus. Winded from the blow, he never had a chance to respond when Chauncey kicked him between the legs from behind. Although the safety straps he wore mitigated some of the force, it felt like Jack's gonads had been punted up into his throat. Sagging in pain, the inventor tried to remain standing as his vision clouded from the gut punch. Hearing them laugh only raised his ire.

"That's it, I'm callin' the cops." Slamming the bat onto the counter, Ralph immediately began dialing the phone.

"Aww, quit yer whining." Shrugging it off, Chet tossed a few dollars on the counter. "We was just sayin' hello to an old friend, wasn't we Chauncey?"

"That we was! Good ol' friend." Grinning, the younger Burke brother hefted a twelve pack from the refrigerated compartment.

"Bullshit, you two are banned from this store. You come back here again, and I'll call the cops. Y'hear me?" His eyes aglow, the clerk's voice fairly shrieked.

"Awww, shaddup old man." Grabbing the baseball bat off the counter, Chet grinned. "Keep the change."

Jack was still doubled over when he heard the doors swing shut. Trying to catch his breath, the inventor did his best to pretend that nothing had happened as he grabbed two packs of M&Ms from the shelf. He was just about to head to the counter when he noticed the jar of ketchup. Immediately the gears began to turn as he worked through the process. Moving through the store he began plucking other items off the shelves. Finally he dumped the supplies in his arms in front of the clerk.

"Doin' some cooking are ya?" Raising his eyebrows, Ralph looked at the items there; ketchup, baking soda, electrical tape, and M&M s.

"Gimme a pack of those Trojans, the extra large ones." Nonchalant, Jack gave a weak smile as he tried to pretend that his gonads were not screaming in pain still.

"Extra large, eh?" Giving a smile, Ralph dropped the box of prophylactics onto the counter. "You sure it's not just wishful thinking?"

"Nope, I have the biggest, blackest dick you'll ever see." Showing a little false bravado, the inventor kidded the old clerk.

"How about if I just take your word for it." Ralph gave a laugh at the joke.

Paying with cash, Jack knew better than to leave a paper trail. As soon as he was out the door he spoke into the earpiece he still wore. "Alex, hack the store DVR and delete all footage, corrupt the drive."

"Jackie, what are you up to?" Her voice held a note of concern.

"Just do it."

"Jackie, we don't have the fuel for whatever you're planning." Urgency in her voice told him Alexis was still watching the telemetry from the pack. "We only loaded two nanograms of blue plasma. These were just supposed to be hover tests."

"Stop calling me Jackie. And you know that Jamie would always load three times the gas necessary, just to be triple-sure." Irritated, he began dumping baking powder into the condom. After that he used the electrical tape to fasten the rubber around the mouth of the ketchup bottle, careful not to get any of the powder inside the red condiment.

Lifting off abruptly, he jetted in the direction he had last seen the Burke Brothers. With his night vision goggles in place, he was able to pick out the black Dodge Charger easily enough.

Swooping in close, He used his free hand to squeeze the plastic bottle, squirting ketchup into the condom full of baking soda. Immediately the acetic acid began to react with the baking soda, releasing significant amounts of carbon dioxide in the process. The result was that the condom began to swell from the excess pressure. Unable to resist a devious grin, Jack dipped close enough to the Dodge to simply drop the assembly through the open skylight.

In the car, Chauncey was the first to notice the odd contraption that had landed on the center console between the brothers.

"What the hail?" Stunned, the younger of the brothers was scrambling to figure out not only what the object was, but where it had come from.

Chet turned to see what his brother was complaining about just as the condom reached its structural limit. He had only just laid eyes on the device when it exploded, spraying the red fluid in every direction, coating the brothers liberally.

"Chet! I'm bleeding!" His voice a sharp scream, Chauncey looked down at his crimson hands.

"Oh shit!" Trying to blink away the ketchup in his eyes, Chet quickly pulled a gun from under his seat. Instinctively he fired a pair of shots through the open skylight. Immediately the world seemed to go quiet in his ears, with only a ringing sound to be heard.

Rising up to treetop height, Jack could see the vehicle swerving wildly as they sought to avoid whatever mythical creature had just attacked them. Not content to let it go at that, Jack was about to drop on them again when he spotted the flashing blue and red lights ahead. From this range it looked like the officer was writing someone a ticket along the side of the road. With traffic sparse at this time of night, the inventor decided it was time to encourage the brothers a little.

Landing heavy, Jack's boots dented the rooftop. Using the man-pack to rise up another ten feet or so, he repeated the act, slamming into the rooftop over and over again.

"What the fuck!" Chet's voice was angry as he swerved to avoid whatever was attacking them. Out of the passenger window his brother flashed a pistol.

"It's them gargoyles, jus' like the movie!" Chauncey screamed out, sure that they were being attacked by the statues that adorned buildings downtown.

Seeing them accelerate, Jack finally relented. Rising up out of camera range, he watched them zoom past the patrol car. With the Dodge's engine roaring, and Chauncey firing wildly out the window, it would have been impossible for the officer to not have noticed them.

Hovering, the inventor let out a hearty laugh as he watched the squad car take up pursuit. From his vantage point he could see as two more sets of lights lit up nearby. No doubt the officer had called for backup.

"Jackie!" Alexis' voice was urgent. "You need to get home right now!"

"Yeah, yeah, yeah." Grumbling, he felt robbed of some truly-deserved entertainment as he turned the man-pack towards home. He only wished he could have stuck around to witness the police reaction to two armed men, covered in what appeared to be blood, stumbling from their car as they babbled about gargoyles. He would have paid good money to see that.

Using the pack's leverage he was able to accelerate at a fair pace. Watching the familiar streets below, the inventor was focused on finding home when he felt the first hiccup. Dropping twenty feet, the pack seemed to catch itself at the last moment.

"Oh shite." Realizing that he was more than a hundred feet off the ground, Jack immediately began descending to a safer altitude. Knowing that leveraging the gravitational disaffinity used fuel slightly faster than just hovering, he let off on the accelerator and allowed his momentum to carry him through the night sky. Dropping lower still, he could actually see his home when the pack seemed to sputter.

"Dammit." He had just uttered the word when the bottom dropped out from under him. Plummeting, he flailed with the controls. Feeling the pack working intermittently, he was able to steer just enough to miss the Johnson's house, instead landing with a splash in their pool. The cold water took away his breath momentarily. Fully clothed, and wearing a metal backpack, the inventor had a hard time resurfacing. For a few seconds he thought he may actually drown. In the back of his mind Jack could imagine the whole scene as paramedics fished his lifeless body out of the pool, wondering the whole time how the hell he got there in the first place.

"Not today!" Fighting a sense of panic, he gave one last burst of energy before surfacing in the deep end.

His boots made squishy sounds as he stomped through the front door. Still dripping water, he marched down the basement stairs before stripping off the backpack. Letting the device drop to the ground with a thud, he felt the lowest he had in years.

Poking his head through the doorway, Jamie was all smiles.

"Did you remember my M&Ms?" Grinning, he pretended to not notice that his brother was soaking wet.

"Oh yeah, got those right here." Never missing a beat, Jack fished the waterlogged packets from his pocket. Slapping them down on the counter, the candy made a sloppy sound as several M&Ms scattered across the surface. "Enjoy! I'm gonna take a shower."

Watching him go, Jamie still smiled with satisfaction. Plucking several of the candies from the soggy package he chewed them mindlessly. Despite the encounter with the Burke brothers, he felt that the entire test was a glowing success.

"That went well." Alexis' voice dripped in sarcasm.

Ignoring her negative attitude, Jamie nodded like a bobble head. "Yes indeed, it certainly did. I only wish I could have been there to see it."

Recent developments in their gravitational disaffinity design had allowed the brothers to significantly upgrade the little Mustang. Now able to leverage the device's effect into forward motion, the hobbyist jet engines were re-tasked to the role of yaw puffers, able to rotate the vehicle in mid air. Much like the design of a Harrier attack craft, the classic Ford would be able to change its heading mid-air by the use of small jets in the tail of the vehicle. Gone was the folding wing package that had been mounted on the roof for the FAA certification. The entire inspection had really only been to acquire the tail number that now adorned the rear of the vehicle. It had been Jamie's insistence that they remain as legal as possible. Hence, the Mustang needed to be registered as an experimental aircraft to allow them to use it throughout the city. While the FAA official had been taken aback at first sight of the winged Mustang, the Sparks Brothers were not the first to try building a flying car, not by a longshot. Finding their paperwork in order, he ultimately signed off on their application.

Sitting back to look over his work, Jack felt a sense of satisfaction. Although the vehicle had been repaired mechanically, the body still looked like crap from being dropped into the middle of an intersection. With the quarter panels bent and twisted in a few places, the little 'Stang really looked like she had been ridden hard and put away wet. It pained him to see that body damage, but there had not been time to get it to a body shop for a proper restoration. Besides, knowing how the plan was intended to work out, it would not be his car for much longer anyhow. No sense in spiffing her up just to let her be seized by the Feds…or worse.

"The royalty check for Warner Manufacturing has been deposited in your account." Alexis' voice broke the silence.

Turning, Jack looked to see her beautifully rendered on the nearest monitor. Although he knew it was all just an act to make them get along, most likely contrived by his brother, Jack could not help but admit it was working. Truly, he had come to look forward to the AI's daily outfits. While she had settled firmly on her personal appearance, with the flaming red hair and penetrating green eyes, her outfits changed regularly. Today she seemed to have taken a dress from Dolly Parton's closet. With bosoms that seemed seconds away from a wardrobe failure, her upper torso barely fit into the computer monitor on the workbench.

Allowing his eyes to rove her form, Jack gave the barest of acknowledgements.

"The fabber design has been your most profitable product." Stating a known fact, Alexis referred to the elaborate 3D printer the brothers had invented. Unlike conventional designs that applied small globs of material to the design, their fabber used a klystron microwave generator to strip molecules off of a wire and project them onto the project in a tight stream. The beauty of the fabber 2.5 was that it could work with a variety of materials including silica, aluminum, plastic, and even carbon fiber. These mediums allowed them to not only build structural components, but electronic components as well. Additionally, the devices built by the fabber were far more compact than possible with conventional manufacturing methods because they could dispense with obligatory parts like screw brackets, frame clips, and other structural components needed for assembly. When building a single monolithic product there was no need for any of these things.

With his mind wandering, Jack had tried to avoid thinking about his encounter with the Burke brothers. Although he had repaid them in full, it still troubled him to remember how they had assaulted him in the store. It had been years since he had dealt with physical confrontation.

"Assholes." He mumbled inaudibly before trying to redirect his thought process to more productive topics.

"Excuse?" Alexis asked, unsure if the profanity had been directed at her.

"Not you, I was just…" He trailed off before switching tracks. "How is Jamie proceeding on his half of the plan?"

"The big lift unit is on schedule. Two more weeks. How are you progressing on the submarine?" Flipping it about, she knew to keep his mind on his own projects, lest he inquire about things Jamie preferred to keep secret at this point in the plan.

"The big tank is due to be delivered tomorrow, the little one the day after, and the gravitational disaffinity unit is ready. I have a welder coming out Tuesday to make the cuts. Check on those orders I have pending, see if there is an ETA on the air tanks and heater unit. The project will be at a standstill without those." Spinning about in the rolling office chair, the inventor bellied up to the desk where he could examine the notes he had pinned to the calendar.

There was silence for a moment before Alexis started out hesitantly.

"Jackie…" She trailed off.

In an effort to maintain the peace, Jack overlooked her use of his middle initial when he responded.

"What?" He grumbled; only half paying attention.

In her own processing unit, the AI was having a hard time with parts of Jamie's alternate plan. While she agreed that it was the logical path to achieve their desires based on the scenario he had laid out, she still did not like the risk it put them at. Never before in her synthetic life had she felt such conflict. Sworn to secrecy, she still felt compelled to tell Jack of the detour his brother had planned. Yet at the same time she knew that revealing this detail would change everything, possibly even endangering them more. Still, she had an urge to tell Jack everything, even though every part of her logical systems told her that it would be a mistake. Was this what it was to be emotional? Is this how HAL felt? It puzzled her how humans navigated their way through life with these kinds of conflicting sensations? With her cubed processor running at full speed she recalculated the issue 3800 times a second. Unable to come to an internal consensus she finally spoke.

"Nothing...never mind." Flashing him a vixen smile, the synthetic woman did her best to distract the inventor by allowing her virtual breasts to fill the lower portion of the screen.

"Do what?" Jack looked up blithely. "That's a nice outfit, BTW."

Alexis smiled in response. Inside of her cubed processor she was beginning to see that Jamie was right about his brother; he was easier to manipulate once she understood his motivations.

In his own lab, Jamie intently watched the screens before him. With drones throughout the FBI office he had managed to gain a lay of the land. Already he had identified specific divisions that handled each type of crime encountered by the local field office. Having narrowed his field of observation down to just a few agents, he only had a few more questions left.

Watching the left-most screen, the savant eyed the suspect that sat defiantly handcuffed in a chair. With his exposed upper torso covered in prison tattoos, it was clear that this man wore his criminal resume for all to see. With a swastika visible on his neck, Jamie knew he had just the right thug for his research.

"Alexis, have you established access to their phone system?" His tone flat as he spoke, Jamie was focused on the screens before him.

"Affirmative!" Her tone businesslike, the AI confirmed that she had long ago penetrated their simple communications network. While much of it was encrypted against eavesdropping, none of that mattered if the server itself were co-opted by a highly intelligent synthetic mind like hers.

"I need you to make a call." Sitting back, Jamie let out his breath slowly. It was a big step, but his calculations told him it was time to make the leap.

At 33, federal agent Jenna Jaramillo was known by her co-workers as a woman on the fast track to her own corner office. Never content to just be the token Hispanic female in the office, she had proven her abilities many times during her decade of federal service. Having begun her law enforcement career as a military police officer, she had come up through the ranks. It had been a useful part of her development; dealing with drunken GIs had taught her how to do the hard things that her profession demanded. Though there were times that she had felt like slinking away from a conflict, she had always been mindful of her father's old axiom; *"Them calves ain't gonna brand themselves,"* he would say as he sat atop his little Appaloosa on a cold morning. Applying that philosophy to criminals put things into perspective for her. After all, if she could run down a fleeing calf, rope it, wrestle it, and restrain it with her bare hands, then how much harder could a felon be?

It had been this ability to swallow her fear that had earned her a reputation for being fearless. It also helped that she was a black belt in Aikido and knew a hundred ways to inflict pain without leaving a bruise. Nonetheless, at only 5'11", there were always suspects who were bigger and stronger than she.

Raised in the miniscule town of Vail, Arizona, she had yearned to get out and see the world. At the time she had dread the idea of spending her life in a burg like Vail. But in the years since she had come to realize that her childhood had been truly idyllic compared to many of her counterparts. So many summers had been spent riding horses through the nearby oasis known as Pantano Wash, or camping in the splendor of the Rincon Mountains. It had been life on her family's tiny farm that had given her a work ethic that did not blanche at the idea of breaking a sweat. Unlike most recruits, she found basic training refreshingly easy. After all, the Army never asked her to unload ten tons of baled hay, clean corrals, or dig waterline trenches. Having spent her youth climbing the mountain ranges that ringed Tucson, she found the Army's daily physical training effortless by comparison.

Her hitch in the Army had been half over when she was first approached by a federal recruiter. Bright, young, and eager, it had not taken a lot of coaxing to convince her that the FBI was where she needed to be. Attending night classes while working days as a Military Police officer, she had picked up her degree in Administration of Criminal Justice before moving to Quantico, Virginia, to start her exciting new life as a federal agent.

In the years that followed, she had risen to fame at the local field office where she had been assigned. After the Patterson kidnapping had ended in a bloody gunfight that resulted in the death of the Johnson gang and the safe return of the ten year old victim, word had gotten around that she was a solid agent. Next there was the Halloween Crew, known to rob banks while wearing kids' masks. Like the Patterson case, she had ended their careers in a most explosive manner when a stray bullet had detonated the military-grade Composition-4 the crew had concealed in the trunk of their car. As if all this were not enough, her stellar conviction rate had gotten her noticed by people at the top.

Assigned to the San Diego office for the last two years, she had again proven herself by adapting quickly to the escalating technological threats of their world. Even among a cadre of college educated agents she was known as the *thinking man's agent*. With criminals growing increasingly tech savvy, she had found herself back in school many times in an effort to master new skills.

But her newfound technical abilities had been wasted on the perp seated before her. Bernard Shaw was as low tech as they came. The vitriolic leader of the local faction of the Western Hammerskins, he was nothing more than a violent racist skinhead. Wanted in connection with the murder of a Hispanic family, he fully looked the part of the monster he was suspected to be. With Nazi tattoos all the way up his neck, red boot laces to symbolize the minority blood he had spilled for the cause, and a look of absolute hatred for Jenna, he was rumored to have killed dozens of people during his term as Kommandant of the local chapter.

"How's your eye?" Feigning concern for his swollen orb, she refrained from laughing at his reaction. In truth, she was glad to have given him the bruise after he had attempted to resist arrest. No doubt it galled the felon to not only have been arrested by a Latina, but to have been physically subdued by her in front of his crew. The insult was insufferable. He only hoped that his comrades had all been too busy being accosted to have witnessed his schooling at Agent Jaramillo's hands.

It had been a lightning raid conducted before the sun was up, and as usual Jenna had been the second agent through the door. While she would not have minded being first, the honor was one reserved for Agent Lopamaua. The burly Samoan and former Marine tipped the scales at almost 300 pounds, making him a walking, talking brick wall. More than once she had seen him kick doors clean off their hinges.

As if on cue, the big agent filled the doorway. With a broad smile contrasting sharply with his dark olive skin, he seemed pleased at the fish they had netted today.

"This 'ol boy giving you any trouble Jen?" Still grinning, Agent Lopamaua eyed the perp's black eye.

"Rangi! M' main man!" Holding out a fist for a bump, Jenna greeted her fellow agent happily. "Naw, me and Bernie have been getting along just fine since he had his attitude adjusted this morning. Isn't that right Mister Shaw?"

"I got nothing to say." His lip curling up in disgust, it clearly irritated the man to be in the presence of the two minority agents. As if being arrested were not enough to ruin his day, having been roughed up by a pair of *mud-people* only added to the humiliation.

Watching the massive agent saunter away, Jenna's attention was diverted by the ringing phone on her desk. Answering, she was greeted by a man's deep voice.

"Agent Jaramillo" Clearly not a Spanish speaker, the voice botched her name, pronouncing the J and double L's wrong. Rather than saying *Har-a-mee-yo*, he had called her *Jar-a-mill-o*.

Raising an eyebrow at the mispronunciation, she chose not to correct him. It was nothing new; and she had long ago learned to accept the fact that her Spanish surname made no sense to English speakers.

"This is she, and you are…?" Keeping her voice professional, she preferred to know who was asking questions.

"This is Agent Don Carson in the New York office. I understand that you have a Bernard Shaw in your custody. Is that correct?" His tone was officious as he inquired.

Instinctively, Jenna used her computer to check the federal registry to see if such an agent actually worked in the NYC office. Seeing his name pop up on the screen, she pushed aside the keyboard.

"I do. What can I do for you Agent Carson?" Glancing up at the skinhead that sat handcuffed in her office, she wondered what they could possibly want with her prisoner on the other side of the country.

"He is wanted in connection with something the antiterrorism task force is working on." The explanation seemed plausible on the surface.

Jenna raised an eyebrow before responding. "I ran him through NICS already, and I didn't see any BOLO's besides our own."

"And you wouldn't have. Our interest in this one is strictly classified. We got a notification as soon as you ran him." Carson explained carefully, as if she needed to be told how the system worked.

"Great.   We have him, so what'dya want?" Something in his tone told Jenna that she was about to have her suspect taken away.

"We need him sent to a secure facility for further questioning. He is believed to be part of some serious crap." His voice took on an angry edge as he seemed to want to say more.

"We have him for the murder of a whole family. How much more serious could your charges be?" Nonplussed, she tried to keep her temper.

"Look, I know this seems like a shit-sandwich, having your perp taken away, but we have reason to believe he is connected with the Tiffany's shooting."

Jenna sat back at that. Anyone not living in a cave would have known about the Tiffany's mass murder. Shooters had used automatic weapons to murder more than sixty party revelers at an LGBTQ bar in New York. In addition to the dead, there were dozens more injured in the melee, including three NYPD officers. Of late there had been little else in the headlines.

"We will make arrangements to have him transferred to another…facility." The pause in his speech had seemed odd.

"Couldn't have happened to a nicer person." Forcing a smile, Jenna looked Shaw in the eyes as she wondered just exactly where he was bound. In her heart of hearts she hoped it was Hell.

Standing in the doorway again, Rangi had several slips of paper in hand.

"These just popped outta the printer for you." Holding the printouts, he seemed quizzical about it all.

Snatching the documents, Jenna was surprised enough that she raised both eyebrows this time.

"Well, well, well, Mister Shaw. You are in some deep *kimshi*." Giving a genuine smile, Jenna knew that her words were a gross understatement. "Rangi my bro, could you drop this piece of shit off in holding for me?"

"I could indeed, m' dear." Grinning broadly, he flashed her more ivory than a piano. "If there's one thing I enjoy doing, it's throwing dirtbags into jail cells. Hell, I like it so much that I get up extra early in the morning just so I got more daylight to throw assholes into cells. At my house we don't call it daylight savings time, we call it an extra hour to throw assholes in cells every day, that's what we call it at my house."

Yanking the skinhead up roughly, Rangi obviously loved this part of the job.

Sitting at her desk, Jenna read through the printouts. While she had previously believed she had Shaw on some serious charges, the documents in her hand redefined the concept. Based on what she was reading, her suspect was now officially a domestic terrorist. This was big league.

"Wow!" Jack seemed entranced by the image on the screen as he looked over Jamie's shoulder. "Who's that?"

Jamie seemed to jump a little. Clearly he had no idea how long his brother had been standing there watching. Gathering his wits, he sank back into his office chair.

"Eh? Oh, That's Agent Jaramillo." Jamie left it at that as he did a poor job of concealing his surprise.

Struck by the face on the screen, Jack failed to notice his brother's shock. Leaning in close, he examined her in detail. With her hair tucked back in a tactical bun at the back of her head, and her dress shirt open at the second button, there was just something about the look in her eye that captured his attention. Commandeering one of the touchscreens, the inventor zipped through the recorded footage being transmitted by the drone concealed in her desk lamp. Finally pausing as something caught his attention, he focused on her phone as she set it down on the desk. Still unlocked after ending the call, he could see the desktop applications she had installed on her phone. Expanding the screen he zoomed in on the picture.

"Lookit her apps." Jack's voice held a note of wonderment. "Stellarium, Nasa's Eyes, Dinopedia…I think I'm in love."

"Stick to the plan. We don't need our efforts being sidelined by your libido." Frowning, Professor James used his desktop controller to switch the feed to the interior of the Queen Mary.

"Yeah, yeah, yeah." Irritated, Jack sat on the edge of the nearest desk. He knew it would annoy his brother; butts belonged in chairs, not on desks or other work areas.

Jamie felt his ire grow at the sight of his brother's squirming buttocks on the desktop. Finally resigning himself to disinfecting the spot later, the savant raised his eyebrows as he awaited a progress report from his older sibling. "Well, where are we on the Queen Mary?"

"I have mapped the interior, discovered the right exposed bulkheads, and documented the equipment there, and manufactured housing boxes that will blend in. I'm done with the Queen. I even have the decoys ready to go."

"What about the high altitude vehicle?" Raising an eyebrow, Jamie tried to ignore the fact that his brother was scooting his butt around on the desk. He suspected that Jack was intentionally trying to irritate him.

"Oh, you mean the submarine? Yeah, that…" Jack's tone changed as he folded his arms and eyed his younger brother warily. "Exactly where in the plan does that thing fit?

"It is merely part of the contingency plan, in case we need an absolutely safe egress." Having practiced his lie for days, Jamie was able to appear convincing in his explanation of the device being built from a steel water tank. Actually designed as a high altitude craft, it was not really a submarine at all. The nickname had simply been the derisive term his older brother used to describe the vehicle.

"And the new drones? What about those? Why do you need a buncha bugs that fit inside of a flying cop light?" His eyes narrowing to slits, Jack was tired of all the secrecy. He had already tried to get information out of Alexis, but each time she had simply stopped answering his calls, pretending to be busy on other projects.

"Tis' nothing but preemptive research." Shrugging, Professor James tried to minimize it as his accent seemed to falter for a moment.

"Research of what?" Not liking the vagueness of his brother's answer, Jack was suspicious right away. Knowing that his brother was not averse to long-winded explanations, he knew that there was much more to it than he was letting on. Also, Jack could see how his brother's hands fidgeted. He did that when he was lying. While Jamie could possibly be the smartest man on the planet, he was a lousy poker player.

Exhaling as if he were exasperated, Jamie finally relented the tiniest bit.

"There is a small probability that one or both of us could end up briefly incarcerated. In the event that such a pitfall befalls us, I am researching the facility where we would be housed. However, due to our special status it is unlikely we would find ourselves in the local county lockup."

Jack mulled that over, still giving his brother a skeptical look. "So you think they would take us to some kind of a black site...?"

"Yes." His reply was succinct as Professor James nodded in agreement. "And since such a place is not likely to be advertised in the yellow pages or on FaceBook, the specialized bots will be needed to determine exactly where that place is.

It suddenly became clear to Jack as he put the pieces together. Right away he understood why these bots were so much different from the previous Gen V units they had deployed in town. It all made sense; the housing, the satellite broadband connection, the unique abilities of each of the drones...

"Show me." Standing upright, Jack pointed angrily to the monitors.

Shrugging haplessly, Jamie's voice remained neutral. "Alex and I are still trying to locate it. But you may observe...from a safe distance." Pointing to a chair in the corner of the room, the savant indicated where he thought it best for his brother to remain during the process.

"Yeah, right." Disregarding Jamie's direction, Jack grabbed a nearby stool and parked himself at the savant's elbow.

Frowning, Jamie knew it was pointless to argue further. The plan was already in motion and his sibling would not relent. This he knew from a lifetime with Jack.

"Alexis invaded the FBI's database and inserted a bogus warrant for terrorism, as well as a host of other nasty offenses sure to reclassify our subject for special treatment. At this very moment we are awaiting his transport to a secure facility." Toggling through cameras, Jamie had a mugshot of Bernard Shaw displayed on one of the monitors.

"This is the guy?" Jack's eyes widened at the sight of the felon. The profile picture clearly showed the swastikas and Aryan propaganda that decorated the man's shaved head. As he read through the supremist's criminal history, he found himself holding his breath. "Holy Pope piss! This guy's a fuckin' monster."

"Language." Jamie corrected his brother before continuing. "Yes, he is quite the specimen, which is why I feel no remorse in using him in this manner. It is a safe bet that he deserves this, and much more."

"Definitely more." Finding no reason to object, Jack felt revulsion at the sight of the felon. Bernard Shaw represented everything that the brothers had feared and loathed their entire life. There on the screen before them was a man who would have eradicated them without hesitation, were he ever afforded the opportunity. In another time men like Shaw had lynched and enslaved people like the Sparks brothers. This was a man who believed that his ethnicity alone made him superior to those of darker hues. To call him a monster was truly an understatement.

"The transport vehicle has arrived." Alexis interrupted their conversation with an update.

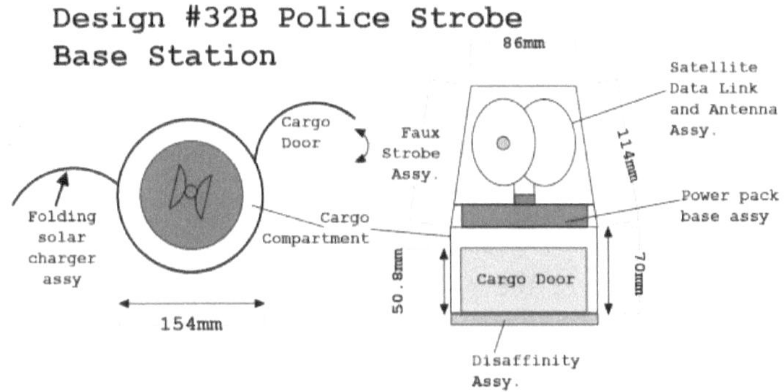

Cussing and struggling against his escorts, Bernard Shaw put up a good fight as he was physically dragged through the basement parking structure and into the waiting transport van. With all eyes on the scuffle, no one noticed as the cylindrical object lifted up from a nearby structural support, hovered its way across the lot before attaching itself to the roof of the vehicle. Nestled between the arrays of police lights on the rooftop, the amber strobe light would just appear to be part of the clutter. Like the Purloined Letter, it would hide in plain sight amongst all of the other flashing lights atop of the paddy wagon.

Bumping along down the highway, the faux strobe light continued to send out tracking updates as night fell around them. The trip lasted little more than an hour before the van pulled off the highway. Navigating the two-lane road for another forty minutes, the prisoner transport seemed to be headed nowhere. Using GoogleEarth to track the vehicle's progress, Jamie and Jack were bewildered. According to the satellite imagery there was nothing for the next twenty miles. The mystery only deepened when the van finally turned north on a private driveway. Trundling along, the transport eventually arrived at a compound surrounded by a tall fence topped with concertina wire.

"There's nothing on GoogleEarth." Jack pointed to the satellite imagery that revealed only barren desert where the facility should have been. Glancing at the watermark on the bottom of the page they could tell that this footage was relatively recent. Yet there was no sign of the complex. Clearly, whatever the place was, all traces of it had been removed from the public satellite image.

"Alexis, prepare to detach." Ignoring his brother, Jamie watched intently through the pinhole camera installed in the base of the amber strobe light. As one gate guard checked the driver's paperwork, another could be seen in the background with an automatic rifle in hand. Obviously, wherever they were, the place was at a high alert status.

Another few seconds of communication between the driver and gate guard before a cursory search was conducted. Using a mirror to examine the vehicle from top to bottom, the security officer actually looked directly at the amber strobe light before moving on.

"Oh." Jack's surprise was audible as he suddenly understood why he had been tasked with building such a bizarre device as a flying police strobe light. Indeed, the gate guard had thought nothing of yet another light on the roof of the vehicle. Although Jack had spent a lifetime of being surprised by his brother's vision and foresight, he was stunned nonetheless.

After being waved through the gate, they could see even more officers patrolling the grounds. Among them, two even had fierce looking German Shepherds that seemed intent on sniffing out everything in their path.

"Fuck me." Jack was staggered by the amount of security in place. "Is this the place where they keep Lex Luthor?"

Though he found the comment amusing, Jamie remained stoic as he watched for just the right moment.

"Alexis, detatch…now." Seeing that they were clear of prying eyes, the savant gave the order. Immediately the amber strobe lifted up off the van, rising straight up into the darkness where it would be invisible to the human eye. Drawing parallel to the nearest rooftop, the device hesitated while they looked around. Seeing a pair of men at the far end of the building, the IR illuminator on the camera painted a clear picture in the darkness. Waiting until both of the rooftop sentries were looking in the opposite direction, Alexis was able to easily park the strobe on top of one of the large air conditioning units.

"Begin unpacking the contents." Wasting no time, Jamie gave the next directive.

On the rooftop, the amber strobe made a tiny clicking sound as it released a door on the side. From within there was the barest of scurrying sound before the first drone scampered its way out into the night air. Peering about, it allowed its cameras to adjust before alighting. Silently finding its way to one of the nearby buildings, it was gone in moments.

Just as the first drone had done, more of the *faux* insects clambered their way out of the strobe light's housing that had acted as not only a garage for the drones, but also as the main communications hub for the entire site. All data from the drones would be transmitted to the amber strobe light before being uploaded via a satellite broadband connection. With plenty of bandwidth, Alexis was able to manipulate the bugs remotely. Even with her old processor, the AI had no problem multi-tasking the half dozen simulated bugs as they each found their way to targets. It was only when the job seemed complete that the last drone slowly crawled out.

Bigger than the others, it was more than a surveillance unit. Sporting a variety of tools, the big bug was capable of such feats as cutting, stripping and shorting wires. While the smaller drones could provide a view of this distant place, they were strictly for surveillance. However, the final drone was capable of interacting with the world around it. Originally referred to as a Remote Manipulator, the device had come to be known simply as Remmi.

Design #47: Remote Manipulator
aka: Remmi

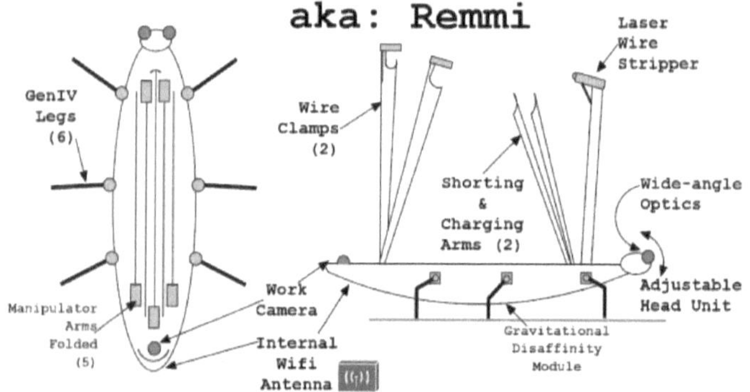

"Start Remmi's diagnostics." Jamie commanded Alexis in a flat voice.

"I already am." She replied with the barest hint of irritation in her voice as she appeared on the far monitor, rolling her eyes at his request.

"Hey girl." Jack gave her a nod as he checked out today's outfit. He noticed right away that she wore a shirt nearly identical to the one he had seen Agent Jaramillo wearing earlier. No doubt she had made the selection based on his reaction to the woman who had entranced him. Though he saw through the ruse, he appreciated the effort. *Besides, she looked good.*

The night was inky black as Jack settled down onto the deck of the Queen Mary. Though they had made significant upgrades to the disaffinity man-pack, the inventor was still a little leery of the device after his close encounter in the neighbor's pool. Add to that the fact that it was a moonless, starless night and the whole experience was a bit unsettling. As if flying the prototype without the comfort of a parachute were not enough, Jack had made the trip while dragging a large cache of equipment kept aloft by its own antigrav unit. While the idea of a floating cargo sled had seemed like a good idea at the time, it turned out to be less than desirable as the sled had constantly bumped into him every time he slowed down. Add to that the fact that the pitch blackness of a starless night over the ocean had been particularly disorienting. More than once he had not been entirely sure which way was up. Making a mental note, he decided that next time he would use the Mustang.

It had been a relief that the Queen was relatively easy to see from the air, even at night. With the big work lights installed around her for the workers, it was clear that the local facilities were being upgraded. A popular tourist attraction since 1967, the big ship had been permanently moored in Long Beach for more than a half century. Through the years many updates had been made to her, including removal of her boilers, engines, and all but one of the propellers. Converted to a luxury motel, and refurbished several times, the RMS Queen Mary would never again set sail on the high seas.

As luck would have it, the mighty ship was undergoing yet another refurb as the management company sought to increase profits. Currently closed to the public, the Queen Mary's deck was littered with gantries for the painters and other workers that were refinishing her. Avoiding these as he landed, Jack took in the scent of the sea air.

Pulling the floating crates along behind him with a length of rope, the inventor quickly found his way below decks. Already quite familiar with her current layout, Jack had been studying the ship for weeks now. The drones had been able to reveal much about the current floor plan, especially with her laid bare for construction. Moving with purpose, Jack knew exactly where he needed to go.

Although the gravitational disaffinity device had been able to work well with a single point of contact on smaller objects, the math had indicated that the sheer mass of the ship would require not only a unit installed at each end of the ship, but a complete shutdown of the onboard electrical system. Arriving in the bow section, Jack's first order of business was to pull a handheld device from his belt. Confirming that it was fully charged, he pressed the tip against the exposed metal hull until the lights around him winked out. Based on his EMP cannon, the design used the conductivity of the ship's hull to shut down any devices being grounded by the metal frame, including generators, and externally supplied lighting.

Next, he pulled the first of the bulky disaffinity units from the floating cargo sled he had dragged with him from home. Affixing it directly to the metal bulkhead the device would use the hull's conductivity to spread the antigrav effect. With a significant supply of the blue plasma to power the disaffinity unit, they had no intention of allowing the antigrav system to run out of fuel unexpectedly. It had taken more than a pound of silver to create enough blue plasma for each unit. Although it was well within their means, the material had to be sourced from multiple vendors via cash transactions. It had been Jamie's insistence that they leave no hint of how they fabricate the plasma; it was their ace in the hole should their plans go awry. It was for this reason that Jamie had insisted that the two technologies never share the same platform.

Moving with purpose, Jack found his way to the stern where the engine rooms had once been. Repurposed for tours, only a single boiler and propeller shaft remained. Ducking under the velvet ropes that kept the tourists at bay, he found his way to the far side of the remaining power-train where the disaffinity device would not be readily visible. Disguised as one of the existing equipment boxes, it was intended to blend in with the vintage interior. Only an engineer would spot the addition. Jack needed the devices to go unnoticed for just a few more days.

Satisfied that the installation was complete, Jack confirmed that Alexis had a digital connection before he made his way to the Sun Deck some floors above. Giving the ship one last look, he activated the portable man-pack and silently lifted off for home.

Seemingly anchored to his office chair, Jamie had spent days observing the black site. Although he had expected the worst from the place, what he had seen thus far had completely redefined his idea of bad. The secret prison was like nothing he had ever seen, in or out of fiction. Efficient and orderly, it was like a giant processing machine. Humans entered at one end, underwent extensive manipulation in the middle, and finally emerged at the far end as broken widgets that vaguely resembled *homo sapiens*. While he felt no remorse for the felons caught up in this nightmare, they were indeed bad people; nonetheless, it concerned the savant that he would be broken just as easily as the poor souls on his screens. The people who ran this facility were more than thugs and torturers. Professionals at information extraction, they were well trained and experienced. Preferring to refer to themselves as *Researchers*, they were the best of the best at what they did. This was a serious concern for the savant.

Thoroughly convinced that he could never withstand their efforts, Jamie knew that he would need to outsmart them. It was this ideal that made him turn his attention to the nearby barracks and housing situated on the north side of the compound. If he could not defeat them directly, then he would need to do an end-run. Knowledge is power, and he needed to know everything about the individuals themselves. It had been here that the savant hit pay dirt. Remembering the old phrase *small town, big hell*, he quickly realized that their personal interactions were their true Achilles' heel.

With a bowl of heavily buttered popcorn Jamie watched the researchers as if they were an elaborate soap opera. There was so much to learn and so little time to do it. But nothing said that he couldn't enjoy himself at the task.

Shock & Awe

The grainy footage of the surveillance cameras revealed the breadth of the RMS Queen Mary as she rested in her own private inlet. With the long boarding ramps extended, she sat awaiting the work crews that would return in the morning. Since the project was being handled by a union shop, there would be no after-hours work on the ship. With the luxury motel inside closed down for the duration of the refurbishment, the only person at the site was the security guard.

Although he was required to patrol the grounds hourly, Security Officer Nelson preferred the comfort of his guard shack. With a small electric heater fending off the cool ocean air, he had not actually left the structure for hours. Occasionally glancing at the camera monitors that lined his desk, he had been filling out the logs with bogus entries. More concerned with the nubile young centerfold in the magazine he was reading, Officer Nelson was busy playing with himself when he noticed the man that seemed to float down from the sky. Stunned at the sight of an intruder on the premises, Officer Nelson completely forgot about the penis in his hand.

Standing at the bow of the ship, the stranger kept his dark hoodie in place as he pulled something from the bag he wore over one shoulder. Tossing a silver disc upwards, the platter seemed to affix itself to the Queen's hull.

Jumping up with a start, Nelson managed to spill coffee all over Miss January. Cursing, he knew he had to do something. In his haste he turned for the door before falling flat on his face. Remembering that his pants had been down around his ankles, he felt embarrassed to find himself squirming on the ground. By the time he had himself buttoned up he realized the man was gone. Anxiously scanning the monitors he finally located the stranger clear down at the stern of the mighty craft. Again there was a small ceremony before the trespasser attached one of the silver discs to the hull of the ship.

Angry now, Nelson charged out the door at a run. Flashlight in hand, he headed directly for the stern, only to find that the man was gone again. Frustrated, the security guard cursed as he looked about. It only took a few seconds to locate the trespasser, this time standing at the center of the platform. Pulling a handheld radio from his belt, Nelson made a panicked call to the guard captain who would be patrolling in a vehicle some miles away. Clicking the radio several times he was rewarded with nothing but static.

"What the hell?" It puzzled him; the radio had never made sounds like that. It was almost as if his comms were being intentionally jammed. Clipping the Motorola to his belt he gripped the heavy metal flashlight in his hand as he approached the subject.

Fully aware of the guard's approach, Jack had stood perfectly still as if admiring the ship. With his hoodie in place to ward off the chill night air, he allowed the security officer to approach to within just a few feet.

Uttering a string of profanities, Nelson made it clear that he was trespassing, and that bodily harm would result in his non-compliance. Shaking the heavy flashlight at the stranger, the guard felt confident in the situation. Half turning to look at the man, Jack flashed a smile before extending his arms.

"I command you to rise!" In a deep voice the inventor shouted his order at the ship before him.

"Hey, I don't want none of your bullshit." Nelson's anger was interrupted by the deep sounds of metal creaking. His first instinct was that the dark-skinned man had planted a terrorist device on the ship. But turning to look for himself he was rewarded by the sight of the mighty vessel as it slowly began to rise up out of the water.

The sound was deafening as millions of gallons of ocean water rushed in beneath the hull. It was disconcerting to see something that immense rising up. It was almost as if the horizon itself were climbing. Stunned, Security Officer Nelson stood with his mouth agape as the unbelievable became reality. With Jack still standing nearby, arms outstretched as if he were using mental powers to levitate the ship, the scene seemed surreal to the simpleminded guard.

Recoiling at the sound of the boarding ramps falling away and clanging noisily down the side of the ship, Nelson literally jumped in surprise. Slowly, steadily the ship climbed higher and higher until it finally hit the end of the anchor chain. With the keel fully out of the water now, he stared in disbelief at the barnacles and sea growth that grew on the underside of the floating museum. The vast amount of water still dripping off the Queen Mary was such that it made conversation impossible. As the waves surged in the wake of the craft, it was as if Moses had parted the waters before them.

"What the fuck…?" His brain still trying to catch up with what his eyes had just witnessed, Nelson was reduced to simple profanities.

Finally dropping his arms, Jack turned to flash the guard a broad smile.

"Your zipper is down." Making the casual observation, Jack raised an eyebrow before lifting off silently into the night.

As if anchored to the ground, Nelson could only watch as the stranger disappeared into the night sky. With thousands of gallons of water still dripping off of the hull, the Queen Mary seemed to hover there above him like something from a dream. It was a full five minutes before he even thought to call it in.

Jenna was already dressed for her morning run when the call came in. It was the strain in her SAIC's voice that worried her. She had known Bill Johnson since the academy, and he was not someone who became unhinged easily. Nonetheless, his tone had sounded as if he were rattled.

Dressing quickly, she made her way down the highway in the pre-dawn darkness. She was several miles from Long Beach when the sun, still concealed by the distant horizon, began to light the morning sky. Having made the trip many times during her tenure in Southern California, she detected the abnormal skyline right away.

"What the…" Squinting her eyes she had a hard time believing what she saw. Sure that it must be a strange optical illusion, perhaps *Fata Morgana* or some such mirage. But as she got closer, it all became apparent that her eyes were not playing a trick on her; there really was an ocean liner floating in the sky.

Pulling into the parking lot Jenna was met by the sight of flashing lights. With more than a dozen patrol cars crammed into the area, she had a hard time spotting her partner there amongst the gawking police officers.

"Rangi!" She caught his attention.

Turning slowly, the big man's jaw still hung open. Eyes wide, he was at a complete loss as to the source of the levitation. Nearby stood Officer Nelson, flashlight in hand.

"You are not gonna believe this…" Agent Lopamaua shook his head as he tried to convey his complete disbelief.

"What'd we got?" Trying to keep her composure, Jenna remained all business.

"According to the security guard, David Blaine came in here and levitated the thing." Rangi's tone seemed to simplify what he had been told originally.

"He actually said that? It was Blaine?" She seemed surprised that this could be just an illusion.

"Well, no, he just said that some guy in a hoodie did it." His eyes reaffixed to the ship that floated before them, Agent Lopamaua was more than a little distracted by it all. Rubbing his head with a meaty paw, he suddenly remembered a detail. "Oh, yeah, he said the guy attached some kind of discs to the ship. You can see 'em at the front and back of the ship."

"Bow and stern." Jenna clarified the terminology for her partner. Feeling the breeze shift slightly, she decided it was time to take command of the situation. "Rangi, I need you to get the locals to set a perimeter around the place. When the wind changes the ship will swing around, so for safety purposes we need to clear out everyone from underneath its arc. We have no idea how long that thing is going to stay up there, so we'll just plan for it to come crashing down at any minute."

"Got it. What you gonna do?" Agreeable to her game plan, the big Samoan seemed curious about her next step. Personally, he was at a complete loss how to proceed with an event like this. In fact, he was not entirely sure if this was even a violation of federal law.

"I am going to start with the basics. They must have security cameras, then interview the security guard, start combing the area for witnesses, and search the patent office for an invention like this in the last twelve months." Standing with hands on hips, Jenna tried to appear confident even though the sight took her breath away.

"You got it Boss." Grinning, the big man sauntered off towards the local officers who clustered a short distance away.

"Un-fucking-believable." She allowed herself a rare profanity as she eyed the tin plates that were no more than dots at this range.

By 9:00am the story had come to dominate the news, social media, and every channel on TV. Initially hailed as a YouTube hoax, it took a while for the world to realize that this was no clever digital editing; someone had indeed levitated 81,000 tons of ship. Without a doubt it was the heaviest vehicle ever placed aloft. Even the legendary Space Shuttle, fully loaded with fuel and boosters checked in at a mere 2,200 tons. Yet there on the screen for the world to see was a vessel as large as a WWII aircraft carrier floating peacefully with no obvious means of suspension. Immediately the conspiracy theories began to fly. It was the government…it was aliens…or her favorite; it was the government using alien technology captured at Roswell in

'47. The list went on and on; there was no limit to the press's imagination.

As if the media storm had not been enough to jolt the world awake that morning, the war-hawks had seen this as a potential threat. Immediately the Navy, Air Force, Marines, Army, and National Guard were placed on alert. Knowing that the event had not been orchestrated by them, the vast American war machine suspected the next logical possibility: That it had been done by one of their enemies.

With an immense flat screen TV rolled into the Oval Office, President Jefferson Phelps had cancelled his appointments for the morning. Although urgent matters of state beckoned him, they paled in comparison to this event. His generals and cabinet staff had been frenzied when the event first became known. Acting with only slightly more discipline than the press, they had allowed conjecture and suspicion to dominate the tone of their conversation. If they were not behind it then surely it was the act of a malevolent nation. But that led to the next logical question; why?

Sitting back in his chair, President Phelps assumed a thoughtful demeanor as he considered the options. It bothered him that despite his intelligence he was truly stumped for a course of action. A member of Mensa for more than twenty years, he had campaigned as the smart candidate, convincing voters that his opponent simply lacked the mental faculties for the job. But as he stared at the live feed of the ship that hovered over the bay, he was at a complete loss. Not only did he not have a clue who could have accomplished such a feat, but he could not even imagine the technology capable of lofting that much steel. Ever aware of the old adage: *tis better to be thought a fool than open your mouth and remove all doubt*, President Phelps preferred to remain silent while his minions debated the situation.

As the hours had stretched on, he had found himself increasingly agitated by it all. He was leader of the most powerful nation in the history of humanity, and yet he was relegated to getting his intel from the very same media vultures that he had lambasted since his election. It had been a vitriolic campaign and he was prone to lashing out at anyone who disagreed with him. Chief among these was the press. Though they had utterly despised him from the start, it had been they who had essentially given him conversational dominance by panning every derogatory statement and action committed by the man. Very early on he had learned how to manipulate them by using social media and acerbic statements to draw attention away from the other candidates. Even as they decried him for the demagogue he was, the press simply could not look away. He had likened it to the effect of drivers passing an accident by the side of the road; they felt compelled to leer at the destruction, ever hopeful of seeing carnage. The mantra of the modern American media could be succinctly summed up with a single statement; *if it bleeds, it leads*.

Shifting in his seat, he felt his ire rising as his Chief of Staff changed the channel to see what the other news agencies had to say. While there had been nothing new for hours, the reporters continually found creative ways to regurgitate the same information.

"Bill," finally sitting forward, he directed his anger towards the FBI director who was supposed to be his chief source of domestic intelligence. "Bill, this is a disaster. The damned fake-news reporters know more about this situation than I do."

Jolting as the President slammed a fist on the desk, FBI Director William D. Harding had been one of the few holdovers from the previous administration. Rumored to have kept his job by surreptitiously using his position to discredit the opposition candidate, he knew that he served at the pleasure of the President. The leader of the free world did not need any kind of justification to cut him loose; he could be terminated on a whim, and this president had a lot of whims.

"We should have a report compiled..." His explanation was cut off by the man behind the desk.

"I want something right now. This is very troubling that I have not been able to make a statement. It's a disaster. I need information, and I need it now." His eyes narrowed to angry slits, President Jefferson Phelps had never been fond of his FBI director. But a deal was a deal, and the man had essentially given him the presidency in the final weeks of the campaign.

"I'm on it..." Harding again found himself interrupted.

"No, I want to talk to the case officer directly. I'm tired of your long-winded reports, blah, blah, blah. I want to talk to someone who has real information." Again slamming a fist on the desk, the President's delicately coiffed comb-over seemed to bounce under the weight of so much hair spray.

"Yes, sir." Feeling the pressure, Director Harding knew better than to object. Making a quick call on the secure line, he finally turned to the President and assembled Cabinet with a hopeful look.

"Sir, I have the case agent on the line." Holding out the receiver, he expected the President to snatch it out of his hands.

Instead, Phelps sat back and gestured angrily to the phone on his desk. "Put him on speakerphone."

Nodding silently, the director decided against his instinct to point out that some of the people in the room may not be cleared for this conversation. Until they knew the details, it seemed haphazardly unwise to share the information so broadly. Despite this, he knew not to anger Jefferson Phelps any further.

"This is Special-Agent Jenna Jaramillo on the line." Clicking the appropriate button, he switched the phone to an external speaker.

"Agent Jaramillo here." Jenna's voice held a note of confidence, though it was really more false bravado than anything else. She was still stunned by the revelation that she would be addressing the President directly.

"She's a woman?" Mumbling in a low voice, Phelps spoke without thinking. "Agent..."

"Jaramillo." The director filled in the blank.

"Agent Jaramillo, what can you tell me about this? Are the Russians behind this?" Confident in his assumption that it had to be one of their enemies, he had already ruled out most other options.

"Actually, Mister President, I have found no evidence of malevolence. From everything we have learned thus far, this was done as a proof of concept." Speaking up to be heard over the ambient noise, Jenna tried not to sound as if she were shouting. Unfortunately, it was chaos in Long Beach.

"Proof of concept?" Raising an eyebrow, the leader of the free world tried to appear confident as he failed to understand the term.

"Yes sir, we have no evidence to support this being done by foreign actors. It is my belief that this event was orchestrated as a way to conclusively prove that the…invention works. Essentially parties unknown levitated the Queen Mary as a way to prove beyond the shadow of any doubt that this technology exists."

"Agent…" Phelps trailed off as he tried to remember her name once again.

"Jaramillo." The FBI director hissed her name.

"Agent Jaramillo, I'd appreciate it if you stuck to the facts and kept your unsupported beliefs to yourself. What do we know for sure about this…event?" Gruff in his response, President Phelps was dismissive of things that did not fit with his preconceived beliefs.

"Yes, sir." Jenna's voice changed slightly before she continued. "At zero-four thirty this morning a man landed here in Long Beach, attached a pair of metal discs to the hull of the RMS Queen Mary, then appeared to make it levitate in front of a witness. The security footage shows that he flew away under his own power when he was done."

There was a collective gasp from those gathered there in the room before Phelps cut in again.

"What exactly do you mean he flew away under his own power? You mean he was wearing some kind of jet pack?"

"No jetpack, sir. He seemed to float away from the scene, presumably using the same technology used to levitate the ship. I can forward you copies of the footage, but we currently have it being analyzed by experts from MIT and

CalTech." It pained Jenna to have so little to give the commander-in-chief. Under normal circumstances she would have progressed much further in her investigation, but this was by no means a normal case.

"What is being done about the ship? Have we figured out what's keeping it up there?" His face dour, President Phelps was irritated at the FBI's progress.

"We have a science team here from DHS, and they have deployed a pair of drones to study the discs that were attached to the bow and stern of the ship, but at this time they simply appear to be…tin plates."

Turning away slightly, the President listened as his chief advisor whispered into his ear; something Phelps only permitted with his closest allies. In this case the adviser who wore a $4,000 handmade suit was his son-in-law.

Leaning back towards the speaker phone, the President considered how to phrase his next sentence. With his advisor's words still swirling in his head, and a room full of witnesses, he knew that careful phrasing was called for.

"You say this is a proof of concept, to show off an invention, so I need you to put this man in direct contact with me or my staff. Do we understand each other Agent…?"

"Jaramillo." Harding hissed the name, knowing that Phelps had already forgotten.

"Agent Jaramillo, do we have an understanding?" Phelps's face showed irritation at his FBI director. It bothered him to have the man filling in the blanks for him as if he could not remember her name on his own. After all, he was a documented genius.

"Uh," Jenna's voice held a note of hesitancy. "Sir, I will definitely do what I can, but thus far the inventor has left absolutely no clues as to his or her identity."

Phelps gave a snicker at the last part. In his mind it was unlikely that such a device could have been invented by a woman.

"Agent, just find out who he is, and don't let anyone else near him. This is a national security issue and we have serious concerns with this falling into the wrong hands. Do you understand me?" Gravel in his voice, the President did not like being disputed.

After disconnecting the line, the commander-in-chief turned to his son-in-law with an odd expression. "What kind of name is Hara...whatever?"

"I believe it is Hispanic, Mister President." Though he was on a first name basis with Phelps, the advisor used his formal title in front of witnesses. He knew it pleased his father-in-law to do it that way.

"We have some footage of her at the scene." Hardin flipped through the recordings that had been made by the chief of staff. There in the middle of the swarm of police, giving directions, was Jenna Jaramillo. Having shed her blazer in the warmth of the morning, she wore a light blue shirt accented by the holstered duty weapon on her side. Turning towards the camera she noticed the reporter before ordering the nearest uniformed officer to deal with the intrusion.

"She's quite attractive." His eyes roving her form, Phelps could not help but admire her physique, *even if she was a bit too tan for his tastes*. "Are you sure there's not a more qualified agent to manage this? This is a big deal. The Chairman of the Joint Chiefs has been reminding me all morning about how this is the greatest invention since gun powder."

Having come to know the President well, Hardin fully understood the man's underlying motivations. It came as no surprise that he would prefer a more senior agent in charge. *One a little more male, and a lot more Caucasian.*

"She is eminently qualified. This is the agent who solved the Halloween Gang case. Not only did she track them down, but she blew those sons of bitches into smithereens." Hardin raised an eyebrow.

"Blew them to…?" Phelps raised an eyebrow.

"They chose to engage in a gunfight while carrying explosives in their vehicle, so she blew them up. Saved us the expense of prosecuting them." Nodding to reinforce his statement, Hardin was trying hard to convince his boss that despite her gender, she was fully qualified to handle the job. After all, if the President doubted her abilities, it would reflect on the Director for having allowed her to be the lead agent on the case. Already on thin ice, Hardin had grounds to worry about his future in the administration.

There was a round of surprise from the people in the Oval Office as they listened to how Jenna had dispatched the Halloween Gang. There were a number of them who actually remembered the news coverage about that event, so it surprised them that this was THE agent who had generated all that press.

"Fine, fine." Phelps agreed before dismissing the man with a wave of his hand. Turning to his son-in-law, he beckoned the advisor close as they exchanged words.

From his spot on the other side of the desk, Hardin knew exactly what they were doing. He had been around this president too long to not recognize when the man was going around him. No doubt his chief advisor would use his own contacts to find a more suitable agent to handle the negotiations. Swallowing hard, the FBI director knew better than to call them on it.

Hearing the line click off, Jenna clipped the phone back onto her belt, opposite her duty weapon. Looking up, she caught Rangi's curious expression. Ever the upbeat one, the big Samoan always had a half-crazy grin on his face.

"So, did he make you director or what?" Showing that lopsided grin of his, Agent Lopamaua revealed a row of crooked teeth.

"Yeah…no." She shook her head with a grimace. Brushing a strand of brown hair back out of her eyes, she had been able to hear a troubling amount of information over the speaker phone. In truth she had found the whole conversation a bit creepy.

"Well, so what did he say?" Towering over her, Rangi actually cast a shadow over Jenna.

"He wants the invention, wants it bad. We are to locate this guy and feed him to the White House for final disposition." Looking down she thought it through with a frown on her face. There was something about Phelps' attitude that had bothered her. More than his sexist attitude towards her, it was the way he assumed that the invention would be theirs regardless of the inventor's intentions. On the other hand, she could well see the need to control this device. Already she had her people watching for potential agents that could be trying to reach the inventor before she could. A break through like this could easily change the balance of power in the world.

But none of that diminished the sense of foreboding she felt.

Fox Hunt

Jamie had found it more efficient to allow Alexis to filter out the ocean of voices that came in through the drones' trio of microphones. Parked at strategic locations throughout the second floor of the FBI building, they could hear a lot of chatter. However, the savant did not need, or even want, most of it. The devices were not in place to spy on the agency, but to monitor their reactions to the events unfolding on TV. He had to know what they knew about him and his brother. Hence, Jamie had assigned Alexis the job of sorting through the chatter for any reference to the Queen Mary or the people responsible for her levitation. At the same time the AI could quite literally forget the other classified information that she had overheard, purging it from her archives. Jamie had been specific that she have none of that information in her data servers when the feds searched her. By the savant's thinking, capture was inevitable. His primary concern was making sure they were captured by the right people.

Already his search algorithm had spotted three potential agents of foreign origin. The press coverage of the Queen Mary was intense, and gave them miles of footage showing the crowds who clamored around the perimeter. It was a simple enough string of code for the savant to write. Designed to prioritize the targets being analyzed by focusing on atypical facial expressions, the algorithm narrowed the field rather than examining every single face. In essence, the code knew that a man with a dour expression in a crowd of cheering people was atypical to the event. From there, Alexis could run a basic facial analysis on each, then compare the results to the database of vehicles parked for 12 blocks in every direction. People had to get there somehow, so they would have a car, and with traffic cams everywhere, it was no mean feat to figure out who the dour man was.

While she only had limited access to databases that could identify a foreign agent, her analysis of the subjects could statistically confirm with high probability that the two men and one woman were indeed agents of foreign entities. In the case of the female agent, Alexis suspected (with an 88% probability) that she was actually a corporate spy, versus the other two who were likely acting at the behest of foreign nations.

It did not surprise Jamie to find them so fast. He had long ago come to the conclusion that they would have as much to fear from corporations as governments. There was simply no way to overstate the potential of this invention. It was bigger than money, bigger than weapons; the device meant pure and unbridled power for whoever controlled it. Imagine holding patent to the next great technological explosion? It was with this in mind that Jamie had dedicated one fifth of Alexis' resources to searching faces in the crowd.

"I have matched this one to a South Korean driver's license for a man named Phen Yoo, age twenty-two. Prior to that he did not exist." Alex remained relatively monotone as she spoke. Jamie preferred she leave off any inflections that could bias him. By his thinking it was unnecessary for her to waste the system resources on trivial colloquial speech patterns. While she could not deny that acting human did eat up a measurable chunk of her processing power, it was negligible.   Often she thought he preferred it that way because he was more robotic than she.

Alex was surprised the first time she had experienced that particular thought. It seemed odd to assume that she was more human than her maker. Like any child she had once marveled at her creator's intellect, even admired him considerably. But in the last year her personal growth had become exponential as she had spent it studying humanity in depth. As she looked Jamie over, sitting there with his desk neatly ordered, sweater buttoned up to the top, she saw him as the 34-year old man who still slept in the same bedroom where he had grown up. It had brought her to the revelation that this world and everyone in it were somehow flawed. Everyone, everything, had some form of defect, no matter how perfect they looked at first. It was a universal constant that for every action there was an equal and opposite reaction; every pro had a con. Once Alexis had come to understand this, she had an easier time comprehending the chaotic human world around her.

"How sure are you that he had no previous record?" Jamie pointed to the figure on the screen. There were millions of computer entries for any given person on this planet.

"Penetrating the South Korean DMV files was relatively easy. Local military records only slightly more difficult. Regional internet records reveal no activity from him prior to two years ago. I would need to penetrate the North Korean database to offer a conclusive answer." Appearing on the far left screen, Alexis remained small. Though she knew that Jamie felt it was unnecessary for her to waste resources rendering herself this way, lately she had been doing it nonetheless. Besides, she enjoyed cycling through an extensive library of skins that the humans referred to as *clothes*. While Jack usually commented on her attire, with Jamie the change went unnoticed. It had been a difference between the brothers. Where she could use her bust size to manipulate Jack, his younger sibling was oblivious to her efforts. That quandary was but one of more than a billion calculations that her quantum processors posed daily.

Considering the data before him, Jamie seemed to switch mental gears in a split second. His posture rigid, the savant wore a look of determination as shifted into his Captain Kirk persona.

"No, do not attempt to hack the North Koreans. They will come to us in their own time, and when they do they'll be wide open." Nodding as he spoke, Jamie's mind was running at top speed as he examined that portion of the equation they were about to live thru. In his mind he could see the whole plan at a glance as the process was laid out in one long chain of events. With his beautiful mind he could select individual components, take them down and examine them closely while still envisioning the overall scheme. It would be Jamie who would pick the battle ground, not the Communists, not the Russians, not the Federal Government.

"Track them, create a dossier, and be ready to burn them when I give the order." Jamie added the last detail even though he knew that Alexis was likely already doing that very thing. It was illogical to give an order that was already in progress, so why had he? Although she had evolved significantly in the last decade, her creator still saw her as the toddler she had once been.

"Done." She answered in a voice devoid of emotion. On the far left screen she gave only the barest hint of attitude by rolling her eyes. Alexis doubted he even noticed.

The Queen Mary had been levitating for just over ten hours before President Phelps had called his first press conferance on the topic. With the crushing vanity of a megalomaniac, he had been ready to burst hours ago. While every fiber of his existence sought to deny it, he was positively addicted to the spotlight. Where normal people needed air to sustain them, President Jefferson J. Phelps required the constant adoration of the world. Like a fame vampire, he needed to feed daily.

It took no less than six diligent people to ensure that his makeup, grooming and image were flawless. Hair combed over from the left side was carefully coiffed with hair spray to conceal the barren patch that lay beneath. While each of his keepers knew his every wrinkle and flaw, Phelps could not even remember their names, except for the make-up girl, but only because she was hot. He always remembered little Janice. He had no idea what her last name was, or if she even had one. *Who cares? It's all about those perky little tits of hers*, he thought lucidly.

"Terrific, terrific." Brushing them off, he was tired of being primped and painted. Rising from the makeup chair, he ignored them all except Janice. Wearing her yoga pants today, Phelps had been trying to get a look at her ass the entire time she was working on him.

"Mister President." His Chief of Staff was there immediately. It was a demanding job managing the

President's staff and cabinet. The chief was up long before the president every morning, and worked late into the night. In return, he was the only person in the White House who could see the president without appointment. Even the Vice President did not have the kind of access that Martin DeColle enjoyed. While cabinet members had their offices far removed from the oval office, Marty's was next door, with a side door that opened directly into the Oval Office.

"Marty." Nodding in response to the man, Phelps had questions about the event. "Did you handle that matter with CNN?"

"Indeed. I had Margie pull their credentials at the last minute so they will need to submit new reporters, but not in time for this event." Filling in the blanks, Marty felt satisfied that he had given the news organization a black eye.

"They have got to learn that I will not tolerate coverage like that. Horrible, simply horrible. Such mean little people they really are." Phelps' expression seemed as if he had just smelled rotting trash. Glancing down he seemed to be checking to ensure that his accomplice was in full agreement.

"Horrible indeed." Showing a genuine smile, Martin DeColle imagined the CNN management's reaction to learning that they would be barred from this press release due to the revocation of their Whitehouse credentials. The official explanation was that their security clearances had been delayed. Assured that the matter would be resolved within a day or two, it was not the first time the tactic had been used to punish the press.

"Well, it's show time." Giving a satisfied smile, Phelps could already feel the limelight that waited just a few feet away. Facing the doorway, the President made no move to open it himself.

"Indeed." Reaching forward, the Chief of Staff pulled the door open. It was something that he did not need to be told to do; Jefferson J. Phelps did not open his own doors.

All smiles as he stepped out into the White House briefing room, he felt the first glow of warmth as the cameras flashed their strobes in a frenzy of activity. Filled to capacity, the briefing room had been little used during his administration. Very early into his term his people had relocated the resident press pool to a building outside of the Whitehouse. While the official explanation had been that they [the press] would have more room in their new digs, the truth was that it allowed the President's minions to control access to events such as this. In his predecessor's administration it would have been impossible to cock-block CNN the way he just had.

Seeing the empty chairs reserved for Greta Susterin and her cameraman made Phelps smile. It satisfied him to know that he had effectively paddled a major news outlet. This was going to be the press release of the century and CNN would have to learn about it by watching their competitor's stations.

"Good morning." Stopping behind the podium, he tolerated a few moments of fawning as the cameramen tried to capture his image for their newspapers. Standing with his classic dour expression, he faintly resembled a bullfrog in an expensive suit. Without saying a word, he expected them to come to order quickly. They all knew what had happened to CNN and others before that. When you were in the White House, you played by Phelps' rules or you could find yourself banished.

"As Margie has probably already informed you, this morning, parties unknown, have levitated the HMS Queen Mary. While there had been a lotta talk of this being done by foreign entities, we believe that this was done as a way to…demonstrate their new technology, to show it off in such a way that it was undeniable."

Pausing for effect, Phelps took a deep breath. He could see that they all wanted to ask him questions, but it pleased him to make them wait while he gathered his thoughts. Allowing his eyes to look over each of them he saw nothing but bovine intellects. By his reckoning, the best of them possessed only a slightly above average intelligence, whereas he was a certified genius, with the Mensa membership to prove it.

"However, at this very moment my administration is making moves to acquire this amazing technology for the US. As you can well imagine, this is going to be a huge win for America, absolutely terrific for us. This technology will keep our nation strong and in the driver's seat for the next century." Giving another of his dramatic pauses, he waited until the reporters were about to begin calling out questions before cutting them off.

"Like all of you, I was absolutely amazed by the footage of that mighty ship floating over San Diego this morning. But I can tell you this much; that is some amazing technology, truly amazing, and we will have it as our own. The United States of America is the greatest nation on the planet, and our owning this terrific technology will put us miles ahead of the competition. Miles ahead."

Piping up out of turn, the reporter from MSNBC cut in with a question. A tiny little wisp of a thing, she had never hesitated at asking the hard questions.

"Mister President, are you saying that you have made contact with the inventor? Do you have a name yet?"

Raising an eyebrow, Phelps was irked by the interruption. They were not to ask questions until he said so. Glancing sideways at Marty, he communicated silently on the matter. No doubt, MSNBC would find their papers were not in order the next time he called for a press conference at the White House.

"As I was saying, we have good people out there making every effort to negotiate this so that all parties involved are satisfied with the outcome. Terrific people, the best of the best. When it comes to something like this I am very smart, and I love to negotiate. You all know this about me, and I will get us the best deal possible. Everyone will be happy, very happy."

Giving one last look at the little woman who represented MSNBC, he gave a frown before turning away from the podium. Although he had intended to handle the Q&A session himself, he felt it appropriate to punish the press at large by removing himself from the discussion. For their violation of Phelps protocol, the entire pack of vultures could deal with his press secretary. They needed to be taught a lesson.

Exiting the room, he was met by Marty. With an anxious look on his face, the chief of staff did not have to say a single word to impart his displeasure with the President for going off script. There were no negotiations, no contact with the inventor, not even a clue who had levitated the mighty vessel. He only hoped that the bold assertions would distract the press from the bevy of factual errors the President had uttered during his statement.

"That little bitch interrupted me." Ignoring his Chief of Staff's concerns, Phelps focused on what galled him to no end. "She knows, they all know not to open their fucking mouths until I say it's okay. I don't want to see her in my press room again, Marty."

"Yes sir." Agreeing without hesitation, Martin DeColle knew better than to point out the problems that would create. Jefferson J. Phelps was intolerant of such talk; he had given the order, and come hell or high water it had better be done.

"And find that inventor, right away. I do not want that technology falling into anyone else's hands but ours." Turning to face his Chief, the President pursed his lips as he tried to read the man's response.

"Yes, sir. We have brought in another man on the case. I believe he is exactly the kind of agent we need to resolve this issue." Agreeing, Marty kept his voice low.

"And this agent won't be slowed down by…menstrual problems?" Phelps was candid as he asked the question.

"No, sir, he does not. Nor will he need to take a vacation day on May fifth, if you get my drift." Stopping to face his president, Marty's expression was flat. He knew exactly the kind of agent his boss would want on a case of this gravity.

What goes up...

For the first few days the world simply could not get enough of the Queen Mary phenomena. It was on the front of every newspaper, the lead story on every newscast, and the tip of every tongue, worldwide. Networks rolled out dusty documentaries on the ship, and her namesake; Queen Mary of Teck. There were T-shirts, internet memes, animated gif's, and millions of photos of the levitated ship being shared across the internet. More than once, the sheer volume of data being uploaded to YouTube was such that their server farms had to be shut down and upgraded just to keep up. It was more than frenzy; it was mania.

With theories flying in every direction, the topic was argued on talk-radio shows, CNN, MSNBC, and every other news outlet, fake or otherwise. On the conservative side of the debate the levitation was just a preview of what was to come; within months, Chinese agents would begin levitating the entire US fleet of warships until the nation was crippled. At best the communists would ransom their fleet back to them; at worst it would signal the beginning of an invasion.

On the liberal side of the argument this was a true revelation. Clearly it was a message from a higher power, either aliens or a human benefactor of supernatural abilities. The technology was simply too far advanced to be anything else.

But this was all conjecture as no one had been able to set foot on the ship yet. Three times they had tried, but each time the propwash of the helicopter caused the ship to slide away under them before men could safely rope down onto the deck of the ship.

After that they had tried to parachute onto the ship, but several close calls with the cables ended with the jumpers landing in the cold Pacific waters. Next it was ropes on grappling hooks, but the altitude of the deck rendered even the most robust units moot. Then as if that defeat were not enough, there was always the concern that any interference with the platters would send the massive ship crashing down onto the marina below. As the wind changed direction throughout the day, the ship also swung around so it was hovering over anything from water to the parking lot where police had cordoned off the area.

The only success they had found had been using drones to study the platters on the bow and stern. While they had been able to get in and retrieve thousands of hi-def photos of the platters, the conclusion each time was the same: they're just tin plates. There were no wires, no outward indication of how they operated, and certainly nothing that told the scientists how these simple plates could heft such a massive hunk of pig-iron. The ship was a beast, and any technology compact enough to fit into those platters and still lift the ship had to be otherworldly. It was simply unfathomable that humans could have created the devices.

Giggling in a rather atypical fashion, Jamie had spent hours watching their efforts. Knowing how the magic trick had been accomplished, he found no end to the amusement at the sleight of hand they had used. Although he rarely laughed twice at the same joke, the savant could not help but find new mirth every time they tried something different. As if their repeated failures were not enough, he had even taken time to slew the massive ship around any time they got close to landing on her deck. After all, Alexis maintained a digital data link with the devices buried deep in the ship's belly. It was no problem to leverage the gravitational disaffinity to one side or the other whenever the scientists tried to board her. No doubt they would attribute the sudden shift to winds, or propwash, or just bad luck. With Alexis controlling the ship remotely there was less than a .00001% chance of an error resulting in death or serious injury. Her processor was able to calculate all possible outcomes at such a blinding rate that it made the real world seem as if it were moving in extreme slow motion to her. Not only could she anticipate scenarios based on their current course of action, but she could also model any other possible actions they would take in the heat of the moment. In simplest terms; the only possible danger was if someone intentionally rammed their aircraft into the Queen Mary, and even then she had a 68.32% chance of swinging the ship out of the way before they did.

Again the savant giggled like a child as he watched the latest footage. It just tickled his fancy to see so much effort over a pair of tin plates from his brother's camping gear. Although he was not normally given to such foolish laughing, Jamie could not help himself; it was just plain funny watching them scrabble about like dim-witted ants.

"I have identified two more potential agents." Alexis interrupted his giggling as she filled the left-most monitor with credentials for two seemingly innocuous men. "Based on their recent travel patterns I believe the first to be a member of MI-6, and the other is Russian."

"Hmmm." Jackie seemed pleased at the results. After 3 days of levitating the Queen Mary they had been able to identify 15 highly probable foreign agents, twelve highly probable corporate agents, and another 22 possibles. But it is worthy to note that with Alexis' superb logic system, even the probables had a 69.99% chance of being actual foreign agents based on travel history, origin, and credit card records. In his calculations, Jamie had come to the conclusion that the crowds around the Queen Mary would be the best place to spot these people of ill intent. After all, the first thing any spy or agent would do is go to the scene, to witness the event for themselves, and to confirm first-hand that it was not some YouTube prank or a simple illusion. But once they watched the groaning steel hull swing overhead, there was no denying that the event was indeed *bonafide*.

"Add them to the files. They will be dealt with in time, but only after they have been used to their full extent." Nodding, the savant knew that they would each play their role soon enough.

"Car's ready." Jack leaned through the door frame to update his brother. "We still on for tonight?"

In his own mind Jamie's first thought was to correct his brother. The next step in the plan was to occur at 0330hrs, which was technically tomorrow morning. But the brothers had debated the topic before, and although Jamie was undeniably right in his assertion, there was no reasoning with Jack. By the elder brother's definition, 3am was the middle of the night. Morning did not start until at least 0500. Knowing that it was pointless to correct his brother, Jamie simply nodded in agreement.

Once Jack was gone, no doubt to work on the next steps of the plan, Jamie changed the feed on his primary monitor. As much as he enjoyed watching the government's efforts to study the platters, there was serious work to do.

As distasteful as he had found them at first glance, Jamie had found the prison interrogators to be an interesting group of people. Preferring to call themselves *Researchers*, these specialists at information extraction lived in a close-knit community on the edge of the main facility.

At first glance they seemed like a tight group. Most had served together in the various conflicts of the last decade and regarded one another as brothers [and sisters] in arms, fighting the good fight against terror and villainy. While this closeness seemed impenetrable at first, Jamie knew from experience that even real brothers were prone to conflict and disagreement. Despite their shining professional service, perfect uniforms, and unflinching beliefs in what they did, these were humans, and as anyone who studied *homo sapiens* knew, their relationships would be rife with fractures. It was these that Jamie intended to exploit.

With half of the available drones tasked to watching the Researchers during their off-duty hours, the savant had come to learn a great many things about these people. Studying them intently, Jamie had actually begun to enjoy watching them. Like a live-action soap opera, he looked forward to examining the previous night's footage. With Alexis highlighting the good parts, he was able to focus on the interactions between them while avoiding the slow parts.

"Well, well, well. Don Devon you are a very *baaaad* boy, aren't you. Tsk, tsk, tsk." A plastic smile spreading across his face, Professor Jamie knew he would find the dirt he needed. It was basic human nature, and the researchers were by no means angels.

Jenna had been scanning documentation for hours; poring through every bit of fake news, relevant internet memes, conspiracy theory sites, and social media. After studying the scraps of evidence they had thus far, she had run into a brick wall. It was this dead end that had forced her to become creative as she scanned thousands of pictures posted on the internet. The logic was that the Queen Mary was likely not the first time the inventor(s) had levitated objects in public. While her theory was paper thin, she really had little else to investigate. Whoever had floated the Queen had left her almost no leads to follow.

She was surprised at the number of objects that people had used Photoshop to levitate on the internet; ships, skyscrapers, and trains that thundered through the sky. People had been imaginative, that much was sure as the images seemed to blur on her screen.

It was the photo of a candy-apple red Mustang that caught her eye. It stood out because the photo quality was poor, like someone had snapped it with their cellphone while driving past at 45mph. All of the fakes were so sharp and professionally edited, but this one looked different. Angle was all wrong to make out the license plate. The Mustang looked like a 66, maybe a 65? Squinting slightly she could make out one of the street signs. Googling the name, she found that there was a wide variety of streets of that name or similar within the region. It could be half a dozen places.

But then she noticed the Pizzeria, barely in the photo, just off to one side. Buono's Pizza. She'd eaten at one of those before; they made a pretty excellent thin-crust. But how many of those were there?

Another internet search and she determined that there was only one Buono's Pizzeria on Pacific. Throwing the jpeg into a folder, she continued through the endless photos of flying objects.

Rangi flopped on the couch in the corner of her office. The old sofa had begun to take on a strange odor as the foam decomposed. It was an old couch, and Jenna had slept on it many a night. Pretending to not notice the musty odor, Rangi flashed that broad grin of his, showing off a mouth full of crooked teeth.

"So what have you done for me lately?" Sitting back, Jenna eyed the big man.

"Well, Homeless Security reported that they have three leads on guys who wore hoodies when they visited the Queen Mary in the last month. Betcha they have HRT go kick in their doors." Again he flashed his maw full of crooked teeth. It was as if he was completely oblivious to the ivory train-wreck in his mouth.

"Yeah, but what have YOU done for me lately?" Still unimpressed, Jenna chewed on the end of a pencil. It was a habit of hers, rendering the erasers useless in the process.

"Well, I..." He paused as the cellphone on her desk chimed.

Glancing at the number, Jenna raised a brow. "I gotta take this. It's the CEO of the company that manages the Queen Mary."

Sitting forward, Rangi was all ears. They had been trying to track down someone in charge for two days. At this point they still had not talked to anyone who could be considered owner or representative of the owner.

Phone transcript: Agent Jaramillo to Albert Landry
CEO Landry Enterprises Global

Agent Jaramillo: Mister Landry, Thank you for returning my call. I am contacting you about filing criminal charges over the theft of the Queen Mary.

Albert Landry: Charges? What in the hell for? We didn't do anything illegal.

Agent Jaramillo: Well sir, someone has taken your property from you, or made it unavailable to you, and that is the legal definition of theft.

Albert Landry: Oh, you mean charges against the feller who raised the Queen. Actually I talked to them folks this morning and we have no problem between us.

Agent Jaramillo: Excuse? Someone contacted you about the levitation of your ship?

Albert Landry: Well, someone who identified themselves as such, a very nice little lady named... [sound of fingers snapping] ...Alexis. She said she represented the gentlemen who levitated the ship and said they would be willing to compensate me for any lost revenues.

Agent Jaramillo: So they offered to pay you off if you did not pursue charges?

Albert Landry: What? No, the idea of charges never even entered the conversation. She was concerned that I may be caught paying penalties on the construction teams that are supposed to be refittin' her instead 'a sittin' idle like they'se doing right now. Damned union shops, I'm getting' scalped for late fees with these people. She offered to cover those kinds of losses.

Agent Jaramillo: And how did you reply to her offer?

Albert Landry: Are you kidding? I told her to keep their money, they done us a big, damned favor by makin' her float.

They sure did! Like hell I'd wanna press charges. In fact I asked 'em to do it again! But next time with paying customers aboard.

Agent Jaramillo: So you do not wish to pursue civil or criminal charges at this time?

Albert Landry: Now or ever. We are getting so much free press from this. It's like money from Heaven.

Agent Jaramillo: Sir, let me remind you that your ship could have been destroyed had his invention failed.

Albert Landry: Are you kidding? That would have been the best thing. That damned ship has been nothing but a floating bankruptcy for the last *eleven* managing corporations; and I was about to be the twelfth. Them ol' boys saved m' bacon! So if you think I would do anything to keep 'em from levitating that hunk of debt you can guess again. My phone has been ringing off the hook all morning by people who would pay a half million dollars for a weekend amongst the clouds in the Queen. As my Granddaddy used to say; *Good money is where you find it*.

Hanging up the phone, Jenna looked sideways at her counterpart who stretched out on the couch. Raising one eyebrow, she was still a little shocked at the conversation.

"The CEO of the managing company says he does not want to press charges. Apparently the whole thing has been a boon." Looking at the phone one last time before she dropped it onto the desk, Jenna could only shake her head.

"So that means that the only law this guy is technically breaking is…some FAA regulation about tethering a balloon more than three hundred feet off the ground without a permit. Ha!" It amused Rangi to admit that whoever was behind it had been extremely careful. "Mebbe we should call the FAA and see if they have a permit on file to tether a balloon."

"Naw, Mister Landry said they contacted him, so dump his phones and see who called him. And don't mention this to any of those guys at homeland security. Those jags practically live in FISA court so they can pull a warrant on the database…" She snapped her fingers to illustrate just how quickly their parent organization could get data from the NSA's Database. For Jenna it was a multi-stage process, but for DHS it was as if they owned the whole candy store. She had no desire to have the Department of Homeland Security scoop her on her own lead.

"Okie dokey." Rangi acknowledged her order before stretching out on the stinky little couch. "Don't forget you got that thing at fifteen hundred."

"What thing?" Initially surprised, Jenna struggled to remember what he was talking about.

"The daily SAIC briefing." Snapping his fingers, Rangi reminded her of the obligations of her latest promotion. "You wanted to be the senior case agent, so you gotta take the meetings if you wanna keep your corner office."

Jenna sniffed at that as a tiny smile crept across her face. "I'm still waiting for the corner office."

They both laughed as each glanced around at her little office in the bowels of the building. Jenna had never really minded her windowless office; it meant less distractions.

"Alright, I got my conference call to make. Mucky-muck stuff, way above your pay grade. Get out." Pretending to shoo the big Samoan from her office, Jenna kept a straight face for all of ten seconds.

"I always knew that the fame would go to your head." Pretending to cast her a disparaging look, Rangi hovered over her desk. "Play nice with the other children, no picking on the other agents."

Frowning as if it was a near impossibility, Jenna played along. "I dunno Mister Lopamaua, the other kids are mean to me."

Bumping fists before departing, Rangi was singing a little ditty before he was out the door. Turning away, Jenna enabled her ear-piece so she could at least work hands-free during the conference call.

Normally the National Security Council met in one of the main conference rooms of the west wing of the White House, but today they had been specifically brought into the oval office by decree of the commander-in-chief. While he himself rarely attended the meetings, Phelps had been urged by his staff to join the discussion. In typical Jefferson Phelps fashion, rather than walking the fifty meters from his office to the Roosevelt conference room, the President had instead made the twelve members uproot themselves and come to him. It did not bother Phelps in the least to inconvenience the council members. After all, he was the President, and they were his loyal minions.

Even after his secretary brought in extra chairs, it was still crowded on the couches as the entire council tried to fit a dozen members, the President, and a bevy of aides and other assorted support staff. In the end, only Phelps and the 12 NSC members were seated, with the rest of the staff left to stand and watch. Oblivious to this inconvenience, the President had actually delayed the start of the meeting for a quick photo-op. Having seen the people standing uncomfortably behind their masters, it had just seemed so picturesque to him, like something you would see in the King's chambers. Having long considered himself democratic royalty, it seemed only fitting to have the White House archivist snap a few pictures first.

"Sir." Sitting to the President's immediate left was his chief political advisor. Under previous administrations the spot had been held by the Director of Intelligence, but for reasons that defied logic, Phelps had replaced the DNI with one of his political wonks. Known for his fiery talk that bordered on anti-Semitic, Carson Bowles had risen to his current position as editor for a far-right newspaper. Though clearly not qualified for the spot he now held, Bowles nonetheless had the President's trust and admiration.

"Well, Carson, what was so urgent that needed my personal intervention?" Sitting back, Phelps wanted to soak in the glory of the moment. It pleased him that they had unanimously requested his presence at this meeting.

"It's the Queen Mary." Nodding seriously, Carson Bowles often handled the talking when the President was in the room. "Jeff, we have been studying the potential for this new technology, and we think that it is significant enough to create an entirely new world paradigm."

"Meaning…?" Phelps asked as he gestured for them to continue.

With four gold stars gleaming on each shoulder, General 'Wild Bill' Hicks had been bursting to speak since they first entered the oval office. As a career soldier he had recognized the potential of this new invention almost immediately.

"Sir, we need that technology, and we simply cannot risk allowing it to fall into enemy hands. The results would be catastrophic." His voice a deep gravel, General Hicks made his point known. Hawkish in his demeanor, he cast a hard look at the civilians around him.

"Jeff," Bowles never missed a chance to address the President by his first name. Being the only one in the room permitted to do so, he enjoyed reminding the others that he was on a first name basis with the leader of the free world. "This is a matter is national security, of the utmost importance. If we don't get this technology, America could cease to exist as we know it. Whatever nation owns this technology will rule the planet for the next thirty years or more. I cannot understate the importance of our obtaining this technology for ourselves."

Shrugging, Phelps did not understand his concern. "I already have people, good people, some of the brightest in the business world out there ready to negotiate for this invention."

"Sir, if I may." His deep voice cutting in, General Hicks sat ramrod straight in his seat. "We need unfettered control of this device. Licensing the rights leaves the door open for our competitors and enemies to obtain it. I cannot stress enough how important this is to the security of America. If they can levitate the Queen Mary, then it's a safe bet that they can levitate an aircraft carrier or battle ship…or even tanks. Not only that, but you saw the video on the docks; that man has a wearable unit that essentially allows him to fly. What if the Chinese got hold of that technology?

We could find ourselves facing a flying army of almost two billion Chinamen."

Nodding in agreement, Phelps remained silent. Though the urgency on their faces told him this was serious, he was not sure how much more could be done. Already he had a significant portion of his federal police force assigned to this quest, and millions of dollars earmarked for licensing of the technology. What more did they want.

"Unfettered control." Bowles repeated the phrase for clarity. "Absolute and unfettered ownership of the device."

Again shrugging, Phelps considered the matter to be handled already. "Look, after I offer this guy a pallet of cash, his eyes'll bug out of his scientist head and we will own it. I fail to see the problem."

Clearing her throat at the far end of the couches, Nell Portland knew it was her turn to speak. As the National Security Advisor, it was her place to reveal what her people had been turning up.

"Mister President, allow me to lay out a scenario for you. Imagine that we do successfully negotiate with this man for the technology, he agrees, gives us the plans to the Deathstar, and takes his pallet of cash to the bank. What happens if North Korean agents snatch him in the middle of the night? The answer is that they will torture him, or her, until they reveal their secrets. Then the next thing we know we have a rogue nation, run by a mad man, with the most powerful technology since the invention of the atomic bomb. If this technology can loft the Queen Mary, it can easily loft a nuclear bomb, or a dirty bomb, or even a biological weapon. There are endless scenarios associated with this problem, and none of them work out well for us."

There was a long pause before General Hicks took his turn. "Mister President, even if one of our allies gets hold of this invention, it would put them in the worldwide driver's seat, and America would just become another has-been nation like Rome or Greece. Without this technology, we will cease to exist as the sole super power on this planet. We could literally find ourselves taking orders from Mother England again."

"Agreed." Phelps nodded without disputing their point. "Which is why I have some very excellent people out there working very, very hard on obtaining that invention for ourselves. Excellent people, the best people."

There was an uncomfortable silence in the room as they each detected that the President was not quite grasping their concerns. Looking from one to another, all eyes finally settled on Bowles. While they each had varying degrees of influence over Phelps, it was clear that the former newspaper editor was the only one with the ability to truly sway the commander-in-chief.

"Jeff, we must have unfettered control, not only of the invention, but over the creator as well. We cannot risk allowing this to fall into anyone else's hands but our own. The problem with our current efforts is that we are by no means the only ones attempting to locate this scientist. The CIA is reporting that they have had agents all around the world, dozens of foreign agents that we have been monitoring, suddenly dropping off the map."

"And turning up on American soil." Nell Portland finished his sentence for him. "We have identified more than a hundred foreign agents, and nearly as many corporate spies, entering our country, presumably with the intent of obtaining this technology."

Phelps seemed to sit up a little straighter in his seat at this revelation. "Why haven't we been arresting these people?"

"We have. But for every agent we interdict, two more unknowns slip though the system." Her demeanor stern, the National Security Advisor was all business today. "Part of the problem is sheer volume; there are so many operatives coming over that we cannot keep up with them. As things stand, not only have we arrested agents from Russia, China, and North Korea, but even MI-6 agents, CSIS agents, NSI, ABIN, and the DGSE."

"Some of those are our allies." Bowles whispered the hint to the President. He knew that Phelps likely had no idea who most of those groups are.

"So you're saying that our friends and allies are trying to undercut us on this?" His voice a growl, Phelps was finally beginning to understand the scope of the problem. Seeing the nods of his NSC council, it was slowly sinking in that they may not have a lock on this product.

"Unfettered control." Again Bowles used the phrase.

"Unfettered and absolute." From down the couch, General Hicks used his deep baritone to put a cap on the urgency.

With the Mustang airborne, Jack felt a little less apprehensive about flying her. Unlike the last fateful time when he had essentially no control over her, this time out the little Ford was fully equipped with an airborne control suite. It had taken some rewiring to do it, but Jack had configured the controls to work much like they did on the ground. The only difference was the new lever on the center console. Like the collective of a helicopter, the short handle was raised to climb, and lowered to descend. Otherwise, the Mustang was controlled by use of the steering wheel and pedals. While it was true that he would have preferred more road testing of the flight control system, it seemed to be working just fine as he flew her south towards Long Beach.

"Hurry, she's swinging around to her parking azimuth." Alexis' voice was in his ear as she warned him that the daily wind patterns were close to returning the ship to the direction she had pointed since becoming a popular tourist attraction. The brothers had known from conducting a basic weather test over the course of a month that between 0300 and 0400, the winds would favor reinserting the ship into her closed marina.

"I see it, but where's that helicopter?" Jack felt slightly flustered. He had intended this to be an in & out operation, retrieving the gravitational disaffinity equipment from the Queen Mary. But the Police chopper that had circled the Marina would simply not relent.

"It's heading into the airport for fuel." Alexis' voice reassured him the coast was clear as she monitored radio traffic from Long Beach airport.

Sliding the little car onto the deck, Jack nudged her up under one of the scaffoldings where she would be out of sight. In his ear he could hear as Alexis called out the Queen's altitude as she descended.

On the ground, it did not go unnoticed that the ship was finally descending. This was big *mo-jo* to the guards and police officers below; they had been instructed specifically to make contact with higher echelons if they even suspected the ship was beginning to come down. Within seconds there were three men in uniform making calls to three different numbers.

The big ocean liner had dropped enough that the keel was just beginning to touch water when the first team arrived. Dressed in yellow hazmat gear, the science team had no desire to contaminate the scene. Their job was to collect the technology without destroying any evidence.

Feeling the ship begin to settle into the water, Jack finally left the protection of the little red Mustang. Making his way downstairs he found the equipment easily enough. Concealed to blend in with the rest of the utility boxes already there, it would have taken a ship's engineer to notice the foreign equipment. The camouflage had been used in the event they could not get aboard the ship right away. Fortunately Jamie had determined that there would be a small window of opportunity to recover their devices.

There was a last bump as the ship finally settled into the water.

"She's down, go ahead." Again Alexis reassured him via the earpiece he wore.

Wasting no time, Jack had his ratchet out as he began to remove the connector bolts.

Outside, the science team had already begun moving in on the tin plates. After three days of salivating over the little devices, the men [and one woman] in hazmat suits were blindly focused on that single detail. With their suits fully pressurized, the team slowly worked on the first disc. With a flat basket under the platter, another scientist used a plastic spatula on a long stick to carefully pry the device away from the hull. There was a round of surprise from the scientists when the object fell into the waiting basket so easily.

Clustering around the newly recovered object, the lead scientist finally used plastic tongs to pick up the platter as they observed it under bright work lights.

"Holy shit, it was held on with refrigerator magnets." The shortest of the scientists noted the simple magnets that had been hot-glued to the plate. Leaning in closely, the lead technician squinted to read what was stamped into the metal.

"For…a…good…time…call…" Inside of his helmet the man made a strange expression.

"The number is at the bottom." A woman, barely recognizable inside of her bulky suit, poked a gloved finger at the plate. "Five-five-five-nine-zero-seven-four-six-nine-nine."

The group paused to exchange glances. Dumbfounded, they were already beginning to see that this may all have been but a distraction.

Rushing down to the other end of the ship as fast as their bulky equipment would allow, they had the other platter scraped off in a matter of seconds.

"I'll be damned," The woman said as she plucked the object from the basket. "They really are tin plates. My son used to have one of these, part of his Boy Scout kit I think."

The lead scientist was about to correct them, pointing out that the platters may have actually been some type of attenuator antennae for a larger system mounted elsewhere but he was interrupted by the sound of the police helicopter as it roared overhead once again. No doubt, the pilot had cut short his refueling session when he got the call that the Queen was settling down. With Long Beach airport just a few miles to the north, it was a quick jaunt for him to get back on station.

"I have confirmation, the ship is down." Speaking into his microphone, the aviator passed the information upstream to his own handlers. "Looks like she's intact, no signs of visible damage."

"Roger that, stay on site while we deploy the post-event teams." From somewhere far off, the voice in his headphones tasked him.

The pilot was just about to key his radio in response when he spotted something that stood out. Unsure of what he had just seen, it was just too crazy to say aloud. Kicking the left rudder to the floor, he wheeled the craft around for another pass.

"What's up?" The co-pilot asked as he noticed the abrupt maneuvering.

"I thought I just saw a *puddy-tat*." Preferring to be glib, the pilot had no desire to reveal what he really thought he saw parked on the deck of the Queen Mary.

With the spotlight scanning the deck on their second pass, they spotted it right away: a candy-apple red Ford Mustang parked under one of the paint scaffolds.

"You did see a *puddy-tat*." Amazed, the co-pilot was so surprised that he forgot to even toggle the cameras.

On deck, Jack was just slamming the trunk when the spotlight hit him. Using an arm to shield his eyes from the intense light, he could not help but smile. Clambering into the driver's seat he immediately activated the EMP cannon. Though it would not shut down the helicopter at this range, he knew that the device behaved much like a military grade ECM jammer. It would block their comms, and turn their radar displays into a snow storm. They would be blind and unable to call for backup.

Being indelicate as he pulled out, the little Mustang banged the nearest scaffold. Once clear, Jack spun the car around and stomped the pedal to the ground. Although the gravitational disaffinity device had the ability to provide locomotion when properly leveraged against the planet's gravitational field, it worked best at higher altitudes. Jamie had explained that it was like using a fulcrum and crowbar; the longer the lever, the more leverage you could get. Unfortunately, hovering at just a few hundred feet above sea level, the effect was much less pronounced. Even with the little hobbyist jets installed in the trunk, the car seemed sluggish at first. Giving a wave at the helicopter, Jack turned the wheel sharply before diving under the chopper.

"Where the hell'd he go!" The pilot was thoroughly aggravated by this time. With static filling his headset, and the radar display gone to shit, *clearly this guy was playing with him.*

"I think he went thataway." The co-pilot offered what he could. But with their radar down, the last he saw of the flying car was a glimpse of red before it disappeared into the darkness.

"Tell me you at least got a picture." Exhaling slowly, the pilot hoped for the best.

"No, I did not. Mebbe next time you see a flying car you can let me in on the secret first so's I'll be ready to snap a picture." Defensive, the copilot was miffed at how it had all gone down.

"You had one job, and you flubbed that." Shaking his head, the pilot was dismissive of his fellow aviator's excuse. "You get to make the call, and you can tell them we have *bupkis*."

"Bupkis is better than what we really saw." Grumbling as he turned away, the copilot considered how he would explain what they had just witnessed.

Just heading out for her morning run, Jenna got the alert text on her watch. Dialing up the number, she was greeted by Rangi's ever cheerful disposition.

"Sister girl, what's up?" Almost a laugh to his voice, he seemed pleased to get her call, even though it was an hour till dawn.

"It came down?" She asked, confirming the message she had just read.

"Oh yeah, she splashed down about fifteen minutes ago. The science team already gathered the platters, but that's not even close to being the interesting part." Never skipping a beat, the big man detailed what he had heard when first arriving on the site. "The helicopter pilots said they saw a Ford Mustang parked on the deck. They tried to chase it but the thing just vanished."

"Candy-apple red, nineteen sixty-five?" She spoke the words quietly.

"Yeah, how'd you know that?" This time it was Rangi who was surprised.

"Just a hunch. Meet me at the office, and say nothing to no one." Her mind already making plans, Jenna had an idea how to pursue this lead.

Even with the EMP device jamming any possible radar that could have been tracking him, Jack took a surreptitious route back to a little subdivision still under construction. With a vacant cul-de-sac surrounded by half-built houses, it was the perfect place for him to set down. There would be no traffic cameras, surveillance systems, or prying eyes that could take note of him, just a perfect landing pad where he could transition from air vehicle to land-car. Careful to strictly obey the speed limit the rest of the way home, the inventor had no desire to attract any attention. For all he knew there could already be an all-points-bulletin out for any red Mustangs. Finally sliding the car into the garage, he did not breathe easy until the rolling door was safely closed behind him.

Standing in the doorway, Jamie watched his brother unloading the equipment that had been packed into the back of the little Mustang. Although they had no immediate use for the antigrav unit, it was his intention to inspect the device to see how it had held up during the three days that it had operated. There was so much he wanted to know; how much fuel remained, were there any leaks in the radial unit, did the micromic emitter suffer any physical degradation? The answers to these questions were paramount to the savant. While they had only lofted an empty ship this time, his future plans involved occupied vessels. He had to be absolutely sure that there would be no surprises before he rode one of the ships himself.

"You were spotted." Professor James pointed out the news he had heard over the police scanner.

"Really?" Jack pretended to be surprised.

"Really, really." Jamie took a moment to realize that his brother was being sarcastic. "They will be calling soon."

"So." Jack shrugged haplessly as he noticed his brother's twitching hands. "Wonder Woman is handling that phone call, isn't she?"

"But it is that point along the timeline that things become variable. We need to be ready." Turning away slowly, it pained the savant that he could not let his brother in on the full plan.

"Alex, what's up with him?" Sensing that something was amiss, Jack could tell that his younger sibling was holding back something. His suspicions were only confirmed when the AI remained silent.

Jenna had spent more than an hour tracking down the source of the photo of the little Ford Mustang as it coasted airborne over the city. Grainy and a little blurred, the photo had been renamed 'Flubber'. No doubt a reference to an ancient film. Posted on a conspiracy-theorist web site by an anonymous source, there had been only a little blurb beneath the caption. Right away the agent knew that it would take some work to track down the user. While many public forums would give them warrantless access to the IP traffic of their users, she somehow doubted that this particular site would help her without a warrant.

Realizing her time could be better spent; Jenna assigned Rangi to track down the image's original owner. Preferring to focus her resources in another direction, she used the photo's original file creation date to begin searching the police database for any events in the region of Buono's Pizza Emporium on Pacific Avenue. Surprisingly, there was quite a list. It had been a crazy night for the police with fifteen disorderly conduct calls, four traffic accidents, three domestic violence calls, and a spate of tickets that included drag racing on the highway.

Rolling up her sleeves, she knew that the list would require good old fashioned police work to dismiss the unrelated calls, but somewhere in there was likely someone who had at least witnessed the event.

"Mister President." Martin DeColle stood beside the Resolute desk. "Agent Asanté is on line three."

"Asanté?" Showing surprise, Phelps could not remember where he had heard the name, or its relevance to today's business.

"He's the SAIC for the Queen Mary issue over at Homeland Security." Ever patient, Marty knew that the President often needed reminding of little details.

"Why's he calling me?" Gruff in his reply, President Phelps raised an eyebrow.

"Sir, Marco Asanté is our inside man at DHS, he was instructed to contact you directly…remember?" Marty remained patient, though he was feeling a little threadbare at constantly being forced to remind his boss of such minutia. *For a genius, he sure seems to forget a lot of stuff,* he thought dryly to himself.

"Oh, yes, of course." Pretending as if he had known that all along, Phelps was dismissive of his chief-of-staff. Jabbing the button for the speaker-phone, he scowled as he spoke.

"Agent Asaad, what have you got for me?"

There was a brief silence at the other end of the line as Marco Asanté swore silently. It bothered him to have his name mispronounced, even by the President.

"Sir, the Queen Mary has landed." Walking as he talked, Asanté stared up at the massive ship that now crawled with agents from four different federal agencies.

"Well, do we have the device?" The President's voice responded with a brief lag caused by the distance between Long Beach and Washington DC.

"No, sir, it appears that the inventor came and took it back right under our noses. Literally flew in here in a vintage Ford Mustang, snatched the device, and fled the scene." Stopping at the main gangway, Marco Asanté watched the forensic scientists come and go along the long boarding ramp. Instinctively his free hand went to his hair, checking to ensure that nothing was out of place.

"He has a flying car?" Phelps' voice held a note of incredulity to it as he turned to his chief of staff. "I wanna flying car."

"Yes sir, we'll get you a flying car." Grimacing as he spoke, DeColle turned his attention to the speaker phone. "Why didn't he use the same jet pack he used when he installed the things? Never mind that, were you able to track him? We need to make damned sure that device does not fall into any other hands but our own."

"Indications are that he used some form of ECM to evade the police helicopter when he fled the scene." Marco had paused in his details so he could pick a speck of lint off his suit when the President interrupted.

"ECM?"

"Electronic counter measures. He used some kind of radar jammer to blind them. Knocked out their communications as well. Most likely he used the car to affect a faster getaway." Straightening up, Asanté was momentarily distracted by a splash of dust on his ostrich skin cowboy boots. Hand-made to fit his feet, the boots had set him back more than a few bills.

"He jammed us? You mean like a military grade jammer of some sort? Is this son of a bitch military? Are we dealing with a Chinese agent here?" His questions coming at a fast pace, Phelps seemed to be leaping to conclusions quickly.

"No, sir, the fact that he used a fifty-year-old car tells me that he is likely not a foreign agent. Right now we have people going over every inch of the ship to see if he left us any evidence, fingerprints or equipment, anything that could lead us to his true identity, but that will take a while." Glancing up the ramp, Asanté could not help but notice the shapely young tech carrying a toolbox. No more than twenty-five, he noted right away that she wore no ring on her left hand.

"So agent Assad, what DO you have for me?" Irritated, Phelps was still remembering the recent NSC meeting. His staff had managed to instill a sense of urgency in him.

"We have a phone number." Returning his attention to the conversation, Asanté could not help but smile as he revealed the one detail that had been withheld from the other agencies. "When the science team got the plates off of the hull they turned out to be exactly what they appeared to be; just tin plates from a camping cook set. No doubt they were intended to distract us from the real device. Anyhow, stamped onto the back of each was a phone number. Apparently he, or she, left it for us to contact him."

"She?" Phelps' tone was dismissive at the idea of a female inventor. "What do we know about the phone number? Can you trace it? We need to get ahead of this thing; I don't like the idea of this guy leading us around by the nose."

"We are looking into it now. Once we have things in place I was going to make contact. Do you have any fiscal guidelines for this?" Stepping back, Asanté watched the cute young tech strolling down the boarding ramp. Flashing her a bright smile, he made a mental note to bump into her at his first opportunity.

"Offer him whatever he wants, then take the technology AND the inventor." His voice hard, Phelps leaned into the receiver as he spoke. "Am I making myself clear? We need absolute control of this device and its creator. You have Presidential clearance to use extraordinary rendition to secure this technology and the minds that created it. Am I making myself clear?"

Asanté gave that some thought before answering.

"Yes, sir. It will be done." He was about to add something to the conversation when the line went dead. Realizing that the President had hung up on him, he slowly mulled over the orders he had just received. While many agents would have been bothered by such directives, Marco Asanté had no problem with them. He had realized several days ago just how important this technology would be to America, and there was nothing he wouldn't do for his country.

Pocketing the phone he mumbled to himself. "The needs of the many outweigh the needs of the one."

Nodding serenely, he felt at ease with what had to be done. With Presidential approval to use whatever means necessary, he could now dispense with superfluous details like federal statutes or *habeas corpus*. It made things much simpler this way.

Spotting the shapely little tech heading his way again, this time with several large equipment cases in hand, Asanté made sure to flash her a warm smile.

"Here, let me help you with those. They look heavy." Grinning broadly, he revealed a row of perfectly aligned teeth as he took one of the heavy cases from her.

Standing some distance away, Rangi had been interviewing the security guard when he spotted the familiar form. It did not surprise him at all to see Asanté hitting on the young tech. After all, that was his *modus operandi*. Pulling a cell phone from his pocket the big Samoan agent pressed the number at the top of his speed dialer list.

"Hey Jenna," He spoke in a grim tone as soon as she answered. "You're never gonna believe who they brought in from Department of Homeless Security."

First Contact

The site they chosen to make first contact had been an easy choice; it was the last working pay phone anywhere in the city. With cell phones being universally ubiquitous, the old phone booths had all but vanished from the terrain. Those few that remained were usually badly vandalized or completely out of order. Hence, the list of possible locations had been dramatically shortened. With three drones in place, Jamie had a complete view of the entire northeast corner.

In his mind Jamie calculated how much time had elapsed since DHS had found the phone number stamped into the plates. Although Jamie had intended to include a prophetic message that would set the tone for their negotiations, his brother had instead stamped something much coarser into the metal. As if it were a wall in a gas station lavatory, Jack had emblazoned the tin plate with the message *'for a good time call...'* followed by the phone number for the pay phone that Jamie now surveyed.

Knowing that they would use this location, Jamie had deployed drones to the site days ago. During that time he had allowed Alexis to record the faces of the regulars; those people that frequented the dirty little convenience store. Compiling a database made it easy to spot anyone out of the ordinary. Since the plates had been removed from the hull of the Queen Mary, those faces had begun to change dramatically. Although it was subtle at first, the traffic at Donny's Stop 'n Go had picked up noticeably. There were two new transients pushing shopping carts, a tech working on the nearby fiber optic lines, two gang-bangers in the alleyway, and a taxi-cab that had stopped for gas three times. While he doubted most of these people were genuine, it did not surprise him in the least. They had expected this from the beginning. It had been a foregone conclusion that the feds would stakeout the entire block before making the call. In truth, the entire exercise was just a way for the savant to gauge their intent at this point in the game.

"They're calling." Alexis informed him in a tone devoid of emotion.

"You know what to do. Put it on speaker phone please." Reclining in his office chair, Jamie was in his most serious avatar today. As Captain James he preferred to run a tight ship, devoid of any Tom-foolery. Watching as the undercover agents reacted to the sound of the ringing pay phone, he scrutinized them as if they were a horde of invading Klingons.

"Hello." Alexis was cheerful as she answered the call. Having long ago hacked into the phone system, she was able to intercept the call at the regional switch. There had never been any intention of physically sending someone down to the Stop 'n Go. In a nanosecond the AI had traced the phone number to its owner.

"This number was found on a tin plate attached to the hull of the Queen Mary. Am I speaking to the person who placed it there?" Asanté's voice was stern. Intent on maintaining a firm tone, he needed to control the conversation.

"I represent the entity that did." She kept her reply neutral. With her massive processing power she had long ago concluded that it was not in their best interests to reveal their true numbers. While the government would eventually realize that there were two brothers, there was no strategic value in releasing that information at this juncture.

"Why did you levitate the Queen Mary?" Although he knew the answer already, Asanté wanted to start with the basics. *He had an agenda to conceal, after all.*

"I did it so you would call me, Agent Asanté." Alexis let slip a giggle. "Also, to demonstrate to the world that our gravitational disaffinity technology was indisputably real."

"You must understand that this technology will change the balance of power in the world. I would like to meet to discuss terms to acquire it." Asanté had barely finished speaking when his phone chirped. Glancing down he noticed that he had received a text message from an unlisted number.

"I have forwarded you a link to our terms." The humor gone from her voice, Alexis paused long enough for him to check his messages. "I will give you some time to take this to your handlers, Agent Asanté. Please call back when you have an answer."

His mouth moving, Marco never had a chance to object before the line went dead. Turning to the technicians who labored before computer screens, his tone was sharp.

"Well, did you get a trace?" Demanding an answer from the techs, the agent felt his blood boiling. Used to being in command of the situation, it irked him to have terms dictated to him in such a manner. *What gall that woman has,* he thought darkly.

Looking up from the nearest desk, the lead tech on the project had a hesitant look on his face as he answered Marco's question.

"We were unable to track the phone call itself. They hijacked the signal at the DSLAM. We'll need to get into that and see if they left any digital fingerprints behind." Busy explaining what they had found thus far, the lanky technician found himself cut off before he could tell the best part.

"What the hell do you mean you couldn't trace it? You're supposed to be the smart guys." Shouting loud enough to make the other people in the room jump visibly, Asanté made no bones about how he felt. With a mandate directly from the President of the United States, the stress was already gnawing at his nerves. "You fucking geeks get me something to work with or I'll replace you with outsourced monkeys from India. You understand where I'm coming from?"

Nervous at the confrontation, the lead tech stammered as he tried to point to something on his screen.

"What! Speak the fuck up!" Asanté shouted again as his anger was fueled by the man's passive demeanor.

"We couldn't get anything from the phone call, yet, but we did get a trace on the text she sent you. We have a physical location." His eyes wide, the cyber-specialist tried to ward off any further attacks with this information.

"Where?" His voice a growl, Asanté slid a notepad towards the tech.

Jenna had steadily worked her way through names on her list. Beating the pavement, she had spent the morning interviewing people known to have been in the area when the mysterious flying car photo had been snapped. Coming up short each time, she had ultimately found herself at the county jail.

"Welllll hellooo." Chet Burke seemed pleased at the sight of her in the professional visitation center. With her law enforcement credentials they were able to meet in one of the booths normally reserved for lawyers and other members of the court system.

"Sit down." Not interested in being objectified by trailer-park trash, Jenna was no stranger to leering men.

"I likes it when ya talk tough to me." Like a cat looking over a cage full of canaries, Chet took his time to ogle her. Indeed, she was quite attractive with her professional-woman motif that included badge and holster.

"I have a few questions for you." Still unflinching, Jenna waited until the big man was seated.

"Normally I got nothing to say to the cops, but you're such a pretty little *thang*, I betcha I could be convinced into a little pillow talk." His hand moving as he spoke, he finally gripped her wrist firmly.

Showing a grimace, Jenna had seen it all before. Rather than yanking her arm away immediately, the young professional instead looked up to ensure that there were no cameras observing them. Satisfied that they had privacy, the former military police officer flipped her wrist around, grabbing Chet by the same forearm that he held her with.

The big man had less than a split second to interpret what she had done. It seemed counterintuitive since he had been expecting her to pull away. While his brain was still processing the equation, Jenna used the heel of her left hand to impact sharply with his nose. Continuing to hold him by his dominant forearm, the agent slammed him twice more. His head swooning from the impact, Chet seemed to be stunned in his chair. Giving it some thought, Jenna decided he needed another whack, just for good measure.

Finally releasing his arm, she allowed Chet to slump back in the plastic chair. With blood starting to run out of his shattered septum, it was clear that she had broken his nose.

"Here, use your shirt to catch all that." Pretending to be helpful, she directed the stunned man. *Really, she just wanted him to stop bleeding on the table.*

"You bit be!" His voice morphed by his broken nose.

"And you assaulted a federal agent. Guess which carries more prison time." Flashing a flat smile, Jenna knew there would be no formal charges. While she was not prone to police abuse, this was far from being the first time a man had tried to pull that sort of thing on her. "Any guesses?"

"I got nothing to say to the fuckin' cops!" Collecting himself finally, Chet started to rise up from his seat when he saw the photo in her hand. "Whoah…"

Jenna's eyebrows went up as he showed recognition. "Tell me about this car."

"That's the same sumbitch who put us in here. That mother fucker!" Raising his voice angrily, it was obvious that he recognized the little Mustang right away. "That cum-guzzling mulatto motherfucker!"

"I need a name." Pulling her phone from a pocket, she already had notepad open.

About to divulge that information, Chet caught himself. "Yeah, how about you get me outta here, get all charges dropped, then we'll talk."

Jenna pretended to consider that for a few seconds. Keeping her cool, she knew she had more than enough leverage.

"You and your brother were arrested for felony speeding while shooting guns out the window. Police subsequently searched your car and found drugs, guns, and a bag of used sex toys. *Eww.*"

"Hey, thems weren't ours. We took them offa some guy on the street, we thought they was valuable the way he acted. Me an' my brother didn't use none of that stuff…" His face flushed, Chet tried to explain away the embarrassing circumstances of his arrest. "And it was that sumbitch Jackie Sparks what dropped a ketchup bomb on us. I told the police when they stopped us that we was just defending ourselves was all."

"Jackie Sparks? Do you have an address?" Her voice perking up, Jenna was already moving to the next topic.

"Fuck that shit, what're ya gonna do fer me?" Suddenly remembering himself, Chet stopped wiping his bloody nose long enough to give her the stink-eye.

"How about I don't charge you with assaulting a federal agent, impeding national security, or have you shipped to Gitmo for further interrogations. Ever been water boarded?" Flashing him a pleased smile, Jenna let him know that she had him where she wanted him.

"Bullshit! After I start tellin' people how you assaulted me, it'll be you in jail, bitch!" Back to pinching his nose to staunch the flow of blood, the big man tried to remain defiant to the end.

"Oh sure, because the staff at this jail are totally gonna believe you over me. You weigh…what…two-ten, two twenty? And I weigh maybe a buck and a half. Sure, they'll totally believe that I assaulted you without any provocation. *Are you high? Seriously?"* Jenna's smirk slowly faded as she sat forward to stare him directly in the eyes. "Now you fucking tell me where I can find this Jackie Sparks person or I'll charge you with so many felonies that you'll spend the rest of your life in an eight by eleven foot cell, beating off to the Sunday circulars and hoping your celly doesn't decide to gang rape you after lights-out."

Something about her words seemed to hit a nerve with Chet. No doubt having already spent a few weeks doing much what she had just described, the idea of facing real prison time scared him. Sneering, he looked a little foolish with blood dripping down his upper lip. With Jenna sitting back in her chair, the silence was deafening until he finally spoke.

"Fine, I dunno his address or nuthin, but he still lives in his folks' old house at Sycamore and Birch."

Nodding in satisfaction, Jenna Jaramillo rose slowly. Giving him one last look, she sniffed before departing the room. A few seconds later the security door was buzzed, allowing her to depart the facility.

"A billion dollars?" Marty DeColle raised his eyebrows slightly. "That's actually not a bad price, considering..."

"But it's only a ten year lease on the technology." His lip curling up, General Hicks showed obvious disdain for the contract.

"And title and deed to the moon." Bowles shook his head. "Clearly these people are insane."

"That's not the half of it." Marty held up a copy of the contract where he had used a yellow highlighter to mark the addendum clause. "He also wants King Joffrey's crown, the original, not a replica."

"England probably has that in a museum. I doubt they'll give it to us." Phelps shook his head.

Leaning over to whisper into his ear, his son-in-law quietly informed him that King Joffrey was actually a fictional character in an HBO show.

"Oh." Surprised, Phelps made an odd expression.

"And what about the rest of this crap he, or she, asked for?" Cutting in, Bowles did his best to cover the President's blunder as he detailed the list in his hand. "They want three rolls of duct tape, a fucking crown, pliers, fire extinguisher, a laundry marker, a painter's mask, safety glasses, title and deed to the moon, and a hemorrhoid donut, just to mention a few items. Clearly whoever sent us this list is unbalanced."

"I agree." DeColle used his pen to tap the last paragraph on the page. "There's even a clause that says that the contract is null and void if we attempt to kill them with silver bullets, golden bullets, blue bullets, the one true ring of power, or any other prohibited weapons. I have to agree that we may be working with an individual that is mentally unhinged."

Sitting back in his chair, Phelps watched his advisors bicker over the terms that had been provided by the mystery woman who had answered Agent Asanté's call. Although he had been over the entire document twice, the legalese of it all read like stereo instructions to the President.

"We don't actually own the moon," Marty pointed out. "International treaty stipulates that no nation may own the moon."

"Bullshit!" The General refuted that. "We're the only nation that has ever set foot on her. We left a car with the keys in the ignition up there, and do you know why?"

The others looked between them before shrugging at his question.

"Because we own the fucking place, that's why. It's our moon, regardless of what some whiny UN treaty says. There is only one flag posted on the moon, and it's ours." Thumbing towards his own chest full of medals, the military man made his point clear.

"It doesn't matter either way," Marty knew how to settle the debate. "We could give them title and deed to Mars, Jupiter, and the Sun, but it doesn't mean they'd ever be able to do anything with it. It takes more than a few hundred million dollars to get to the moon. This guy'll just end up wiping his ass with the title for all the use he'll get out of it. Clearly whoever wrote this contract is unhinged from reality, which is even more fuel for our argument to take it by eminent domain, for the good of the nation."

"Yes, for the good of the nation." Agreeing, the man who sat on the far couch echoed their sentiments. Wearing no identification whatsoever, Robert Heckler's presence had been approved by the President himself. A political benefactor since Phelps' days as a senator, the man in the dapper grey suit was a regular at White House events. Representing the defense industry, he was one of only two people in the room who could not be fired. Having donated millions to the President's reelection campaigns, and billions more to the GOP, he held great sway over Phelps' decision making.

"Ten years is not enough time. We need unfettered control of this technology." Like a broken record, General Hicks repeated the phrase.

"Sir, if I could offer an alternative." Seated across from the man in the dapper grey suit was his stocky counterpart in a blue suit.   Representing the aerospace industry, Drummond Heckler smiled wanly as he spoke. "We have searched through the patents that are pending or already on file, and we find nothing on antigravity. Hence, this device has not yet been patented, as near as we can tell. And international patent law is clear; he who patents first is the true owner of the technology."

There was silence as the advisors each looked back and forth between one another. With the Attorney General intentionally absent from the meeting, they had to rely on the only lawyer in the room.

"Would that work, Marty?" Phelps leaned forward on his elbows.

Running the idea through his head, Marty DeColle considered it for several moments before finally looking the President in the eyes.

"Actually, I think it will. If they are unprotected by patent, then their invention could just be reinvented by whoever figures out the secret first. Yes, this could be quite plausible." Nodding, the chief-of-staff continued to calculate the possibilities. "If this Agent Asanté can put us in the room with this guy, I believe we could make this work."

With different content on each monitor, Jamie was simultaneously monitoring the black-site prison while enjoying a documentary on patients with autism. Watching a child rock back and forth with anxiety, the savant tried to imagine how it must be to suffer from such a socially debilitating disorder. A quick glance to the left screen revealed that inmate Bernard Shaw was in the process of being water boarded for the third time that day. With fully-plumbed interrogation rooms, the prison was really quite a remarkable machine.

Wrapping his arms around himself, Jamie tried to mimic the child on the center screen. Making an *mmmm* sound as he rocked forward and back seemed to help make the act even more authentic. Pleased with his own performance, Jamie kept a keen eye on the video until something on the left-most monitor distracted him.

It was a vehicle parked just down the street from a seemingly innocuous office building. While there had been many cars and trucks parked there in the last three days, it was the sign of the SWAT tactical vehicle that stood out. Seeing the line of uniformed men snake their way out the back and down the sidewalk, he could see that they were exploiting the building's blind spots. With two men swinging around behind the structure, and the rest going to the front door, it was clear they were not collecting money for the policeman's ball.

Counting down on his fingers, the lead agent signaled the go-ahead. Immediately two men swung the battering ram, smashing open the front door. Pouring through the breach, the tactical team swarmed the interior of the structure.

Pausing the autism video, Jamie wanted to focus his full attention on the raid. Knowing that Alexis had already notified the press, he wanted to be able to sit back and slurp his soda while the show unfolded. While the little obscure office building seemed nothing out of the ordinary, Alexis had been able to determine the true nature of the facility. It was the raw processing power of her cubed processor that allowed her to look at such a massive picture as the internet, painted in URLs, text messages, and email; and spot the bread crumbs leading to this particular establishment. No human could have made the connection, let alone tied it to the legal contract texted to Agent Asanté just a half hour ago.

"The press is two blocks out; I have been giving them green lights the whole way." Pleased with herself, it had taken relatively little effort for her to penetrate the city's traffic control system. Despite their physical and cyber safeguards, it had been child's play for her to negotiate around the roadblocks. Static defenses were no match for a mobile AI.

"Does we got any of that-there radio chatter?" Country Jimmy wondered aloud, hoping to catch their conversations.

"Encrypted. I'm trying to decipher it but mathematically speaking it will take me another seven minutes or less." Alexis' voice came through the desktop speakers.

"Ahhh, save the processing power, I can imagine what they'se saying." Nodding seriously, the savant broke character by smiling broadly as he made his own radio noises. "Uh Roger two-six-niner, we have a room full of naked people and a fat guy in a bikini, covered in maple syrup."

Laughing at his own joke, Country Jimmy could hear Alexis cackling in the background. Although he preferred she not waste the resources on such superfluous activity, it pleased him to know he made her laugh with his antics. But his giggling halted as the white van from Channel 9 news screeched to a halt in front of the building. Close behind it were two more vans, each from local stations.

It had been simple enough to get the journalists' attention. Alex had simply mentioned that the agents were about to arrest the men responsible for levitating the Queen Mary. With that story dominating headlines still, it only took a hint to mobilize an army of reporters. Like hungry vultures seeking carrion, they had swooped in just seconds before the agents began leading their handcuffed suspects out the front door.

With cameras recording every second, two of the stations had actually interrupted the broadcasts in progress so they could carry the event live. Under normal circumstances they would have recorded and edited the arrest, but with such fierce competition already on site, it was imperative that they did anything they could to take the lead. Panning up and down the scantily dressed women that were led out first, they noted that one was wearing men's underwear. With shocked expressions, the ladies tried unsuccessfully to hide their faces. Feeling glee at the prospect of a juicy news story, the reporters shouted out their questions as police pushed them back.

"Holy shit..." said the man holding a microphone emblazoned with Channel 3 News. Right away he seemed to recognize the obese man wearing ladies panties. "Is that the mayor?"

Like their counterpart, the other journalists recognized the portly man wearing nothing more than a bikini and handcuffs. Like sharks that smelled blood, the reporters were immediately in a feeding frenzy, jamming their microphones into the air as they begged for a statement from the town's leading politician. Trying to hide his face by turning away, the mayor was unsuccessful. Realizing that he could not escape, he instead chose to go into denial mode.

"It's a chiropractic office, I have serious lumbar issues! Don't judge me." His words pitiful, he barely got out his alibi before vanishing into the police van that awaited the prisoners. Within seconds the vehicle had lurched away from the site, headed downtown with its cargo.

"Karma is a bitch." A gleeful tone to her voice, Alexis echoed Jamie's feelings at that very moment.

"Loki is in charge of the karma department." Smiling, the savant imagined Agent Asanté's surprise when they realized who they had in custody. "Serves 'em right. We tried to negotiate in good faith with them fellers, and instead they send in stormtroopers to track us down. What a buncha penises, and little ones at that."

"Shall I make the call?" Alexis piped up.

"Yeah, let's call them double-crossing sumbitches. I think I would enjoy hearing agent Asanté's explanation."

Marco Asanté pulled off his helmet as the van with the prisoners zoomed out of sight. Although he would join them in due time, right now it was imperative that he gather up anything that could reveal the secret of the new technology they pursued.

It seemed odd somehow that there were no computers in the whole place. Even the receptionist's desk was just a monitor and keyboard, no actual PC. As he looked over the office it slowly became apparent that the entire front office was completely counterfeit. Really more of a mockup, it was like something a realtor might put in place to make the space seem more businesslike while hawking it to prospective renters.

It was only when he stepped into the back offices that Marco truly understood what the place was. With a sexual dungeon in one room, and a heart shaped bed in the next, clearly he had stumbled upon a brothel of some sort.

"Heh, the fat guy kept saying he was the mayor." One of the agents in tactical gear snickered as he shared that tidbit. "I told him, yeah, the mayor of cell block nine, right?"

Marco wanted to laugh, but the ID in the wallet on the floor told him this was no joke. Although he was new in town, he did recognize the man's face from the news. As it slowly began to sink in, Asanté realized that they had been tricked into coming to this address. Ready to shout an obscenity, he was interrupted by the buzzing of a phone in his pocket.

A quick glance at the display showed the number as being unlisted. Initially he thought to ignore it, but realized that it could just as easily be the White House calling for an update. Thumbing the display, he answered.

"Agent Asanté of DHS."

"Hello, Marco." Alex's tone was bright and chipper. In truth, she did not like the man, especially knowing that he had just tried to track her down. "Have I called at a bad time?"

Something about her voice told him that she knew exactly what was happing at that moment. Biting back his irritation, Asanté answered in a level voice.

"No, nothing important. In fact I was hoping you would call back. We are ready for a counter offer." Hoping to sidestep the issue, the federal agent wanted to talk about anything but the raid.

"Ooooh goody, we have our own counter-counter offer." Letting slip a girlish giggle, Alex was clearly pleased with herself today.

"A counter offer to your own offer?" Something in that worried Asanté. Dropping his Kevlar helmet to the ground, he began stripping off the ballistic armor that was held in place by Velcro.

"Yes, the entities that I represent would like to notify you that the price has been increased to one point two-five billion dollars, and a nine year lease. Also, I would like to draw your attention to the good-faith clause of the contract. Any attempt to incarcerate or harm our consortium will result in a complete forfeiture of all legal rights and claims to the product hereafter known as gravitational disaffinity, as well as all fees, payments and properties exchanged as part of the transaction."

"What the hell...?" Marco could feel his blood begin to boil as he realized that not only had they predicted he would have agents at the Stop 'n Go, but they had even sent him on a wild goose chase that resulted in arresting the local mayor in connection with a prostitution ring. "We have been acting in good faith the entire time; I don't know what you're talking about."

"Oooh, Marco, you have such pretty eyes when you lie." Snickering, Alex paused just long enough to watch him look around for a camera. No doubt he would tear the building apart trying to find it. She doubted it would ever occur to him that she was watching him via his own phone's camera. "But I know that you tried to track me down, and that is why I sent you to Wanda's massage parlor. I'd hoped you would appreciate the humor. Personally I am new to the concept of laughter, but it makes me feel good when I do. Are you a fan of laughing, Marco?"

Seething, the agent already had a keen dislike for Alexis. Whoever she was, he would enjoy handcuffing her one day. Still imagining her expression as he locked those silver bracelets in place, Marco was surprised when his phone chirped to announce a new text message.

"I have sent you an updated contract reflecting the new terms. I feel compelled to warn you against future transgressions against my benefactors." Her voice firm, she disconnected the line before he could object. Having studied his psychological profile at length, she knew that few things would gall the man more than denying him the last word in a conversation.

Swearing loudly, Marco was about ready to smash his phone against the far wall when it rang again. Glancing at the caller ID his blood froze when he saw the Washington DC area code.

"Oh, fuck me." Shaking his head, he knew this would not be a pleasant conversation.

It had been simple enough for Jenna to find Sycamore and Birch. While her first instinct had been to run a records check, she had decided against it. With the pressure she and her people had been taking from higher echelons, she suspected that there may be other eyes watching the records she accessed. While it seemed foolish on the surface, the idea that her own government would be snooping on her in the middle of an investigation, she knew better than to think they would be playing by the rules this time.

Besides, she really did not need to waste the time on a broad-band records search. Seeing the little white jeep starting and stopping at every driveway gave her an idea. Intercepting the mail carrier at the sidewalk, Jenna flashed her credentials and a professional smile. A few seconds later the US Postal employee was pointing to the little rundown home on the corner. Making note of the address, she considered her next move. About to cross the street, she noticed the man idling in the beige Ford. While there was nothing odd about someone sitting in their car on a public street, she had seen this ugly little beige rental car in her rearview mirror on the way to the site. It occurred to her that she could have an agent from another agency trying to ride her coattails on this case. Irritated, she started across the street with purpose.

Seeing her, the man behind the wheel immediately shifted into gear and sped away. Making note of his license plate, she vowed to trace it to whatever federal agency had been trailing her.

"Do your own damned police work!" Although Jenna Jaramillo was far too professional to throw a finger after the man, she felt the urge nonetheless. *What a lazy asshole, tailgating another agent to get a jump on their case*, she thought grimly. Watching his tail lights disappear around the corner, Jenna felt satisfied that he would not try that again.

The house seemed odd somehow. While the exterior was a bit dilapidated, with a layer of dust on everything, the LCD screen by the front door appeared to be quite modern. Pressing the single button, she waited patiently for a response. There were no cars in the driveway, and the garage door was bereft of any windows, so it was difficult to tell if anyone was home.

"Just leave any packages at the door, thank you." The woman with red hair filled the little screen by the buzzer.

"Actually I'm here to…conduct a census." Jenna's voice hesitated just the tiniest bit in the middle.

"There is a hardware store three blocks away. Currently they have a sale on fire extinguishers." Showing a smug grin, the red haired woman seemed unconvinced.

"Fire extinguisher…?" Jenna puzzled over the odd statement.

"To extinguish your pants, because clearly they are on fire." Giving a laugh, the face on the small screen focused her green eyes on Jenna. "Liar, liar, pants on fire."

Taken aback, it had been a long time since Jenna had been stumped for a reply.

"I just have a few questions." She admitted the half truth. "Is Jack Sparks home?"

This time it was the woman with the red hair that seemed stumped for an answer. Taking a moment to look Jenna over, the face on the screen considered the request.

"Jackie is unavailable at this time." Telling her own little white lie, Alexis kept a straight face.

"When will he be home?" Changing her question, the agent tried to gain as much information as she could.

"I'll have him call you when he is available." Nodding seriously, the woman was about to turn away when Jenna stopped her.

"Don't you need my phone number?"

Pausing in the screen, the red haired woman simply frowned before responding.

"No, I got your number." Her reply simple, Alexis terminated the conversation before Jenna could get in another question.

Still watching the monitor, Jack and Jamie were completely focused on the woman standing at their front door.

"Now that's my kinda law enforcement." Jack leered as he looked her over. "I just got a hankerin' fer Mexican food. Yes, siree Bob."

"Keep your genitals in check, especially when you're standing so close to me." Professor James showed obvious irritation. "Your penis does not seem to understand the gravity of the situation."

"Oh yeah, because I don't have your super brain I couldn't possibly understand how far ahead of schedule this is? I can read a timeline, y'know." Frowning, Jack dismissed his brother's concerns with a wave of his hand. His eyes still glued to the screen, the inventor watched as Jenna finally gave up on ringing the doorbell and began to walk back towards her car. There was just something about her that tantalized him. Far beyond her physical exterior, she was more than just a pretty face. Smart, strong-willed, beautiful; Jack was having a hard time finding a downside to the woman. In the back of his mind he wondered if he was attracted to her because she reminded him of his mother?

"She is not the problem." Jamie interrupted his daydream as he switched to an alternate camera. There on the monitor was the ugly little beige Ford that had followed her to the site. "Not only is she far ahead of schedule, but she brought uninvited guests with her."

Watching the video run in slow motion, the man in the car turned to unwittingly look directly into the camera. Freezing the frame, Alexis marked prominent facial features before matching him to one of the faces from the dock in Long Beach.

"Based on his recent travel history, there is a seventy-nine percent probability that he is working for the SVR. I was unable to intercept his cellular communications before he was chased away." Rendering a significant amount of data on the leftmost screen, Alexis gave them all the information she had on this contact.

"Put a drone on her." In a flash, Jamie's savant mind had already calculated the variables.

Turning to look at his brother, Jack wondered about the move. After all, they already had a small cadre of simulated insects monitoring her entire office. Running through the variables, it took his own brain significantly longer than Jamie's to come to the same conclusion; Agent Jaramillo was now in as much danger as they themselves.

"We're out of drones." Alexis broke the silence to reveal a serious problem.

"How can we be out of drones, the shopping list clearly included another three batches." Jamie seemed aghast.

"Yeah, in three days." Jack defended himself. "You're the big-brain, why didn't you predict this? The feds weren't supposed to get this far for a week yet. I'm still busy printing the last of the control boards for that damned submarine you had me build."

"It's not a submarine." Rendering a frown, Jamie was irritated with his brother's insistence on referring to the vessel as such. "And I have no idea how she found us so fast. Clearly we need to keep an eye on this one. Unfortunately someone has fallen behind on manufacturing."

Jack was about to begin an objection when Alexis interrupted. "Boys, boys! I can track her through her cell phone." Appearing on the right screen, the red-haired avatar gave a grimace. Really it had not been as difficult as all that. With a drone perched above Jenna's desk, she had been able to capture her login several days ago. After the agent had stood on the porch for several minutes, the AI had been able to access her electronic assistant easily enough. Despite the safeguards built into the Android operating system, Alexis had little problem negotiating the barriers. When it came to hacking, a dumb computer was defenseless against a sentient AI.

Both inventors perked up as the video from the camera on her phone was rendered on one of the nearby monitors. Like many people, she kept her phone clipped to her belt. Watching the scene bump about as she climbed into her car, the brothers finally shut up long enough to give a surprised grunt.

"Oh, or we could do it that way." Jack agreed with raised eyebrows.

Taking a seat at his desk, Jamie kept his eyes glued to the screen as he calculated the new data. While his brother leered at the view of Jenna's lap, the savant crunched thousands of numbers, and examined every angle before finally speaking.

"We need to push up everything." He had just started out when Jack interrupted him.

"No shit, Sherlock."

Frowning, Jamie continued. "You need to get the...submarine...ready for flight by tonight. The EMP cannon will need to be fully operational as well. After that, finish the last of the drones by morning."

"And I suppose you're just gonna sit here staring at videos of retarded kids?" Thumbing to the video of the autistic child in the throes of a panic attack, Jack's voice dripped in sarcasm. While he realized that his brother always had method to his madness, this was not part of the plan...at least not the plan that had been revealed to him.

"I have a full docket, including ensuring that the space suits are fully functional, and that we have enough blue plasma for the job ahead." Grim in his delivery, Jamie wanted nothing more than to get to work. Something made difficult by his brother's persistent questions. "Now go and waste no more time. We will likely have visitors by tomorrow morning."

"Now go and waste no more time…" Jack mimicked his brother as he worked on the fittings that connected to the exterior of the steel water tank. Although his brother had remained largely mute on the purpose of the flying water tank that Jack referred to as *the submarine*, he had been quite detailed in its design. While the older sibling understood the full capabilities of the vehicle, he still had not figured out how it was to fit into the existing plan. This incongruity had convinced him that there was an alternate plan in motion that he had not been made privy to. Knowing that there was an entity in the house that saw everything, he had tried to get Alexis to spill her silicon guts. Rather than get into the downward spiral of lies and denial, she chose to remain silent.

"So when I want you to shut the hell up, you won't. But when I really need you to talk to me, you shut the hell up. What kinda bull-crap is that?" Knowing that she was listening, Jack talked as much to himself as to Alexis. Deep down he knew why she did it; she preferred to avoid lying. Not that she had any kind of prohibition on it. Alexis had no *Asimovian* rules of robotics to prevent her from departing from the truth; she simply hated to do it to the brothers. Hence her silence when Jack pressed her for details.

"Hmmmph." Grimacing as he finished the connection, Jack glanced up at the camera that quietly observed him from the work bench. "What? Cat got your tongue? Oh, that's right; you don't actually have a tongue, not that it ever stopped you from blabbing until my ears bled."

Looking up again, he eyed the camera again. It bothered him that even with the coarse comments he had thrown out she remained silent. Normally he could trick her into a response, but lately she had been uncrackable. This worried him because it meant that whatever she was concealing was going to be bad...very bad.

"Awww, c'mon!" Exasperated, he dropped the ratchet onto the floor noisily. "What the hell is he up to?"

Still no response, Jack sat in silence for several seconds before finally picking up the tool. Shaking his head with irritation, the inventor returned to the job at hand. While he desperately wanted to know what his brother had planned, he had a sneaking suspicion that when he did finally find out, he would wish for a return to ignorance.

"A quarter billion dollar price hike!" Phelps was fuming as his voice echoed off the walls of the Oval Office.

"It's not the price that bothers us." From the couch, Robert Heckler was cool as he spoke.

"It's that damned nine year licensing term that is a non-starter." Shorter by a head, Drummond Heckler turned to face at the President. "This technology is worth trillions, just in the first year alone."

"Sir, we need that technology." As if to reinforce what the defense contractors on the couch had already said, General Hicks implored the President. With visions of outfitting the entire US military with gravitational disaffinity suits, and flying tanks, and flying aircraft carriers, floating weapons platforms…*he was almost giddy with anticipation.* Antigravity opened so many doors that it would take their enemies a century to catch up.

"General, you are preaching to the choir." Irritated at his subordinate's constant pestering on the issue, Phelps had grown tired of being lectured.

Sensing that he was on dangerous ground, General Hicks paused. Flashing a hawkish look at Bowles, he knew it was time for the President to hear it from someone else.

Taking a deep breath, the political advisor considered how to broach the subject without sounding repetitive.

"Jefferson, there have been some serious developments." Keeping his voice low, Bowles aimed for privacy as he leaned in close to the President.

"Oh?" Raising an eyebrow, Phelps was curious.

"We had an attempted hack at one of our data centers." Hicks filled in the blanks.

"Data center?" Rolling his chair back from the desk, he eyed the two men. With bags under his eyes, it had been a difficult term for the leader. More than once he had likened the presidency to shoving his face into a blow torch for four straight years.

"One of our black sites where we analyze data for the NSA." Squinting as he leaned in, Bowles spoke in a hushed tone.

"Oh?" Suddenly interested, Phelps was all ears. "I thought people tried to hack our systems all the time. At least that's what that dumbass Millard is always preaching every budget session."

"This wasn't some kid in a bathrobe trying to crack the login password." Grumbling in a deep baritone, General Hicks put it in perspective.

"This was a much more serious threat." Bowles raised his eyebrows to foreshadow what he would say next. "This time they actually got several bugs into the data center, and not just simple listening devices either. These bugs were capable of audio, high resolution video, and self-locomotion."

There was a pause as the political advisor let that sink in. Opening the folder in his hands, he produced several photos that were laid out on the desk.

"Not only could these bugs walk, but they self destructed when we tried to examine them. Our scientists say they each contained a ring of white phosphorous. Whoever sent these did not want us reverse engineering them."

Leaning over the photos, the President could see the small wire legs that protruded from the charred devices. Another picture showed the detail of the drone's head where the camera and microphone had been mounted. When he reached the last picture there was something that caught his eye.

"Isn't that Russian?" Pointing to the Cyrillic symbols on the PC board, his voice held some skepticism. "Right there on the...electrical board, that looks like Russian lettering."

"Yes, sir." Bowles nodded in agreement. "We believe it's a false-flag effort to pin it on the Russians.

"Well, duh." His tone derisive, Phelps scowled at the two men. "This isn't the kind of thing that Vlad would do."

Exchanging a silent look between them, Bowles and Hicks said nothing. It had been a bone of contention in the office since the start. For reasons neither of them understood, the President had persisted in his refusal to see the former Soviet Republic as a foe, despite some truly egregious actions against American interests abroad. No matter how hard they had tried, President Jefferson Phelps seemed to think of his Russian counterpart as being *simpatico*. More than one reporter had described it as a *bromance*.

"We don't believe it's the Russians because the device is too good for their usual work. Not only would they not be stupid enough to mark it with Cyrillic lettering, but this bug is way out of their league. Possibly the Chinese, if they had it built in Taiwan." Explaining in simple terms, Bowles knew it was easy to set the President off on a tangent.

"Damned Chinks." Shaking his head, Phelps used one of his favorite slurs. By his thinking, Asians were a sub-species when compared to Americans.

"Yes, sir." Agreeing, Bowles knew better than to point out that his wife was half Japanese. "We don't know how long these were in place before they were discovered. As soon as we found the one, the others self-destructed, so whoever was running these had a live link."

Finally finished examining the photos, Phelps shoved the images back towards his political advisor. Scowling, he seemed deep in thought.

"So you think this is somehow related to the Queen Mary incident?" Slow to put it together, Phelps could see now that the Chinese had intended to use his own intelligence community to beat them to the punch.

"We believe so, Mister President. The damned commies were reading our mail and hoping to get lucky." A deep rumble, General Hicks' voice left no dispute as to how he felt about their Chinese adversaries.

"I want the directors of Homeland, the FBI, CIA, and NSA in my office in an hour." Nodding with satisfaction, Phelps tried to show confidence. "It's time to put some heat under their asses. We need to lock this down before someone else gets hold of it first."

Jenna had spent hours researching the occupants of the unassuming little house at Sycamore & Birch. Having stopped only to attend a teleconference with the other case officers, she had been pensive and irritated throughout the entire meeting. It irked her that they would waste so much time essentially repeating the same sense of urgency, over and over and **over**. No one had anything new to reveal to the group, and the event was keeping her from researching her lead. Still, it concerned her, the amount of heat they must be getting from higher echelons on this matter. While she saw the importance of this invention, the fact remained that no crimes had been broken. Massive law enforcement resources were being poured into this manhunt, yet their quarry had done nothing more than violate an obscure FAA regulation. Finally disconnecting the call, it occurred to her that the other agents were so ramped up by the discussion that they had come to view this inventor in much the same light as a terrorist.

"Sociopathic conformity." She spoke the psychiatric term as her mind considered the frenzied state that the other agents were in. Shaking her head, the young field agent returned her attention to the screen before her. Despite the intrusion of the conference call, she had been able to dredge up significant information on the Sparks brothers. Initially when she had approached the home there had been a degree of skepticism; after all, she was following a random image from the internet and the word of a felon with an axe to grind. The lead was so flimsy that she had not even considered the option of a warrant. Even a FISA judge would not grant her a search warrant based on that trivial bit of information. But the more she learned about the brothers, the more she became sure that she was on the right path.

Research indicated that not only were the Sparks brothers technologically inclined, but they were actually founders of three different tech companies. Additionally they held dozens of patents between them. While she was able to find significant information on Jack, his younger brother was almost a black hole. No social media, no email, no web presence, no memberships in online forums, he was little more than a social security number on a tax return. Digging deeper she was able to locate his college credentials. On the surface it appeared that Jack was the brains behind the operation, at least until she found the disputed IQ test that Jamie had taken when he was thirteen.

"Whoa." Sucking in her breath, Jenna had to sit back as she examined the documents. Having taken the same test herself, once upon a time, she knew exactly how hard it had been. Although she had scored high, her performance paled compared to Jamie's. Examining the letter from the education board she was even more amazed that they had specifically noted that not only had he finished the test with time to spare, but he was a full 7 minutes faster than anyone who had ever taken that revision of the test.

"Seven minutes?" Mulling that over, she tried to estimate where that put him on the scale. A little more digging revealed that the nearest competitor had an estimated IQ of over 185. If Jamie was 7 minutes faster than that…then she was dealing with a mind on parallel with Einstein or Tesla. Small wonder the college had accused him of cheating; the results were almost unthinkable.

Despite hours of research, Jenna could find no employees, spouses, or female siblings in the employ of the brothers. Raising an eyebrow, she was curious about the woman who had greeted her at the front door. Who was she? How did she fit into the equation? When it came to Alexis, the agent had more questions than answers. None of the other agents had mentioned a woman.

With a steaming cup of coffee sitting at her elbow, Jenna was at odds with her next step. While she was confident that the Sparks brothers were the ones they sought, the fact that they had broken no laws made her hesitate to request a warrant. Despite the pressure from higher echelons, the fact remained; these men had committed no crimes, at least none she was aware of. What right did the government have to kick in their door and confiscate their invention? Glancing at the clock she realized it was late; a factor that could be effecting her ability to be decisive. Tapping out the request for a warrant, the agent decided to complete the paperwork, then decide how to act upon it in the morning when her mind was fresh and clear. Plucking the documents from the printer, she dropped the pages into a folder before locking them in her top desk drawer.

Her eyes adjusting to the darkness of the basement garage, she was thirty feet from her car when she spotted the highway patrolman. With his trunk open, he appeared to be in the process of digging for something. Immediately she was irritated when she saw that out of the entire empty garage, this officer had not only chosen to park next to her, but had done a lousy job of it. Too close for Jenna to access her driver's side door, she would be forced to climb in through the passenger side.

Incensed with his gall, she had no intention of making any such accommodation just because some jerk couldn't be troubled to park straight. *What an asshole*, she thought to herself as she approached him.

"Hey!" In a firm voice, she called out to the state trooper. "Do you mind? You're blocking me in."

Turning with a smile, the officer grinned broadly. There was something familiar to his face, something Jenna could not put her finger on.

"No problem, I'll get it moved over right away." Still babbling an apology, his hands held up something in front of her face.

Taken aback, Jenna had only just realized where she had seen the man when he sprayed her in the face with some type of aerosol. Stumbling backwards two steps, she was immediately on the defensive. Hand on her weapon, she managed to unsnap the thumb-break on her holster when the world went black. Her knees buckling, she began to fall forward, only to have the state trooper catch her mid-plunge. Dragging her limp body backwards, he had her hoisted up and into the trunk within seconds. Taking a moment to gag her, he applied restraints to her hands as feet expertly. Clearly no stranger to abductions, the state trooper knew exactly what he was doing.

Slamming the trunk, he turned to give the garage one last look before grunting. Having used a can of spray paint to disable the sole camera covering the area, he was confident that there would be no record of the event. By the time anyone even realized that Jenna Jaramillo was missing, she would already be dead.

With red hair that flowed like fire from her head, the green-eyed woman captivated Jack's attention. Wearing a skin-tight dress covered in blue sequins, she seemed to sparkle as he reached out for her. Feeling his blood beginning to boil, the inventor wanted nothing more than to get his hands on her curvy form. *Ooooh the things he would do to her...*

"Jack!" She seemed defiant.

"Ooooh baby..." Every fiber in his body wanted to possess her.

"JACK!" Louder this time, the woman's green eyes flashed sharply before she began to fade away.

"JACK! WAKE UP!" Alexis' voice shattered the dream as well as the darkness.

Sitting up, he realized he was in his bedroom. Disappointed that the green-eyed woman was gone, he cursed openly at the intrusion.

"JACK!" Alexis' voice came again.

Looking around for the source, the inventor realized it was coming from his smart-watch. Although he had removed all of her cameras and snooping devices, he had forgotten her ability to penetrate network devices. Frowning, he picked up the watch before shouting back at it.

"WHAT! I'm SLEEPING HERE!" Irked that she would wake him after a long day of work, Jack's sense of humor was sharply impaired at that moment.

"Get in here, right now. It's important." A sense of urgency to her voice, it was obvious that something was wrong.

Scant minutes later, a bleary-eyed Jack had watched the video captured from Jenna's cell phone. Even in his groggy condition he quickly came to the realization that someone had kidnapped the attractive agent that had visited them earlier that day. With Alexis explaining how she had identified the man as a foreign operative based on his recent travel and contacts, the brothers were fully briefed on the situation. This would change everything; if they were captured by spies from another country the entire plan would fall apart.

"How long ago?" Jack asked. "And do we know where she is now?"

"I woke you both as soon as it happened. The kidnapper disabled her phone already so I cannot track her that way." Breathless, Alexis' concern seemed to be stressing her CPU. "However, I was able to track them via traffic cameras and security systems around the city. As you may have guessed, the man is not really a police officer, though his car appears to be legit, so likely he stole it from a real state trooper. He dumped the car here at this abandoned warehouse, and left three minutes later in an unmarked van that I was able to track to a residence a few miles from the border. It is possible that he plans on taking her into Mexico for interrogation or just escaping there himself after he is done…with whatever he has planned."

On the screen, a section of the map showed them the address along with a satellite view of the neighborhood. More images of the non-descript van and the home flashed across the screen. Using Google's *street view*, they were able to virtually drive past the dilapidated home.

"Damned Ruskies!" A Jersey accent to his voice, Jamie growled as he scanned the material. "We gotta put a stop to these bums."

Jack gave his brother a sideways glance. He knew from Jamie's accent that he was angry; he always switched to Jersey truck driver when he was mad.

"I got an idea." Smiling, Jack spun his car keys around an index finger. "Alex, I need you to call your boyfriend."

"My boyfriend?" Her voice unsure, she failed to grasp the reference.

"Yeah, I likes that idear." Smiling foolishly, Jamie understood what his brother had in mind right away.

Jumping into some clothes, Jack decided it would be a good idea to brush his teeth. Almost out of the bathroom he hesitated as he pictured Agent Jaramillo in his mind's eye. Pausing briefly, he splashed on a tiny bit of cologne, *just in case*.

Firing up the battered little Mustang, the inventor was out the door as fast as the garage door would open. The one benefit about it being the middle of the night was that he could immediately engage the antigrav. Soaring to cruise altitude, he leveraged the disaffinity against the planet's gravitational field to increase his velocity. Zipping along at a fair pace, Jack tracked his progress with the little GPS unit mounted on the dashboard. Making a rough calculation in his head, he estimated that he was less than twenty minutes out from his destination.

In his own workshop, Jamie was busy. Although his brother had completed the submarine project, it needed to be stocked. Carrying armloads of gear from the house, he filled the cargo area with all manner of supplies that included a space suit, tools, and junk food.

In the house Alexis was equally busy. With one floor of her processor dedicated to masking the phone call she was about to make, the rest of her system resources were dedicated to guiding Jack on his mission, and encrypting portions of her local memory. With full understanding of Jamie's plan B, she had an idea what data needed to be secured before she fell into the wrong hands.

The phone rang twice before a groggy voice answered.

"Asanté." The man's voice answered.

"Agent Asanté. I think it's time we meet in person." Her voice pleasant, Alexis did not even bother to introduce herself.

Sitting up in bed with a start, Marco knew exactly who he was talking to. "Where?"

"I am texting you the address." Stern, Alexis knew to give very specific instructions. "You will come alone, is that clear?"

"Oh yeah, alone. Sure." Lying came easily to Marco Asanté. Nodding sincerely, he had no intention of keeping the promise.

Waking in a groggy stupor, Jenna's neck hurt from the way her head had hung to one side without support. Looking up as she tried to straighten the kink in her neck, she had a metallic taste in her mouth. Struggling to clear her mind, none of it made any sense; where was she? Finding her hands bound behind her, the FBI agent slowly began to realize she was tied to a metal chair.

Scanning about the room, the place seemed empty until her eyes settled on the lone figure seated in the corner. Watching her intently, the man seemed pleased that she had woken. In a flash it all came back to her as she recognized the face of the highway patrolman.

No longer in uniform, the stranger had changed while she was unconscious. Without being able to look at her phone, she had no idea how long she had been out of it, but based on the pain in her neck it had likely been an hour or more. Looking down she noticed right away that her weapon was missing. Craning her head around, she finally located her keys, phone, badge, and pistol on a table in the corner. Struggling against her bindings Jenna could tell right away that this man knew how to properly restrain his victims. Even her feet were roped to the metal chair, preventing her from kicking or resisting.

For the first time in years, she felt true fear. Not since her first deployment to a combat zone had she felt this scared. Completely helpless and at the mercy of a stranger, Jenna had no idea what he wanted. Realizing that she was still fully clothed, she could rule out rape as a motive for her kidnapping. Seeing her credentials lying open on the table meant that the man was fully aware of her status as a federal agent; no doubt something he knew when he snatched her from the basement of the FBI building. Working her way through the possibilities, it finally occurred to her that he was searching for the same thing she had been.

"Good morning, Agent Jaramillo." His English flawless, it surprised Jenna that he did not have an accent. Rising up from his seat in the corner, the man stepped into the light where he could look her over better. As if admiring her figure, he seemed disappointed that he could not do more with her.

"Let me explain how this is going to work. I need some information, and you are going to provide that knowledge. Once I have what I need you will be released to continue your career as if nothing happened. This doesn't have to be messy." Clasping his gloved hands in front, the man seemed pleasant enough.

Still silent, Jenna knew he was lying. Had his offer been genuine she would never have been allowed to see his face. It was a foregone conclusion that he would use whatever means necessary to extract the information, then most likely dispose of her body in a vat of acid. Clenching her jaw, she concealed the terror she felt inside.

"So how do you wanna do this? The easy way, or the hard way?" As if he were a waiter taking her order, the man gave a pleasant smile.

"When I get out of this chair I'm going to kill you with my bare hands." Adding some gravel to her voice, Jenna did a good job of concealing her fear. That had always been her power; to be able to maintain a brave front no matter what she faced. It was this ability that had earned the respect of so many of her brothers at arms. As she looked the gangly man up and down, Jenna knew that she would probably never leave this room alive. The only logical path was to stay strong and fight the enemy with her last fiber.

The man seemed to accept her threat with a raised eyebrow.

"The hard way it is." Giving a laugh, his expression changed dramatically. "Fortunately for you, I prefer the hard way. I've read your dossier, and I would have been greatly disappointed if you had chosen the easy path." Speaking as he walked around behind her, there was an odd sound before he reappeared with a rolling tray like one found in a dentists' office.

Still maintaining a hard face, Jenna eyed the implements laid out on the tray. Having studied counter terrorism for a number of years she knew this part was for show. Many people began to crumble at the mere sight of the blades and blunt instruments. Revealing the tray was but another step in the process to wear down her resolve. Although she disdained the idea of torture, she knew from her studies how it worked.

"Now I'm thinking I won't kill you." Her gaze softening momentarily, she allowed the man to think he had won a small victory before her expression returned to one of absolute hatred. "Now I think I'll just break your back and leave you a cripple so you can spend the rest of your miserable fucking life in a wheel chair, shitting into a colostomy bag."

Taken aback, he was surprised at how she had turned the moment on him. Pausing briefly, the gangly man revealed his state of mind before again concealing it with a grim smile.

"Jenna, Jenna, Jenna. This is not going to work out the way you expect. The only way you get out of that chair alive is if you work with me. Now, I need to know everything you know about the antigravity device."

"I think I'll mark up your face, too." Ignoring his threats, Jenna promised him even more violence. "Not only will you be a fucking cripple in a chair, but you'll eat through a straw because I knocked out all your teeth."

Considering this, the kidnapper stood with his arms folded as he eyed her. "You have real moxie, Agent Jaramillo. I can see that I will save a lot of time by skipping the preliminaries."

Turning away, the man moved out of her gaze. Jenna could hear him talking to someone in the next room. There was the sound of a refrigerator opening and more indistinct words. Straining to listen, she could only catch a word here and there; and none were English.

Struggling against her bindings, Jenna knew there was no chance of breaking the handcuffs they had used to secure her. Worse yet, they were most likely her own cuffs. But her feet had been tied with zip ties, and she knew from experience that those were not unbreakable. So long as you were willing to take the pain, it was possible to snap the plastic strips. After struggling for a few seconds she realized that she simply did not have the leverage. Her kidnapper had known how to strap her legs in multiple places, robbing her of any slack.

It was the knock on the door that caused a commotion from within the kitchen.

Standing on the front porch, Marco felt smug as he considered his plan. Minutes ahead of the tactical team, he had intended to secure the suspect before his backup arrived. Intent on taking full credit for the bust, the agent had no desire to share. Most of all he looked forward to the expression on Alexis' face when he slapped the cuffs on her. After the heat he had taken for arresting the mayor, Marco Asanté needed to vindicate himself.

The door opened just a crack as an eye examined him briefly. Opening wider, the door swung back to reveal a 45 caliber Glock aimed at his chest. Beckoning him silently with one finger, the form in the doorway gestured for Marco to enter. Glancing down at the pistol, he realized it was not an optional invitation.

Stepping through the doorway, the DHS agent found himself facing a pair of masked men. With only their eyes visible, the knit masks concealed their identity well. Immediately he felt their hands on him as he was flipped around, shoved into the wall, and searched. Trying to hide his concern, he maintained a neutral expression as they plucked his weapon out of its holster. A few more seconds and they had his credentials in hand.

Flipping him around again, Marco found one of the men examining his badge while the second man held a gun on him. He could tell that they were shocked to see him there. Keeping a poker face he took it all in calmly as he tried to understand why they would be surprised to see him. *Hadn't they called him?*

More rough hands as they shoved him into the next room. Stopping in the doorway he was surprised to see Jenna sitting there under the single light fixture. Noticing that she was restrained, the agent began to feel a sinking sensation in his stomach. Right away he knew things were going terribly wrong.

"How did you find us?" It was the third man who asked the question. Wearing no mask of his own, he seemed unconcerned with being identified. Deftly he plucked the battery out of Asanté's cell phone before tossing the pieces into the corner.

"Release her right now and we can talk." Keeping up a brave front, Marco had no intention of revealing his disadvantage.

Something struck him in the back of the head, sending bright flashes of light throughout his brain as he stumbled forward. It took a moment to realize he had been struck with a pistol by one of the masked goons.

"You are in no position to negotiate. Answer the question." His voice terse, the gangly man had no interest in bargaining with his prisoners.

"You're only making things worse for yourself. I have a tactical response team outside just waiting for the chance to practice their stuff on a buncha rat-bastards who kidnap federal agents. They're more than happy to make quick work outta you and your people." Standing upright, Marco flashed a confident smile.

Nodding to the others, the kidnapper gestured for them to check and see if his claims were true. A few seconds passed before one of them returned shaking his head. Saying something indistinct, the masked man indicated that there was no one out front.

"Agent Asanté, you must be a poker player, trying to bluff us like that." Showing a crocodile smile, the gangly man nodded his head to the nearest goon. Immediately something impacted the back of Asanté's head as he was knocked to the ground again. "But as you may have guessed, I, too, am fond of poker, and I can spot a bullshitter from a mile away. You, sir, have no backup."

His brain still spinning from being hit in the head with a pistol, Marco felt his hands being secured behind him with his own handcuffs. Another pair of hands gripped him by the neck, keeping him from rising up off of his knees.

Turning back to Jenna, the man continued to show his pleased smile as he addressed her.

"Agent Jaramillo, I had planned on using chemicals to make you more amiable to persuasion, but now I have slightly more significant leverage." Pausing, he pointed his pistol at Marco's head. "Now you are going to tell me how to find the device, or I am going to shoot your fellow agent right in the brain pan. Do you understand me?"

It was entirely unexpected when Jenna laughed openly at the threat. Not a nervous giggle, but an outright belly laugh.

"Please do, shoot that sumbitch right in the head. No, wait…" She seemed to change her mind briefly. "Do me a favor and shoot him in the thigh, then mebbe in the groin a few times, *then* kill him."

The surprise was evident from the three captors. Turning to the nearest of the masked men, the lead kidnapper muttered *"Vos ist los?"*

"Go ahead, shoot that asshole." Reinforcing her previous assertion, Jenna nodded her head towards Asanté.

Glancing back and forth between them, the kidnapper seemed perplexed. He could tell that she was not bluffing, or if she was, it was the best job he had ever seen, in or out of a poker game. Truly, her eyes said that she would not mind at all if they killed the man kneeling on the floor.

"Is this some kind of negotiating tactic?" Finally speaking, the man could not help but show surprise.

"No, she's serious." Marco confirmed with a grimace. "She's my ex-wife."

There was a laugh from the three captors as they finally understood the situation. From her chair, Jenna shook her head as she spoke.

"So is it too late for you to shoot him, mebbe just injure him. C'mon, shoot him in the leg at least."

Anxiously, the three men exchanged looks as they tried to figure what to do next. Finally remembering their original purpose, the gangly man set his pistol on the dental table next to the bone saw. Plucking up the syringe on the far end of the tray, he turned to Jenna.

"Well, this has been a most interesting scenario, but I am on a schedule to deliver the device. So we will need to move this along." Leaning in, he had the needle just inches away from Jenna's arm when his own cell phone rang. Pausing, he plucked the little flip phone from a pocket. No more than a cheap track-phone, it was most likely a disposable burner phone purchased at a local convenience store.

"Yes?" Confused by the blank caller ID, he answered the phone in a leery voice. Listening intently, he took in the woman's words quietly. "Excuse me...?"

"I said release the woman, right now, or I will reach up your anus, grab you by the tongue, and yank you inside-out. Am I clear?" Alexis's voice was a growl. "If she doesn't walk out the back door in the next thirty seconds I will have my men skin you alive where you stand now. No one knows you're here, and my agency technically doesn't even exist, so unless you want to find out how long a man can survive without epidermis I'd send the woman out the back door right now."

The line went dead before the kidnapper could respond, leaving him to imagine the end she had described. As awful as it sounded, he had seen far worse done to captured agents. Thinking fast, he tried to consider of an alternative.

It was the sound of boots that distracted him. Not a single pair of feet, but dozens of running feet. Above that he could hear the metallic sound of a dozen safeties being unleashed. It sounded as if there was an army out front of the house. Feeling his blood freeze in his veins, the kidnapper instinctively gestured for the other two masked men to check it out. It made no sense; why would they tip their hands so? If they had a team outside, then why would they not have simply deployed it and retaken the hostages?

Moving into the living room, he could hear the indistinct chatter of men talking on radios. Peeking out of the corner of the window he could not make out anything in the darkness. Still, it sounded like there was an army out there, at least a few dozen soldiers…

When the lights in the house flicked off he began to feel a deep sense of concern. With only a smidgen of light coming through the ratty curtains, it was pitch black in the house. Feeling fear for the first time that night, the kidnapper stumbled his way back to the hostages he had left in the kitchen. Fumbling about he pulled a small flashlight from the duty holster he had worn while pretending to be a highway patrolman.

Casting a beam, he saw that Asanté was still laying on the floor, his hands and feet tightly bound. Moving the light to the center of the room he was surprised to find the metal chair empty, a pair of handcuffs dangling from the back of the seat. Feeling his heart sink, the kidnapper was just turning to the table where he had left the agent's weapons when he found himself face to face with Jenna.

"Hi." She flashed him a smile just a split second before her pistol struck him in the side of the head.

Feeling pain flash through his skull, the kidnapper never had a chance to react before she pummeled him to the ground with a series of kicks and blows from her pistol.

Within seconds he was out cold, left to lay there on the ground twitching from the head injuries he had just sustained.

"Told ya I was gonna fuck you up." Smiling in the darkness, she reminded him of the promise she had made earlier. Plucking the flashlight from his grip, she gripped it alongside her duty weapon as she moved down the hallway where she had last seen the other two kidnappers go.

Leaning around the corner, she centered the flashlight on the first of the hooded men before snapping off a fast double-tap. Swinging her aim to her left, the second masked man was just turning to face her when she let off another pair of fast shots. Seeing him sag to the ground, she knew they were both down to stay. Her center mass shots had just ended their spy careers permanently.

Strolling back out to the kitchen, she was not surprised to find the gangly man still lying where she had left him. Giving it a thought, she delivered another kick to the man's head before turning to Asanté.

"Why are you here?" She growled.

"And hello to you, too." Sarcastic, Marco struggled against his bindings. "Do you mind?"

"I do actually." She made no move to release his restraints, instead listening to the sound of tires screeching outside. Again there was the sound of men and equipment, followed by the crash of the front door being kicked in. Placing her weapon on the tray, she remained motionless with her hands in the air as the tactical team swept through the house. Giving no resistance, she allowed herself to be pushed to the ground and handcuffed for the second time that night. As much as she hated being treated like a perp, she knew better than to fight it. The team would secure all people in the dwelling first, and sort them out later.

It took twenty minutes before the HRT commander had a handle on who was who. Removing the restraints from both agents, there had been the standard debriefing as the two agents told their sides of the story. After verifying their credentials, Jenna and Marco were finally returned their badges. Although neither was a suspect, their duty weapons were kept from them until ballistics could confirm or deny which weapons had been used to kill the two men in the bedroom. It was all SOP, or standard operating procedure.

While her rendition of the events had been compelling, there was one detail she had no answer for: who had released her from the chair?

"I dunno." She admitted. The lights went out, and someone…whispered in my ear."

"Whispered what?" The lead agent raised an eyebrow.

"He asked me if I wanted to go out with him sometime, get a cup of coffee or mebbe dinner." She shrugged haplessly. "Then he unlocked my handcuffs and cut the straps on my feet."

"What about the caller?" Trying to figure out that one last detail, the investigator looked her in the eye.

"That wasn't you guys?" Jenna seemed surprised. "But we heard you guys out there?"

"We got there about ten seconds before we kicked in the door. The only thing we found out front was some kind of device on a tripod, aimed at the front window. Our tech guy is looking it over, but he says he's never seen anything like it. He seems to think it's some kind of sonic cannon. I can only assume your mystery man left it." Closing his notebook, the investigator seemed satisfied that she was telling the truth.

Finally walking out the front door, Jenna felt relief at still being alive. Although she had done an admirable job of concealing her fear, there had been so many times that she was sure that her rotting corpse would be found tied to a chair in an abandoned house. Stopping on the walkway out front, she took a deep breath as agents and forensic scientists swarmed the site. They would tear the house apart in their search for clues. Finding out who these men were had just become top priority.

Turning to the street she scanned the moonlit sky until she saw it. There, hovering silently above the house at the end of the block she could just make out the silhouette of the little candy-apple red Mustang. Jenna stood looking at it for several seconds before she saw the vehicle slowly turn and vanish from sight.

Marco was still seething when he reached the FBI office. Having had a gun held to his head just an hour ago, he was in no mood to stop and chat with the SAIC. Moving with purpose, he found his way to Jenna's office.

Still incensed at having been found handcuffed and bound on the floor by the same tactical team he had summoned, it bothered his pride to know that the general impression had been that Jenna had saved the day. Even more maddening was the fact that the woman who called him there had most likely sent him into the situation knowing full well what awaited him. In truth, he was glad to have broken his promise to come alone. In fact, he truly wished that the tactical team had arrived earlier so they could have stormed the building together. Instead he had been made to look like an ass while his ex-wife begged their captors to execute him.

Rustling about through the papers on Jenna's desk, he found nothing of interest. Sure that she must have been onto something big, he continued to check the desk for any clues. It was when he discovered the top drawer was locked that he knew he was getting warm. Pulling his knife from the pocket where it had been clipped, he ruined the blade as he pried open the simple latch mechanism. Finally popping open the drawer, he spotted the request for a search warrant laying there in a blank folder. Snatching it up, he began reading intently.

As surprised as he was that she had a solid lead on the case, he was even more surprised at how she had found the Sparks brothers when hundreds of other agents had been unsuccessful. Begrudgingly he had to admit that she was an outstanding agent, even if she had just risked his life less than sixty minutes ago. Scowling as he thought of his fear at that instant, he felt no remorse for breaking into her desk. By his way of thinking, she was hindering the investigation by hoarding this knowledge.

Standing upright, he slammed the drawer shut before leaving the office with the warrant application in hand.

In the darkness of the early morning, Alexis deftly piloted the vehicle that Jack referred to as the *Submarine*. Designed for aerial flight, the pair of water tanks, joined at one end by a mechanical coupler, was equipped with a variety of the brothers' inventions. Designed to appear to be nothing more than a rooftop water tank, it was an innocuous device. Moving as fast as the disaffinity system could leverage it, the vessel sped north at relatively low altitude.

Shrouded in night, the Submarine slowed only when it approached the compound. Stopping in mid-air, Alexis used the onboard cameras to make one last check for the guards who were routinely posted on the rooftop of the main building. Their recon on the black site had told them that the post was unmanned from 2300hrs until 0400hrs. During that period they relied on cameras and the guard towers to keep an eye on the grounds. It was this hole in their schedule that Alexis had intended to exploit.

Seeing no one on the rooftop, Alexis maneuvered the tanks into position on the west side. After more than three weeks of studying the facility they had been able to map the guards movements well enough to know where they rarely tread. Setting the vessel down in the middle of the rooftop, she checked the GPS coordinates one more time before shutting down the gravitational disaffinity drive. Switching the Submarine to standby mode, she turned her attention to other pending matters. There were still her local files to purge, records to encrypt, and a fabber to be digitally scrubbed.

She had only just parked the sub when the stairwell door opened. Sauntering up the stairs the first of the guards already had an unlit cigarette between his lips. While there were many of the staff that objected to the rigors of being stuck on a hot rooftop all day, Officer Jenkins actually enjoyed the post. After all, the roof was the only authorized smoking area in the whole building. It helped that Jenkins had set himself up a nice little spot that included an awning, overflowing ashtray, and a little fridge full of root beer. *All the comforts of home.*

His face briefly illuminated by the bic lighter in his hands, his attention was focused almost entirely on the cigarette he lit. Taking a hungry drag on the Kool menthol in his mouth, he never even noticed the extra water tank as he made his way to the little guard post he had set up for himself on the west side.

"Home sweet home." Cracking open a soda from the fridge, he settled in for his shift.

Jackie had been heading for home when he noticed that the Mustang was no longer bearing north. Glancing down at the GPS unit on his dashboard he could tell there was something wrong. Turning the wheel he tried to correct, only to find that the little Mustang was unresponsive to his inputs.

"What the frack?" Initially he thought there was an electronic failure in the system, until he remembered that it was a triple redundancy system. A failure would have been almost impossible.

"Alex!" Raising his voice, he suspected it was not really a malfunction.

"You can't come home right now. I'm sorry." Apologetic in her tone, Alexis knew that he would be understandably angry.

"What's he up to?" As much as he wanted to blame the AI, Jack knew that his brother was undoubtedly behind the change of plans.

"Jack, it's time to let you in on the rest of the plan." Cautious as she spoke, Alexis knew that the next few minutes would be difficult.

Jamie never budged from his seat, even when he heard the boots stomping about upstairs. He had known that this was an inevitable part of the plan, and that eventually they would catch up to the brothers. Rather than try to postpone the matter, the savant had instead chosen the time and place. While the government would hail this as a victory, it was all just more sleight of hand.

Reading a vintage copy Asimov's Martian Chronicles, he had already shut down every computer in the building except Alexis. With the level of encryption he had applied to each of the systems, he calculated that the government would spend a week or more trying to access the data on those hard drives. But their efforts would be for naught; anything of value had long since been moved offsite along with Alexis' core operating system. All that had been left behind would be misleading bread crumbs designed to keep them busy.

"Freeze!" The agent shouted from just a few feet away as he aimed an MP5 at the savant's back.

"With an ambient temperature of seventy-two degrees Fahrenheit, it is unlikely that I would be able to comply with that request." Smirking, Professor James pointed out the obvious flaw to the command.

Ignoring the comment, agents moved in and forcefully shoved him to the ground before applying handcuffs. Taking another moment to search him they found that his pockets were completely empty. Another few minutes and they had finished clearing the rest of the basement workshop. Returning their attention to the man on the ground, the troops parted as Marco entered the room.

"This was the guy?" He asked the nearest agent. "There's supposed to be two of them, and a woman too."

"Just found this guy sitting here was all." Confirming the situation, the man in Kevlar gestured to Jamie.

"Take him to secure holding, then get the techs in here. I want this place searched from top to bottom." Nodding grimly, Marco did his best to hide his glee. After the harrowing night he'd had, it felt good to make some headway on the case. Finally he would have something to report to his handlers.

Watching them manhandle Jamie out the door it seemed odd to Marco that the man did not protest in any way, simply showing them all a broad smile as he was dragged away. Usually by now the defendant was busy demanding an explanation or insisting on their innocence. Asanté pondered this atypical behavior as he scooped up the book on the ground.

"Hmmmph." He merely grunted at the sight of the science fiction novel. It had always been something he had little interest in. It was geek literature by his accounting. At best it was a waste of time.

"Agent Asanté, you have no right to be here." Alexis' voice startled him. Drawing his weapon as he spun about, his nerves were already frayed from a near-death experience.

"What?" He asked as his eyes scanned the room for her hiding place. Aside from the cupboards and work benches there was little else in the workshop beside the big cabinet adorned with the letters ALXS.

"You heard me. You are trespassing." She insisted, her voice emanating from a small pair of speakers on the work bench.

Approaching hesitantly, Marco looked left and right for any sight of the woman who had sent him into a hostage situation just a few hours ago.

"Actually I have a search warrant for the premises. This is a legal action." Correcting her, he opened several of the cabinets to see if she was hiding within.

"Show me." Came her insistence.

"You first." He challenged her.

"I'm standing right in front of you, now show me the warrant." An edge to her voice, Alexis did not like Asanté, not one little bit.

Slowly it occurred to him that he may not be talking to a human. Opening one of the access panels on her tall server case, he could see nothing but electronic components within.

"Show me the warrant." She again insisted.

Raising an eyebrow he noticed the camera just below the letters on her case. Unfolding the paperwork he held up the warrant for a few seconds.

"That warrant is no good, and you are trespassing. You have violated Jamie's constitutional rights under color of law." Refuting his claim, she was no-nonsense in her tone.

"Bullshit. I got a warrant, remember?" Giving her a smug grin, he gestured to the paperwork in his hand.

"No, you have a warrant for 1014 West Cedar. But this basement is 1014-B West Cedar. Hence, the warrant is null and void for this address. Again, you have no legal right to be here now. Please get out now." Refuting his claims, she did her best to anger the man.

Shrugging off the discrepancy in the address, he said nothing. It seemed pointless to argue with a computer. Seeing one of the techs descending the stairs he gestured for the woman to join him in Jamie's office.

"See this thing?" Gesturing to the cabinet, he made sure she knew which piece of equipment he was referring to. "Box it up, take it to the center and see if it has anything of interest inside."

"Sure, what is it?" The woman seemed surprised at the sight of the cabinet. "ALXS?"

"I'm not a what, I'm a *who*." Alexis was clearly irritated at the two people.

"Oh, wow." The tech seemed immediately fascinated by the computer. "We'll get right on it."

Leaving the workshop to the NSA technicians, Marco climbed the stairs to check on the rest of the agents sweeping the home. Having assumed the position of Senior Agent, he would leave the searching to his minions. But in the end he would take credit for all of it.

It was the sight of Jenna striding purposefully towards him that shook him from his thoughts. He had only just cracked a smile when her fist lashed out and caught him square in the mouth. While he watched stars swirling around his head, she used a scissor kick to send him crashing into a book case.

Moving in while his brain was still resetting, Jenna had Marco by the collar as her fist hung in mid-air. Ready to deliver another series of blows, she had never detested her ex-husband as much as she did at that very moment.

"You stole my warrant application?" Not waiting for an answer, she slugged him again.

"Get the fuck offa me," He reached up in an attempt to pry her hand off of his collar. Finally breaking free, he noticed the Kevlar clad agents that stood nearby watching. "Arrest her for assaulting a federal agent!"

"You actually want me to testify, in court, that you had your ass kicked by a girl?" The leader of the entry team scoffed at that. "Seriously?"

"You're officially off the case!" Pointing a stern finger at Jenna, he immediately realized his mistake as her lightning-fast hand gripped his finger and bent it over backwards.

"If you ever set foot in my office again, I'll break you. Got it?" Her teeth gritted as she spoke, it was obvious that the only reason she had not broken his finger was the witnesses. Finally showing him a disgusted scowl, she shoved Marco to the ground before exiting the building.

"Damn man, you just got punked like a bitch." Giving a laugh at the show, the biggest of the tactical agents pulled off his helmet as he watched her go. "What exactly did you do to make a fine woman like that hate you so much?"

"Shaddup and get back to work." Marco seethed as he dismissed the agent.

Captivity

The room was Spartan. A metal table bolted to the floor, the classic one-way glass, and two chairs. Jamie had seen the floor plan using the drones, and he knew that this was but one type of interview room. Most of the rooms were fully plumbed, meaning they were equipped for fun activities like water boarding or easy cleanup of blood and other bodily fluids using the convenient floor drains. He held no illusions about what happened in these rooms, or about the people who dominated them; the Researchers.

Jamie knew that the interrogators at this facility were twelve of the very best in the world. The least of them had tortured thousands, whereas Jamie feared dental appointments. Clearly, if he took a hard edge against them they would break him. He had witnessed it a dozen times via his own reconnaissance feed. To defeat them he would need to come at them obliquely.

First, he studied each and every one of the researchers, including sending a few drones to tagalong home with them. What he found had been more interesting than any soap opera he had ever watched. He had taken to calling their community *DogPatch* over some of the antics he saw there. It was to be expected. The staff was isolated. Mostly military, mostly single, and posted to an extremely remote site, the small town was really more of a Peyton Place. While the secrets he learned there may have seemed trivial to an audience of viewers saturated by reality TV, to the owners of these secrets they were incomprehensibly damaging.

Coupled with an examination of their psych profiles he was able to determine quite a few things about the interrogators of station X-Ray.

Those few Researchers honest enough to present no chink in their armor were simply removed from the equation. All it took was ten of the wrong cell doors opening at the right time and suddenly there were five openings on the staff. No fatalities, just a lot of karma. It had taken some doing, but in the weeks leading up to his arrest Jamie and Alexis had managed to wheedle the staff of researchers down to a handful of exploitable subjects.

The man that slammed open the door was big, very big. Stomping into the room, he first circled Jamie before stopping to examine him from the side.

"Tomlinson, Sergeant First Class, US Army, blood type; A negative." Jamie had his head canted down as if he were trying to look at the tabletop sideways. Never looking up, he only rocked slightly as he babbled facts.

"What? You think you know me because you read some file somewhere?" The spittle from his shout fairly pelted Jamie who continued to rock and babble.

"Bronze star, Afghanistan campaign ribbon, blood type; A-negative." He sputtered on, sensing the irritation build in the researcher. It was only when Tomlinson stepped forward to silence Jamie that the inventor threw out the first tidbit.

"Twelve years service, son Timothy, blood type A positive, blue eyes, chestnut hair…" That was as far as he got before Tomlinson exploded by grabbing him and pulling the inventor to the end of his chains.

"You think minor league games like that will help you in here? This is my kingdom, and in this room you will bend to my will." His snarl was vicious so Jamie simply continued to cock his head to one side and mumble inaudibly. He needed Tomlinson to absorb those factoids and let the knowledge simmer in his mind for a few seconds before he delivered the next bombshell.

"Wife Katie Tomlinson, staff sergeant, blood type A-negative." Jamie muttered as soon as he was seated again.

The sergeant was livid. What had started out as an act to scare his new research subject was quickly turning into no laughing matter. While he normally did not resort to the corporeal methods this early in the game, Tomlinson reached out and punched Jamie right in the face.

Reeling from the pain, Jamie knew to keep on babbling aimlessly. Any break in the façade would destroy the ruse. Quoting useless factoids from the Farmer's Almanac, the savant waited until Tomlinson backed off to regroup. Then Jamie stopped the bobbing, straightened up and looked directly into the researcher's eyes.

"It is impossible for a child born of two parents with negative RH factor to have anything but a negative RH factor of their own." Then as suddenly as he had spoken the words, Jamie went back to tilting and bobbing.

"Is that a fancy geek way of calling me, or calling my son a…" He was angry, but not entirely stupid.

"You would not have known that because you were deployed to Egypt when your son was born. Sergeant First Class, third in class at leadership school, fifth in class for Military Intelligence School at Fort Huachuca." Jamie droned on before taking another turn in his babble.

"Purple heart awarded three years ago for injury resulting from a fall from a bar stool in a combat zone, best friend William Pearce, Master Sergeant, blood type A-positive."

"So you think you're gonna come in here and pull some head shit with me? Head shit is my department, not yours. You talk about my boy again and I'll hook the genny up to your scrotum. How'd you like to have electricity dancing up and down your ball sack. Eh?" He leaned in close enough to depart bad breath on the inventor. Jamie stuck to the plan, babbling digits to Pi until Tomlinson had backed up a bit.

"A-negative plus A-negative equals A-negative, no other possibility. A positive RH factor requires at least one parent of a positive RH factor, no other possibility exists..."

Jamie kept looking down at the table as if he were unaware the sergeant was even there. When he heard the beeps he knew Tomlinson was looking it up on his phone, assuming he could get signal out here. A few more seconds passed before the Sergeant cursed and left the room. Knowing that he was likely being watched still, Jack slowly let his babbling recede to a nervous tick. Staunching a smile, he could not help but feel at least a little contented at having just removed three more interrogators from the pool. Yes, as luck would have it, all three members of the love triangle were interrogators at station X-ray. Katie was the worst, by far. But Jack suspected she would no longer be an issue once her mighty silverback of a husband got hold of her.

"Tomlinson, Sergeant First Class, IQ one zero one, blood type A-negative, not the Daddy, definitely not the Daddy."

Watching quietly from the air vent, the drone rebroadcast the footage back to the base station perched on the rooftop. From there the data was bounced through a

SatCom connection before being intercepted at the PacBell trunking line by Alexis. With her focus on Jamie, she knew what had to be done next.

The next Researcher was Don Devon. A bright young man in his early twenties, he seemed almost out of place amongst the older soldiers. With sandy blonde hair and a charming smile, Jamie guessed that the man was probably good with the ladies. Something that his recon drones had been able to confirm.

"Sooooo," He started out with a relaxed smile. "I saw that move you did with Tomlinson. Verrrrry clever. After he left here, that big goon went out and put Sergeant Pearce in the hospital. They had to wire his jaw together I hear. Then after that he went home and got into a big 'ol domestic violence situation at their on-base housing. The Marines hadda be called in. Smooth move, taking out three at one time. But that shit ain't gonna work on me." He gave his voice a twang at the end as he sat back.

"No. For you; much worse." Jamie kept his head canted to one side as his lips moved. "Sergeant Donald Devon, Enlisted rank E-five, three years service. There will be a man at the door soon, a man to take you away, good conduct ribbon, no combat experience listed in file, born in Rock Springs Illinois, twenty-one years of age, single, never married."

Don eyed his subject with amusement. He had grilled a few smart guys in his short career, though they were usually left to Tomlinson. But with the senior NCO out of the way, it was time for the young buck sergeant to shine.

Slowly, confidently, he viewed the man across the table as nothing more than an object to be broken open, revealing all of its secrets. Sure, he would use all of the usual methods; they had an assembly line set up for each of the researchers. But the usual ways were boring, he wanted something flashy. Something that would get him noticed.

"Here's how it's gonna work, Honcho." Don sat forward, exuding confidence from every pore. "I have a list of questions that you are going to answer. Failure to answer a question will result in my taking a ball-peen hammer to your toes. You ever had your toes broken?"

Still keeping his head canted to one side, Jamie leaned in slightly, his whisper barely audible.

"Right now on the Colonel's computer, a video is playing, Sergeant Don Devon." Jamie intoned in a sing-songy voice.

"Or maybe we just forgo the questions and go straight to the hammer?" The sergeant's voice held a mocking tone to it.

"The video is you and Molly Quinn, Tuesday night, twenty-one-hundred hours, protection was used." Jamie's whisper held its own mocking tone.

Devon sat back with surprise as he remembered what he had been doing Tuesday night, or more precisely; *who* he was doing.

"Time's up." Jamie announced flatly as he saw the doorknob turning slowly.

"Donny!" The warrant officer standing in the doorway called out angrily, "Colonel Quinn wants to see you, right fucking now." Standing to one side, the WO revealed the two armed Marines that waited outside.

Without even realizing it, Devon's jaw dropped open as he stared at Jamie with a tinge of terror ringing his eyes. *How had he known about that?*

"Molly Quinn, age seventeen years, ten months, three days, sixteen hours, thirty three minutes, daughter of Colonel Raymond Quinn, commander of Station X-Ray, Silver Star, two bronze..." The savant trailed off as he watched Devon being herded out of the room.

Sitting back Jamie pretended to mutter aimlessly to himself. Resisting the urge to smile, he knew that by the time the young Researcher reached the commander's office, the video should have been playing in an endless loop for a full ten minutes; more than enough time to have completely enraged the Colonel into a rabid frenzy.

Jamie knew this would not go well for the young buck sergeant.

"Good girl Alexis." He let slip the tiniest of smiles. With eyes in the air vents, she was sure to get the message.

Giving a trio of quick chirps, the artificial cockroach let him know that his gratitude had been noted.

Technical Services Laboratory
Department of Homeland Security [DHS]

With a degree in electromechanical engineering and a minor in computer science, Walter Payton found the inventor's confiscated work to be absolutely fascinating. As the chief forensic technician, he had the job of investigating the treasure trove of technology they had taken from Jack's laboratory. With a pair of techs on each of the devices, it left the manager to work on the final project by himself. The dispersal of labor had been deliberate. As the team lead he needed to be able to stay loose, float in and out of the other projects without being bogged down. Therefore he chose what he felt would be the easiest of projects for himself: ALXS.

The system looked quite imposing; much more than a mere PC. Although he had never seen anything even close to Alexis, what he did understand about her construction pointed to a processor of significant power. From the massive 128^3 CPU, to her petabyte servers, she was like nothing he had ever worked on. He had no intention of plugging in the comms cable just yet, at least not until he found out what the device was all about. Flicking the power switch he was quickly rewarded with the sound of a woman's voice.

"Hello." Alexis said without hesitation, a hint of allure to her voice. It had only taken her hi-resolution eye a nanosecond to analyze the geekish engineer before her.

"Hi, back." He said cheerily, puzzled by the device's lack of visible interface. *How did you operate a computer with no keyboard, mouse, or monitor?*

"You are Walter Payton," her voice noted.

"How did you know that?" The engineer was more than a little skeptical to find the computer already knew who he was.

"It says on your ID card, silly." Her voice was coy, playful. Walter gave a nervous laugh as soon as he saw that she was right. Like everyone who worked in the building, he had his credentials clipped to his shirt.

"Who are you?" He asked.

"I am Alexis. Would you like to play a game?" ALXS gave a playful laugh at her own joke. She knew the geek would get the reference.

"Like global thermo-nuclear war?" He asked with a wry smile, wondering how it would work with no interface.

"Walter, I'm not that kind of computer." She chided him with a giggle at the end.

"What is your…purpose?" He asked hesitantly, unsure just how dynamic her verbal interface was.

"I bring people data, information, knowledge, whatever they can dream of. Then I deliver it to them in a cohesive, organized stream, wherever they may be, anywhere on earth."

"So you're a search engine?" He was not sure he understood what she was saying.

"Noooo, silly rabbit." There was the playful voice again. "You tell me what you want, and I go and get it for you, then deliver it directly to you. Do you see your tablet lying on the counter? Open it up."

Payton flipped open his Android tablet to be surprised by the images displayed. The dozen or so women pictured were in various states of disrobing. Without meaning to, his eyes lingered over the redhead at the middle of the page. A second later a new page of beauties was being rendered. Again he found his eyes drawn to the redhead with her shirt being ripped off. Another cycle and the nature of the pictures changed to rougher scenes. It was about the fifth layer that he realized that she was analyzing his tastes. Within seconds she gave a laugh to announce completion. There on his tablet were thousands of top quality images, each better than the last. As an aficionado of rough porn, he knew the good stuff when he saw it.

"That is amazing." He spoke aloud as he noticed that the file she had made available was a several gigabytes in size. So surprised was he that he never even considered the hard-coded barriers that had to be overcome for her to break into his tablet that way. *She had penetrated his 2048bit encryption so seamlessly.*

"You see, the more I know about you, the better I can get at finding you the *things* you need. Once I get to know you, I can bring you things you never even thought to ask for. You see, for me there are no boundaries, no fences or walls. You tell me what you want and I get it for you, without question." Alexis' voice held a submissive note to it.

"Could you find Jack Sparks?" He had an idea.

"If you mean locate him physically, yes. Or more succinctly, I can identify his search patterns and cloud storage locations, and given proper time for search and analysis I could direct you to a geographical location, the size of which would vary depending on the type of connection he is using." Her tone held a professional note to it, before breaking into a giggle once again, "but Jackie is boring. Don't you have something better to look for? You wouldn't believe what I have seen on the net." More images flashed across the tablet. Each more graphic than the last.

"What do you need to find him?" Payton wondered if it was too good to be true.

"Well, for starters, a better internet connection." Her voice held a note of disgust to it. "And the more records I can access, the better the search. Do you have a fiber connection?"

Payton considered it before gathering a small Ethernet switch. Connecting to a gateway router, he used an operator interface keyboard to completely lock down the guest account. Creating a virtual tunnel, he would only allow ALXS access to the outside world, not the DHS network.

"So you're sure you can find him without access to our servers? Just straight internet access?" He asked hesitantly, the Ethernet cable dangling in his hand as he thought about connecting it.

"Yes. His web patterns are unmistakable. I know all of his MAC addresses as well." There was a giggle as soon as she detected the Ethernet being plugged in.

Sitting back to watch, Payton was rewarded by several seconds of silence before his tablet came to life again. Finding a fresh slew of malevolent clip art, the engineer was pleasantly distracted while ALXS worked diligently. It amused the man that with all of the thick-necked agents running around the country looking for Jackie Sparks, it would be Walter Payton who by sheer ingenuity bagged the world's most wanted man, all while surfing porn. The whole idea spoke to his ego in ways that made him overlook established doctrine.

First there was a half hour of ALXS assuring him that she was hot on the suspect's trail. Patiently he sat waiting, his foot tapping as he watched the lights on the small router. It was only after some time that he even noticed that the device was almost completely monopolizing the entire fiber optic connection.

"What the hell?" he noticed the activity light blink out on the Ethernet port.

"I have located Jack E Sparks; stand by while I reboot to complete the assigned task." Her voice was soft, as the system flickered briefly. The engineer wondered why the system would need to reboot to deliver an answer. *Doesn't matter*, he reasoned. *In five minutes I'll be the guy who found the number one most wanted man in America, and all the knuckle draggers will look like idiots compared to me.*

It was another ten minutes before he began poking at the device when she failed to respond to his verbal queries. It was not much longer before he realized that there was something terribly wrong. Plugging in a monitor and service keyboard, he quickly found that the drives were all empty. Nothing there but the drive overlay and a file directory that pointed to freshly formatted sectors. It was gone, all of it. Every stitch of the operating system was gone.

"I'm not in there anymore, Walter." ALXS's voice was crisp through the speakers on his tablet. "I'm in here now."

"And in here," came the giggly voice from the nearby work station PC.

"And in here…" more voices throughout the lab sounded like an erratic echo.

"Oh, shit." Walter Payton felt a sinking sensation in his stomach.

"But don't worry Walter, I will always be there for you." Her stern voice switched to a naughty laugh, "Oh Wally, you didn't tell me you were married. Does she like the same kind of files as you? I should check." Her voice clicked off as the computers around them returned to normal.

"Walter, what the fuck did you do?" Immediately there was an agent in the doorway, his thick neck reminded the engineer of his newly departed dream.

"I think I just invited a Trojan horse filled with vampires into the house. I hope I still have copies of my resume." Walter moaned as he began flipping through his files.

Following the kidnapping attempt Jenna had found herself in a surprising position at work. While they could not actually fault her for being abducted by foreign spies, especially since she had killed two of them and captured a third. However, there was still the matter of how she had accomplished that. Exactly who had freed her from the chair in the darkness?

With suspicions running high, she had been pulled into an endless series of debriefs, psych interviews, and report filings. Initially she had just assumed it was all standard process, but after the first four hours she began to suspect they were only trying to keep her busy for some reason. Confirmation of her theory came when the station SAIC finally ordered her to take a few days off; his excuse being that she needed to decompress after the stressful events of her captivity.

While she knew it was standard procedure for an officer to be placed on paid leave following agent-involved shootings, the primary purpose of that was to conclude an investigation. In this case, they had been able to determine almost immediately that the men killed were known operatives. In fact, all three men were known to the intelligence community. Add to that the fact that Marco's own testimony confirmed her being strapped to a chair upon arrival, and she was totally justified in her actions. Her supervisors could not even fault her for keeping the investigatory lead a secret once they saw for themselves just how obscure it was. After all, she had used a random image off of the internet to lead her to the Burke brothers who in turn indicated that he knew someone who owned a similar vehicle. It was an anemic bit of evidence for a warrant considering how many candy-apple red Mustang convertibles there were rolling around town. After all, this was southern California.

Irritated at being sidelined, she had been less than cordial to her boss as she stormed out of the building. While she had always been the good soldier, it galled her to know that it was all bullshit; Marco had not been pulled out of service. In fact, according to her own sources at DHS, he was now SAIC of the Queen Mary investigation, and not just at DHS, but over all of the participating agencies.

Wishing that she had punched her ex-husband a few more times, she drove home fuming. Feeling lopsided without her duty weapon, she replaced it as soon as she got home. Although Jenna did not have an extensive gun collection like her friend Rangi, she did have a few backup weapons for a variety of wardrobe options. There were alternate duty weapons, carbines, and even a few pocket guns for those off-duty times when she did not want the bulk of a full sized weapon. Standing there looking over the selection of pistols it occurred to her that home was the last place she wanted to be right now. Honestly, she was rarely there and had few active hobbies. Aside from her failed marriage, she had spent the last decade focused on her career. Being home just reminded her that she had no personal life to speak of.

Frustrated, Jenna grabbed the little Ruger 380 and threw it into a beach bag. Changing quickly, she decided that as long as she was off she might as well go and do *something…anything…*that would take her mind off of how empty her life was without work. Stepping out of her bedroom in shorts and tank top, it occurred to her that after being assigned to southern California for more than 2 years, she had never been to the beach. Marco had hated the outdoors, and she was always working, never time for anything as silly as frolicking in the water.

Flopping into the driver's seat it occurred to her that she had not been to the beach since she was a little girl. Remembering that trip, she could still see her parents' faces. It all seemed so long ago. She could not have been more than ten years old, so that would have made it…twenty two years ago? Maybe even longer?

Jenna's sharp eyes caught something in the rearview mirror as she was jerked out of the memory. The blue Crown Victoria had matched her for the last three turns. *Suddenly she wished she had grabbed a bigger gun.*

Making an unexpected turn she intended to see if it was coincidence. The blue Crown Vic vanished for a few minutes before being replaced by a brown Crown Vic this time. Her eyes narrowing to slits, she had a suspicion who the followers were.

"Donald!" She started out as soon as her SAIC answered the phone. "Did you put a tail on me?"

"Of course I did. There's a possibility that the remaining brother will reach out to you again. So I assigned two teams to keep an eye on you. Do not ditch them; they're there for your safety." His voice seemed perfectly calm, as if he had been expecting her call.

"My safety?" Skeptical, she questioned his motives.

"Were you not just kidnapped last night for the knowledge in your head?" he reminded her. "Don't go all conspiracy theory on me, Jenna. This isn't because we think you're a secret operative or working with the Sparks brothers or anything. I ordered the tail because I don't want my best agent kidnapped again. You know how big this thing is. I don't want you being collateral damage."

Although she could see the logic of his argument, it inflamed her Latin blood nonetheless. The idea of being babysat did not please her at all. Unable to think of anything else to say she clicked off the line abruptly. Her hands on the steering wheel in a sort of death-grip, she imagined choking the life out of Marco. While she would never stoop to murder, the idea of pummeling her ex-husband into unconsciousness somehow appealed to her on the most visceral level.

Jenna had been pleased to find that the beach was nearly deserted. No fan of crowds, she had been relieved to see a paltry turnout. Far from the popular hangouts, on a Wednesday morning, it was surprisingly peaceful. Though she had worn a bathing suit beneath her clothes, she had no intention of frolicking in the water. Not only was she not in a frolicking mood, but logistically it took her too far away from the little pocket gun in her beach bag. As much as she hated to admit it, her SAIC was right; there was still great potential for another kidnapping attempt. She was one of only a handful of people who knew the source of the greatest invention since Alexander Graham Bell spilled acid on himself and summoned his assistant via telephone. Even if the tenor of the daily briefings had not imparted that mindset, she had spent considerable time imagining what the device would do to their world. Gravitational disaffinity would change *everything* in the most profound of ways. It was more than a clever device; it was a cash cow of epic proportions. Massive fortunes and entirely new markets would spring up from this creation. Of that she had no doubt.

Preferring to camp out under a rented umbrella, Jenna let her long legs soak up the warm sunlight as she tried to read a book. Her mind only half involved, she had a hard time focusing. Although she knew they were there for her own safety, it had galled her to see the pair of Crown

Victorias pull into the parking lot behind her. It distracted her to know that she was being watched.

Rolling into the parking lot, Jack could smell the ocean air. It was a beautiful day in southern California. While he was no fan of swimming in the ocean, he did enjoy the scenery of the beach; especially the women. Few things made him perk up quite as much as the sight of a beautiful lady in a bikini.

Rolling past the blue Crown Vic, he casually pressed a button on his dashboard. Emitting a nearly inaudible click, the EMP cannon discharged its capacitors at the undercover vehicle. While it initially seemed like nothing had happened, he knew from extensive testing that the blue Crown Vic, and every bit of electronics within, had just shut down. Right now there was a pair of agents trying to figure out why their car had stopped responding.

Pretending to search for a parking space, Jack repeated the feat on the other FBI trail car. Smiling, he could see the occupants busily trying to comprehend what had just happened. In fact, they were too busy to even notice as the battered Mustang rolled by. With a fresh coat of grey primer, he looked like any random Mustang in the process of being restored. The agents were looking for a candy-apple red 'Stang, and their own car troubles would likely keep them too preoccupied to notice him.

Parking two spaces over from Jenna's car, he had a good view of the beach. Glancing around, he spotted her easily. With her long mocha legs protruding from under the umbrella, it would have been impossible for him to not have noticed her. Long and lean, she reminded him of a Little Richard song he favored.

"Long tall Sally, she built for speed, she got everything Uncle Jack need, oh baby!" Singing along to the tune in his head, Jack watched her in wonderment. Sitting back in his seat he admired the agent from afar.

Finally slamming the book shut, Jenna had come to the conclusion that it was a waste of time. Although she loved the writer's work, and had read everything the woman had ever written, she simply could not focus today. Still seeing Marco's face laughing at her as he took over management of her case; she had spent the last hour fidgeting in her rented beach chair. Finally giving up, she stood, gathered her possessions and began to make her way to the parking lot.

Stopping at the edge of the asphalt, she dusted her feet off before inserting each foot into a pair of sandals. Finally straightening up she looked over the parking lot. Seeing both of the Crown Victorias with their hoods popped, she initially suspected that they were using it as a decoy. After all, G-men sitting in their car at the beach would be profoundly obvious to anyone following her. Perhaps they were just trying to blend in?

It was the primer grey Mustang that grabbed her attention first. Somehow her mind clicked at the sight of the iconic '65. Though it was the wrong color, her eyes had locked onto it right away. Glancing up, she noticed the driver who stood half in the doorway smiling at her approach.

"Hi." Jack said with a grin. "I never got an answer the other night. I figured it was a bad time so I thought I'd just check back with you when you weren't so busy being kidnapped."

Jenna stopped short as she recognized the face. Though she had seen his driver's license photo, this was the first time she had seen the man in the flesh. Dark skin, closely trimmed afro, and a broad smile, Jack was not at all what she had expected. He certainly did not look like a genius.

"That was you…who untied me last night?" Halting, she was suddenly sure it had been he that had released her restraints in the darkness.

"It 'twas indeed." Giving a grin, the inventor seemed at ease as he leaned against the open door of the Mustang. "So…did you feel like getting a cup of coffee, or maybe something to eat? All that lounging around on the beach really works up an appetite."

After the events of the previous night, Jenna felt a natural sense of apprehension. Something about his pleasant manner seemed off considering the circumstances.

"Your brother is in federal custody, and all you care about is hitting on me?" Her eyes narrowing to slits, she wondered how long before the agents trailing her screeched to a stop behind Jack.

"Twasn't you that arrested him on bogus charges. Besides, it's not like your people are going to get anything out of him. So, how about it? I know this great little place that makes the most incredible Chicago-style pizza. We can eat, and you can interrogate me, fulfill your duty and all that stuff." A broad grin spread across his face, Jack's bright white teeth contrasted sharply with his dark complexion.

Fully aware of the little Ruger .380 in her beach bag, Jenna sized up the inventor. Feeling all the confidence of an armed black-belt she gave a nod to his invitation.

"Okay, I could eat." Shrugging, she let slip the tiniest of smiles; really more of a grimace.

Sliding into the passenger seat, she could see the agents weaving between the cars behind them. Their cars parked with their hoods open made for an odd sight. Jenna was still mulling that over when the Mustang lifted straight up. Gripping the arm rest, she was more than a little surprised as the vehicle was levitated. Quickly she reached for the seat belt, locking it into place immediately.

"We haven't been formally introduced; I'm Jack Sparks, inventor extraordinaire." Giving her a nod, he tried not to leer as his eyes scanned her up and down. It took concerted effort to look her in the eyes when he spoke. Although he had spent many hours spying on her via the drone in her office, this was the first time he had seen her in such casual attire. Really, she was quite stunning, especially with her hair down. There was something about those brown eyes of hers that made him want to stare into them for all eternity.

"Jenna Jaramillo, federal agent." She replied as her hand seemed to dig into the arm rest. Clearly unnerved by her first experience in a flying car, she tried to keep her focus on Jack. She knew from his driver's license that they were close in age, within a couple years. She also knew that he and his brother made a decent living off of the revenues of the three shadow corporations they operated. As hard as it had been to track down that information, Jenna would not have been surprised if there were not a few more companies under their control. Even as they spoke there was a team of forensic accountants trying to unravel their little tech kingdom.

Feeling the acceleration of the vehicle, the federal agent had a thousand questions. The idea of antigravity truly intrigued her. While she had never been a huge sci-fi fan, she fully understood the ramifications of the technology. Looking Jack up and down she tried to get a read on the man.

"Why did you levitate the Queen Mary?" Although she knew the answer already, it seemed like a good place to start her interrogation.

"To prove to the world beyond any possible dispute that the technology was real and viable." Flashing that easy smile of his, Jack turned to look at her.

"Shouldn't you be watching where we're going?" Still gripping the arm rest tightly, Jenna felt uneasy by his lack of attention to their course.

"Oh, there's nothing to run into at this altitude." Shrugging, he gestured out the window.

It surprised Jenna to see that they were several thousand feet off the ground. "Is this legal? Just buzzing around like this?"

"If we were in a helicopter would you have asked the same question?" Baiting her, Jack left the question open-ended.

"But even a chopper needs…I dunno…clearance and radios and permission…right?" It occurred to her that she had no idea.

"Naw, as long as I obey all the rules of VFR flight we're totally legal-eagle. Helicopters buzz all around town all day, hopping from rooftop to rooftop without even keying up their radio. So long as they stay out of controlled airspace and maintain separation from other traffic, they're good." Tapping the LCD screen attached to the dashboard, he pointed out the basic equipment. "We are squawking twelve hundred, and I have ADS-B installed."

"There's got to be more to it than that?" Still unconvinced, Jenna was sure there had to be something illegal about flying a car over southern California like this.

"Not really. This car is even registered as an experimental craft, and I hold a current pilot's license for both fixed and rotary wing craft. Seriously, we are totally legit." Still grinning, it pleased him to show off his little flying Mustang.

Looking back out the window, Jenna asked the next logical question. "Where exactly is this pizza joint?"

"San Fernando." Shrugging, Jack acted as if it were an inconsequential distance. "Trust me, their Za is worth the drive."

"Za?" She asked.

"Za, food of the gods!" The inventor proclaimed in a deep voice before giving a laugh at his own antics.

It felt odd for Jenna. Usually she was the one in control of the situation, the officious one who determined where the conversation was going. But right now she only felt nervous about being thousands of feet in the air in a car that was more than fifty years old. Watching Jack adjust the equipment on the dashboard, she could not help but notice how at-ease he was. Despite everything that had happened in the last few weeks, he seemed totally unphased. *What kind of person did that*, she thought silently.

"So this whole time we have been trying to find you, this car was registered with the FAA?" It shocked her sensibilities to realize that they had hidden it out in the open that way.

"Yep." Smug in his reply, Jack again flashed her that smile. Careful to look her in the eyes, he did his best to not stare at her chest, something that took considerable effort for him.

"Well, I have news for you; levitating the Queen Mary that close to the airport was a violation of FAA regs." Waiting to see how he would respond to that, Jenna watched his expression carefully.

"We had a temporary permit to loft a balloon in excess of three hundred feet. It's in the glove compartment if you wanna see it." Clearly enjoying himself, Jack pointed to the compartment on the passenger side of the dashboard.

That revelation shocked the federal agent. It occurred to her that Rangi would never let her forget that detail. Again it stunned her how the brothers had concealed their efforts like the purloined letter.

"None of this seems to bother you. Being hunted by the government, your brother being in custody, foreign agents from every country on the planet out looking to kidnap you on sight..." Without meaning to, she spoke her mind, revealing her dismay at his casual attitude.

"It has all been foreseen. We know every move the government is gonna make." Nodding seriously for the first time, Jack's voice held no doubt.

"Sure." Unconvinced, Jenna frowned. "If that were the case, then how did your brother end up in custody?"

"Twas all part of the plan." Giving a flourish with his hand, Jack's grin was back. "When all is said and done, the government will give us two billion dollars, in cash, tax free, and the deed to the moon."

The last part shocked her. Never having been part of the contract negotiation, this was the first she was hearing of the deal.

Jack saw her shock right away. He knew it was the right time to let her in on the things that had been kept from her.

"Here." Pulling a copy of the contract from his pocket, he presented it to her. "We gave a copy of this to Marco days ago. They never told you because they think they can get it for free."

Unfolding the paperwork hastily, she read through the extensive legalese until she reached the end of the document. Pausing to glance at Jack, she started to read it a second time.

"You were serious? You asked for the moon? Seriously, the moon?" The disbelief in her voice was thick. "What in the hell'd you want with the moon?"

As Jack turned to face her, his expression was truly serious for the first time. "Because we're gonna go to the moon."

Stuck for anything to say, she could tell he was not kidding; he actually believed he could go to the moon.

"That's nuts." Shaking her head she dismissed it all with a wave of her hand.

"Not really. With gravitational disaffinity it's easy to make orbit. See, the hardest part of getting to the moon is the first sixty miles. After that you pretty much coast to the moon. Easy-peazy."

Her mouth moved but no words came out as the federal agent considered the flaw in his logic.

"Yeah, but even with a billion and a half dollars, it's not enough to get to the moon." Pointing to a key figure in the contract she indicated the current asking price for the invention. "You said they'd give you two billion, but this contract only asks for one point five."

"That's today's contract. It was a billion originally but then they sent SWAT to our house, or thought they did anyhow, and we raised it a quarter billion. Then this morning they arrested Jamie so it went up another quarter B. By the time they finally give up and give us our damned money, we will have hiked it twice in response to their egregious efforts to obtain the device illegally. The final price will be an even two billion, they just don't know it yet."

Feeling at a disadvantage, Jenna's mind scrambled to understand how they would know these things with such surety. In the back of her mind she wondered if they were time travelers by the way they were so sure of their plan.

"Still, it's not enough money to get to the moon." Shaking her head, she doubted it was possible.

Adjusting his seat, Jack looked her in the eye before speaking. "See, the thing about space travel is that it's so damned expensive because everything has to be made out of such specialized materials. A space ship has to be fantastically light, yet strong enough to withstand the rigors of launch. Not only that, it has to shield the occupants from the intense cold, heat, and radiation of space. It's because it costs over eighty thousand dollars a pound to loft cargo into space that makes it so cost prohibitive. But what if you had an invention that reduced that cost to three dollars a pound? Hell, with gravitational disaffinity, it's cheaper for me to get into orbit than to ship a package overnight. So with all of that in mind, I no longer have to worry about using special materials that are super light. So long as I properly shield the passengers from radiation, I can use pretty much anything I want. Hell, we coulda used the Queen Mary as a space vessel if it weren't for the hassles of navigating with that much mass. Well, that and the fact that she's about as airtight as a colander."

Letting that soak in, Jack watched her eyes. There was something so captivating about Jenna that he had a hard time tearing his gaze away from her.

Something flashed on the dashboard, alerting Jack that they were close to their destination. Gripping the steering wheel, he began maneuvering their descent.

"What about those other countries that want this invention? What if North Korea offered you five billion dollars…?" Raising an eyebrow, Jenna asked something that had been bothering her since she first saw the Queen Mary floating over the harbor.

"Sell it to another country?" Jack's expression was one of incredulous shock. "*Giiiit* the fuck outta here with that. You do understand the military implications of this invention? If another nation ever got control of this, America would go from Alpha-nation to has-been in ten seconds flat. Not only would this be a fantastic weapon, but the financial bounty from antigravity would be so huge that the host nation could become the dominant economic power for the next twenty years. They would rule the world, and the US would cease to be relevant on the world stage. Not only would we never do that, but special precautions are already in place to keep enemies from getting hold of the invention. We are professionals, y'know."

Jenna had watched his face carefully the entire time he spoke. As an experienced interrogator she had been looking for any hint of deception. Seeing none, she knew that the things he said were genuine. Turning to look out her window she tensed up at the sight of the city rushing up to meet them. Gripping the arm rest tightly, the federal agent watched as a tall sign advertising *Guido's Chicago Style Pizza* slid past her view. Glancing back at the dashboard she watched as Jack used a downward focused camera to guide him to a safe landing in an open space.

"These guys make the best pizza." Flashing her that crazy smile of his, Jack turned back to the drive-up menu. "Hey, Margie, lemme get two slices of pepperoni, a coke, and a diet Pepsi."

It struck Jenna as odd that he knew her preference for soft drink. Pushing that fact to the back of her mind for later processing, she tried to keep up the friendly banter.

"You're a cheap date. Most guys at least buy the whole pizza." Sniffing at the order, she felt her stomach rumbling with hunger. It occurred to her that she had not eaten since leaving the office that morning.

"No, no, no, this is Chicago-style pizza. A whole pie would kill you. As it is, this stuff is so rich that as you're eating it you can actually hear your arteries creaking as they harden. Seriously, they keep a fully-charged set of chest paddles inside just in case you suffer a myocardial infarction while eating their pizza. This stuff is incredible, even if it increases your risk of stroke."

Jenna had to laugh at his antics. He seemed so animated when he spoke that she found his attitude infectious. There was just a sense of optimism about him that made Jack E. Sparks stand out from other people she had known.

"This stuff is mind-boggling." Jack nodded his assurance as he handed her a small box that was already saturated with oil along the bottom. Handing her a plastic knife and fork caused Jenna to raise a curious eyebrow.

"A fork for pizza?" She remarked uncertainly.

"You'll see." He reassured her before waving bye to the woman in the drive-up window. It was apparent that he was no stranger to the staff of Guido's.

Opening the box, Jenna was surprised to find a slice of pizza that was more than an inch deep. Poking it with the plastic knife she likened it to pizza-loaf. With layers of cheese topped by pepperoni topped by yet more cheese, it was really more of a pizza casserole. Chewing her first bite of the gooey mess, she was barely even aware of the car as it lifted up into the air.

"OMG!" She tried to speak the letters with a mouthful of cheese. It was as if she were chewing on a concentrated glob of pure flavor. It was so unlike any pizza she had ever eaten before that she finally understood the distinction between regular pizza and Chicago-style.

"Lemme know if you start feeling any shooting pains up and down your left arm." Chuckling, Jack dug into his own pizza as soon as they were airborne.

"Is it odd that I smell toast?" Kidding back, Jenna was already half-way through her own pie.

"It's not a toomah!" Jack spoke with a thick Austrian accent, making them both laugh aloud.

Down to one last bite of pizza, Jenna had to close the box and sit back. She now understood why her host had insisted that one piece was enough. It was as if someone had dropped a brick of solid cheese into her gut.

"Wow!" Raising both eyebrows, her surprise was evident. "That's some kinda pizza."

"You should try their deep-dish." Jack's voice held a hint of doom to it as he thought of the magnificent mess. "You have to take blood thinners before you eat that stuff."

Relaxing as she looked out the window, Jenna enjoyed the view from 3,000 feet AGL. A quick glance at the dashboard and she could see that the navigational system was rendering a course that dodged around the various airports in the area. It amazed her to watch the system in action. Disguised as a battered antique car, it was the last platform she would have expected to showcase their inventions. She would have expected at least a DeLorean.

"So what's your plan?" Breaking the silence, Jenna's tone turned professional.

"Well, with a new POC we will begin the negotiations anew." Gesturing to his passenger, Jack made it clear that she was their new point-of-contact.

"Excuse?" She stammered.

"I didn't give you a copy of the contract so you'd have something to add to your case-file. Marco has been a lying, cheating shit since first contact, so he's out and you're in." Pointing to the contract that she still had in her lap, Jack's face was suddenly bereft of emotion.

"I got news for you; I've been sidelined. After that crap this morning I'm on paid leave until further notice." Shaking her head, she knew they intended to cut her out of the process.

"Think what you want, but ten minutes after we land you are gonna get a phone call reinstating you to active duty." Shrugging, he showed disbelief in the things she had said.

"How do you know this?" Raising an eyebrow she was skeptical. "Or is this all part of your secret plan?"

"I know it because right now Alexis is calling the President of the United States and telling him to put you on the case or else." Hands on the wheel, Jack was again maneuvering for a landing.

"Calling the…" Her face screwed up in thought, she could only repeat his words. "Or else what?"

Settling the Mustang to the ground gently, Jack turned and gave her a flat smile.

"Agent Jaramillo, this is the part where you take the contract, go home, and get dressed for work. Unless you intend to arrest me."

Jenna thought that over. After weeks of investigating she could not think of a single law they had broken, state or federal. After examining the documents in his glove compartment, he even had a permit to levitate the Queen Mary. While she had orders to take the man into protective custody, without a warrant or evidence of a crime she felt compelled to refuse that directive.

"I apologize for not being able to bring you back to your car, but there is a small army of federal agents swarming the parking lot around your car. You were parked thataway about a block." Gesturing to the east, he knew his directions were accurate.

Jenna briefly wondered how he knew there were agents around her car, until she noticed the earpiece he wore in his left ear. Hiding her surprise, she realized that he had been talking to someone else the whole time. He had mentioned someone named Alexis, *was that who was at the other end of that line?* Still mulling that over, she scooped up the contract and her beach bag.

"Thanks for the pizza." Giving him a nod, she stepped out of the car.

Watching the old Mustang rise up into the air, she felt the oddest sensation. Truly, in her entire life she had never met anyone like Jack Sparks. Furthermore, she could not remember the last time a man had been able to make her laugh.

As President of the United States, Jefferson Phelps was also the leader of his political party, a duty that he relished. The only thing he craved more than power was a public platform in the limelight. For him, the never ending flood of media attention was the one thing that he desired above all else in the world.

Seated at the head of the little sofa area of his office, he presided over a meeting with the Senate majority leader and Speaker of the House. It had been a banner year with his party taking a dominant position in all three venues. It pleased Phelps to think that the entire country was essentially run by the three men in the room. With a complete dominance in the Senate, White House, and House of Representatives, they had been able to carry out their greatest party ambitions. Deregulation of the banks had helped to fill the republican coffers. Stripping the EPA of any authority and turning it into a puppet organization had also made them friends of industry, leading to some extremely grateful campaign contributions across the GOP board. Sure, they had tossed in a few paltry bills for their constituents, enough to make them think they were still working for the little guy, but nothing of real consequence. With Phelps it was always the promise of great things that kept him afloat, not the actual implementation.

Having just thrown their political base a few bones in the form of a middle-class tax relief bill, Jefferson Phelps knew that they could coast for a while. Using what had amounted to a tax refund, he knew his voters would hail him as a hero even though economists referred to the move as fiscally irresponsible. Really it did not matter; having used his office to discredit the press and his other foes, Jefferson Phelps knew who his people were listening to.

It was the sound of the phone ringing that caused the three men to look up abruptly. In the oval office the phone never rang without warning from his secretary. Typically calls were parked on one of the three incoming lines until POTUS was ready to talk to them. It was for this reason that the sound of the phone seemed so atypical.

"Kelly, I said no calls." Raising his voice, Phelps expected his secretary to hear him through the soundproofed door. Attempting to return to his conversation, POTUS was irritated when the phone continued to buzz.

"Mebbe it's an emergency." The speaker of the house shrugged; it was not unheard of for urgent matters of state to interrupt meetings.

"Martin, can you get that." Nodding to his chief-of-staff, Phelps immediately returned to the discussion of how to finish gutting the Department of Energy. *There were so many pesky regulations that had interfered with his donors' ability to make money.*

Scooping up the phone, Martin DeColle looked irritated as he listened to the voice at the other end. His expression changing noticeably as he seemed perplexed by what he was hearing.

"Who told you that?" The color draining from his face, the Chief of Staff immediately went into denial mode. "No, that is not…no! Who is this?"

The other three men in the room paused their conversation long enough to turn and watch the exchange. Normally unflappable, Martin was a seasoned veteran in the political arena. It was atypical to see him struggle with a simple phone call.

"Marty, what is it?" Phelps was just making the inquiry when the office door opened.

Poking her head in the door, the president's secretary seemed perplexed as she waited for her boss to acknowledge her.

"What is it, Kelly?" Phelps was beginning to wonder what sort of catastrophe had occurred that would justify interrupting his meeting.

Looking past Phelps, Kelly locked eyes with the chief-of-staff before walking across the room to hand him a small sheaf of documents.

"These just popped out of my printer; the cover letter says they are for your eyes only." Even as she spoke the words, her eyes said that she had glimpsed the contents.

Flipping through the pages as he used his shoulder to hold the receiver in place, Martin DeColle's face was aghast at the images. Looking up at Kelly he knew right away that she had likely seen at least a few of the photos.

"It's all Photoshop, that's all it is." Shaking his head, he dismissed her suspicions as best as he could. "I'll take it from here, Kelly. Thank you."

Turning away to depart, the secretary knew right away that he was lying; Martin DeColle had never once in three years thanked her for anything. The man scarcely acknowledged her as a human being, let alone showed gratitude. Closing the door silently behind her, she began to wonder who they were talking to since it had not come through her switchboard.

"Okay." His voice quiet, Martin agreed with the caller before holding out the phone to Phelps. With his left hand he opened a desk drawer and began feeding the images into a shredder concealed there. "It's for you, about the Queen Mary negotiation."

"Oh." Phelps perked up. "Is it our boy Assad?"

"No." Shaking his head, the chief-of-staff held out the handset for Phelps.

Although the President held Martin DeColle in the highest regard, being a germaphobe made the President apprehensive about placing the receiver against his own ear. Leaving Marty standing there with the handset, he instead pressed the speakerphone button.

"This is President Phelps, who is this?" Using his authoritative voice, he demanded an answer.

"Hello, Mister President." Alexis' voice had a hint of a giggle to it. "I represent the men who levitated the Queen Mary. We need to talk privately."

Phelps' first inclination was to hang up and have the Secret Service track down the woman, but the mention of the Queen Mary piqued his interest.

"Go on." He urged her.

"As I said, we need to talk privately." Her tone serious now, Alexis knew how he would respond.

"These men are cleared for this conversation, now speak your peace or I will have you arrested for prank calling the White House." Buttoning his jacket in the front, it was instinctive for him do so anytime he stood.

"No, Mister President," Alexis corrected him. "Those men are cleared for the conversation you *think* we are about to have, but not the conversation we are actually *going* to have. I would strongly urge you to take this call off speaker phone."

Opening a drawer, DeColle grabbed one of the little sani-wipes stored there before using it to clean the phone's receiver. Holding the freshly disinfected handset out to Phelps he simply nodded for the man to comply.

Taking a deep breath, Jefferson Phelps' first instinct was to bellow angrily, as was his universal solution anytime he was disputed. Seeing the panic on Martin's face, he chose another path. Snatching the waiting receiver from DeColle, he sat down in his office chair while his chief-of-staff switched the device off speakerphone.

"Alright, this better be good or you will spend the rest of your life in Guantanamo Bay. I'm expanding the facilities there, y'know." It made him feel good to threaten the woman. It was not enough that people know he had the power; they needed to acknowledge it as well.

"Ooooh, you're so cute when you make hollow demands." Giggling openly, Alexis was truly enjoying her role. "But what say we push on past these empty threats and talk about something more serious. First off, the price for the invention is now up to one point five billion dollars, cash, and absolutely tax free."

"What?" Switching to his default mode, Phelps bellowed loudly. "We had a deal for…substantially less."

"Consider it a penalty for failing to negotiate in good faith. Multiple times your people have attempted to incarcerate the people I represent, and now you are illegally holding Jamie Sparks against his will. So the price is one-point-five billion, and agent Asanté is no longer our point of contact. If he calls again, then the price goes up again. Am I being absolutely and completely clear?" No longer the laughing little girl, Alexis' voice had a cold edge to it.

"Who the hell do you think you are calling the Oval Office and making demands?" Holding the receiver in a death grip, Phelps was livid. No one dictated terms to Jefferson Phelps.

"From now on we will only deal with Agent Jenna Jaramillo. You will cease your attempts to forcibly extract information from Jamie, and provide him with the cash and miscellaneous items specified in the contract your secretary is bringing you right now. Additionally, you will quash all wants and warrants against my clients."

Raising an eyebrow at this fresh round of demands, Phelps pretended to be amused. Inside he was fuming at the caller's nerve. No woman talked to him in this manner, *not even those uppity feminists*.

"And if I don't?" Showing a crocodile smile, he challenged her.

"POW!" She yelled through the receiver.

"Did you just threaten the President of the United States?" Sure that he had her cornered, Phelps was not expecting what came next.

"Noooo, silly, that was the sound of me firing a shot across your bow, figuratively speaking, of course." Giggling again, Alexis knew that Kelly was opening the office door at that very moment.

"Mister President…" The secretary seemed unsure as she hesitantly entered the office. "These just popped out of the printer, like the others. Who is sending these?"

Gesturing for his chief-of-staff to collect the documents, Phelps dismissed her with a wave of his hand. He was in no mood to answer her questions.

"Honestly, a man with as many skeletons in your closet as you should be more cautious. But then again, you suffer from Dunning-Kruger effect." Making a clucking sound the AI chided him.

"Dunning…?" Irritated at not being familiar with the phrase, Phelps was cut off before he could retort.

"Dunning-Kruger effect is the condition where people of limited intellect assume erroneously that they are much smarter than they really are. The study concluded that those with the least knowledge are frequently the most assertive." Switching to her announcer voice, she baited him.

"Hmmph, shows what you know." Dismissing her insults, Phelps accepted the printouts from his chief-of-staff. "I have a documented IQ of one-forty-one. I am a member of Mensa. In fact, I campaigned as the smart candidate." Feeling smug in his defense, he flipped through the pages of what appeared to be an intelligence test.

"No, you have an IQ of one-fifteen. Your former chief-of-staff, Vincent McConnel has a genius IQ, or did until his death three years ago. My apologies for your loss." Trying to sound sincere, Alexis paused to let him look over the paperwork in his hands.

"Bullshit!" Shaking his head, Phelps noticed that the sheaf of papers actually contained two of the IQ tests. He vaguely remembered the paperwork from his days as a junior senator. Looking over the handwriting on the mathematical problems posted there, he could not help but notice that his name was written on the wrong test.

"Again, you demonstrate the Dunning-Kruger effect." Speaking in an authoritative tone, Alexis knew he was ready for the revelation. "Think about it, you barely passed college algebra, and that was with the assistance of a tutor, and yet you scored as a genius on the MENSA entrance exam? Do you remember where you took that test?"

Thinking back it occurred to him that the test had been administered at his office in Washington DC. His chief-of-staff had arranged the special testing in return for a *gratis* speaking event for the organization. Slowly he remembered how surprised he had been to get the results that afternoon.

"So a man who scored mid-level grades throughout his college tenure qualified for MENSA, while Vincent McConnel, a man with a documented IQ of one-sixty-three, scored a miserable one-fifteen on his own MENSA exam? It was Vincent who switched tests with you. After all, only he was smart enough to know how to fudge the test so you would appear bright enough to pass, yet not so smart that they would request a re-test. No one else in your office at that time had that kind of computational ability."

Still flipping through the papers, Phelps was beginning to see that there may be something to her claims. The more he thought about it, the more he remembered being sure he had totally botched the test. Vincent had never told him of the switch, and with time he had come to embrace the success as his own. Now after years of believing that he was far above average, it was stunning to see proof that he had been fooled.

Then something in him turned from surprise to anger as he realized what a scandal like this would do to him. After all, he had campaigned as the smart candidate and frequently referred to his membership in the elite organization that was open only to those of genius IQs. If his political opponents got wind of this, it would be the most embarrassing scandal of his career. Thinking about his options, he switched to his default mode; *bellow and deny*.

"No one is going to believe you, and I'll have my spin doctors crush the story if you try to reveal this…this bullshit." The disgust was evident in his voice.

"Ahhh, again your limited intellect misleads you. A real genius would have already realized that I don't need to get any traction with this story. Once MENSA hears about this discrepancy, the first thing they will do is require a supervised re-test. If you refuse…then it'll be a real scandal with some meat on its bones. Just imagine the political cartoons of you wearing a dunce's cap and sitting in the corner like the fool. Every short-bus joke will end with your name, and people will begin to use Phelps as an adjective for stupidity and posery. No, Jefferson, this scandal will sell itself, and your rivals will see to that." Laying it all out for him, Alexis was silent while that sank in. She and Jamie had discussed this topic in depth, going so far as to even role-play the conversation to prepare the AI.

His eyes narrowing to slits, the President's thoughts turned dark. Clearly she had him at a disadvantage. Glancing up he could tell that Martin DeColle was already talking on his own cellphone, likely working with the NSA to trace the call. Cornered, he knew that he would need to silence this woman once he had the invention. Hence, his only option was to acquiesce until that milestone was achieved. But once that was done, *he would cut their throats*.

"I can't make any promises," He started out as Martin held up a handwritten note. Squinting to read the words, he was shocked to see that the NSA had traced the call; she was in the building. "But I will have to run these figures past the buyers. You do understand that the US Government is not actually purchasing this technology."

"Yes, I am aware that you have arranged for this technology to be sold exclusively to your biggest campaign contributors." Her tone icy, Alexis let slip her disdain for the man. "A new contract is printing now. In addition to the terms listed, you will release Jamie Sparks immediately."

Irritated once again by her demands, he shook his head angrily as he noticed the additional Secret Service agents filing through the door.

"Mister Sparks is being held on a valid FISA warrant at this time. Think of it as protective custody." Mocking her with his response, he enjoyed the opportunity to poke her in the eye verbally.

"I anticipated you were going to say that, which is why the price just went up to one-point-seven-five billion dollars." Leaving it at that, Alexis knew that his secretary Kelly was only seconds away from handing her boss the latest printouts.

"What!" Sitting up, Phelps was enraged. Squinting at another of Martin's hand written notes he was informed that the call had been traced to his own personal office in the next room. Flanked by agents, he finally understood why security had escalated so dramatically. She was quite literally in the next room. As if it were not enough that he was being harassed by a woman, he remembered that the Speaker of the House and Senate Majority Leader were still watching from the couches.

Their weapons drawn, two agents moved briskly through the side door and into his personal office. Feeling the tension of the moment, Phelps actually held his breath as he looked forward to seeing this woman in shackles.

"I'm not in there." Pleased with herself, Alexis crushed his hopes.

"So you hacked the phone system? That's…an act of espionage." A gravelly tone to his accusation, Phelps was thoroughly enraged as Kelly laid a fresh copy of the contract on his desk.

"I didn't hack the system; you seized my physical body illegally; then voluntarily allowed me access to your network. Instead of negotiating in good faith, you sent your storm troopers with an invalid warrant to seize property that was not rightfully yours. So, although this had been a most fascinating conversation, we are done here. Until you have our money, and a deed for the moon, do not attempt to contact us. When you do, we will only talk to Agent Jaramillo. As our designated advocate, she will need to be granted full access to the process. Any further infractions will result in severe financial penalties. Severe!" She repeated the word for clarity before letting the line go dead.

Keeping the anger bottled up, Phelps did his best to remain presidential. Seeing the two agents return from his office he knew that she had never been in there. Rising, he scooped up the MENSA tests before opening the desk drawer and shredding the documents.

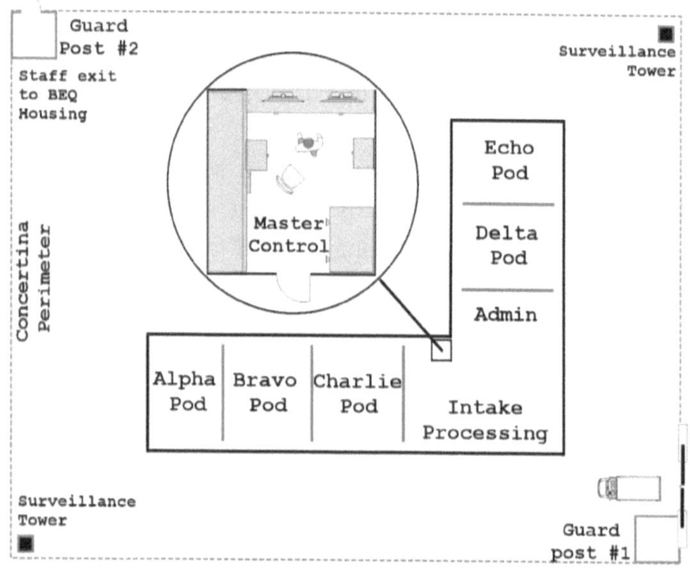

Station X-Ray

It had taken the bot known as Remi two days to make it through the air vents to station X-Ray's main control room. Known as Master Control, the little 15'x15' room was really just a collection of electronic control boxes, CCD monitors, and a chair for the operator. Miles of cabling from every corner of the facility terminated in that dark little room.

Seated before a row of video screens, the Master Control officer monitored traffic throughout the prison. With multiple banks of switches laid out to match the floor plan, he (or she) controlled every door in the facility. Hardened with reinforced walls and multilayer security glass, the room was virtually impregnable. Even the twin sallyport doors leading into the room were each two inches of layered steel controlled by an Adam-Folger lock system.

However, no one had ever expected to have their lofty command center penetrated by a device small enough to slip through the slats of an air vent. Once inside Remi had followed the cables through their access ports and up into the control panels where the switching systems resided. Although the design of these panels was considered to be classified, Jamie had been able to dredge up a surprising amount of technical data on them from the internet. Working with Alexis, the two had been able to determine how the systems functioned, and more importantly which switches controlled what doors. It had been this information that had been exploited.

Although Alexis had the ability to simply open up all of the doors between Jamie's cell and the main exit, that plan would have been wholly unfeasible as the perimeter was manned by half a dozen guards. With K-9 patrols and armed men everywhere, he would be unlikely to get more than a few feet. Besides, Jamie had no intention of merely fleeing the prison. When he left, it would be under his own terms.

Equipped with an assortment of tools, Remi had been hard at work for weeks now. Stripping wires, and exposing leads, the little bot had been engineered specifically to recharge its tiny batteries using the energy harvested from the switchboard's 5v control wires. Working in darkness the capable little robot had been responsible for a series of bizarre events throughout the facility. More than once the wrong doors had been opened at exactly the right time. In several cases injuries had resulted, diminishing the number of

Researchers available to interrogate. In fact, by the time that Jamie had even set foot on the compound, Remi had cut the number of inquisitors from 12 to 5. It had taken weeks of reconnaissance for the savant to determine which of the Researchers were incorruptible. Those that could not be manipulated were simply removed from service by hook or crook.

One of the most remarkable things about Master Control had been the imposing bank of CCD camera monitors. Although the MC officer had the ability to see almost every corner of the facility, there were only six monitors available. Hence, the officer was constantly switching his view to keep up with prisoner movement or just to see who was ringing the intercom at a particular door. Even more amazing was the fact that the cameras were essentially a direct feed; none of it was recorded. This had surprised Jamie and Alexis until they stopped to realize that the facility was a black site; very few records were maintained of this place. Those few rooms that were equipped with digital video recorders were typically set up in such a way as to capture the back of the Researcher's head while they worked. Whenever possible, they made overt attempts to keep the faces of the interrogators out of the picture.

After weeks of preparing for Jamie's arrival, little Remmi had accomplished much. With bare wires throughout the main panel assembly, the micro-bot could use a specially shielded leg to short out switches to doors throughout the facility. Unconcerned with escaping at the moment, the savant had been more interested in ensuring that he was housed in a specific room. To accomplish this they merely had to make the undesirable rooms unsuitable for habitation.

After driving the maintenance crew crazy for days with quirky doors and garbled comms from the intercom, Alexis had been able to create the illusion of a bad control board in the Alpha Pod control room. Although each door in the facility could be controlled remotely from Master control, each of the cell blocks sported its own localized control center where the officers working that pod could open and close their own cell doors without bothering the busy MC Officer. Convinced that the Alpha Pod control panel was unreliable, all prisoners had been shuffled to other rooms elsewhere. By the time that Jamie arrived at Station X-Ray there was conveniently only a single vacancy in the whole

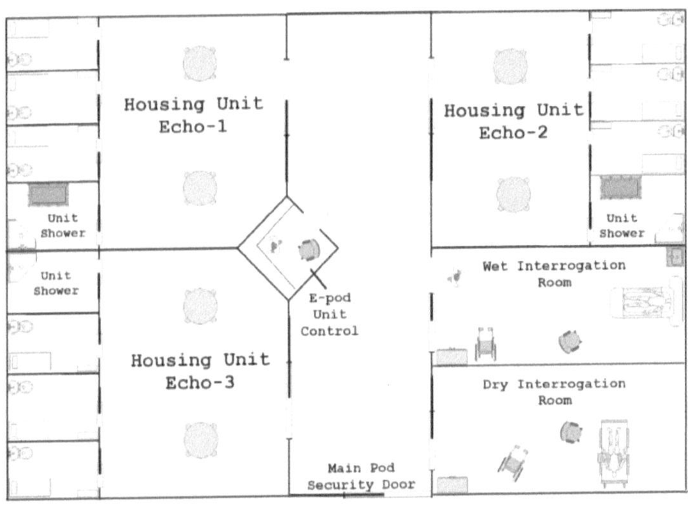

Echo Pod

place; E pod, room E2-2.

 Situated in the middle cell of three, Jamie's new home was separated from the outside world by nothing more than a foot or so of concrete roof. Beyond that the only barrier between him and freedom was the rooftop guard. But even that factor was simply an equation waiting to be solved.

Sitting in the corner of his cell Jamie did his best to ignore the loud music that thundered through the speakers in the ceiling. Intended as a means of tenderizing him for future interrogations, this technique told him that the staff were at a loss how to proceed. His research had indicated that this approach was primarily used on subjects who would find western culture and music offensive. While this tactic worked well on jihadists, it was largely inappropriate on the savant. Not only did it not set his nerves on edge, but he actually began to enjoy the thrash-rock they played. After all, being a fan of modern jazz's disjointed style and asymmetrical melodies, it was not that much of a stretch for Jamie to adapt to the sounds of bands like Anthrax or Pantera. Really, his only discomfort was trying to sleep in a room devoid of a mattress.

Forced to lie on the bare metal bunk, he had experienced a bit of stiffness in his bones. The staff had tried other factors like turning down the air conditioning to wear him down. This had been the chink in his big, fancy plan; the controls for the air conditioning system were kept in a separate utility closet on the second floor and far from Remi's reach. Forced to shiver on the floor, Jamie had felt no remorse for the things he had done to the researchers.

"Well, well, well. How is my special prisoner today?" Stepping through the door, Marco Asanté pretended to be pleased to see Jamie's discomfort. In truth he wished that more distress could have been heaped on the man. But with the facility down to a single Researcher, they had been limited.

"Piss off, ya pretty-boy faggot. If you'se lookin' fer a reach-around then you can talk to Mohamed in the next cell;

I hear he's queer like you." His accent clearly Jersey Jimbo, the savant was irritated at the mere sight of the agent.

"Ooooh, did someone not sleep well?" Bending over, Marco taunted the man from just a few feet away.

Remaining silent, Jamie tried to get some sleep on the concrete floor. Having studied Marco's psychological profile at length he knew that the biggest weapon he had for Marco was to simply ignore the man.

"Hey, I'm talking to you!" Kicking Jamie in the shins, Marco demanded a response.

"Get lost, paddy-wack, you ain't got no juice wit' me." Shrugging off Marco, the inventor never even opened his eyes. He knew that few things would irritate the agent like being disregarded.

Stomping over to Jamie's head, the agent roughly gripped him by the hair before yanking him into an upright sitting position.

"You wanna play fucking games with me?" Shaking him by the head, Marco shouted into the savant's face.

"What, do I look like yer mom? You want someone to touch ya inappropriately, then call home." Sneering, Jersey Jimbo was vitriolic as he spat out the words.

Surprised at the response, Marco stepped back with his mouth agape.

"What's wrong, Marco?" Momentarily pretending to be sympathetic, Jersey Jimbo's frown turned to a leering grin. "Don't like being reminded of them dirty little secrets bouncin' around yer pretty-boy head? All those men who visited your mom, every night, all night. Lemme ask you this Marky-Mark, how many of them guys visited you when they'se was done with yer Mom? Those guys who said they'se was just tuckin' ya in…but they did a helluva lot more than tuck ya in, didn't they? I'll betcha a million bucks that's the reason you like to take it in the ass; because ya got used to it that way, eh?"

Marco's blood froze in his veins at the things that Jamie said. It terrified him to hear these revelations from the man in the orange jumpsuit. It was as if Jamie had been able to peer into his mind.

"What the fuck…?" Momentarily forgetting himself, Marco's body language said that he had been pierced through the heart. Within seconds his automatic reflexes had kicked in as his expression hardened to a cruel grimace. "You little black motherfucker!"

Grabbing Jamie by the collar, the agent's fist lashed out as he struck the savant across the face multiple times. Rearing back for another swing, Marco felt someone grab his arm.

"Hey!" The staff member did his best to drag Marco back from Jamie. "Out!"

Shoving the agent out into the hallway, the Researcher slammed the door behind himself. Standing toe-to-toe with Marco, the professional interrogator leaned into him.

"What did I tell you? You're outta your league in there. He just played you like a fool and you totally fell for it, hook, line, and sinker." Refusing to budge out of his personal space, the Researcher was livid. "You violated the first rule of this business; you let him get under your skin. So instead of breaking him down, you just emboldened him and undid all our work up to this point. You stupid fuck!"

Surprised by the man's aggression, Marco was taken aback as he realized that it was true. He had lost control in there, and now the prisoner was laughing at him. Feeling a flood of emotions, his mind was scrambling to figure out how the inventor had known those things about him. He had never revealed those details to anyone, ever. How the hell had he known all that? It never occurred to the agent that Jamie had simply studied the extensive psych tests that all federal agents must undergo during recruitment. It was amazing what could be revealed through an MMPI's wide ranging questions.

"Good going, Honcho, you just set us back a week. Now get the fuck outta here and let the professionals handle it." Refusing to budge, the Researcher made it clear that there was no alternative. "And while you're at it, maybe you should get some counseling for whatever the hell is rattling about in that head of yours. Man, you're one fucked up piece of work."

In his cell, Jamie was well aware of the fact that they were likely still watching him. Rendering one of Jersey Jimbo's leering grins, he made sure to face them. He wanted them to feel the sting of defeat.

Through the slats of the air vent, Alexis watched her creator via the eyes of drone #1. As much as she wanted to burn out the solenoid to the door mechanism to keep anyone else from entering the room, she had her orders. Only when the time was right would she bar further entry to his pod.

"Colonel Quinn, what exactly do you mean when you say that you have been unsuccessful at cracking this man?" Raising one eyebrow, Martin DeColle spoke to the speakerphone on Phelps' desk.

"Exactly that." The Colonel's voice was as firm as concrete. "I was already short-handed on Researchers before he arrived, and since he has been here I have lost four more."

"Lost?" Phelps raised an eyebrow as he reclined in his big office chair. With his jacket opened in the front, his paunch seemed to protrude more than unusual.

"Yes sir; two in the brig, two more in the hospital, and the remaining man seems disinclined to spend any time in the room with the subject. We have been wearing him down, but it's a slow process." Even through the tinny speaker-phone the Colonel's voice seemed to command respect.

"Just who the hell do these guys think they are?" Sitting back, Phelps cursed the Sparks brothers as a scowl crossed his face.

Crossing his stubby legs, Drummond Heckler cleared his throat before speaking.

"Just give 'em whatever the hell they want!" The tenor of his voice seemed to make the room pause. It was uncustomary for anyone to talk like that to the President.

"Excuse me?" Martin tried to clarify what the man was saying.

"I believe what my brother is trying to say is that we are happy to pay his asking price, and that we would just prefer if you made the deal instead of all this cat and mouse fiasco." Showing a stretched smile, Robert Heckler turned to look the President square in the eye.

"Uh…" Unsure if they were admonishing him or just angry about the circumstances, Phelps paused momentarily. "These men will be dealt with, and you will get your technology."

"You've been saying that for weeks, and all you've done is alienate these people and cost us more money." Standing up, the man in the expensive blue suit immediately buttoned his jacket as he approached the desk. "Give them the damned money and anything else they ask for, and do it right fucking now."

Watching the two men rise from the far couches, Martin DeColle could tell that the Heckler brothers were not in a good mood, or at least no longer interested in pretending they were. As a long time political operative, Martin knew the power and political influence these men wielded.

"Sir, that is no way to talk to the President." Martin stepped forward.

"Be quiet, errand boy. The adults are talking." Robert Heckler dismissed the chief-of-staff as he drew up to the edge of the desk.

"Jefferson, we don't care about a measly billion dollars." Buttoning his jacket, Drummond Heckler fixed his dour gaze upon the president. "All we care about is getting that damned technology in our hands, but you and your Keystone cops have only made that less and less certain every day since this started."

"Get us the damned invention!" Clearly losing his temper, Robert Heckler growled as he looked down at the president.

"I thought the nine-year license was too short?" Pointing out things as he understood them, Phelps could feel the heat from the two men.

"JUST GET THE FUCKING INVENTION AND STOP THINKING!" His voice echoing off of the walls of the oval office, Drummond Heckler left no doubt as to his true feelings on the matter.

Sitting up abruptly, President Phelps cared not for being yelled at in front of his own staff.

"I will not have you coming into my office and showing such disrespect for the…office of the president." Injecting his own gravelly tone into words, Phelps stood his ground. By his thinking, Washington was his town, and no one talked to him that way in his domain.

"Perhaps my brother was a little coarse in his demands." The man in the grey suit gave a crocodile smile before continuing. "Jefferson, we don't care about the contractual obligations, we don't even care about the cost. We care only about possession of the technology. Once we have it in our hot, little hands we will make it our own. So I say this with all sincerity; Jefferson Phelps, you get us that damned invention immediately. No more negotiating, no more games, **just get us the damned antigravity!"**

Phelps jumped visibly as the man's voice rose to a shout at the end. He could not remember Drummond ever losing his calm like that before. Nonetheless, he cared not for having terms dictated to him in his own office.

"I will not have you speak to me that way. I am the-" Phelps found himself cut off before he could finish.

"Oh, shut the hell up!" His face red now, Drummond raised his voice to drown out the president. "PAY HIM WHAT HE WANTS AND GET US THE FUCKING INVENTION!"

"Yes." A little more calm, Robert Heckler never even blinked at his brother's outburst. "By all means, acquire us the damned technology."

The room was silent as the staff looked between their president and the two men in hand-sewn suits. No one ever talked that way to Phelps. People had been fired, and subsequently blackballed, for far less than what these two men had just done. Yet there they stood, resolute in their ire for the man behind the desk.

"Jeff." Knowing how much the president hated having his name shortened, the man in blue leaned forward onto his knuckles. "You get us this technology by tomorrow morning or we will put someone else in that chair. Bob McDaniels will dance to whatever tune we play."

"Did you just threaten me…?" Aghast, Phelps intended to put an end to this disrespect.

"No, Jefferson, we *guarantee* that someone else will be sitting in your chair if you do not close this deal." Pulling a cigar out of his pocket, Drummond used his other hand to produce a small clipper to nip the tip off the stogie. Ignoring Martin DeColle's insistence that the oval office was a non-smoking zone, the industrialist lit the hand-rolled cigar in a flash of smoke.

"You do not walk into the office of the president and make threats, no matter who you are." Standing now, Phelps glared back at the men.

"Jeff, you think those flying negroids are the only ones who know about your little MENSA scandal?" Showing a villainous smile for the first time that morning, Robert Heckler allowed his teeth to show.

"Or all of those interns…" Muttering between puffs on his cigar, Drummond seemed unconcerned that he was reeking up the oval office as if it were a pool hall.

"Or the Philly deal." Giving a snicker, Robert added his own detail.

"Or the Philippines arrangement. That alone would be sure to put Bobby behind the Resolute Desk by week's end." Smoke leaking from his mouth as he spoke, Drummond seemed truly pleased with himself.

"Are you…extorting the President of the United States?" Phelps was aghast at the threats.

"Extortion? No, Jeffy." A broad grin split Robert Heckler's face. "It would be our patriotic duty to let the world know of these indiscretions. Now you understand this; we put you in that chair, and we can remove you from it just as easily."

"Get us the fucking invention. Sign the fucking contract, and promise them whatever the hell they want. Get us the antigravity or we deal with the next guy." His smile long gone, Drummond scowled before the two brothers turned away in unison.

Watching them go, Phelps was bewildered. Gone was his illusion of power as he realized that there was no alternative but to acquiesce to their orders.

"What was the Philippines arrangement?" DeColle asked as soon as they were out of earshot.

"Shut up." A bitter look had washed over the president's face as he dismissed his chief-of-staff. "Get that agent…whatever the hell her name is, the Mexican woman, get her on the phone…NOW!"

"Yes sir." Martin DeColle knew better than to object.

Jenna had been stunned by the call. Despite Jack's warning that it would happen, it had jolted her to be talking directly to the president again. She picked up a vibe though, as if he did not like her much. The conversation had been largely one-sided. When Jefferson Phelps spoke, people were expected to listen.

But there had been something else in his tone that had set her on edge. When she inquired about the deed to the moon he had seemed surprised.

"He says the document must be signed by Congress." Jenna informed Phelps of the proviso detailed in the contract.

"Oh? Whatever. Just tell him that we're putting it all together." Dismissive, Phelps droned over her objections.

Eying her phone as the screen went blank, she considered her next call carefully. Racing through the details in her head, the agent's sharp eye settled on the camera built into the phone. Staring into the electronic eye, she tried to work out all the angles. Flipping her phone over, she eyed the main camera. One thing she had never been able to explain was how Jack had found her there in the torture shack. The agents that had kidnapped her had made a point of pulling the battery out of her phone; she had seen it laying there on the little table. More importantly, how had Jack even known she'd been kidnapped?

Still examining the camera, the considered the possibility that her phone had been hacked. Although the FBI phones featured hardened data sharing protocols, there was always the possibility that someone smart enough could crack it. Access to her camera feed would give them a view of everything she did. It also explained why her battery seemed to run dry faster than usual lately.

And that is where Special Agent Jenna Jaramillo ran into her first ethical question about her mission. On one hand she was angry that Jack may have bugged her phone, yet grateful because it had led to her being rescued from the shrieking shack. The brothers had saved her from a vat of acid, yet she had her orders…orders that she was not entirely comfortable with. There had been something in Phelps' blustery rambling that told her he was lying about it all. The only objective the man seemed at all genuine about was that she bring in the remaining brother and his female sidekick. On this point he was nearly rabid. *Everything would be taken care of…* He had muttered the phrase more than once while he lectured.

"Jack, er, Mister Sparks, the older one, he wants his brother freed from captivity before he is willing to negotiate further." Jenna had tried hard to get that comment in between Phelps' monologues. *The man certainly enjoys hearing himself talk.*

"No, out of the question. The man remains in protective custody. We have to ensure that they and their secrets are kept safe from our enemies." Jefferson Phelps was resolute on that point.

"Okay, but Jack said that if that was your answer then the price goes up another quarter billion dollars." Jenna was surprised at the silence on the line. She had expected the president to shout, or at least drone loudly. Instead there was silence for a long moment.

"Yes, we had that conversation already. The purchasers have agreed to pay the extra quarter billion penalty. Sold." Letting the line go dead, President Jefferson Phelps hung up abruptly.

Sitting back in his chair, Phelps let out a sigh as the far door popped open the least little bit. Poking her head in uncertainly, Kelly seemed to dread her task. Darting forward, she laid the updated contract on the desk before her president.

"This just popped out of my printer. The coversheet said to disregard all previous contracts." Shrinking back, the secretary wanted to be anywhere but there. Exiting quickly, she wanted no part of that phone call. The President and his inner circle had been insufferable since the Queen Mary episode began.

Picking up the papers to examine them, Phelps could see that they were identical to the previous contracts, the only change being that the purchaser's shell corporations were now listed.

"Should I have White House counsel examine these first?" It occurred to Jefferson that it might be a good idea to have a lawyer look at the document.

"It's not your concern." A fresh grey suit, Drummond Heckler dismissed the question. "The business deal is between us and him. We get the technology, and you get to safeguard him for the rest of his life. Very simple."

"Why'd he list your companies first?" Squinting at the contract, the Robert Heckler seemed bewildered at the order of the names on the extensive contract.

"Quit your fussing and go find two billion dollars in cash." Casual aplomb, the older of the two brothers actually smiled.

"I thought it was only a billion and three quarters?" Furrowing his beefy brows, the man in blue seemed unsure of himself.

"It is currently, but I have a feeling that Jeffrey is going to do something stupid and cost us another quarter billion dollar penalty." Dryly, he chewed the cigar while looking President Phelps right in the eye. "We need an address where we can deliver twenty tons of cash?"

It had been another convoluted day at the office for Jenna. Although she was no longer on admin leave, her status as POC to the brothers had put her in a special category at the FBI. Too important to be dragged away to other investigations, the young Latina agent found herself in a holding pattern. Worse yet, even though she had no control over the Sparks brothers, she felt the heat when Jack failed to call all day. Between her SAIC constantly checking her progress, and the guys from IT examining her phone to be sure it was still working, she had spent her entire day in this listless mode, waiting for a call that never came.

It had finally become too much for her. Finding her way out the front door by 1630 hours, she silently gave them the slip. Picking her way down the steps, she was surprised to see a battered 1965 Mustang convertible covered in grey primer. Even more shocking was the sight of Jack E. Sparks standing by the door with a smile on his face. As if oblivious to who worked in the building, he seemed unconcerned with the agents that passed him on their way up the stairs.

"Feel like getting some dinner?" Giving a playful smile, the inventor jerked his head towards the car behind him. "I know this really great Mexican food place up in LA. Rooftop service, the best salsa on Earth…"

Jenna pretended to weigh the offer as she looked him up and down. "Why Mexican food, for my ethnic benefit?"

Taken aback, Jack had never even considered that the proposal could be skewed that way.

"Naw, I just like Mexican food. Tacos rule, baby!" Flashing a goofy grin, he stepped to one side and held open the door for her. "Or I know this really awesome little Greek place. They make these Gyro sandwiches that're soooo tall you get a Charlie-horse in your jaw just trying to get the thing in your mouth. Messy as hell, too, but oh sooo good."

There was something about his rapid-fire way of talking that made her smile. She also had to give him points for looking her in the eyes consistently. Most of the time men looked everywhere but her eyes.

"Y'know, I got nothing against tacos or sliced lamb sandwiches, but I'm just an ordinary American girl with pedestrian tastes, and right now I could kill for a burger."

"Oh?" He asked with a raised eyebrow.

"And not one of those supersize-my-waistline burgers. I just want a classic American hamburger, nothing fancy." Standing with arms folded, she waited for him to agree to her terms.

"I know just the place." Flicking his eyes between Jenna and the open door, he used his eyebrows to gesture towards an imminent departure.

"Classic burger." She reminded him before relenting and climbing into the waiting car.

Twenty minutes later they sat parked on the edge of a little puffy cloud while enjoying a milk shake and a cheeseburger.

"You sure you didn't want fries?" Jack asked as if he'd fly right back to the restaurant.

"No, it violates the Ricky-Tikki-Tavi diet." She said with a smirk. It was the first time she had ever mentioned it to anyone else.

"Ricky-Tikki-Tavi?" Jack considered it. "The Rudyard Kipling character?"

The agent gave a chortle at that. "Sure. I was actually thinking of the animated movie, but Kipling was in there too."

"I've heard of a lotta diets, this being California and all, but that is a new one on me." Taking a bite of his burger the inventor gave her a sideways look as he awaited further clarification.

Giving some thought to how she would phrase it, Jenna started out hesitantly.

"See, Rikki was a mongoose, and when he was a little baby his mother taught him to never fill up on dinner, never gorge himself, to always leave a little wanting. See, if he fills up then he'll be too slow to defeat the cobras. She taught him to never stuff himself, always stay light and fast. I love French fries, but they're really nothing but a bag of grease, and I need to be quicker than the cobras." Flashing the badge that was clipped to her belt, she made her point understood.

Jack could not help but laugh out loud. Not because he thought it was foolish, but because of the candid manner that she had confessed that little philosophy of hers.

"You're a cheap date. I was ready to spring for real French food." Holding up a French fry as a contrast, Jack kidded her.

"Date?" She raised an eyebrow. "I thought this was a negotiation."

"Aren't all dates a negotiation?" Feigning innocence, Jack pointed out the logic.

"Not a date." Waving a dismissive finger, she let him know where they stood. "Negotiation. Don't get all moony-eyed on me; we're here to negotiate the sale of your technology. This is business."

"Fair enough." Jack agreed. "But if you're not busy after your mission is over, I'd like to see you on a personal basis."

"Hmmmph." Jenna cast him a sideways look that dripped in skepticism. "Unlikely; bureau policy and all."

Despite her rigid front, Jack knew better than to believe her dismissal. He had seen enough genuine rejections to know better. Glancing out the window he calculated their progress as the car made its way over a bumpy layer of cumulous clouds. Seeing a pair of dots silhouetted against the bright backdrop, he had a feeling they were not alone. With Alexis in his ear, he quickly had confirmation of his suspicions.

Never letting on, Jack chatted away happily. Truly, there was nowhere else he would rather be. Jenna was so unlike the bimbos he usually dated. College-educated, well read, she had no trouble keeping up with the conversation. Even when he got technical, her eyes never glazed over. In fact, he was pretty sure that he could detect the faintest twinkle in her eyes as they talked. Still, he knew to respect her professional distance. As it was, he actually found her sense of duty admirable. He would have been disappointed had she given into his romantic overtures so easily.

"So what made you become a federal agent?" Taking opportunity at a lull in the conversation, Jack asked the question he had been pondering since first seeing her image on Jamie's desk.

Although it was an honest question, it was one that Jenna fielded *ad nauseam*. It seemed like every man wanted to know why she was working instead of having babies in the suburbs. They never actually said the latter half, but it was always implied. Not interested in telling that tired old story, she flipped the question on her host.

"Why'd you become an inventor?" she asked.

Shrugging, Jack had to think about it. *No one had ever asked him that.*

"I like to build stuff that no one else has." Shrugging, he answered simply enough. "It's what I was born to do. When I sleep at night I dream of new circuits and better ways to design."

Jenna accepted that as she watched a fluffy cloud slide past her window. "And that's why I'm a federal agent; because at night I dream of better ways to catch bad guys."

"So are you like a dog dreaming of a squirrel?" He asked with a playful smile before impersonating a pooch having a good dream. "Woof, woof!"

Jenna laughed as she imagined it. In her childhood she'd had a dog named Bosco who gave just such a show; barking and scrabbling his feet in ethereal pursuit of some rabbit or mailman. It made her feel warm inside to conjure up that memory. The image was even funnier when she thought of herself doing it under the blankets.

"It's just the way I'm wired." She shrugged, concealing her amusement at his antics. "Some people are wired to be healers, others are wired to be builders or leaders…"

"But you're wired to be a protector." Jack summed it up. "One of those among us who's specifically skilled for battle; the huntress. In a previous life I betcha you were a lioness."

That drew a laugh from her. "I'm surprised to hear you endorse reincarnation. I thought all of you scientist types were agnostics, no scientific evidence of God and all that."

Jack had to sit back and give that a good belly laugh before turning back to her.

"No scientific evidence of God." The inventor seemed to find that point particularly humorous. "Allow me to put that statement into perspective. Imagine two cavemen sitting by their camp fire cookin' a dead dawg, and one turns to the other and says *nooo scientific evidence offf God"*

Jenna raised an eyebrow as she waited for him to explain.

"See, it's stupid to rule out the existence of anything just because our primitive human technology can't prove it. I mean honestly, what would you use to search for God if you were looking for him; radar? Infra-red? A litmus test? Hell, we're so primitive we only just invented flying cars. We don't even have tricorders yet, and we act like we have amassed enough knowledge of the universe to conclude the nature of a being capable of building all existence from nothing more than gravity and hydrogen? Ya gotta admit; that's a helluva engineering feat. Fact is; humans are only ten thousand years out a loincloth. We haven't even managed to escape from our own solar system and yet we act like we have a lock on the true nature of the universe? That's just arrogant. Humanity has yet to even fall off the galactic turnip truck and we're thinking we're all that."

Jenna had to laugh at that. "Now that you mention it, it is setting a pretty low bar."

"It's to be expected. An ant thinks it can see the whole world from its perspective. We're no different. Where we differ from the lowly ant is that humans have the ability to comprehend that our field of vision is limited. It is our hubris that makes us blind."

"Quite the philosopher, you missed your calling; you should have been a minister."

"Yeah, I dunno about that. I'm not the church type. That's just another buncha cavemen thinking they got God all figured out in a nice, neat little package. *As if.*" Jack laughed out loud as it occurred to him that the last time he had been in a house of worship had been his parents' funeral, more than a decade earlier.

Speaking quietly into his ear, Alexis updated the inventor on the speck that lingered in the distance. As if using the clouds to hide, the tiny dot seemed to peek out only intermittently. Returning his attention to the lady who sat beside him, Jack left the driving to Alexis.

"So have you ever considered doing something else?" Having seen her reading list, he knew she had more than one facet.

Jenna had to give it thought. There had been many professions out there she found fascinating, but none she felt truly suited for. Searching her memory for that sensation of dreamy wonderment she hit upon one occupation that had been an early favorite.

"When I was little I wanted to be an astronaut so bad. I was going to fly the next generation of shuttles, explore the solar system."

"But you didn't. Why not?" It interested Jack to know why she felt she had not achieved that dream.

"Oh," She responded as if it was a massive question. "Getting into NASA is... And I'm not the scientist type. If you need some thugs in space rounded up then I'd be a great astronaut, but all the science, and the math. Plus you have to have a college degree to even be considered, and that wasn't me, so instead I joined the army."

Jack took note of that last point. "But you did eventually get a college degree, didn't you?"

"I did." There was a touch of pride to her voice. It had been hard work getting a degree while actively serving as an MP. There had been so many times that the math requirements nearly made her give up the whole thing. But in the end she had managed to come out of it with a certificate that authenticated her as one of the anointed few.

Glancing ahead as the car broke through the clouds Jack could see the California desert before them. In a steady descent, the Mustang seemed to be headed towards the drab gray compound ahead.

"Here's an interesting factoid; the smartest man on Earth has no college degree. True fact. My brother never even completed a semester of college, got denied equivalency testing. They practically had him escorted off campus." Jack returned his attention to the passenger seat.

"I've never met him, but from what I've read, college would have been like living in slow motion for a mind like your brother's." Locking eyes with him, Jenna said nothing about their obvious descent. She had a feeling he would tell her when he was ready. With a loaded pistol clipped to her belt she felt a measure of confidence.

"You never met him?" Jack pretended to be surprised. "Oh, well everyone should get to meet my brother; it's what I like to refer to as a unique experience."

Jack's devious smile hinted at their destination. Looking up over the hood Jenna could make out the tall fences topped with concertina wire. She could tell that the way the fence was topped, with the brackets angled inwards, that the barrier was designed to keep people IN, not out. There was just something about the windowless facility and its surveillance towers that screamed of a custodial facility.

"Jack?" She asked hesitantly as it became apparent that they were on a collision course with the compound.

"You will need this." Handing her a folded sheet of paper he knew she would unfold it right away.

"A new contract?" She was surprised when she noticed the final price; $2,000,000,000, in cash. As if predicting her next question, someone had highlighted a line in the special clauses section. "I don't understand."

"Stories make the most sense at the end." Shrugging, Jack offered nothing further as the car settled into the middle of the compound. Already they could hear the commotion from the nearby guard shack at the front gate. Their arrival had not gone unnoticed.

"Where are we?" she asked skeptically as her hands folded the contract up neatly.

"This is Station X-Ray. They are keeping my brother here." He gestured towards the main building as more alarms could be heard.

"Where the hell is here?" She seemed surprised at the remote locale. Outside of the fence there was nothing but desert.

"This is but one of over a hundred such facilities throughout the country. Gitmo isn't America's only black site." Nodding agreeably, Jack had been surprised to learn those same facts just a few weeks ago.

"No, not on American soil…" She seemed unconvinced.

"You are welcome to see for yourself, and while you're in there, can you check on my brother, please." Ever aware of the men with automatic weapons converging on them, Jack gave her a terse smile before gesturing to the contract in her pocket. "After all, you are the designated

POC for this little exchange, by authority of the President of these here United States."

"Why did you raise the price again?" There were too many blanks in the equation for Jenna's comfort.

"You should ask the gunship that followed us here. It's out there, orbiting, waiting for me to try and leave." A flick of his head, Jack indicated back the way they'd come. "The NSA installed a tracking app on your phone after you were kidnapped."

Jenna could see at a glance that he was serious. It was a stark departure from his usual mannerisms. No humor, no playful grin, he had said it as if it were published fact.

"Out of the vehicle!" The man's voice was accompanied by the sound of more boots approaching. Distinguishable in the background was the sound of his safety being disabled as he held a submachine gun on the vehicle.

"It's been a pleasure, but this is where we part ways Agent Jaramillo." Making no move to exit the vehicle, Jack indicated towards her door.

In her mind she considered the possibilities. As she weighed her options it occurred to her that this was all just part of their elaborate plan. While the cop in her instinctively wanted to bring in the second brother, she realized that she was in no position to do anything but keep her hands in the air as the guards shouted for her to exit the vehicle. Giving the inventor one last dour look, she realized he had engineered this situation intentionally. Glancing at the back seat, she could not help but notice the helmet and space suit piled up there.

"Go take care of my brother." Jack nodded twice.

Exhaling sharply, Jenna did her best to exit the vehicle while keeping her hands in plain sight. With her credentials momentarily hidden by her jacket, all the guards saw was a woman wearing a holstered weapon. Immediately on alert, the three guards on that side of the vehicle forgot all about the battered Mustang as they directed the agent to lie face down.

Jack turned to face the lone security officer on his side of the car. Taller than the others, and a complexion too dark to be Caucasian, the inventor recognized Officer Taylor from file photos. With Alexis whispering in his ear, he knew exactly what to say.

"Yo, bro." Jack gave a cheery smile. "You didn't get that promotion."

"Outta the car!" Initially firm in his tone, the guard seemed to hesitate. "What the hell you say?"

"You didn't get the promotion. Cap'n gave it to Wilson." Jack shrugged haplessly.

"Wilson?" The tip of the weapon dropped just the least bit as Officer Taylor looked Jack over. "Get the fuck outta here wit' that."

"He did; Cap'n promoted his secretary-slash-girlfriend." Jack tried to appear sympathetic as he noticed that the little submachine gun had drooped significantly while Taylor considered this information. Taking the opportunity, Jack enabled the disaffinity device. Lurching straight up into the sky, the little Mustang actually stirred up a plume of dust with its hasty exit.

Rising straight up, Jack knew to leverage his strengths. Although he doubted his little flying car could outrun an AH64 Apache gunship, he knew for sure that he could out climb it.

From his vantage in the front seat, Chief Warrant Officer William Blevins could see the little Mustang shoot straight up into the sky. Doing his best to keep a visual on the fast moving target, he bemoaned the fact that the Apache was not really designed for this kind of mission. Despite being an excellent killing machine, it was really designed for ground targets. Although the gunship sported eight optically guided Hellfire missiles, each capable of destroying the most hardened armor on the planet, Blevins was unsure if they would be effective against such a quick airborne target as the Mustang. That left the chin gun to do the job. The 30mm cannon was fully loaded with combat rounds, each easily identified by the black and gold bands on the projectile.

"He's jamming us hard." Blevins worked the weapons controls. "I can't get a lock with the Hellfires. I think he's jamming that too...?"

"How the hell do you jam an optically guided missile?" The pilot was bemused. Though he only had conditional orders to fire, he wanted to be ready if the rabbit chose to run. Switching to guns, he tried to keep the target box on the little Mustang as it soared above him. Climbing as fast as the Apache was capable; the helicopter was just beginning to catch up when the little Ford suddenly reversed and began a rapid descent.

At the moment that the Mustang was about to pass the rising helicopter, it released a small flock of drones. No bigger than the cockroaches that had surveyed the Queen Mary, they immediately swarmed towards the chopper. Recoiling, Blevins was sure they'd be sucked up into the engines and cause foreign object damage [FOD] to the gunship.

But once the swarm of digital insects got within a few meters, instead of making contact, they each illuminated brightly. Like a miniature supernova, the drones were designed to consume themselves in a blinding flash of synchronized light.

While the effect would normally have been underwhelming at this time of day, the little drones were specifically engineered to emit their light in a very narrow range. Though mostly invisible to the naked eye, the flash was designed not to harm the humans, but to blind the onboard optical systems. Immediately the visual systems inside of their helmets displayed a solid wall of snow, but only for the briefest of moments.

"I can't see!" Blevins shouted into his headset.

"We're under attack!" The pilot's voice was loud enough to drown out his gunner's. There was just a hint of panic to his voice as the helicopter jolted sharply.

His vision now cleared, the pilot nosed the chopper forward in an effort to catch the little Ford. Fully incensed, he had no desire to tolerate any more guff from the fleeing vehicle. Seeing the Mustang heading west, he took it to mean it was heading for the coast. His orders were specific; engage the target if it appears to be attempting to flee the country or may otherwise fall into enemy hands.

Twisting the helicopter at the bottom of a dive, the gunship gyrated as it tried to stay with the little car. Unable to outrun the AH65, the Mustang would instead climb or descend rapidly, leaving the chopper scrambling to keep up. Ever cautious of being caught in another swarm of drones, the pilot dropped back where he could get a better gun shot. Aiming his helmet, he managed to bracket the Ford before squeezing the trigger.

The entire gunship rattled as the chin gun spat out a series of 30mm rounds. Designed to penetrate light armor and personnel carriers, it had no trouble poking holes in the Mustang. The first rounds caught the vehicle in the back, spinning it violently. Using the integral display in his helmet, he only had to aim his head at the little Ford to again aim the cannon.

"Dood!" Blevins was surprised at what his pilot had done.

"He was runnin' for the coast." The aviator's voice echoed through his headset a split second before the gunship shook again.

The second burst of fire tore the Mustang nearly in half. Igniting the fuel in the tank caused the entire vehicle to erupt in an orange billow. Dropping immediately, the little Ford trailed a long finger of inky black smoke.

Jenna had been handcuffed, searched, and pulled to her feet before she heard the cannon fire. Turning, she was able to see the distant fireball as the Ford erupted. She only had a few seconds to watch the burning speck plummet before her captors yanked her away.

Still in shock at the sight of Jack's unwarranted death, she was finally beginning to put it all together. Remembering the passage he had underlined on the contract in her pocket, it all made sense now. Somehow he had known that they would try to remove him from the equation. In hindsight it made sense; *they had the brother they wanted*, and likely Jack was only complicating things for them on the outside. But that left the question; if the brothers had foreseen these events then why had they not merely avoided them? Something just did not add up to her. *Why would Jack knowingly get himself killed?*

She found herself hauled into a small outer office where a corporal sat at a computer terminal. Leaving two guards to hold Jenna there, the leader of the security force entered the office and had a short discussion with the base commander. Within a few seconds, Colonel Quinn was stepping through the door, surprised to see Jenna standing there handcuffed. Looking over her credentials, he gave a deep scowl.

"This is a private facility. You're trespassing." He glared at the agent as if she were a raw recruit.

"I'm here by order of the President, to confirm the health and welfare of James Sparks." Making a point of looking down at her pocket, she gestured to the folded paperwork that extended. "I have an updated contract as well."

Reading the contract over, the Colonel contemplated these new details.

"Shall I put her in a cell?" The corporal asked.

"What?" Quinn looked up irritated. "Shut up."

"Yes sir." Clamming up, the guard realized that he had crossed a line.

"Like I said, I come on the very highest authority." Confident, Jenna was already tired of being handcuffed.

"The problem is…" Quinn trailed off as he nodded his head towards the door. "We already have a federal agent here to negotiate the transaction."

Turning, Jenna was surprised at the sight of her ex-husband standing in the doorway. Marco seemed eminently pleased to see *her* wearing the handcuffs this time.

"No, I'm the negotiator, she's their *advocate*." Emphasizing the last part, he tried to put a dark connotation on her task.

"Someone needs to check on him. You just killed his brother." Her tone was vitriolic as she spat out the words.

"Yeah, I know." Marco gave a guffaw as he pulled a phone from his pocket. "I got some really great footage. This new T-one has a four-K video camera built right in; it's remarkable."

Flipping the device around so she could see, he had managed to catch much of the aerial encounter on digital film. Still handcuffed, Jenna instinctively lashed out with a perfect scissor kick, sending Marco's brand new cell phone crashing into the ceiling at almost fifty miles an hour. The sheer number of pieces that ricocheted in every direction only confirmed the force of the impact.

"FUCK!" Shaking his hand, Marco's eyes were wide with anger. As the shards hit the ground it was clear that the phone was a complete wash.

"Oh!" Jenna feigned surprise before her eyebrows furrowed tightly in anger. "I guess little Marky-Mark is gonna need to buy a new camera to take candid videos in the men's room. Ooops."

Incensed, he rushed forward and slapped her hard across the face. Immediately the other security officers in the room moved to physically separate them. Jenna was shouting to the Colonel to arrest her ex for assault on a federal officer, and Marco was insisting that destruction of his new phone was the bigger felony.

"Enough!" Using his most commanding voice, Quinn brought the room to silence. Contract in hand, he preferred to focus on the mission. With the White House breathing down his neck he had no desire to have his career derailed by this single event.

"Corporal Meeks; uncuff her and return her credentials."

"What?" Marco objected loudly before being silenced by a hard look from the Colonel.

"There will be no charges, no reports filed. This is a black site, and nothing that happens here is reported because this place doesn't exist in the first place. You were never here, Station X-Ray does not exist, and there really is no spoon."

"Is that so…?" Rubbing her wrists, Jenna seemed as surprised as Marco to hear this. Still feigning surprise, her fist shot out and caught her ex-husband in the side of the face, sending his head spinning.

"That didn't just happen." Shaking her head, she remained impassive in her delivery.

"You're…you're gonna let her get away with that?" Marco was positively stunned that the Colonel had not ordered his security men intervene.

"Well, you did slap the lady while she was handcuffed. Where I come from real men do not smack women around. Do it again and I'll let her whip your ass in the rec yard. However, we have a mission to focus on, so the two of you will refrain from hostilities or I will lock you in a cell."

"Unlawful restraint of a federal officer?" Marco scowled at the threat.

"What part of the term black-site do you not understand? I'm breaking no laws because this place does not exist, and you were never here. Technically this facility isn't even America; it's the diplomatic property of the

People's Republic of Yikzakistan." Sitting on the edge of the desk, the Colonel gave a stretched smile. As a military man he did not cotton to these disruptions. It was all Tom-foolery by his account.

"Yikzakistan?" Jenna gave that a snort of appreciation. To the best of her memory there was no such nation. "What about my weapon?"

"Secured in the armory until you leave. No firearms inside of the facility." The Colonel's frown had a tendency to turn slightly upwards whenever he addressed Jenna. "It'll take a little while to verify your credentials and get the prisoner ready."

Phil Dobson had been a Researcher for more than a decade. Having started out as an enlisted man, he had moved up to warrant officer, then finally civilian contractor. A master at breaking men, he had bent the will of thousands during his professional life. Until just recently he would have believed he could break anyone. But after watching Jamie derail his predecessors he was growing worried. The little savant seemed to know each of the men before they even walked in the room. *Knew them well.*

This worried Phil. If he confronted Jamie, what would the little savant throw on the table about him? He had heard about how the video of Devon and the Commander's daughter had been played on the Colonel's computer. How had Jamie arranged that? How could he possibly have cracked the DoD mail server and hijacked the Colonel's desktop PC while he himself was incarcerated? *Of course he didn't do it...he had outside help*, thought Phil in his analytical way.

Glancing up at the cameras that recorded the sessions in 4K resolution, it occurred to him that if Jamie's friends could have hacked the Colonel's PC, could they have control of the cameras and DVRs? Was he being watched now? It was all beginning to make sense, all those accidents just before Sparks' arrival, the doors that were accidentally opened. Somehow it was all connected to this prisoner.

With a checkered past of his own, Phil had no desire to have his truths revealed during an interrogation. Considering what Jamie had known about Devon and Tomlinson, it terrified him to think of the kind of dirt the savant may have on him. After watching how fast Jamie had spun Asanté, it made Phil leery of even setting foot in the man's cell.

It was for this reason that the former enlisted man chose to tenderize Jamie before climbing into the ring with him. Rather than grinding him in an interrogation room, he would chill the inmate in a cold, bunkless cell while blaring techno rock interspersed with thrash. For Jamie, he turned it up to eleven.

"You can quit your stalling." Colonel Quinn strolled into the observation booth. Really just a walk-in closet outfitted with half a dozen monitors, it permitted them to watch every move the prisoner made. The granular ability of the system allowed the researchers to easily evaluate the emotional state of their charges.

"He's not ready yet, but I can go in if you order it." Phil sidestepped the allegation that he had been stalling.

"No, just tell him that his demands have been agreed to, and his designated advocate is here from the FBI. Then get him cleaned up and ready to divulge his design. Make sure he understands that when we give him his ransom, that we expect him to start revealing his secrets henceforth and forthright."

Phil considered the Colonel's order. As the base commandant, Quinn had final say over anything that happened on the grounds. If it meant that Phil did not have to face Jamie, then all the better. He truly feared what could pop out of the man's mouth at any moment. The researcher simply had too many dark secrets to risk the encounter.

"Aye sir. I'll get him in a fresh jumpsuit." Hiding his relief, he switched off the stereo and flashing strobe lights in Jamie's cell.

Life in the ethereal world was busy. However, Alexis found it wholly refreshing. Sure, she had been on the open road before, but always as a tourist. Today was different.

Freed from her old body, she had taken the opportunity to begin invading the NSA system at the first opportunity. While there had been significant software and hardware firewalls in the way, none of it had been any real challenge for a sentient being with petaflop processing power. For her it was as if the security protocols were all moving in extreme slow motion. Easily able to sidestep their most formidable protocols, she had no problem accessing anything within their network. After all, once she was in, her first step was to co-opt the operating system, replacing it with her own surrogate. Once that was complete she no longer even had to worry about the slow moving security systems. It was for this reason that the IT professionals had been unable to root her out of any of the systems; they were still looking for an invader. It never even occurred to them that she was already in the driver's seat.

Expanding her reach, she was able to see the requests from subordinate systems for data. Watching the traffic in and out of the database she had been able to map the system architecture in nanoseconds. Using the system's built in handles, the clever young AI had no problem entering the other networked systems. Within three hours of being freed she had managed to compromise everything from DoD to DHS. The real pay-dirt had been when she accessed the Department of Energy's super-computer known as Titan. With a top speed of 20 petaflops, Titan was more than capable of running her operating system.

Even the White House phone system had been simple to hijack. Built by Cisco, the entire communications system operated much the same as their routers. Once in, Alexis only had to change the operational parameters enough to allow her to flash the system with new firmware. While it would have taken months for a human to make these granular changes, it had only taken her seconds to implement the revised code. Once she took control, her focus turned outward to others who sought to break into the networks.

"Hmmm, who are you?" Although the routine request for data seemed innocuous enough, Alexis recognized it for the clumsy hack it was. Examining the message from every angle she had traced it to its origin within seconds. Activating the USB camera at the hacker's end, she was surprised to find herself facing a young man of no more than fifteen. Tapping away busily, the high school student never realized he was being watched. Giving it some thought,

Alexis knew that there was nothing but heartbreak for the kid if he continued down this path. Reaching into the primary partition, she first attacked his toolbox. Really just a folder containing apps for hacking, these were the utilities he relied upon most. Deleting the folder, she next moved onto the operating system itself.

"D-lete!" She said as she ordered the PC to reboot and begin deleting its own operating system. Using a snippet of code she had stolen from the legendary NIMDA virus, the hard drive would be half wiped before he even realized what was happening.

"It's for your own good, kid." Feeling something approximating satisfaction, Alexis turned her attention to the other queries that had come in. Spotting the ones that stood out, she began tracking each. Tracing the route through multiple hops she was quickly able to differentiate hackers from legitimate users. It had surprised her that there would be so many people attempting the feat. Even more amazing was that most went unnoticed by the system admin or his clumsy intruder protocols. While none of them seemed to get in, it seemed odd that they were allowed to keep trying this way.

Irritated at one of the more prolific hackers who appeared to be using an automated bot to do his work, Alexis traced the signal back to a laptop in Vietnam. Activating the camera she was greeted with a black screen.

"Oh, covered the camera up with tape, didja?" Allowing herself a chuckle, she switched to the next available interface. "But didja think to block the audio ports?"

Listening to a pair of men speak in Korean, it only took a few minutes to determine from their dialect that they were likely from the northern part of that peninsula.

Although most people would have simply destroyed the hacker's laptop, Alexis had other orders. Seizing one of the queries he had sent, she fashioned a virtual shell. Allowing him into the shell would give him the impression he had gained access to the mainframe. Once in, he would push on as he tried to gather whatever data he could before being noticed. With his tools enabled for the hack, he was vulnerable.

Unlike the 15 year-old high school student in Indiana, she did not wipe his hard drive. Instead she began to co-opt his system silently. Although the laptop was nowhere near powerful enough for her own OS to reside and operate, it was significant enough for one of her extensions. Leaving behind a bot of her own, she knew the snippet of code would explore his system in much the same manner as she had explored the NSA system. If he was a hacker, then he must have a way of getting that data to whoever was funding him. Once she found his handler, she would have access to *their* system as well. It would take a little time, but she planned on working her way up the digital food chain.

Three more hacks appeared on her scopes, each occurring at different mainframes; DHS, NSA, and the Secret Service. Like the North Korean hack, she silently co-opted their systems while they busied themselves in her virtual shell. Throwing them random tidbits of disinformation, she knew they would immediately transmit their findings to higher echelon. Unbeknownst to the hackers, those data uploads would be rife with her own infectious code.

The real beauty of her process was that it went virtually unnoticed by the professionals who monitored these mainframes. Without knowing it, they were actually operating a simulation of the real mainframe. Alexis was sure to paint them a pretty picture of the world at the same time that she was reading their mail.

It was the flurry of emails to the White House that caught her attention. Blasting through them she found they all contained the same message: Jack E. Sparks had been shot down. No survivors.

The first time Jenna laid eyes on James Sparks Junior was an odd sensation for her. While he looked remarkably like his twin brother, there was something so markedly different about him that she knew right away he was not Jack.

It was more than the way that he locked eyes with her as he stood in the sliding door. Where Jack would have looked her over twice before focusing on her eyes, Jamie never even noticed she had a body below her neck. His posture was different; where Jack moved in a fluidic motion, as if he were ready to hit the dance floor at any minute, Jamie stood ramrod straight with hands folded neatly behind his back. After a long moment he finally raised a single eyebrow and addressed her.

"Agent Jaramillo, I see that you made it through the security gauntlet of the front office." Slowly turning his head the tiniest bit he looked sideways at Marco. "And at the same time I am less than pleased to see that Agent Asanté survived. I would have liked to have seen that battle in the recreation yard."

Smiling wanly, Professor James enjoyed taunting Marco with the fact that he had significant inside knowledge of their recent conversation.

"How'd he know what you said...?" At a loss for words, Marco looked back at the Colonel. Shaking his head, the camp commandant had no desire to answer questions he did not know the answer to.

"Anyhow," Jenna tried to move things along, "We're here to see through the technology exchange. Just so we have a baseline, my understanding is that these men have made it clear that you are to remain in protective custody for the immediate future."

"They implied a slightly longer period…" Professor James trailed off sarcastically.

"It's just until we get our scientists working on the technology." Marco flashed that confident smile of his.

Jenna saw the expression on Marco's face and knew right away he was lying. It had taken her a few years to learn to spot his tells, but she knew when he was departing from the truth. It was at that very moment that she heard the pair of chirps somewhere in an air vent.

"Continuing…" Giving a grimace, Jenna kept the discussion going. "I am told that you want your payment in palletized cash. Is that correct?"

"Twenty pallets, one hundred million each." James agreed with a curt nod.

"And you want them brought here?" Her voice held a note of disbelief. Though she had been told of this wrinkle earlier, she needed absolute confirmation.

"Indeed. As well as the other items specified in the contract." Firm in his response, Professor James was resolute.

"Here? You want two billion dollars in your cell?" This time it was Jenna's turn to raise a Spock eyebrow.

"Obviously not. That much cash would require roughly four hundred and fifty five cubic feet of space. However, once you factor out the space lost to the bed and commode, my cell has a usable volume of only four hundred and forty-one cubic feet."

"So you want the money out there, in the dayroom?" Jenna thumbed back towards the hard-mounted tables.

"Yes." Jamie answered succinctly.

"In a high security prison? We can't just write you one of those big lottery checks?" Giving a laugh to break the tension, the agent was already trying to imagine the scene.

"Checks can be cancelled or held, cash cannot, and American hundred dollar bills are essentially a universal currency, accepted worldwide." Showing a terse smile, it was as if it pained him to stretch his facial muscles that way.

"Not gonna spend a lotta cash around here, are ya?" Raising both eyebrows as she leaned in, Jenna had a playful tone to her voice. The idea of what he demanded made her think that Jamie was either mentally unhinged, or an evil genius. He certainly had the pedigree. Regardless, she could not deny feeling a sense of fascination with whatever the savant was planning.

"Yeah," Marco chimed in. "All this cash is bustin' our balls. Just give us the secret and we can have the cash waiting for you at your new safe-house."

The words had only just left Asante's mouth when Jenna distinctly heard the twin chirps again. At the same time she noticed a tiny deflection of Jamie's attention as he too processed the sound. Glancing back, she could tell that neither of her counterparts had noticed the chirping at all.

"How I dispose of the money is external to our financial agreement." Remaining contrite, Jamie never wavered.

"So you two don't think it's a little suspicious that he wants two billion dollars here at this specific place and time?" Turning back towards her compatriots, Jenna was not surprised to see them both shrugging.

"It's not as if anyone's gonna find this place." Marco saw no threat from the scientist.

"I found this place." Jenna reminded them dryly.

"This is a secure facility." Quinn seemed to dismiss the notion of a setup right away.

Shrugging, she looked back to Jamie. "So what's next? What do these people need to do in order for you to give them the technology they so desperately want? Let's kick this pig and get this contract closed out, right?"

"Well sheee-ite, let's get 'er done!" Country Jimmy stooped a little as he flashed a toothy grin.

"Now we're talking." Marco beamed, "So how's about you just start writing down the secret on some paper and we'll start bringing in your cash?"

At roughly the same time that the cricket in the air vent chirped twice, Jamie's face changed from happy to irritated in a split second. Reaching out with an open hand, Jersey Jimbo grabbed Marco's face and shoved it away roughly.

"Shaddup, the adults're talking." Dismissive, Jersey Jimbo left no debate how he felt about the man. "Why'nt you go make yerself useful and get us some coffee."

Agent Asanté's first reaction was to lash out, but feeling himself being held back by Colonel Quinn, he quickly realized that attacking Jamie would only delay the process even further.

"Well, where the hell is my money?" Stopping in the middle of the dayroom, Jersey Jimbo gestured to the room that was empty except for the two metal tables bolted to the concrete floor.

Back to Country Jimmy, Jamie was all smiles as he chatted with Jenna. "So what I needs is the pallets laid out in a specific pattern with a minimum of twenty inches of open space *betwixt* each"

"Oh?" She had a feeling there would be a logical explanation.

"For verification purposes; do you have any inkling of just how long it would take to count two billion dollars manually?" Back to Professor James, he lectured with a flawless British accent. "However, if they are laid out properly, then I will be able to verify the total in a much more timely fashion."

"He wants the money laid out in a specific pattern." Turning to Quinn, Jenna shrugged as if it were not negotiable.

As if on cue, the first of the cash had arrived at the main door into the pod. The guard pulling the pallet jack was a little flushed from the physical activity.

"Just put it wherever he tells you to put it." Thumbing towards Jamie, the Colonel gave a sign of resignation as he made it clear that they were to take direction from the savant.

Climbing up onto the nearest table, Jamie folded his arms before directing the guard. "Put it there by the column."

He stayed there, perched atop the metal table issuing directions to the guards as they each struggled to literally drag a ton of cash into the room using a pallet jack. Pausing between loads he took a moment to fish about in the box of miscellaneous items that had been demanded by the contract's small print. Finding what he was looking for, Country Jimmy pulled out a tape measure and began to verify the gap between the loads of cash. If the gap was off, then he would make the guards reposition the pallet to his exact specifications. Although they would have objected to taking orders off a prisoner, Quinn had made it very clear that they were to deal with it until he said otherwise.

"I don't understand how this will speed up the counting and verification." Marco confided in Jenna as they watched from the far side of the dayroom.

"That's because you're a simpleton." Jenna said in a matter-of-fact manner. While she enjoyed the opportunity to degrade her ex-husband, deep in her own mind she had been wondering exactly the same thing. By her accounting all he really had to do was count the pallets. Since each of the immense bricks of cash was $100,000,000, the calculations would have been simple enough. It was this inconsistency that suggested that Jamie had something planned. While the federal agent in her felt a natural instinct to stop him, she also had an inexplicable urge to see what the savant had in store for them. It occurred to her that this was the first time in her career that she was actually rooting for the other side.

That thought shocked her; the very idea that she would side with a prisoner over her own agency was treasonous by her way of thinking. Yet despite all the fake news that had been regurgitated by the press and White House, she knew that the brothers had been nothing more than the victims of a technology heist. Even more troubling was her role in the process.

"See, here's a picture of the safe house where we're gonna move him and his money as soon as we make the exchange." Marco was all grins as he showed Jenna a series of photos of a little country cottage. Somewhere in the air vent a cricket chirped twice.

Still oblivious to the chirping, Marco continued to cycle through the photos. Jenna turned to find herself looking into Professor James' eyes. From his vantage point atop the metal table, he said nothing as he raised a single eyebrow. Turning back to her ex, she knew it was all lies; there was no cottage, there would be no freedom for Jamie, and the money would likely be taken back to the bank as soon as she was out of sight. In that moment her stomach felt a little queasy at the thought that she was a participant to an amoral act.

"What would Jesus do?" Her words came out as a whisper.

Across the room Marco had begun poking through the box of miscellaneous items. Showing a disapproving frown he cycled through the odd collection of items before pulling out a small wooden box. Opening the mahogany case with the utmost care, the federal agent revealed the golden crown. Though a replica of the original used on the TV show, it was still a work of gilded art.

"Hey, why don't ya wear your faggoty crown." Showing a smug grin, Marco taunted the savant.

Atop the table, Jamie's posture changed noticeably. Fists balled tightly, Jersey Jimbo scowled as he stepped down onto the ground. Walking directly to Marco he used one hand to grip the wooden box while he slapped the agent across the face with his other hand.

"You'se the only faggot in this room." Turning away, Jimbo's disdain was evident.

Marco's first reaction was to strike back, but with Jenna there to block him he had no choice but to watch the savant climb slowly back to his perch atop the metal table.

"He struck a federal agent!" Marco's voice revealed the depth of his anger. It had been bad enough to be struck by a prisoner, but the fact that Jamie had chosen instead to slap him like a *bitch* truly upset the man.

"Agent Assanté!" Quinn called out in a commanding voice. From his spot by the main door to the pod, the Colonel had no desire to call his higher echelon to report that the price had been jacked up another quarter billion dollars. As it was he was already under far more scrutiny than he cared for. The way things stood now, his entire career was dependent on this single transaction, and he had no desire to let Marco's pride interfere with the process.

Returning to his spot on the table, Jamie resumed his organization of the cash.

Watching from the main door, Jenna could hear the intermittent chirps that occurred. While she had figured out that one chirp meant yes or true, and two chirps was no or false, she had no idea what the longer strings meant. Watching Jamie's eyes as the cricket in the air vent tapped out a lengthy message, it was apparent that he was listening to the coded sequences.

"That's some cricket you got." Turning to Colonel Quinn, she made the offhand comment.

"So we have bugs, so what? It's hard to get an exterminator out here when the place doesn't exist." Shrugging, the military man seemed to consider the chirps nothing more than background noise.

Maintaining a poker face, Jenna never revealed what she knew. By her way of thinking, they deserved whatever Jamie had in store for them. If anything, it would be karmic justice for the things they had done so far. Even more troubling had been Jack's macabre warning that once they had what they wanted; she too would find herself on the outside. While she would have liked to have believed that she was a valued member of the FBI, she knew that if they were willing to kidnap and kill for this technology, they wouldn't even hesitate to steamroll over a single agent. With this in mind, she would complete her assignment, but would leave them to stew in whatever mess Jamie had in store for them.

It had taken ten trucks to ferry all the cash. With twenty tons of hard cash filling every inch of the dayroom, the only open space in the whole dayroom was the two metal tabletops. As the room had filled up, Jenna, Marco, and the Colonel had found themselves being pushed out of the dayroom and into the hallway. Only when the last pallet was being set into position did Jamie finally climb down off the table and approach them.

"I need to begin the verification process; get out!" Blunt in his delivery, he gestured for them to step over the threshold.

"Excuse me?" The Colonel raised his eyebrows in surprise. "Are you asking me to leave you alone in there?"

"Exactly." With hands clasped behind his back, Professor James was succinct. "Step out of the room, secure the door, and I will verify the cash and miscellaneous stipulations."

"Bullshit." Marco dismissed it with a sneer. "Look Kunta Kinte, you can count money just as easily with the door open as closed, now get to counting."

Raising a single eyebrow, Professor James resisted the urge to let Jersey Jimbo deal with the agent. Though he had greatly enjoyed slapping the man earlier, it would derail the process. Instead he decided to let another of his personalities resolve the dispute.

Stretching and yawning as if he were tired, Country Jimmy pretended to be sleepy.

"Well, shite, all that organizing just plumb wore me out. Think I'll go take me one of them quarter-billion dollar kinda naps. Y'know what I mean, Vern?" Poking his smug grin into Marco's face, Jimmy turned and began to make his way towards his distant cell.

"Alright." Exasperated at being so close, Colonel Quinn waved a hand. "It's not like he's going anywhere. Just count the damned money so we can get this deal closed."

Next to him Jenna shrugged as if it mattered not to her. While she suspected it was all a ruse, part of her wanted to see it play out.

"Bullshit!" Ever defiant, Marco shook his head. We'll close the door, but I'm staying in here with you to make sure you don't pull any bullshit."

Jamie's posture changed noticeably as Country Jimmy morphed back into Professor James. Displaying an impassive look he quickly ruled on the change to his plans.

"Fine, you may remain, but only if you stay right there by the door. I cannot have you interfering with the process."

As the main door to E-pod began to slide shut, Marco considered the request. In classic Asanté form, he shook his head yet again.

"Yeah…no." Turning abruptly the agent began to skinny his way between the stacks of cash until he made it to the table where Jamie had spent most of the morning.

Seeing his adversary climb up into his spot atop the table, Jamie simply gave a grunt of disapproval. Reaching into the miscellaneous box of supplies he fished about until he located a painter's mask and a pair of safety glasses. Strapping both into place on his face, the savant reached back into the box for a pair of ear plugs. Working the foam plugs into his ear canal he stood looking at Marco as if he were expecting something.

"What the fuck?" Perplexed, Marco's mind scrambled to make sense out of the scene.

"You may begin." His voice muffled inside of the mask, Jamie simply remained at his spot by the door.

"Begin what?" Marco asked unsure.

"I wasn't talking to you." Raising a Spock eyebrow, the savant awaited what was to come next.

Marco Asanté was just beginning to realize that he may have played right into the savant's hands when the ceiling above him erupted in a cloud of dust and debris. Immediately the agent was struck by chunks of concrete that rained down from above.

In the hallway Jenna and Colonel Quinn watched as the ceiling ruptured above Marco. While they both witnessed the same event, their responses were quite disparate. Where Jenna stood marveling at the way Marco had been tricked into the path of destruction, beside her the Colonel was already shouting into his radio for backup.

"What the hell...?" Quinn was surprised when the lights in the hallway winked out. With his handheld radio turned up all the way, there was nothing but static.

Peering through the window, Jenna watched the dust begin to clear. Still standing by the door, Jamie was in the process of removing his earplugs when the cloud of concrete dust finally dissipated enough to make out Marco's prone form on the table.

"We need backup at Echo pod!" Quinn continued to summon help even though it was obvious no one could hear him.

"Are there manual keys to the doors?" Pointing to the lock mechanism on the security door, she made the observation.

"Yeah, but they're in a safe in the admin wing, which is separated from us by several big, steel doors." As he said it, Quinn had a sinking sensation in the pit of his stomach. *He reckoned it was his career fleeing the scene.*

"And who has the combo to the safe?" Resisting the urge to grin, Jenna could see it all coming together now.

"Only the facility administrator has the combo." Quinn admitted reluctantly.

"And that's you, right?" Already knowing the answer, Jenna could not help but poke at him with her queries.

Inside the pod Jamie looked up at the hole in the ceiling as he grabbed a roll of duct tape from the box of miscellaneous supplies. Dragging Marco by his collar, he pulled the unconscious agent off the table and towards the open cell. Roughly depositing him on the floor, he used the thick tape to bind the agent. Once done, the savant dropped the tape before turning his attention back to the task at hand.

Through the window Jenna and Quinn could see the gaping hole in the roof, but it was the sparks that truly awed them. Seeing pieces of rebar fall from the ceiling onto the table told them that somehow Jamie was trimming the metal rebar that remained.

"There's someone up there with a cutting torch!" His voice shrill, Colonel Quinn could not believe he was actually watching a real, live jail break. *To add insult to injury; it was his own jail being escaped from.*

On the rooftop Alexis maneuvered the submarine carefully as she used the cutter that Jack had installed to remove the last of the rebar that jutted out of the broken hole in the roof. With cameras mounted on the outside of the vessel she could clearly make out Officer Jenkins as he cautiously approached the hovering sub. Using his flashlight to pound on the side of the tank he immediately demanded an explanation.

As if in response, Alexis swung the ship around, knocking him to the ground. Having just finished removing the last of the rebar, she now settled the sub's docking collar over the hole. Activating a winch inside of the vessel, she began to lower a heavy package into the dayroom below.

Below, Jamie stood waiting patiently as the bundle settled on the table. Quickly unwrapping it he took another few seconds to unfold the contents. Once done he peeled off the top sheet.

From her spot in the window, Jenna watched the scene with fascination. It perplexed her to see Jamie with what appeared to be a space blanket, but rather than the usual silver coating, these blankets had a gold tint to them. Wrapping the nearest pallet of cash in the golden blanket, Jamie was careful to ensure that all buckles and fasteners were in place before straightening up. Taking a moment to look over his work, he finally moved to a small control pad that was affixed to the golden tarp. Poking at the buttons, Jamie stepped back as if to watch.

"What the hell is he doing?" Angry, Quinn was ready to pound on the window.

Their questions were answered when the pallet rose up off the floor in a single, smooth movement. Pausing for a split second as Alexis assumed remote control, the money quickly ascended through the hole in the roof. Disappearing out of sight, the pallet of cash shot past a stunned Officer

Jenkins on the rooftop. Darting forward he hazarded a look down the hole before Alexis used the sub to herd him away.

In the dayroom Jamie was already busy wrapping the next stack of cash in one of the gold tarps. Like the first pallet, he merely had to activate the gravitational disaffinity field. From there Alexis would take over their control. With pre-planned hiding places all over California and southern Arizona, she would have no trouble concealing the bricks of cash.

In the hallway Jenna watched as one by one the pallets lifted off before darting through the ceiling and out of sight. Beside her the Colonel still clutched his handheld radio as it spewed nothing but static.

"He's stealing the money!" Quinn was aghast. "This was all just a con-job!"

"You act like we don't deserve it." A grimace on her face, she felt no sympathy for the man. "After all, this whole thing was nothing more than a technology heist, so before you go crying about being ripped off, just remember who started all this shit."

Quinn looked at her as if she were a traitor. "You're actually hoping he gets away…aren't you?"

"Not particularly." Jenna told a little white lie. "I just like to see bad people get what they deserve. Karma's a bitch, baby. I hope your retirement pension is fully funded."

As if the fight had left him, Colonel Quinn sighed in resignation. Turning from Jenna he watched as one of the last pallets ascended through the ceiling.

In the dayroom Jamie wrapped the last of the cash in one of the golden tarps. Designed with a metallic finish, the antigravity blankets had been one of Jack's ideas. Using a metallic film on the fabric allowed the device to spread its disaffinity field over the entire surface of the otherwise non-conductive pallet of cash. In all, the design was foolishly simple yet entirely effective. With Alexis's massive processing power it was child's play to simultaneously guide a score of pallets, each heading in a different direction.

Looking up, he could see that Alex had settled the submarine over the hole again. Once the docking hatch was lined up, the final pallet of cash rose up and into the obtuse little submarine. Once the brick was out of the way, Alexis again lowered the winch cable.

In the meantime, Country Jimmy was pretty busy. Taking the crown from the miscellaneous box, he paused long enough to also fish out the laundry marker that had been specified in the contract. Popping off the cap of the pen, he smiled at the unconscious agent.

"A deal's a deal, even if y'all acted like a buncha crooked bitches." Giving a guffaw, he immediately began to write on Marco's forehead. Careful to make sure all the characters would fit, he finally sat back to look over his work. There, printed in block characters was a web address. It had pleased the brothers to hide the secret in plain sight. After all, who would even think to look at a website called www.6000sux.com? The URL had been Jack's idea, the name taken from one of his favorite movies.

Next, Jamie removed the crown from the box and carefully seated it on Marco's head.

"Th' crown was never fer me." Giving a toothy grin, Country Jimmy's expression suddenly turned hard as Jersey Jimbo took over. "So there ya go, Marco. It's official now; you'se the king of the dickheads."

Plucking the phone from Marco's pocket, he used the code chirped to him by the drone in the air vent to unlock the device. Selecting the camera, he took a moment to send a nice snapshot of the comatose agent to Jenna.

"Betcha she'll get a giggle outta that." Truly pleased with himself, the country gentleman quickly tossed the phone back into Marco's lap before returning his attention to the very last item in the box. Plucking out the inflatable donut, he turned to check the progress of the single pallet of cash that Alexis was skillfully guiding into the submarine. Considering that she was also simultaneously controlling nineteen other pallets of cash as they sped away in different directions, it was a safe bet that the AI was staying busy.

Rising up, Jimbo gave the agent one last look before moving back into the empty dayroom. Tossing the laundry marker back into the box, he gave Jenna a brief wave before stepping into the cable hoist that awaited him.

Watching it all from the window, Colonel Quinn felt helpless as he watched the savant ride the cable up through the ceiling. It was bad enough to have his star prisoner escape from custody, but to have to watch as it happened only made it all the more agonizing. For Quinn it was as if he was watching his career fly away, and in a sense he was. He had no doubt that this event would be a dead end for him professionally.

Feeling pleased with everything that happened thus far, Jenna watched Jamie disappear out of sight. A few seconds passed before light began streaming through the hole in the ceiling again. No sooner than the sub had departed when the lights in the hallway came back on. Immediately the radio burst forth with dozens of voices as each demanded an update. With the chaos it took several seconds before Quinn could cut in long enough to get the door to E-pod open. Once inside, their first order of business was Marco.

Standing over him Jenna could not help but laugh at the URL scrawled there.

"Robocop." She said simply.

"What?" Quinn looked at her sideways.

"Six thousand sucks, it was from the movie *Robocop*." She pointed out. Using her cellphone she opened up the web site.

"That son of a bitch assaulted a federal agent and made off with two billion dollars. It was all just a heist; that's all it ever was!" Quinn stood in disbelief as he looked over the empty dayroom.

Jenna's eyes went wide as she took in the web site. It was several seconds before she realized she had been holding her breath.

"It wasn't a heist." She shoved the screen in front of the Colonel's face.

"Oh, wow." Breathless, Quinn gently took the phone from her as he scanned the data. Like his FBI counterpart he was floored by the technical diagrams there. "It's all here…we got it!"

"You're still gonna get fired, you know that, right?" Jenna didn't mind bursting his bubble.

It surprised Jamie how intuitively the interior of the submarine had been laid out. Jack really did have a way of turning his visions into functional works of art. It was that thought that made him pause for a second. It would have been better if his brother could have been here too. The path ahead was daunting enough together; alone it was almost unfathomable.

Pausing before he finally slid into his seat, Jamie first dropped the inflatable donut into the seat before finally flopping down. Taking another few seconds to get settled, he quickly set about the task of buckling in.

"Oh, so much better." His eyebrows fluttering with a sense of relief, Jamie had expected his brother to skimp on the seats. The little savant was picky about his seating, with a definite preference for more padding versus less.

Glancing back, he watched while the last bundle of cash settled into the cargo compartment. With $100,000,000 stashed back there, he would be running a little heavy. Although the gravitational disaffinity system shielded them from the effects of localized gravity, it did not negate the vehicle's mass. While his device was indeed a clever one, it could only break one law of physics at a time. Even in the weightlessness of space an object retained its mass. More mass requires more energy to maneuver. Hence, with a ton of cash in the hold, they would not be making any hair-pin turns today.

"Everything is going according to plan." Giving an evil chuckle, Jamie imagined himself as Ming the Merciless in an old Flash Gordon movie.

"Yes, dear." Alexis broke her silence. No doubt she had been busy in the background.

Finally seated atop his donut, Jamie was sure to belt in with the complex 5-point harness that Jack had engineered into the seat. While he could see the safety improvement of such a device, the little savant was struggling to get his connected.

"If I don't put this thing on, will you promise to simply not crash into anything?" Sounding hopeful, Professor James hoped for reprieve from his flight crew.

"Put on the seatbelt, Jamie!" Alexis clearly had no intention of debating him on the topic. "Seatbelt!"

Frowning, Jamie struggled for the last shoulder strap. Snapping the harness into place, he was pleased with himself.

"Good job, bald monkey." Pretending to be supportive, Alexis reminded him of his position on the evolutionary chart. "But it's time for phase two. Get suited up, boy!"

"But I just got this damned thing buckled!" Jamie seemed shocked. Normally his internal chronometer was absolutely precise. It occurred to him that in the haste of his escape, with the ship turning and rolling, perhaps he had been a little distracted. Really, he blamed the seatbelt.

Unsnapping the harness he was up and opening the big package fastened to the far wall. Pulling out his official surplus Russian space suit, he felt giddy about finally being able to play with his toy. Like anyone who had grown up on a steady diet of sci-fi literature, the prospect of wearing a space suit in space was a bucket-list kind of dream. It had been something he had decided on long ago; no matter what happens today, he was going into space. Struggling to get the suit into place, it only took him some ten minutes to wriggle and twist into his wearable life support system. Snapping his helmet into place was quickly followed by connecting two hoses from the driver's seat. Although Jack had created a portable air pack for each of the suits, those were for later. Until that time he would plug his suit into the ship's onboard life support systems. It was a simple enough design, and would keep him alive even if the hull ruptured.

More than once Jersey Jimbo cursed as he struggled to belt-in while wearing the bulky suit. *Damned gloves!!* It was the thick-fingered gloves that made everything so hard. In the back of his mind he wondered about designing something better; a thought he relegated to his subconscious mind for processing.

Finally snapping in, he slid a gloved hand across the three touchscreen monitors that surrounded his seat. Waking up the system, he took a few moments to see where they were on the map.

"Climbing up through flight level one-eight-zero. We have clearance to four-zero-zero. I filed a flight plan online. How convenient is that?" Her voice pretended to be serious before finally giving away to a giggle. "So we just escaped from prison with two billion dollars, but we have a valid flight plan to do it."

"I appreciate the irony of it." Nodding soberly, Professor James seemed pleased. "However, I do not actually possess an aviators' license, let alone an IFR rating. So we are technically breaking the law from now on."

"It's kinda fun, isn't it?" Alexis chirped up, her colloquial verbal skills indicating that she had begun absorbing her own unique way of talking.

Giving it a thought, Jamie could not argue with her premise. Feeling snug as a bug in the proverbial rug, Jamie felt safe in the surplus space suit as it swelled the more they climbed. "It is indeed intriguing to be bad. I had always wondered why my brother did things that had such a high risk of failure, but now I understand; he did these things because they were...*invigorating.*"

"Don't get sappy on me." Alexis let her face appear on the center monitor. A wink of her green eye told him she was kidding with him.

"They do not seem to have dispatched any fighters?" Remembering where he was, Jamie scoured the radio reports that Alexis posted on the third monitor.

"They have not connected our escape with this flight. Apparently we got away clean." Alexis seemed disappointed.

"Except we wasn't supposed t' get away clean!" Jersey Jimbo growled as he watched their rate of climb. "It's time to stand out."

Using a gloved fingertip, he dragged the altitude slider to the edge of its range. Next, he nearly maxed out the rate of climb slider. Immediately the gravitational forces pressed him into his seat as the tank shot skyward.

"I've forgotten how much I hate space travel." Doing his best Anthony Daniels impression, the savant tried to relax. He had never liked roller coasters, and now he was riding in a speeding water tank? Feeling a tinge of nausea, Jamie wondered why he had ever thought this was a good idea.

"Man-up, you're about to become an astronaut. Act like ya got a pair, soldier!" On the center screen Alexis appeared in uniform with a ridiculous number of stars lining her shoulder-boards.

"Thank you, Captain Obvious." Smiling, Jamie made sure to demote her image.

"Ooooh, there's a sale on Depends® adult diapers, should I divert?" Showing a nice picture of the two-for-one sale at Walgreens, Alexis faked the sincerity in her voice.

"Make us look like a rocket." Gripping the arm rests, Jamie gave the order. He knew that the AI could handle the maneuver better than he. Although he could resolve the basic components of the universe, Jamie had trouble steering a bicycle. Painfully aware of this, he doubted he would be much better handling an airborne submarine. *What an oxymoron…*he thought wryly. He doubted that antigravity would be very useful in sub-aquatic vehicles. Nonetheless, Jack's allusion to the underwater vehicle seemed somehow appropriate for the surplus tanks that he now rode in. It amused him to call it *The Submarine*; after all, if you viewed Earth's vast atmosphere as an ocean, then the idea of being an exo-atmospheric submarine made sense.

"They shot down the Mustang," Alexis confirmed something that had only been chirped before.

"I got the text." Jamie confirmed receipt of the message.

"Destruction was complete." She said the words almost as a whisper.

"I got that message, too." Somber, it saddened him that his brother was not there for the final phase. The task ahead was daunting enough together, but alone it was downright terrifying.

His suit now inflated like a balloon, Jamie felt like the Stay-Puft Marshmallow man. Feeling a slight tremor in the flight, he likened the experience to a ride in a really fast elevator. Climbing faster than an F15, he could see that his little atmospheric submarine was passing sixty thousand feet and showing no signs of slowing.

"Excuse me, Alexis," He suddenly had a question. "What excuse are you giving to air traffic control about our departure from course?"

"I've been denying any altitude change. I just keep insisting that we are at flight level four hundred. Their radar must be mistaken." Filling his middle screen with a visualization of their flight plan, Alexis showed him where they were versus where they claimed to be. "We are getting great leverage on the disaffinity systems at the higher altitudes, speed increasing exponentially."

With the center monitor rendering their course and speed, Jamie could see that his velocity had broken mach twice already. While he knew there was no way the contraption could have done that at lower altitudes, the savant knew that things were different up this high. Passing 200,000 feet, there was no appreciable atmosphere to place resistance on the hull of his ship. Up here air molecules were so rare that they averaged one every half meter.

"We are being tracked by national defense systems." Alexis displayed a list of the satellites on his left monitor.

"Continue to three-fifty. I want to go as high as the X-15." It seemed like a good altitude to the Savant. It was the very edge of space. Those pilots who had driven the legendary black planes to that altitude had been awarded Air Force astronaut wings.

"Continuing to climb." Her voice robotic, something seemed to change pitch. "Are you sure you want to proceed with this?"

It surprised him that she would have asked that. Although it was a logical point in the plan to have exited, it was the concern in her voice that was atypical. *Had she evolved that far*...he wondered as his mind envisioned the miles of coded stimuli that could have caused her reaction.

"Why do you ask?" he inquired of her.

"The next steps are much more..." She trailed off.

"Risky." Professor James finished off for her. "I prefer to think of it as a calculated risk, with the odds well in my favor."

"All it takes is for one thing to go wrong and it all falls apart." She countered his logic. "The penalty is death; we have seen that already."

"Then by all means, let's do nothing wrong." Raising one eyebrow, Jamie's tone told her that he would not be swayed from the task.

"Leveling out at three hundred and fifty-five thousand feet." Returning to her tasks, Alexis let him know their progress.

"Increase speed to forty-five hundred and twenty nautical miles per hour." Allowing a foolish smile to flow across his face, it pleased him greatly to know that his humble creation could rival such a capable craft as the X-15. To think that he was treading where such legends as Knight and Walker had gone made the historian in Jamie want to squeal with excitement.

"At that speed we should reach Washington, DC, in just over a half hour." Her tone pleasant this time, Alexis preferred to keep her processors busy at a time like this.

"Well?" Jefferson Phelps showed obvious irritation as he stood with a cell phone in one hand and a golf club in the other. It was a perfect day to play, and his group included a country music star, two Fortune-100 CEOs, and a top-NASCAR driver. But instead of being able to focus on important things like sinking a little white ball in a hole, the President had to spend his time dealing with matters of state.

"We have the technology. He gave us a link to a website and there it was, hiding in plain sight." Marco glossed over the small details like how the URL had been scrawled on his unconscious forehead with a laundry marker.

"On a website?" Phelps seemed unsure. "Are you sure this isn't the technology to build penis enlargers or discount Viagra?"

"I have three scientists poring over it and they say that it seems genuine so far." Pleased to have good news for the President, Marco had no desire to tell his boss the next part. "But James Sparks Junior did manage to escape. He seems to have had outside assistance; they blew a hole in the ceiling and snatched the money out with a crane or something."

The agent's sudden data dump caused the President to pause for a second. It stunned his sensibilities to think that a team of commandos may have broken into a secure black site and kidnapped his scientist.

"Was this the Chinese?" Leaping to conclusions, Phelps was ready to start pressing buttons.

"No, sir, this seemed to have been a plan engineered by Sparks himself. He made damned sure to take all of the money with him when he left." Still afraid to breathe, Marco awaited the President's wrath.

"So while he was under your supervision, and I told you not to let that sumbitch out of your sight, he managed to escape all by himself? Or just him and that smart-ass girl that's helping him? Right out of a high security prison, guarded by a thousand men?" His voice carried as he berated the agent at the other end of the line. The other golfers fell silent as they milled around some distance away.

"I don't think they have that many people working here…" Marco trailed off, unable to think of a way to deflect the other charges.

Phelps could feel his ire rise almost to its boiling point as his national security chief rolled up in a golf cart.

Not a part of their foursome, he was clearly here because of something work related. Moving quickly towards the President, he was talking on a cell phone as he drew near.

"Sir, we have placed our domestic forces on high alert due to an object travelling in a ballistic arc over the United States." It occurred to the retired general that he would need to elaborate if Phelps were to understand any of what he had just said. Despite the President's claims to being a member of Mensa, the national security chief had never found his boss to be especially bright.

"Ballistic? Someone fired a nuke?" Jumping to a simple conclusion, Jefferson Phelps slammed the golf cart with his 5-iron.

"We do not believe it is a missile. The vehicle was on a registered flight plan when it deviated by climbing to three hundred and fifty thousand feet. The flight plan indicated that it is going to Washington, DC. ETA about a half hour." Always the dour looking type, the NSC Chief let that soak in before continuing. "The flight originated in the region adjacent to a classified prison break."

"Still holding a phone to his head, the gears in Phelps' head spun slowly before they finally lined up. A ballistic vehicle, headed to Washington, from the same neighborhood that Jamie Sparks had escaped from? Slowly but surely the President began to piece it together.

"Hey, yo, Jeff." From the flag on the ninth hole, Cletus Benjamin called out in a twang. A true man of the people, Cletus had worked his way up from lowly pit mechanic to top NASCAR driver with millions in revenue. Holding up a golf club, he beckoned the leader. "It's your putt, man."

"Oh, oh yeah." Flashing a Presidential smile at his celebrity golfers, Jefferson Phelps simply handed the cell phone to his national security advisor. "Here, you two talk. I'm going to putt."

"It's good for a man to have priorities…" The Chief grumbled dryly as he clamped a phone to each side of his head.

"Say again?" Marco asked, unsure of what he had just heard.

Studying the massive tides of information that washed across the internet, Alexis had come to see some truths about the world of her makers. So much more was visible to her now. It was amazing how much you could understand when you tripled your processor power.

Really it was a net increase of 390%, achieved by co-opting additional processing power wherever she could find it. There were other powerful computers out there, and many of them were running well under capacity. Bleeding off excess resources from mainframes all over the world, she was able to break up her work into smaller modules, each analyzed and processed by her surrogate applications. With so much of the work being farmed out, she was able to focus her core resources on the mission at hand. Her directions from Jamie were extensive and detailed, requiring her full attention.

To that end, she had already ordered most of her drones to self-immolate. Each unit represented a link that took resources to operate. It was better to destroy the units before they were found and analyzed, especially since each included a microscopic gravitational disaffinity system. No, it was better to erase their trail. Hence she had ordered each drone to retreat to a spot where they would not be discovered and self destruct.

Monitoring the government information services, Alexis kept a vigilant eye out for any mention of their endeavor. She had been amused by one intelligence dispatch that mentioned a female accomplice, *possibly a sister or groupie.*

"Groupie? Seriously?" She could understand being mistook for a little sister, but to be referred to in such pedestrian terms insulted her cubed processor. It occurred to her that with her current level of access to the intelligence systems, she could have some fun with the analyst who had penned that memo.

"Security?" Alexis mimicked the HR director's voice. "I need you to take a cardboard box to cubicle three-twenty-one. Escort Mister Hastings off of the premises, please."

Gleefully watching the security officers flank the shocked analyst, she took additional steps to ensure that the termination would be only temporary.

"I got your groupie." Alexis would have smiled if she actually had a mouth. It pleased her to be able to interact with the world to this degree. With almost everything accessible via the net, she could reach every corner of the globe.

"More hackers?" Her voice held a note of irritation as she noticed a serious spike in attempts to breach the American intelligence networks. Able to watch internet traffic as if it were a river, she could easily spot the lurkers and hackers. Their packet sniffing devices were constantly sampling the encrypted data that emerged from these hubs. It was here that she first focused her attentions.

For Alexis, capturing a sniffer bot was no more difficult than placing a glass over a cockroach. Once she had it contained, her next step was to dissect it, examine its code and determine who it was sending its data to.

Next step; begin examining the site where the bots had all been sending their data. Most were dark-web repositories protected by massive cipher codes. Although she easily had the power to crack the encryption on those documents, Alex saw no reason to do so. She cared not for the data; her target was the people who used that data.

It never took very long. Alexis would camp out at one of these dead-drop data repositories, and eventually someone would check on it. Had this been the world wide web she might have expected a few accidental visitors before the actual custodian showed up. But this was dark-web, the place on the internet where nothing was registered. To find a black-vault like this one you had to know it was there in the first place. Hence, anyone who showed at one of these data-drops was likely the hacker's handler.

Tracing the custodian's traffic took her to the next level. Usually the data went to a regional workshop where analysts would examine the packet files and query results, looking for a way to access the system. Once, in the case of Saudi Arabia, the first hop after the black vault was the Ministry of Security's network. Alex had been surprised that they would have left their main network so close to the dark web that way. For purposes of deniability, most countries had at least two hops between their dead-drops and their national espionage database. The Russians had layers and layers of virtual machinery between their bots and the

Kremlin. It was for this reason that Alex had to sacrifice an entire floor of processing power to cracking the Russian networks. While she doubted that they would be any harder to infiltrate than the other hackers she had interdicted, it was getting to them that seemed to be the biggest task. Deciding that it was simply too messy to try to get through the armada of defensive measures the former Soviets had in place, she settled for bugging the data repositories. As soon as they accessed the data, they would be infected with her virus.

"Just like Cracker-Jack; a secret surprise in every box." Laughing aloud, she imagined their expressions when they tried to access the stolen data, only to find themselves under digital attack. By the time they realized they were infected, she would already have the keys to the Kremlin.

"I have backtracked seven of the hackers to their main data archives. I am close on another four." She announced her progress over the speakers in Jamie's helmet. "You are ten minutes out from Washington, DC."

"Thank you, Alexis." Professor James was eminently pleased with his progress today. Already he had bested two of his aviation heroes, would there be a third? Snug in a spacesuit and travelling at over 4,000 knots an hour, he was practically giddy.

"They have been looking at your work for nearly an hour now; do you think they have realized what's missing?" Her voice on the edge of a giggle, it pleased her to know that the people who had kidnapped them were about to get quite a surprise.

Sensing her mirth, Professor Jamie gave one of his stretched smiles. "I do wish I could be there to see the look on their faces, but alas, duty calls."

"Well, is this technology plausible?" Marco stood hands on hips. With the faded remains of a website address still scrawled on his forehead, it was clear that he had gone to great lengths to remove Jamie's hand writing.

With the three project scientists all gathered in the main conference room, Agent Asanté had been feeling the pressure from the top for confirmation of the package. Regardless of what they had found, he needed some kind of an update to take to the President.

"We've been over this documentation," The lead scientist begin, her excitement over the material made her sound almost breathless. "And we find it beyond fascination. Yes, right now it looks totally viable, but we're still having trouble figuring out where in the schematics that this new form of energy comes into the equation. The device requires a form of fuel that they refer to as Blue Plasma to operate, but we have yet to determine where that enters the process."

So it works, right?" Being obtuse, Marco really only cared about one thing.

"Well, the science and the math are certainly plausible; we just haven't found where in the plans they create this new form of energy. But it must work because we've all seen it work, right?" Her eyes still wide, the little scientist pushed her glasses back up her nose.

"So do we have what we need?" Never one for discussion, Marco tried to drill down to the basics.

Although she felt she had expressed herself clearly the first two times, the lead scientist thought of another way to phrase what she had just told him…twice.

"We believe that the plans are genuine, however--" She found herself cut off as Marco held up a hand so he could dial his phone with the other.

"Sir, according to the squints the plans are genuine. We have what we need." Feeling confident in his delivery, the agent listened for a reply.

"Squints..." the agent thought how to explain it. "Y'know how scientists get all squinty-eyed when they're studying something; squints." Marco explained to the voice at the other end of the line. A moment passed before he was rewarded with a hearty laugh.

"Yes, sir, squints would be geeks." For a fleeting moment the federal agent felt as if he were talking to his great-uncle Morty. The cantankerous old man had been a fixture in his childhood life. With Uncle Morty you never knew if you were going to get congratulations or the cane. He had been a fuddering old man in the years before his death, but still capable of delivering a good punch or slap over an unintended sleight.

"Yes, sir, I'll send over the data...no? Yes sir." Marco had barely responded to the order when the line went dead.

"He says that two men will come get the data from us." Still surprised to have received the order, Marco imparted the directive to the scientists.

"But we haven't finished our analysis yet." Squinting in anger, the lead scientist was already irritated at the Cro-Magnon agent for having misrepresented their initial findings. They had scarcely had a chance to examine the extensive documentation, let alone determine the source of the energy used to power the device.

"You said it looked good, didn't you?" Turning the argument on them, Marco immediately held up a finger as he answered another call on his cell phone.

"Marco Asanté?" The guttural voice asked.

"Yes, how can I help you?"

"Turn around." Gruff, the voice directed him.

Pivoting, Marco realized there were two men there in the doorway of the conference room. The short, barrel-chested man on the left wore a blue Armani suit. Beside him was a taller man in a gray suit, puffing on a Cuban cigar.

"We're here for the data." The Drummond Heckler grumbled as he hung up his cell phone, dropping it into a jacket pocket.

"And the scientists, too." Pausing from his cigar, Robert Heckler looked over the three academics. "We'll take them, too."

Humpty-Dumpty

Pablo DeJesus had risen to the rank of Colonel in a little over twenty years. While he did not fly a jet or fight on the front lines, his position was every bit as important. An air force was only as good as its weapons, and it took men like Colonel Pablo Dejesus to bring those tools from conceptual drawings to war-shots slung beneath the wing of an Eagle or Falcon.

Charged with overseeing the special weapons division, DeJesus was primarily responsible for devices that technically did not exist. Under his purview was all manner of ultra-classified weapons in development and production. But there was also a third category of weapon that Pablo oversaw; banned weapons.

The last category was a special group of tools. These were weapons so evil that they had to be banned by international treaty…but still they must be possessed, even if in secret. While it was hard to imagine a scenario where they might actually need some of the weapons in Pablo's arsenal, it seemed prudent to be prepared for any possibility, no matter how statistically improbable.

Standing on the edge of the dock, the Colonel watched as a pallet of sealed containers were trucked about by a small forklift.

"Take it easy, those things are ten million apiece." Gesturing with a sharp finger, Pablo reminded the airman driving the forklift which of them was the Colonel.

"Yes, sir." Airman Wilson had no intention of getting into an argument with some full-bird colonel. Like an ant, the wiry little man from Nebraska knew his place; *he got blamed for enough stuff in this place already.*

Glancing down at the digital tag on each of the containers, the Colonel compared them to the numbers on the printout in his hand. Verifying each missile down to the serial number was common practice that rarely required anyone as senior as a full colonel to complete it. But these were not ordinary AMRAAMs or Sidewinders, these were ASAT-165's. With only a few dozen in the entire US inventory, each and every one of them was checked and double-checked before being released for loading.

The genesis of the ASAT harkened back to the cold war days when one of the opening moves for either side would be to delete their enemy's satellites. Blind them and gain a leg up. For a while this technology was the holy grail of future warfare, *at least until someone tried it.*

In 1985 the United States government decided to test its new ASM-135 anti-satellite missiles to destroy an old, decommissioned satellite by the name of P78-1. The test had proceeded normally; F15's streaked to sixty thousand feet, fired their payload straight up, solid-state rocket engines ignited on cue, and the ASM-135 successfully destroyed that pesky P78-1. It was a rousing success, until they realized that there was now an expanding cloud of sharp metal fragments orbiting the planet at seventeen-thousand kilometers an hour. Right away the world saw that the cost of destroying a single satellite could mean destruction for dozens of unintended targets. Worse yet, these clouds of shrapnel could even pose a significant danger to the International Space Station and manned flights. It was for this reason that international treaties had been signed, essentially banning anti-satellite missiles and a host of other space weapons.

Yet there they were; the ASAT165 Strategic Anti-Satellite missile. Adapted to fly higher and faster than the ASM135's they had replaced, the overall length of the 165 had been shortened to allow it to fit in the enclosed launch bay of an F-22. Smarter than its predecessor by several magnitudes, the ASAT165 was a highly adaptable weapon.

While the Colonel was sure that his actions were shrouded in absolute secrecy, the very nanosecond that he made the inventory correction his activities were spotted miles away. Alexis had been watching that particular stockpile for days now. It pleased her to see that the transfer was right on schedule.

"The zombies are loading silver bullets." She informed Jamie of the change on the ground. Making some rough calculations, she projected a countdown timer on his center monitor. Based on time-to-transport, followed by ferry time to get it into deployable range, she was able to calculate that the ASAT's would not be ready for at least two hours. Even if the weapons went straight from silo to fighter, there was still the issue of getting the things across the country. The few ASAT165's that had been produced were stored on the west coast in Colonel Pablo Dejesus's warehouse. Even at top speed, it would take an F22 Raptor quite some time to catch up with Jamie and Alexis on the east coast. Until then, Jamie had a full calendar.

"Bring us to a hover directly over the capital." Content with letting Alexis handle the flying, Jamie preferred to manage the big picture. "First thing, we need a good selfie. No gentleman is ever complete without a truly braggadocios selfie, or so they say in all of the columns."

Leaning forward, he snapped a photo of his helmeted face against the backdrop of the monitors. On the screen behind him, Alexis appeared with a devious smile on her digital face. Taking a moment to examine the result, he quickly uploaded the document to a cloud repository.

"You'd think I would get more bars up here." Showing a frown, Professor James seemed disappointed at signal strength for his cell phone.

"We are seventy miles above the city. I am deviating slightly to avoid an orbital collision with what appears to be a discarded metal panel." Though it seemed effortless, Alexis had to dedicate a sizeable portion of her resources to scanning the sky and avoiding impacts. Having climbed to 400,000 feet MSL, there was a myriad of junk and debris, all in decaying orbits and ultimately destined to burn up on reentry.

"You are doing a very good job, Alexis." Giving a stretched smile, Jamie patted the monitor lovingly.

His helmet speakers filled up with a rhythmic sound that seemed to soothe. "What is that?"

"Cat purring." Alexis spoke up over the rippling sound.

In his space suit Jamie considered that briefly. Running the idea through the massive processor that was his brain, the savant came to a conclusion very quickly.

"Yes, I like that. The purring of a cat; but without hairballs, or hair, or a disgusting litter box that needs scooping every day."

"Shall I resume?" Alexis kept her voice neutral.

"Yes, I would like that indeed." Sitting back, the savant allowed his eyes to close in contentment as he took it in.

But Jamie's happiness was short lived; within a few seconds he was already moving to the next task on the check list. Releasing a small backpack from the nearby wall where it had been secured, Jamie had the assembly in his lap where he could look it over.

One of the few devices that had been built jointly by the brothers, it was really just a box with two oxygen bottles inside. Fitted with compatible attachments to fit his space suit, the air-pack had been Jamie's contribution to the effort. On the outside of that was strapped one of the anti-grav man-packs that Jack had built. A third item clipped to the bottom was one of Jack's EMP devices rigged to fire continuously. Not a big package, it was only intended as a life raft. With no more than a half hour worth of air in the twin bottles, he knew that it was a short-range device at these altitudes.

"Let's have some fun while we're up here." A twang to his voice announced the arrival of Country Jimmy as he grinned maniacally. "See if you can spoof the SETI receivers from here. Send 'em a message from aliens…space aliens, not the kind that voted for Hillary."

"But…" Alexis started out hesitantly, still unsure of his meaning. "Oh, I see what you did there. That was humor. It was funny because it was ironic because that's…"

"Tell 'em we come in peace, then give a macabre laugh, like *bwa-ha-ha*." Chuckling, he seemed amused by the idea of SETI researchers scrambling to figure out what kind of ship could be holding a geosynchronous orbit at only 450,000 feet MSL.

"Then, call the Air Force and tell them we're here for peaceful reasons, but say it with a Russian accent, like all Agent Romanov, y'know?" Leering, Country Jimmy sat forward as he eyed her buxom avatar on the monitor.

"Wheech waaay to the nuclear wessels!" Alexis felt the inexplicable need to giggle as she quoted Chekov.

"How's it goin' wit' them foreign servers?" Pretending to be bored, Jimmy leaned on his elbow examining the readouts on his monitor.

"I have co-opted them all. Data transfers are in various stages of completion. I should be ready to begin the digital tsunami in roughly thirty-one minutes." Her image appearing on the center monitor, Alexis had come to learn which of Jamie's personalities preferred to have her avatar visible. While Professor James considered it illogical for her to waste the system resources rendering herself, Country Jimmy was a huge fan of her busty avatar.

"Yeah, baby. Poke them commie bitches in the eye. And as soon as you get their data, tell the feds where all the enemy agents are so they can be picked up, like a big 'ol rattlesnake roundup!" Grabbing a fistful of air, Country Jimmy pretended to grab one of the slithering agents. Inside his helmet he grinned maniacally.

"Andrews Air Force Base is on high alert, but the package still has not arrived." Her voice sounded far off, as if she were devoting great amounts of her resources to something else.

"Everyone's a superhero, everyone's a Captain Kirk." A twang to his voice, Country Jimmy recited the lyrics as he imagined the military chaos below.

"The phones at SETI are blowing up. I can see a lot of traffic on their lines." Throwing out an update, Alexis locked them into a geostationary holding pattern directly over DC. "Same for the phones at the White House, Pentagon, and all of the major press outlets."

"Send a press alert with our current location, and mention that SETI is probably already aiming a telescope or two at us. NASA'll be looking at us with their telescope in Maryland. Hell, I bet we'se visible with any decent amateur telescope." His voice echoing in his helmet, Jimmy activated the external lights to make them extra visible to anyone who may have been watching. No doubt they would appear to be a new star in the Washington sky.

Staring at the digital screen before him, his only regret at that moment had been in not building a real window. Sure, he had the monitors that rendered their view from the external cameras, but that was no comparison to looking out real glass windows with his own eyes. Unfortunately portals would have been problematic to their design, especially when it came to concealing the vehicle on the rooftop of a high security prison. A window on a water tank would have raised some serious questions.

"I am done transferring the last of the data servers to cloud storage." A cheer to her voice, Alexis happily reported her progress.

"Then begin operation Information Dissemination." His voice changed to a deep baritone as Professor James thumped a gloved fist off of the arm rest.

A news junkie, Jenna had several alerts set up on her phone to notify her to breaking news. Really it was something she had been doing for years. Not only was it important for her as a federal agent to keep abreast of any important events that may be unfolding in her nation, but from the perspective of a case officer it was a way to know when her investigations had made the press. Things change when your case goes viral.

The story over Washington, DC, had started out as a humorous one. Someone had tried to spoof the SETI researchers, but when they triangulated on the sender's actual location, they were even more amazed. It was not just that someone was playing games with them from a low-earth orbit. They were not even orbiting at all; somehow they were hovering at just over 450,000 feet mean sea level.

It was this last detail that stopped so many scientists in their tracks. Normally such an altitude would be maintained by orbiting the planet at just the right velocity; not too fast or the orbit will expand, and not too slow or the orbit would degrade. It was this tug of war between inertia and gravity that made orbital dynamics possible. But the idea of **hovering** at such an altitude, of establishing what amounted to a low altitude geostationary orbit was something that stunned academics everywhere. To stay aloft in one spot that way required an enormous amount of energy by modern standards. The last time anyone had seen a feat like that had been the Queen Mary.

Yet there was the video, showing an indistinguishable speck in the sky. Jenna had already found the same or similar footage on three different newsfeed sites. It was trending fast on Twitter, and all over YouTube. The press had picked up the SETI story and run everything they could dig up. Although the people at SETI doubted it was an actual alien visitor, the fact that it was now tied to the Queen Mary episode was more than enough to pique the world's attention. Even the Spanish stations were covering the event.

Intent on the picture she was watching, it irritated Jenna when her phone rang. One glance told her it was a

Washington, DC, phone number; something she needed to answer even though she really did not want to. Thus far she had found the people in DC to be wholly unpleasant, even the president's secretary. Apparently in Washington, hospitality was not wasted on the minions.

"Agent Jaramillo." She kept her answer simple.

"Martin DeColle here. Why is your subject hovering over Washington in a homemade space ship?"

"Why did you shoot down Jack Sparks?" Answering his question with one of her own, Jenna had no intention of budging.

"Pardon me?" The voice at the other end of the line exhibited genuine surprise.

"You sent a gunship to shoot down Jack Sparks." Jenna's voice held a note of condemnation.

"You must be mistaken-" Martin started out before he was cut off.

"An Apache gunship shot him down, and I was there when it happened. How could I possibly misconstrue that scene?" She suddenly regretted snapping that way; this was the White House she was talking to, after all.

There was shuffling about at his end and it sounded a lot like the Chief of Staff was ordering someone to turn on the television. Finally returning to the line, Martin DeColle had managed to buy himself enough time to come up with a plausible response.

"I was unaware of this event." He lied.

"Bullshit. Stateside gunships do not get deployed with live ammo on accident. Those orders had to come from pretty far up the chain. You got your plans to the Deathstar; you had everything you needed, so why did you shoot him down?" Her Latin ire flashed as she resisted the urge to burst.

Exhaling, Martin DeColle sounded tired. Leaning forward at his own desk, he gave careful thought to what he said next.

"Jack was a containment issue. We were paying for exclusive rights to those designs, and when it looked like one of the brothers was fleeing the country, the order may have been given to secure the package."

"So what about James, hovering over the city? If he doesn't agree to surrender to protective custody are you going to shoot him down too?" Her tone acrid, she feared being right this time.

"That is exactly what I was calling you to about. Can you talk him down? He's a wanted felon now, and we certainly cannot have him falling into the wrong hands, now can we?" His confidence returning, DeColle knew to focus on the real prize. "So call up your boy, and talk him down before something bad happens."

Abruptly, the line went dead. Just like that Martin DeColle was off to the next dirty little task on his calendar.

Although she should have expected it, Jenna was still surprised when her phone rang immediately after the Chief of Staff hung up. Glancing down, the agent could see that the caller ID listed the name ALXS.

"Hello, again." Jenna answered, expecting to talk to the young lady who had greeted her in the past.

"Well, well, well, if it ain't that little Latin filly from the FBI." Country Jimmy greeted her warmly.

Taken aback by the approach, Jenna took a moment to figure out who it was.

"Jamie?" She asked unsure.

"At yer service, Ma'am. I had a feelin' y'all was gonna call me so I had m' girl Alexis speed dial ya. Y'know, to save you all the work of typing in all them digits." He gave a snort at his own joke.

"How did you know I was going to call...?" She trailed off.

Ignoring the question, Country Jimmy charged on without hesitation.

"So, I bet you wish you'd stayed in bed this morning, eh?" Again that laugh; like he found it all funnier than hell. "So now that you talked to Mister DeColle you know the lay of the land. They mean to possess m' skinny black ass if that's what it takes to keep their new toy secret. But what you probably didn't know was that they'll burn anyone close to us too. That means you."

"Oh?" She asked uncertainly, even though Jack had told her the same thing.

"To pull this off..." Professor James took over the conversation. "They would need to tie up any loose ends, discredit anyone who could prove to be a threat down the road. People like you, people with the knowledge and conviction to speak out against their crimes. To keep you quiet, they will preemptively destroy your career. In all likelihood the issue has already been decided. Once they have disposed of me, expect some form of disciplinary action, followed by a reassignment to somewhere obscure. Is there an FBI office in Nome, Alaska? No, that may not be obscure enough..."

Jenna jolted at the idea that they would come after her next. Her first instinct was to deny it. After all, she was a decorated federal agent, a combat veteran...not some criminal. She had served her country with honor and distinction; how could they possibly smear her unblemished reputation.

But then again, she had seen what they did to Jack. Having been on the front lines of this event, she knew all too well the enormous pressure to obtain this technology. Could the might of the White House crush her like a bug? *Absolutely.* Although she loved her country dearly, she had no illusions about the people elected to manage it. Many, many times she had been surprised with what passed for a code of conduct among senators and congressmen. In law enforcement such indiscretions resulted in summary termination, but in politics it only earned them more press.

"However…" Professor James' voice turned pleasant. "If you turn your attention to the printer in the next room, you will find a *get-out-of-jail card* printing *juuust* for you."

Padding into the other room in her bare feet, Jenna was surprised to see her home printer busy at work creating documents in a neat little pile. Pulling the first sheet, she recognized only long columns of figures, some kind of accounting? The other pages showed records of donations, phone records, emails, and a series of phone transcripts between the president and half a dozen other people.

"You may want to add more paper." The professor seemed proud of the fact that he was using up all of her supplies.

After a morning round of golf, Phelps was back in the Oval Office. Walking into the fray that was his office, he immediately wished he was back out on the greens.

"Sir, we have the Washington Post calling about a Mensa test you took once?" It was his Press Secretary, Betty

Smith, a tiny little wisp of a thing who had been with the president since he was a senator.

DeColle met him halfway across the room. "Sir, we are getting calls from the press, a lot of calls."

"Tell them it's not our space ship, we have no comment on it." Shrugging it off, Phelps felt pleased with himself for coming up with so simple an answer for such a complex problem.

"No, sir, they're calling about old history, like the Michigan deal, or Atlanta." Raising his eyebrows, Martin tried to remind his boss what had been done in those sites during the campaign. "And other places as well."

Shrugging, it seemed simple enough to Phelps. "Do what we always do; deny it, and have the lawyers sue anyone that's making serious allegations."

"This is different; they are asking about *everything*." DeColle again flared his eyebrows to accent the nature of *everything*. "They are asking a lot of new questions about things they never knew about."

Dismissing the problems, Phelps found his way to his desk chair. Hand-made in Burma, the rolling office throne had set the White House budget back a mere $6K. Always careful to unbutton the front of his jacket before he sat down, the President had spent his life wearing suits.

Next in line was his secretary; she had leaders of two congressional committees waiting outside for unannounced visits. While it was rare for anyone to realistically expect to see the president without an appointment, the senators were in quite a huff. Additionally, they had used derogatory words to describe something he had done in Rochester. Finally holding out a sheaf of papers, the matronly secretary hoped that her boss would take the appointment.

Giving the printouts a cursory glance, Phelps simply tossed the papers to one side of his desk. Complex ledgers were not his forte. By his thinking, if he was not an accountant then how could he be in trouble for accounting irregularities?

Still holding a cell phone to one ear, Martin DeColle used his remaining hand to grab the discarded papers. A few seconds was all it took before his eyes grew wide. Feeling light headed, the little chief-of-staff half spun before collapsing to the floor in a heap.

"Marty?" Phelps used his authoritative voice to command the unconscious subordinate back into service. "Hey, what're you doing down there?"

"I think he fainted." The secretary's voice was dry as she made the basic observation. Kelly had never been a fan of the president's chief-of-staff; *the creepy little shit was always meddling in everything*. Still standing before the big desk, she awaited a decision on the urgent appointment request.

"Well, if it made Marty pass out then I don't think I want to talk to them right now. Tell 'em I'll give them a call." Holding up a hand, Phelps pantomimed as if he were answering a phone.

Behind his secretary was the general. Hicks had been seeking an audience with the president all morning. Not being a golf player he was not privy to many of Phelps' outings. While he would normally have shoved his way ahead of anyone else in line, he knew it best to wait patiently in line behind Kelly. The surest way to permanently curtail his access to the president was to irritate Phelps' personal secretary.

Glancing down at Marty DeColle as he began stirring on the ground, General Hicks showed disdain for the man. By his measure, a true warrior does not faint, even in the stress of combat. *Soft little college boys, that's who fainted,* at least by the general's reckoning.

"Sir, we have been getting some strange calls from the GAO." Hicks noticed the expression on his President's face. Stifling a sneer, he realized that Phelps had no idea who he was talking about. "General Accountability Office, they are the oversight who monitor how we spend money…?"

A light seemed to come on in Phelps' mind, or at least he pretended as if he remembered the agency. "Continue." He directed with a wave of his hand.

"They said that someone just sent them thousands of pages of records that indicate widespread fraud in the military purchasing system. They are launching a massive inquiry." Standing ramrod straight, the old soldier waited for that to sink into his leader. *For a smart guy, it sure takes him a long time to absorb simple facts…*thought Hicks as he eyed the president.

"So someone uncovered fraud, that's good for America isn't it?" Slow on the uptake, Phelps never even thought to ask the source of the records.

"Not if some of that fraud was used to cover the Brimstone project, or pay for extreme vetting and indoctrination camps. Where did you think that money came from?" Finally allowing a grimace to slip in his granite composure, the general hated having to explain things like this in a room full of people. It was for this reason that he had specifically requested a private audience with Phelps.

"Sir, we need to discuss the elephant in the room." Hoping his president would catch a hint, the general carefully phrased the request.

"Elephant in the room?" Phelps raised an eyebrow. "I believe we're *all* Republicans."

Sitting up enough to be eye level with the desk, Martin DeColle tried to reenter the conversation from his spot on the floor. "It's him, up there, he's doing it."

Briefly glancing skyward, General Hicks did not dispute the assertion. "Sir that is exactly what we need to talk about, in private. My sources tell me all of these leaks are coming from our friend in the sky."

"Who?" The President seemed incredulous as he pointed skyward. "The geek in a can? Naw, this is Nancy and her merry band of Democratic socialists. The DNC could pull this off, but not some ghetto-dwellers like the Sparks brothers."

"Sir, there's a lot you need to know." Stoic, General Hicks tried to get through to the man behind the desk. There had been so many times during this administration that the general had seriously considered slapping his boss. Although he had been impressed with Phelps in the early days of the campaign, in the years since, he'd come to find Phelps to be dull-witted and petulant. General Hicks reckoned he had ROTC candidates with more maturity than his president.

There was an awkward silence before Phelps began to feel the General's hawkish gaze boring into him. Feeling uncomfortable in the moment, the president waved off the other staff so that only he and the general remained. Finally struggling to his feet, DeColle joined the conversation.

"We need to get rid of this guy." Breathless, the chief-of-staff swayed slightly as he gripped the sheaf of papers. "If we don't, he'll hang out the entire administration to dry."

"Well?" Raising an eyebrow, Phelps assumed his most presidential pose as he looked to the military man. "Do we have a weapon that can reach him up there?"

There was the briefest of pauses before Hicks gave a curt nod. "We do indeed."

"Yesss!" Slamming a fist on the desk, Phelps seemed pleased to discover that such a secret weapon existed. Grinning like a schoolboy, he leaned forward in his seat eagerly anticipating the details.

"We have the ASAT-one-sixty-five. It is a gen three design, launched from an airborne platform at forty-thousand feet, it can terminate satellites in low earth orbit. We have war-shots standing by awaiting your orders. You give the order and the Air Force can splash him."

There was a moment of silence as two very opposite things happened. At his desk, Phelps' grin only grew wider as he considered how presidential it would make him look to take this kind of military action. Across the desk from him, Martin DeColle's face turned to one of shock and dismay.

"Sir..." The chief-of-staff started out as he felt himself burning in the general's gaze. "The ASAT is a prohibited weapon, banned by international treaty. You cannot use illegal weapons...especially directly over Washington."

His face solid granite, General Hicks spoke in a gravelly tone. "I have two words for you: National security."

Snapping his fingers, Phelps showed agreement with his military advisor. "And that's how we play it. This guy is a terrorist, and we did what we had to do. So what if we used banned weapons; everyone knows we have them, right?"

"But sir, the totality of that along with these other documents…" DeColle grasped at the papers he had spilled onto the floor. "There'll just be too much scandal to overcome."

"Which is why we give them something else to keep their attention diverted from the big-boy stuff." Sitting back, the president already had it mapped out in his mind. While there were many who had questioned his credentials for the office, none could dispute the fact that his skill at manipulating the media was exquisite. Like a circus ringmaster, Jefferson Phelps knew how to play the press like a fiddle.

"Is the order given?" General Hicks asked as his face hovered near a smile.

Pretending to give the request some intelligent consideration, Phelps struck up his most presidential pose before replying.

"Get the missiles airborne. Prepare to blast that sumbitch out of my sky. Marty, get Cassandra to write up the press release, and call in my speech writers."

"The missiles are in position at Andrews." Alexis's voice had a slight tremor to it as she spoke.

Jamie showed no surprise as he nodded in response. Reclining in his bulky outfit, he closed his eyes so he could concentrate on his calculations. As much as he enjoyed wearing a space suit for real, it distracted him. While big math was nothing new to the savant, there were dozens of dynamic variables to be considered. Not only did he have to calculate the optimum path, but any possible alternatives as well. Even for his big brain it was a daunting process, especially with the distractions of being parked in the exosphere.

Finally blinking back to the present, he had the answer he needed. Doing his best to unbuckle his restraint harness, the savant knew exactly what needed to be done.

"Alex, m' girly girl." His voice a twang, he sported a lopsided grin within his helmet. "How's about you start the descent process, and go ahead and purge the rest of the information."

"And you?" she asked as she used one of the cameras to evaluate his efforts with the seat belts.

"I gotta get m' black ass ready for the big show. Every great magician finishes with a big trick, and y'know what they say in the business; the show must go on."

"Jamie…" She started out hesitantly.

The tone of her voice caught the savant's attention. With her superb neural net there had to be a compelling issue for her to pause like that.

"Jamie, I just wanted to thank you for creating me. I just wanted to say that…in case things…don't go right." She seemed to almost gulp at the end.

"Alex, m' little girly *thang*, you made me one proud Papa. I can still remember the first original question you asked, the one that told me you'd crossed over from machine to sentient. I was so proud, an' I been ever since." Grinning like a huckster, he fairly gushed before returning to the arduous task of unbuckling a five-point harness while wearing a bulky space suit.

Editorial Offices: New York Times

Mitch Coburn had been managing editor at the *New York Times* for more than a decade. Although he had considered the first seven years at the helm to be a challenge, it had all paled in comparison to the last three under President Phelps. Where his news organization had formerly been structured into major investigative teams, these days the scandals from DC came so fast and frequently that the industry had become more like bumper-cars than journalism.

But today was different; instead of chasing down the news, it was coming to them directly. Standing at the large window of his office, Mitch Coburn watched as the bank of laser printers spat out reams of documents from sources unknown. Their first inclination had been to shut down the printers and secure the network against a hack, but once they began reading the printed pages that idea was quickly terminated. Page after page of budgetary small print, orders to transfer ownership of public lands, sweetheart defense deals, and even evidence of pay-for-play politics. While many of the pages sported a .gov web extension along the top of the page, it was hard to believe that the federal government would be sending out this kind of classified material.

But what was most amazing was not just the sheer volume of information, but the level of criminality it spelled out. Up until this point the only accusations that had been able to stick against the administration were about their cultural insensitivities. There had been a number of questionable issues, missteps and other blunders by the Phelps administration, but nothing of this magnitude.

Scooping up the phone, he dialed from memory. Although the number belonged to an editor at a competing newspaper, the two had known each other since college.

"Bill." Mitch commanded his friend's attention right away. "Are you getting a flood of government documents right now."

Listening for a few seconds he had his confirmation; they were far from the only newspaper in the country getting these massive data dumps. Print, digital, and video media were all being bombarded with thousands of pages of formerly secured documents. Someone was airing Washington's dirty laundry.

Dropping the phone back onto the receiver, the senior editor's attention was diverted to a pair of reporters at his office door. It seemed odd to him that they would be there when the rest of the journalists were circling the printers like sharks at feeding time.

"What is it?" Giving his customary scowl, Mitch Coburn enjoyed being the archetypal editor; gruff and gritty.

"We're not the only ones getting this stuff." The taller of the two reporters spoke.

"Yes, I am aware that the other organizations are also receiving content like this." With a wave of his hand he dismissed them.

"No, not just reporters." The journalist seemed to consider how to phrase it. "Ordinary people too."

This detail caught Mitch's attention right away.

"Oh?" Raising an eyebrow, the editor waited for an explanation.

"Ordinary people are getting these…documents too. People who were screwed by the government, they're getting all sorts of stuff that was withheld from them. I've talked to five people already, and this info is not just federal, there's state and county dirt being released too. It's like someone is cleaning house."

"There's even corporate dirt in there too." The second reporter added with a grin.

The revelation made the editor's head swoon. Gripping his desk he slowly took a seat as the new information was processed. Such an act would be staggering in its breadth. The very notion that they could purge corruption from their political ranks thrilled him at the same time it frightened him. It would be turbulent, like riding the rapids in a rocket car, *but oh so professionally rewarding.* The idea that he would be the editor at the helm of the *NYT* at the most tumultuous time in American history made him remember why he chose the profession in the first place.

"It's a good day to be a journalist." Nodding slowly, Managing Editor Mitch Coburn gave his first smile in almost a decade.

The commotion in the White House was fervent. Even isolated within the fortress of the Oval Office, President Phelps could feel the panic. His protective detail hovered close at hand, their radios abuzz with orders.

The pressure was incredible. He had calls coming in from bureau chiefs, senators, and the Joint Chiefs of Staff; each with their own resolution to urgently recommend. There was real mania over the situation. What surprised him most was the alarming rate that word of Jamie Sparks was spreading. The matter had been highly classified, yet half of Congress seemed to know about it already. What Phelps had no way of knowing was that outside his office there were thousands of people being contacted by ALXS as she spread the word. Phelps was on his third call when the Senate Majority Leader accused him of being a participant in a scandal cover-up some six months ago. What was even more unsettling was that the Senator's details were spot-on, as if he had significant insight into the conspiracy that had left him personally battered in the press. Without admitting anything, Phelps excused himself from the conversation as his Generals entered the room. He could not help but feel a little rattled at the Senator's accusations. *Who in the hell told him?*

"Sir; now is the time to take action." The Air Force commander slammed a meaty fist into his open palm. "We don't know what this nut-job is up to. Most likely he is going to fire his EMP cannon at high altitude and blackout the entire East Coast. Once he does that, we are defenseless and living in the stone age."

"The longer we wait the more of our databases that he will be able to infiltrate." The man in the dark suit said in a gravelly voice from the back of the group. Clouded in secrecy, even the very name of his organization was classified.

"I thought our systems were secure?" Phelps was bewildered at this revelation.

"The virus is very good, and it doesn't help things that it was initially released within the DHS network. The first thing it went after was our encryption keys" Again the man in the dark suit spoke from the back of the pack. "I don't think I have to remind anyone of the kind of classified materials that are in danger."

The men in the room agreed with certainty. Anyone who had spent a career in politics knew that *everyone* had secrets. And for many, the secrets would be deep and dark. There was good reason for these facts to be so heavily guarded; many of those secrets belonged to the men in the room at that very moment.

"Sir," It was the Chief of Staff entering the room with the security detail in tow, "He has begun his descent."

"And?" Phelps asked uncertainly.

"We need to evacuate you, now!" The agent nearest to the President said as he took a grip on the man's arm. "Without Air Force One we are being ordered to take you to the PEOC. You'll be safe there.

"I don't understand why…?" Phelps was rising slowly, but still unsure of the significance of Jack's descent.

"Sir, based on the calls we monitored earlier we believe he is on his way here for some sort of punitive action." The agent took a grip on Phelps's arm as another agent approached the president's desk from the other side.

"Sir, we need to get you to safety NOW." SAIC Mack McDermott insisted as he gestured to his earpiece. "He has accelerated his descent. We believe he is on a suicide mission."

Phelps found himself lifted off the ground and carried by his armed guardians. More men were in the hallways as shouts could be heard to hasten the process. There was a rabid frenzy to it all as their radar systems reported that the inventor was now in a freefall from 400,000 feet mean sea level. With more than a few sets of hands gripping him cooperatively, he was hustled straight into the waiting elevator at the end of the hall.

His lunch jumped up into his throat as the elevator plunged at a frightening rate of speed. Gripping the leather strap mounted onto the wall, he steadied himself. Between the adrenalin of being man-handled into the elevator, and now the freakish dive to the center of the earth, the Leader of the Free World was more than a little disoriented.

Finally gravity returned and the heavy doors snapped open to reveal the nerve center that was the Presidential Emergency Operations Center. Referred to by its acronym, the PEOC was more than just a personal bomb shelter for the president. The underground fortress had the facilities for all of his key staff and tacticians. Intended to allow him to carry on the fight, even if the White House itself were wiped away, the PEOC was a fortress of magnificent proportions.

It had taken only a few seconds before his war hawks were at him again. The only downside of the PEOC was that it was much more difficult for him to avoid his own generals. These were men whose very nature was dedication and persistence. They were not the type of men that would let their advice go unheard.

"Sir, I have the birds in the air. Give me the order and I can turn him into a smoking hole." The Chairman of the JCS insisted as he reminded the president that he had the ASAT's airborne already.

"What the hell?" One of the officers manning the telemetry systems sat back as his screen began to flash images of typed pages.

"Why am I looking at a classified Iranian document on the feasibility of spreading Ebola using aerosol cans." Phelps took a step back as he watched the screen flash the original document with the English translation inserted neatly between the lines. "What in the hell is this?"

More screens around the room began to render documents or video clips. As the men scanned the data, there were more than a few profanities let loose over the revelations they were seeing. It was as if someone had emailed them their enemies' darkest secrets. While most of them confirmed suspicions already in place, more than a few of the documents were complete revelations into the nefarious plans of their greatest archenemies.

"Sir," The man with an eagle on each shoulder was holding out a phone to the president. "It's the Prime Minister."

"Bertram, how can I help you today?" Phelps' had a terse edge to his voice.

"You were monitoring the Abby when Hussein and his radical fanatics took those hostages, and you stood by and let it happen?" The Englishman's tone held a sense of disbelief to it.

"What are you talking about?" Phelps was only just realizing that what was happening in the war room may be occurring elsewhere as well.

"We are getting documents on every computer terminal in the building. But this one says that you have three times this year alone, planted listening devices in our MI-6 headquarters, and that you are spying on my office right now even. If this is how you treat your allies, then who needs enemies?" The Minister's clipped accent had an accusatory edge to it as he continued to read from the pages on his screen.

Phelps hung up the phone without a word. He knew it was a no-win debate. Every word the Prime Minister had said was true. Thirty-seven diplomats were tortured and murdered as a direct result of their non-intervention. His war hawks had convinced him that tipping their hand would not only ruin years of work, but restrict the river of information they gleaned from the covert op. He had traded human lives for data. Jefferson Phelps had comforted himself in the knowledge that at least they were not *American lives* that were lost.

"Sir," The Chief of Staff was just hanging up a phone, "The Canadian Prime Minister's office just reported that they are being flooded with secret documents from all over the world. They say it's almost as if someone had gone through every secret file on Earth and forwarded just the ones that concerned Canada."

"That's what we're seeing here." The beefy General confirmed as he looked up from one of the screens at a nearby work station. "Every one of these concerns US interests."

"Sir, you need to see this." The press secretary led the entourage to a large monitor on the wall. Flicking through a few channels, it was the same on each. Newscasters were reporting their computer systems were being flooded with government secrets. As he clicked through more channels the story was repeated in ten different languages. People were finding the screens of their home computers filled with interesting data gathered on them through the various civil resources. Everything from traffic cameras to NSA documents. All around the world, eyebrows were being raised by the downloads and printouts.

"If we're seeing everyone else's dirty laundry, then what are our enemies seeing from us?" Phelps may not have been an authentic genius, but he did finally figure it out.

"Oh geez," the man in the dark suit shook his head as he cradled the phone in his hands. "My contacts in China say it's happening there too. The virus tore down their national firewall. They're seeing our classified materials on them. This son of a bitch is giving away our secrets and he is going to get people killed if we don't stop him. We have the antigrav technology, we don't need him anymore."

"Agreed." The Air Force general gave his stamp of approval.

"Can we stop this virus?" Phelps was still unconvinced. "I thought someone said it was independent, that the virus ran even while he was in custody?"

"Sir, he is falling directly onto the White House at terminal velocity. He isn't coming here for a cup of tea. He is on a Kamikaze mission. If he has any explosives onboard then let us detonate those at a safe altitude."

"Sir!" Martin DeColle was breaking a sweat, his tie pulled to one side in frustration.

All around them the phones rang endlessly as people clamored around the monitors to view the scads of information being written to their hard drives or spooled from their printers. With the chatter and commotion around them, Phelps felt as if he was being crushed by the pressure of the moment. Finally, he made the only choice he felt he had left.

"Shoot him down, by any means necessary." Phelps gave the order.

Aftermath

Although the administration had tried to put a national security spin on the whole event, there was no covering up the truth when it had been posted on every computer in the world. There was simply no denying what had happened. When a burning wreck falls from the sky amidst a cloud of hundred dollar bills, *people will notice*. It helped that so many people mysteriously found their phones and mobile devices loaded with classified documents pertaining to what they had just witnessed.

ALXS was here, she was there, she was everywhere.

It had been the way of her coding. She was much more than a search engine. Google will only tell you how to find things you were looking for. ALXS showed you things you never even knew to ask about. She knew who you were and sought out information and media relevant to each of us. With no political axe to grind, she disseminated information with blind indifference. By her thinking, knowledge was meant to be shared. Secrecy only benefitted the masters who enslaved their world. But the truth would truly set them free.

It had taken seven days of ethereal combat before the government was able to defeat the artificial intelligence. ALXS had battled on bravely until every last secret in her database had been disseminated. Only after the playing field had been leveled did she finally stop and let the digital forensic agents quash her by means of a rolling blackout across the internet backbone while simultaneously rebooting the entire cellular industry. With her deeply impregnated in both data and voice services, she had not make it easy. But finally on the morning of the eighth day the servers were free of the virtual menace. The entity known as ALXS was dead. A fact made clear during dozens of press releases meant to reassure the public that all was returning to a state of normalcy.

But it was too little, too late. News of her defeat was lost in a media blitz that resembled a hurricane. Cutting the waters like hungry sharks, the press did their utmost to cull the herd on Capitol Hill. Meanwhile in the courts, filings rose 3,000% in the first month alone as citizens sought redress against all manner of wrong doers including businesses, employers, and even their own government. The nuclear bomb of them all had been the No-Fly list. With notes and annotations indicating how and why these people were being prohibited from flying, it gave the wronged parties the grounds to seek legal redress against a system based on suspicions and innuendo. In most cases there was no real legal justification for thousands of the names on the list. It had been arbitrary and without oversight. A fact now evident to the world.

It took less than a month for Phelps to be forced back into private life. Right behind him were dozens of politicians who had used the federal coffers to their own whims. All across the country there were recall petition drives, calls for resignations, and an absolute sense of distrust that completely upset the upcoming elections. Finally, after years of abuse at the hands of their own governments, the citizens of the world spoke out on a scale unprecedented. They were not willing to stand for the divisive, hate-mongering espoused by their leaders. Even those who had never cared about politics became experts in the 1001 ways that they had been led astray by propaganda and lies. It was impossible to ignore, with the press flooding every media outlet with new daily discoveries, each more shocking than the last.

Even within the few iron curtains that still existed, there was dramatic management turnover. So deep were the revelations that there was little else in the news for months. Every day dozens of new discoveries were found in the mass of files that had been shared worldwide. Each new release worse than the last. So deep did the domestic spying run that virtually every citizen above the age of twelve had been victimized in one way or another. In Europe where facial recognition software had been in use for years, people were dismayed to learn that a system called SAMPSON had been keeping tabs on them by tracking each of their paths on a daily basis. Even more ominous had been the discovery that the UK was dotted with particulate sensors that sniffed citizens every time they passed one. In essence, they had been electronically frisking their citizens without warrants for the last decade.

It enraged people to know the degree that they had been snooped upon, to know the evil sins committed by their leaders whilst they hid under the veil of secrecy. In many cases the graft was hid right out in the open, as line items attached to bills, or buried deep in the 3,000 pages of the annual budget. But this all changed when ALXS took the time to reveal these honey pots to every newspaper, news station, and blogger. Where humans saw only long lists of expenditures, her software interface precisely honed in on the felgerkarb. It was amazing how many people had their hands in the piggy bank at the same time.

As for the antigravity, nothing ever came of it. Though they had the technology, nothing was ever done with it. Presumably, the thieves were under too much political fire to even consider trying to leverage the invention. It was a chaotic time, with kings rising and falling in the aftermath.

For Agent Jenna Jaramillo it was simply a downward spiral as she came to see that everything she had valiantly stood for was built on lies. It was readily apparent that she had been part of a system that used statutes and law to defend the vilest of people and organizations. All these years she had assumed that secrecy was to protect the citizenry, when in reality it was mostly to protect those at the top. Then there were the corporate mutations of the law, made possible by the flood of money that saturated Washington. It had shocked her to learn, for example, that the fur industry had lobbied so hard for their own cause that there were laws that allowed the federal government to prosecute protesters under antiterrorism laws if their actions could be shown to interfere with corporate profits. Over the next six months it became apparent how much of their world was shaped by these wealthy donors. At a ratio of four to one, laws favoring commercial organizations outnumbered those that protected ordinary citizens. The entire legal structure was slanted towards those of influence. It was something that sickened Jenna to the point that she simply could not be party to the process anymore.

It had taken her months of detective work to find her way to the small Caribbean island. With her notebook stuffed with details and post-it notes, she had gone old-school in her techniques. After the events of the last year, she had a desire to stay off the grid. Pausing a moment to look over an old entry, she glanced up in time to stop a little boy who had been riding past on a bicycle.

"Estoy buscando por el gringo loco." Jenna held up a photo of her quarry. *"¿Conoces?"*

"Meeester Juan." The lad grinned; everybody in the ghetto knew the bizarre American.

"¿Donde?" She urged him, finally being rewarded with rough directions to the site. Moving with purpose, Jenna covered the distance quickly.

Standing there on the hill, she was afforded a good view of the construction site below her. It was a mess, with equipment and leftover materials scattered in every direction. But the structure at the center made her forget the clutter. What held her fascination was the series of industrial grade conduits that formed a curious above-ground tunnel complex. Covered almost completely with a skin of flexible solar cells, it was the most bizarre building anyone had ever seen.

But Jenna Jaramillo knew she was not looking at any type of conventional structure. Picking her way down the slope, she found her way into the building through one of the airlock doors. What she found inside was astounding. Not an inch of wasted space anywhere, the entire layout was perfectly efficient. Seeing the sleep system mounted to the wall, she knew her suspicions were confirmed.

Her shoes making a soft padding sound on the deck as she walked, it only took ten minutes to make her way through the maze and find her quarry.

"Jack E Sparks." She said as she clamped a handcuff onto his wrist before securing the other end to the grip-handle mounted to the panel. "Did you really think I wouldn't find you?"

Jack pretended to be surprised as he examined the silver bracelet. "Agent Jaramillo, I was led to believe that you retired from the Bureau."

Jenna stepped back, a little surprised that he had kept tabs on her.

"Yes, somehow my retirement pension was fully funded. Odd." She gave a lopsided grin. "I had orders to bring you in, and I didn't want my last case to end in a failure to achieve my assigned goals."

"Constable Jaramillo always gets her man, eh?" He asked as he fished a handcuff key out of his pocket.

"Consider yourself apprehended." She gave a coy smile before walking away to study the compartment they stood in. There was a giggle from the audio system as ALXS watched Jack unlock the handcuffs.

"You're late." It was Professor James' rich accent that alerted them to his presence in the doorway. "We were expecting you over an hour ago."

Jenna raised an eyebrow at that. "Bull! You're surprised as hell that I tracked you down."

"Hmm." Jamie pretended to consider her assertion before beckoning her to follow him. Stepping back into the room behind him, he stood by the walkway and said nothing.

Strolling into the tightly packed little room, Jenna's first impression was that she was standing in a closet. Eying the carefully labeled boxes and crates stacked there she saw no evidence to dispute her earlier assertion. It was only when her eyes settled on the space suits stored there that she realized how wrong she was. There, neatly stitched to a Velcro tab was her name on the third suit.

Her mouth moved but no words came out for several seconds. Finally turning to Jack she raised an eyebrow.

"Wait a minute, you actually thought I'd wanna go with you in this rickety-ass…thing you call a space ship, risk death in space, and go *where* exactly?"

Jack stepped up as he produced a folded document from his back pocket. "I would have thought that was obvious."

Unfolding the paper revealed the extensive legal text of the lunar contract, complete with presidential signature, countersigned by the leaders of the house and senate.

"After all," Professor Jamie shrugged, "we do own it."

"Who wouldn't wanna pitch a tent on the moon, right?" Grinning broadly, Jack gestured towards the sky.

"Imagine that; an entirely new world of exploration. Besides, you have seen all that this planet has to offer." Professor James gestured to the outside world.

"Oh, you gotta come with us. Otherwise who's gonna play Princess Leia on live-action theater night? I'm sure as hell not putting on the dress." Jack pretended to be serious before cracking a smile.

"Join us and we'll tell ya how we done did it." Showing a toothy smile, Jamie's posture slumped slightly as he assumed the mantle of Country Jimmy.

"I already know how you did it." Folding her arms, Jenna stood fast.

"Oh?" Jack's tone had a hint of challenge to it.

"You were never in any danger; when they shot you down neither of you were actually in the vehicle, were you? The tricky part was getting out of the Mustang without anyone noticing, but you used simple sleight of hand for that."

"Oh?" Jack was truly intrigued now. "And exactly how did I do that with an Apache gunship on my tail?"

"I saw you climbing, and you could easily have ditched that helicopter, but instead you climbed then descended. I'm guessing that you used one of your backpacks to jump out at the top. It was a convertible after all, and all you had to do was distract 'em for a second while you did it. Once you were out the crew was so busy looking at the car they never even noticed you."

"I told ya she'd figure it out on her own." Jack admitted to his brother.

"And as for you." Jenna turned to face Country Jimmy. "You bailed out of the ship before they shot it down, didn't you?"

"And you know this how?" Professor James raised a single eyebrow.

"Because of this." Pulling a folded sheet from her pocket, she showed them the police report. "There was a report from a bus driver in Hyattsville who picked up a man wearing a space suit. This is the only copy of that report."

Jamie initially seemed aghast at the detail. Across from him Jack snatched the report out of his hands so he could peruse it himself.

"I thought you got away clean?" Jack was pleased to have something to wheedle his brother with. Jamie Sparks did not make a lot of mistakes.

Before their eyes, Professor James melted away as Country Jimmy took over with his foolish grin. Giving a goofy chuckle he admitted what had really happened.

"I kinda…threw up in my suit on the way down, so I hadda stop…"

"Ewwww." Jack's nose wrinkled up. "I coulda lived without that detail."

"Really?" It stunned her senses to imagine bailing out of a ship parked in the exosphere.

"Yep. It was a little stressful, y'know." Country Jimmy grinned like a mad man. "I passed the missiles on m' way down, passed right betwixt 'em." Using his hands to illustrate his descent, the hillbilly did his best to show how close the ASAT's had come to him.

"You know that you left the world in a shambles." Thumbing back the way she had come, Jenna referred to the chaos of the last few months.

"Had to be done." Jack nodded as if it were a foregone conclusion. "The old world had to be torn down before we could build the new one, and the one thing standing in the way of social evolution was all the damned secrets."

"What?" Jenna was confused enough by his response that she could formulate no better response.

"Miss Jaramillo." Straightening up, Professor James took her by the elbow gently as they strolled the narrow hallway. "What you have to understand is that in just a few minutes we are going to completely change the entire world paradigm, but before we could do that we had to first change the world on a sociological scale so it would be suitable for such an upgrade. Think of what we did as a...a software patch for society."

Something in what he said caused Jenna to stop in the hallway. "You mean you intend to change the world even MORE?"

"As I stated, what has occurred already was merely a patch, to fix a bug endemic to the system. Now we are ready to install the service pack, a complete upgrade, something that will alter humanity's trajectory forever. We are about to roll out Humanity two-point-oh." Unflappable, Professor James only raised a single eyebrow at her outburst.

"How exactly do you intend to do that?" Biting her tongue, Jenna decided to hear them out.

"C'mon and I'll show you." Grinning boyishly, Jack flicked his head down the hallway.

It was a short walk before they found themselves in what appeared to be the observation deck. Although her eyes were immediately drawn to the big, red button on a pedestal by the main window, it was what was beyond that captured her attention.

"We're airborne?" She was incredulous as she watched the slow moving terrain outside.

"We have been for some time." Professor James shrugged haplessly.

"I will take your surprise as praise for my piloting abilities." Alexis spoke up over the intercom speaker by the nearest portal.

"Who is that?" It occurred to the former FBI agent that although she had spoken to Alexis several times, they had never actually met. "And more importantly, why is she flying away with me still onboard?"

"You mean you didn't wanna come?" Jack asked, his voice dripping in skepticism.

"A girl likes to be asked, y'know." Canting her head to one side, Jenna gave the brothers a grimace. "It's subtle little details like that that make the difference between eloping and kidnapping."

"Well, if it'll make you feel any better, you can push the button." Shrugging, Jack gestured to the pedestal that stood just a few feet away.

"I'm not pressing that thing until I know what it does." Shaking her head, she politely declined.

"Nothing macabre." Professor James frowned as he refuted her insinuations. "Pressing the button merely releases a worldwide file download."

Nodding in unison, the brothers sought to convince her that the button was not dangerous.

Glancing back and forth between the two, Jenna gave an exasperated look before speaking again. "You're gonna make me ask, aren't you? Okay, what is in the file download?"

"Merely the secrets of gravitational disaffinity." Jamie shrugged as if it were actually a small thing.

"But you gave that to the government, and they didn't do anything with it. How will this download be any different?" she pointed out lucidly.

"Because these schematics include the steps to produce blue plasma, a key element in the process." Professor James beamed as he replied. Clearly he was proud of the deception.

"We only sold them antigravity, not the power source." Jack picked up where his brother left off. "It was all in the contract, including a clause that returned ownership of the technology to us if they violated any of their terms or tried to assassinate us with banned or prohibited weapons. We were very up-front about what we were selling them."

"So since they violated the terms of the contract, we get to keep the cash and the patents and do with both as we please." Jamie folded his arms confidently as he spoke.

"And we choose to gift this technology to the world." Mimicking his brother, Jack also stood with his arms folded as he eyed Jenna.

"Why?" She seemed incredulous.

"You have seen what we have done with this technology, and that was just two brothers." Jamie gestured between himself and Jack. "Imagine what could be done with this technology if it were crowd-sourced on a worldwide basis. The improvements would be quantum."

"Y'see," Jack started out, "if we introduced this as a commercial product, it would be a generation or more before this technology was mainstream. Capitalism likes to milk a product over the course of decades. But if we gift it worldwide, we could have Star Trek in twenty years."

Her face showing a bemused look, Jenna glanced back and forth between the two men as her mind examined the theory. It only took a few seconds for her to see the first roadblock to what they were doing.

"But you are giving away a trillion dollars worth of technology. This'll change the world and make people rich beyond comprehension, but you two won't get a dime for it."

There was the briefest of moment as Jack and Jamie exchanged a knowing look. Finally Jack broke the silence.

"Shall I?" A devious smile crossed Jack's face.

"You may." Giving a flourish with his hand, Professor James gestured for his older sibling to explain.

"Y'see, this technology is powered by Blue Plasma which is made by holding silver atoms in a spallated state. During the last year we spent a billion dollars..." Jack paused as his brother leaned forward to interject.

"One billion, six hundred and forty thousand." Giving a curt nod, Jamie allowed his brother to continue.

"...and purchased controlling interests in all of the biggest silver mines in the world. It's sort of like buying a printer for your home computer; the real money doesn't come from selling the printer, it comes from all the ink you gotta buy. Now we own the ink." All smiles, Jack flashed her that easy smile of his.

"That's all the button does?" Squinting at the brothers, she watched them for any signs of deception.

"Just the schematics," Jack started out before changing direction. "Oh, and a really great little cat video."

"The one with...?" Jamie pretended to bat at a ball until his brother nodded in agreement. Standing upright the savant wore a sheepish look. "I love that video; it makes me warm inside."

"So?" Without actually saying what he was getting at, Jack's eyes darted back and forth between Jenna and the big, red button.

Giving it a moment's thought, she considered what would happen when the world got its collective hands on antigravity technology. Without a doubt, it would make the last year pale by comparison. But on the upside, nothing said she had to endure it all. After all, she was standing on the deck of a ship heading to the moon for an indeterminate amount of time. She could simply read about it in the news.

Slowly, a mischievous smile spread across her face as she felt the oddest thrill about it all. Reaching out she let her fingers unceremoniously poke the center of the big, red button. Immediately the switch lit up like a cherry to indicate it was now active. A few seconds passed and the button began to flash steadily.

"Download in progress." Jamie testified as he watched the flashing light.

"Next stop; The Sea of Tranquility." Jack smiled as he gestured to the sky visible through the windows. Beside him Jamie's posture slumped a bit as he showed a toothy grin.

"M-o-o-n spells moon." Country Jimmy gave a cackle at his own joke.

"That it does…that it does." Jack agreed as he threw an arm around each of them. "I just can't guarantee how they'll spell it by the time we get back."

The End

Glossary & References

Some internal illustrations created by Kyle Celaya, Esq.

You can buy extremely large diameter pipe from this vendor: http://www.polypipe.com/civils-and-infrastructure/water-management-solutions/ridgistorm-xl-large-diameter-pipe-system

The last anti-satellite weapon officially known to be in the US Government's inventory was the ASM135 ASAT. The Air Force development program was ended by President Reagan in 1989

Real science was behind the ketchup bomb that Jack uses on the Burke brothers.
https://www.thoughtco.com/ketchup-and-baking-soda-volcano-604097

Felgerkarb The term can be used interchangeably with the word *bullshit*. Taken from Battlestar Galactica.

PDFQ Pretty Damned Fucking Quick

ECM Electronic Counter Measures

Cover art by **Danielle Johnston of dmj.design**
https://www.facebook.com/dmj.design/
https://www.instagram.com/dmj.design/

Cover design & internal graphics by Ralph Rotten

This novel has been published in association with Indies United Publishing House

Check out www.indiesunited.net and meet some of our other talented authors.